Hau Tree Green

Bob Bickford

Hau Tree Green © 2017 Bob Bickford

ISBN: 978-1-943789-65-8

Published by Taylor and Seale Publishing, LLC
3408 South Atlantic Avenue
Unit 139
Daytona Beach Shores, FL 32118

Cover layout by WhiteRabbitgraphix.com

Cover photographic element by Donnez Cardoza, used with permission.

Seven of Hearts
for the Doctor
"This is not an argument."

Part One

"Pink Heart, Green Tree"

-One-

Monday, March 31, 1947
Santa Teresa County, California

The knock on her bedroom door insisted. It stopped, just as she woke up enough to understand what it was, and then it started up again. Beatrice Stone sat up and smoothed her dress before she crossed the room and opened the door. The chauffeur stood in the hall, hatless. He gaped at her and kneaded his hands.

"What is it?" she asked.

"You didn't answer the bell, Miss Beatrice," he explained. "They sent me up to get you."

His name was Herb, but he called himself 'Jackie's Brother', which often made her wonder if he might be a little bit simple. Still, he had always been nice to her. It was a rarity in this house, someone being nice.

"It's my day off, and I'm allowed a nap. What's wrong?" she asked. They stood, looking at each other. His eyes got sad.

"You'd better get on down there, Miss Beatrice," he said.

"They're waiting for you in the conservatory."

She listened to his shoes going down the stairs. Slightly groggy, she splashed her face with water from the washbasin in the corner and patted it dry with a towel. It didn't help much. On the way out, she glanced back at the tall wooden dresser and stopped, considering. She wanted what hid in the top drawer.

The bottle lay beneath her underthings, dark green glass trimmed with gold. Keeping one eye on the open door, she uncapped it. She took a short bracer, and then like a second thought, one more. An old friend, a secret promise that never disappointed, the heat moved from her throat to her stomach, and then to her blood. Well-being flooded her.

"That's better," she murmured.

The gin was warm, and tasted like perfume. She wouldn't drink perfume, though, and she giggled a little at the idea of it. She slipped a scented lozenge from the tin box in her pocket and put it under her tongue. The taste of violets goes well with gin, she thought. In her mind, the two fragrances were pleasurably connected, ghosts holding hands.

She went into the hall. Herb the chauffeur had gone. She locked the door behind her and put the key into the pocket of her dress. She always kept the door locked. The cook lived at the other end of the hall, and she didn't trust her. As she went down the flight of wooden stairs, a young woman in a maid's black-and-white uniform came up. When they met, Bea put a hand on her shoulder.

"They've summoned me," she said. *"On my day off. Can you imagine?"*

The maid became instantly worried, *"Do you think . . .?"*

"Who knows?" Bea shrugged. *"I don't think so. I'm not*

worried."

"Maybe it's about your drinking," the young woman offered, half-hopefully.

"What about my drinking?" Bea snapped. *"That old bag drinks morning to night. She has nothing to say about my drinking."*

The maid squeezed her hand, and tilted her head for a kiss on the cheek. It lingered and started to turn into something else, until she moved imperceptibly away.

"Come and tell me how it turns out," she said. *"It's probably nothing—they just like to be able to bother you on your day off."*

They kissed again, quickly, and Bea finished going downstairs. She passed through the kitchen with its enormous pantries, ovens and sinks, and passed through double doors into the main hall. The conservatory squatted at the rear of the house, next to the library. She took a deep breath and let herself in.

Bea hated the plants that filled the space. She had no idea what they were called, but they were all the same species. Growing in containers on every available surface, suspended from the ceiling by delicate chains, they sent stems and leaves over the sides of their pots. They looked like large spiders lowering themselves from dusty webs to attack. The flowers were fleshy, somehow female, and smelled dreadful. The place overflowed with their stink.

She closed the door behind her and walked to the middle of the room, facing two older women who sat in wicker chairs with a table between them. The slender one was named Olive, which always struck Bea as a peculiar and dreadful name. The other, fat *and blind, was Chamomile. Bea thought she made most of the decisions, even though the thin one did all the talking.*

They had the same last name, even though they weren't sisters. Olive had married old Mister Gaynor, Chamomile's brother, when she was in her twenties. She had supposedly been a great beauty. By all accounts, even when they were young, the two women were inseparable. Bea had her own ideas about what the curious arrangement actually might be, and she stifled a giggle.

Olive Gaynor stared at her, and then pointedly at the buzzer button she kept close at hand. Chamomile stared, too, but at nothing, since she had no working eyes.

"Yes, ma'am?" Bea ventured.

The woman took a deep breath, hitching her face at the end of it as though it pained her. She had a glass of ruby port wine in front of her, and a matching decanter within reach. She drained the glass, and carefully refilled it before she spoke.

"It took you a long time to get here, Miss Stone," she said. "As usual. That kind of inefficiency isn't what we expected when we engaged you."

"I didn't hear the bell—"

"Quiet!" Olive snapped.

A sparrow had been trapped in a small cage on the table. It let out a small cheep, as if to underline the point. Chamomile began to move her hands. She played constantly with an oversized glass marble. She always had it with her, and claimed her vision got restored when she held it. Sometimes, Bea believed that was true, even though it was the invention of a crazy mind. The ball clicked against her rings gently as the blind woman passed it from hand to hand.

"I'm searching for some explanations," the older woman started. *"I'm trying to understand why I find myself in this position."*

Bea felt the first stirrings of fear, sharpness in her groin that made her feel as though she might wet herself. She simply couldn't lose this job.

"How long have you been an alcoholic, Miss Stone?"

She felt as though a hole had opened in the floor in front of her, a chasm of fear and guilt. The room and everything in it took on the quality of nightmare.

"There's constantly alcohol on your breath, underneath the candies that you eat, even in the mornings. We know about the bottles in your room, the empties you slip into garbage cans."

"I'm not," she stammered. *"I'm not that. What are you talking about?"*

"More importantly, how long have you been a— degenerate?" Olive Gaynor stared at her triumphantly. She smacked her lips before she went on. *"You thought we didn't know, but we know everything that goes on in this house. You are morally corrupt, and you have corrupted another young woman in our employ. It won't go on any longer."*

The hole in the floor opened wider, and Beatrice Stone began her long, long fall.

"How dare you?" she stammered. *"You, of all people . . ."*

"Your belongings are being packed right now," Olive said. *"My car will take you into town and drop you wherever you say."*

"You don't have my permission to touch my things," Bea said. She felt a flash of panic, thinking about the half-bottle of gin in the dresser drawer, and the empties stashed in the closet. *"I can*

pack myself."

"I won't have you further corrupting my home with your filth," the older woman went on. "You don't have my permission to be here even a moment longer. Give the chauffeur your new address, and we will mail your last check to you."

"Obviously, I don't have a new address. How could I?" Bea felt desperation clawing. She had nowhere to go, and no money. "If you want me out, get my pay. I won't leave without it."

Olive glared at her. Bea forced herself to hold her ground, to not turn and flee. After a moment, the woman rose from her chair.

"Very well. Since I have just fired my secretary, I'll go to the office and make out a check myself."

The conservatory hummed with silence, except for the tiny clicking of the glass balls in the blind woman's hands. Bea went to the table and drained the abandoned glass of port, then poured another glass from the crystal decanter, toasted the room with it, and tossed it down. She looked at the blind woman. Chamomile was pathetic, as funny as hell, and Bea laughed.

"What do you think about all this?"

The woman didn't answer. The filmy black veil pinned to her hat obscured her face, but Bea knew her eyes were so pale they were nearly colorless. She went to where she sat and took her hands. They felt like animal paws, soft and unresisting.

"Can I see this?"

Bea pried the glass orb loose, and held it up. About half the size of a baseball and not quite transparent, it caught the light from the windows and changed it into colors. It was pretty. On impulse, she slipped it into the pocket of her dress. The blind woman made a mewling noise.

"Ready to go, Miss Beatrice."

Bea glanced over her shoulder. The chauffeur stood in the open doorway. He didn't act like he had noticed anything.

"I put your things in the car," he said. "I put some things you might not want in the trash. Won't nobody bother with them."

A dozen empty gin bottles were hidden in her closet, and she felt absurdly grateful he had spared her that humiliation. She looked around the room, glad she wouldn't see it again. She would never again read the old woman's meaningless mail out loud to her or take any more endless dictation. She also wouldn't see the maid again, and that was painful.

"Thank you for that," she said. "Let's go, then. No time like the present."

She quickly poured and drank two more glasses of the port before Herb Robinson took the decanter from her and put it back on the table. Then he held her gently by the elbow and led her to the waiting car.

The blind woman patted the birdcage, weeping, and had nothing to say about any of it.

-Two-

Thursday, September 4, 1947
Corazón Rosa, Mexico

Baskets hung from the balcony railing, trailing vines. The building had a stucco face, like all the other buildings on the street, but washed pink. A wooden sign over the door said *'Pez en un Árbol'*, which I read as 'Fish in a Tree'. It didn't make much sense, but the letters were badly faded and my Spanish wasn't very good, so it might not have meant that at all.

It was the place I wanted though, so I set my suitcase down.

Inside, the cantina was cool and dim and quiet. The ancient cement walls were soaked with the odors of spilled beer, dark coffee, and peppers fried in oil. Ceiling fans turned slowly and paddled the warm air. A tin advertisement fixed to a column sported a blue-and-yellow parrot, sitting on a branch. Surrounded by green leaves, peeling letters spelled "One Hundred Percent Unbleached" in English.

In the farthest corner of the room, a woman sat at a table, with her back to me. Plain muslin covered her head, with her face hidden by the fringe. The loose drape of her dress ended just above elegant ankles and bare feet. A lemon sat on a plate in front of her beside the knife she had used to slice it.

She sat absolutely still as I crossed the room slowly to her. My balance felt off, and I heard my own pulse. I was afraid she would vanish before I got to the table.

There were no colors, and yet she seemed to radiate every color, lit in the center of her own rainbow. When I stood beside her, she glanced up at me. Her skin was honeyed, and her eyes were liquid and impossibly dark.

"It gets a little cold here at night," Annie Kahlo said. "Still, it's pretty wonderful. Why not stay here with me, for good?"

"You know I'm leaving," I said. "How did you know?"

Her smile was perfect. She gave the smallest shrug. It didn't break her stillness.

"Since when do you have to tell me anything out loud?"

I scraped a chair back on the stone floor and sat across from her. I took the telegram from my breast pocket and spread the flimsy yellow paper on the table. She didn't look at it.

"Back to California," I said. "We left owing some favors. Things have to get squared away, sooner or later."

"Fin sent for you?"

"Telegram is from him," I nodded. "When the old gangster crooks his finger, he expects obedience. I'll be glad to get out from under owing him."

"I like him," she murmured. "I haven't made up my mind if he's good or bad. You don't give him enough credit."

"There are also some open case files on my desk, and we could use a little money. I'm going to start driving back tonight, while it's cool. I should cross the border in the morning and be in Santa Teresa in a couple days."

She carefully cut a slice from the lemon and squeezed it into her glass.

"Are you glad?" she asked.

"To be going back?" I asked. "I'm here because I want to be. I belong with you."

"For the full nine innings?"

"Yes," I said. "The whole nine."

The only reason Annie hadn't been executed was that the police in California thought she had already died. She had killed at least a half-dozen people. All of them had needed it, as far as I was concerned. The cops had chased her into a crash, and a dozen of them had watched her car burn until only a shell remained, with her inside. She hadn't been inside the car though, and now she lived here, in Mexico. A judge had signed a paper that said she had died, so nobody hunted for her. Fin had helped engineer the whole thing, so I owed him.

I lived here too, as much as I could manage. I didn't want to go anywhere but wherever she went. The newspapers said she was dangerously crazy. I thought she was dangerously wonderful.

The light outside began to fade, and water-colored the street outside the cantina door blue and gold. When the sun set, the walls of Corazón Rosa turned pink. I wanted to see it, but there was no hurry. There would be other evenings.

"I think you're going to need my help," she said. "I'll come when you need me."

"You can't go back to the States, Annie, ever again. If they find out you're alive, they'll put you in the gas chamber and make you dead."

"I'll come when you need me," she repeated.

She finished her drink. I watched her throat work, and wondered why everything about her seemed so completely graceful. She set her glass down, and looked at me, ready to leave.

"Remind me of everything I've wanted to tell you, forever," she said. "Deal?"

I nodded, and pushed back my chair.

"Deal."

~*~

A couple of days and a whole lot of miles later, I stood in the parking lot of a motor court hotel called 'The Sand Castle'. The beach across the street probably accounted for the name. The sign in front promised the rooms were air-conditioned. I stretched my sore back. It was late afternoon, and I was tired.

The outfit catered to tourists who wanted to wade in the surf and see the sights on the cheap, the kind of place where the maids wiped dirty drinking glasses with used bath towels, and slipped them into paper sleeves that said, 'sanitized for your protection'. As long as it had a working ice machine in the hall, I didn't much care.

Behind me, the Ford's engine ticked as it cooled. I had left the Mexican border at sunup, and after a day behind the wheel I wanted three things: a cold drink, something to eat, and a quiet place to close my eyes for a few hours. It didn't matter what order they came in.

My house sat only a few blocks away, but I wouldn't go home tonight. My funds were dangerously low and I had a job I hadn't gotten around to before I went to Mexico, a divorce case. I needed to get the goods on a man named Highland who brought his secretary here for fun a couple of times a week. After meeting with his wife, I didn't much blame him, but taking sides wasn't part of the job. I planned to take some photographs and get paid for them. I wouldn't ruin his marriage; he had already done that for himself. The photos were to make his divorce settlement a little bit fatter, and I didn't see anything unfair about it.

Santa Teresa looked about the same as it had when I'd left it a couple of weeks before. An hour or so north of Los Angeles, it worked hard on its Spanish missionary charm, with plastered walls and flower baskets. The red-tiled roofs slid down the side of a worn-out mountain right to the sandy beach.

The ocean never changed, and that made the slight differences in cars and people on the street unimportant. The breeze from the water was warm but getting cooler. Across the street, people were leaving the beach for the day. The amusement park, a block down at the pier, still went full speed, and I could hear the roller coaster rattling and the faint screams from its riders. They sounded like they were having more fun than me.

I got my suitcase from the back of the car and set it down. A line of small trees decorated the edge of the lot, and littered the ground with fallen blossoms. They smelled dark green, a strange fermented perfume that went well with the air coming off the ocean.

A woman left the sidewalk and moved across the lot toward me. When she got close enough she stood still to let me get a good look at her. She moved as though she had just gotten up from a nap. Her blue dress was dingy, her lipstick appeared hurried, and I caught a whiff of booze. On top, it smelled fresh, but underneath it carried the stale reek of bad habit.

"You staying here, mister?" she asked.

I admitted it, and she glanced at my suitcase and shifted her weight from one foot to the other.

"You want some company?" she asked. "Buy a girl some dinner and a drink, maybe?"

Company was the last thing I wanted, but I was too slow saying so, and something like hope crossed her tired face.

"I could use a bath first," she said. "A place to lie down for a little while."

She was awfully young, and somehow didn't seem the type. She was pretty enough. If she was cleaned up and pampered a little, she might have been more than just pretty. Her complexion showed a slight coarseness though, the kind that comes from sleeping too often in unfamiliar places. I wondered about her story, but only briefly. You hear a lot of stories in my line of work, and you learn not to get interested in them unless you're being paid for it. Maybe she and I weren't all that different. I fished out my wallet, and handed her a five.

"Get yourself a bath, a place to lie down, and some dinner," I said. "It will have to be without me, though. I'm busy right now."

The hurt in her eyes surprised me. She took the money I held out, though. The fingers that brushed mine were ice cold.

"Suit yourself," she said. "Thanks for the date."

I watched her stroll back across the parking lot. When she had almost reached the sidewalk, she turned around. "What's your name?" she called.

"Nate," I called back. "Nate Crowe. Like the bird. What's yours?"

"Beatrice." She stuck out her tongue, unexpectedly playful. "Nice to meet you, Mister Blackbird. My friends call me Bea, as if you care."

I waved her goodbye and picked up my bag. I wondered what came next for her; it made me feel even sadder than I usually did.

The office had a bell over the door that jangled when I opened it. The noise didn't bother the hunched-over man behind the counter, who was busy listening to a baseball game on a portable radio. I set my suitcase down and watched him not look up at me. After a minute, I decided not to be in any hurry either, and I went over to browse a wire rack of postcards standing in the corner.

"Help you?" the man finally asked.

I ignored him. The cards were mostly colorized shots of the Santa Teresa beach from the air. A few of them had images of families splashing in bright swimming pools, laughing children with movie-star fathers and pin-up girl mothers. Some sported pictures of dolphins and whales. All of them were things I had never seen in southern California.

"Help you?" he insisted, and this time I stared at him.

"When you're good and ready," I said. "I don't want to bother you."

"What do you want to be a wise guy for?"

He stared at me, faintly offended, like he didn't get it. He wore a short-sleeved plaid shirt opened at the collar to show off a dingy undershirt. The light reflected off his glasses. He looked nearly as exhausted as I felt, and when I got close he smelled faintly of beer and salami. I felt almost sorry for him.

"I don't want to be a wise guy," I said. "I can't help it. I've been driving for three days straight and I need to lie down somewhere before I fall over."

"Why'ncha say so, then?" he shrugged. "Three bucks-ten. Checkout's at noon."

"I need a room with a window that overlooks the front entrance and parking lot," I said.

"I got a couple empty with ocean view," he offered.

"Parking lot," I repeated. "I'm a private investigator. I need to see the street entrance from my room."

He stared at me, taken aback.

"We don't like trouble here," he said. "The owners run a quiet place."

"No trouble," I said. "I don't like it either."

I took the pen he gave me, and filled out the registration card with an address in Corazón Rosa, Mexico. When I finished, I slid it back across to him with three singles and a dime. He picked up the card and moved his lips as he read it carefully.

"Crowe," he said. "That isn't a Mexican name. You live in Mexico? You don't look Mexican to me."

"How should I look?" I asked. "I'm willing to give it a try."

He stared at me, uncomprehending. Since I had the room key in my hand, I didn't see any profit in continuing the conversation. The bell over the door rang goodbye as I went out. I found the room number that matched the tag without much trouble, and after jiggling the lock, let myself into stale air. The room was like a thousand others I had been in, just not as clean. I tossed my suitcase on the bed and made a trip back up the hall to the ice machine I had hoped for.

After I bought myself a drink from the bottle in my suitcase, I pulled the drapes open and dragged a chair over to sit in front of the window. I checked the film in my camera. The Highland character drove a beige Cadillac Sixty Special. I knew he was a sharp-dressed dandy who wore bow ties. I didn't know anything about his secretary.

An electric fan on the dresser hummed lies to me about tropical breezes. Across the street, the sky over the water turned twilight, and I wondered if Annie Kahlo was looking at the same ocean from someplace cleaner, a thousand or so miles to the south.

I hadn't seen her for twenty-four hours. It had been a full day since I had kissed her goodbye. She liked it in the small Mexican town she had run to. She also liked it that everyone thought she had died. She spent her days painting pictures and walking on the beach. We had something, once. Maybe we still did, but now she lived there and I lived here, and neither of us seemed to know what to do about it.

My one-man detective agency kept my days full. I had an office on State Street, and an empty house a few blocks away on Figueroa. I kept them because I didn't have anything else. My work was mostly dull, but there were dangerous moments. I knew that not having my heart in it made a good way to get myself killed, sooner or later.

I had been thinking a lot about death lately. It had been much closer to me than it was now, but never worried me as much. I blamed Annie that it bothered me. She turned me sentimental.

'I'll be on the other side of your last breath.'

I had promised her that, a long time ago. I kept my promises, even when I didn't know how.

The ice finally did what it was supposed to, and the glass was cold. I took a long sip of bourbon, slipped my shoes off and closed my eyes.

"Your last breath . . ." I murmured to myself, or maybe to her.

After a little while, I slept. I didn't wake up, even when the sky outside went fully dark and the glass fell from my hand onto the carpet.

-Three-

When I woke up, full night showed outside the window. The dark smelled like mold and stale cigarettes. I had slid down in the chair. I rubbed a palm against the pain in my neck, and cursed myself.

The long drive and half-glass of bourbon had knocked me out like a dose of ether. The sodium lights in the parking lot showed only the black humps of sleeping cars. The camera sat in my lap, but nobody had stuck around to get caught in the act. The beige Cadillac had probably come and gone, and the guilty lovers were back in their own beds by now.

The dollars that had just flown away weren't coming back until next Saturday night, at the soonest. I pushed myself from the chair and cursed myself again. I decided to check the parking lot on the off chance the big sedan still sat there. If it did, it would be risky. Photographs would be dicey in the dark, and if they didn't develop I would have tipped my hand. My lovebirds would find another nest. I had no other prospects sitting on my desk, though, and there were bills waiting for me.

Instinctively, I didn't turn a lamp on. I laced my shoes in the dark. I had no clue where I had tossed the room key. The door was ajar, anyway. I didn't remember leaving it that way, but I left it and went outside without the key. The traffic on Cabrillo Boulevard had dried up. A lonely car followed the yellow of its headlights slowly by; in their beams I could see the early morning fog beginning to roll in off the ocean. There were voices from across the street. It sounded like two women arguing. I didn't see anyone, and after a minute the shouting stopped.

The parking lot was only half-full, and I walked it and checked the cars. This wasn't the kind of place that saw many Cadillacs, and there wasn't one parked there now. If my birds had come in earlier, they were gone now.

At the edge of the lot, the fermented green smell of the trees wafted strong in the cool air. On impulse, I crossed Cabrillo to the beach side. The boardwalk was deserted. The lights set on poles to illuminate it weren't doing much good; they disappeared in either direction, lost in the fog. I found an empty bench where I could sit to smoke a cigarette. When I patted my pockets, I realized I had left them behind. I sat down anyway.

I killed a half-hour staring out at black nothing. I couldn't see the ocean, but I could hear the whisper of surf. In the dark, it sounded like breathing. My wristwatch said half past four o'clock, the hour I liked best. It's down-deep-dark time, the hour when the world pretends that people never came along. The black is just blue enough to see without being seen. The three o'clock monsters are in retreat, the bars are closed, and the pretty people have all gone off to strange beds they'll try to forget when they're old.

I spoke Annie's words, like a charm against the strange things that rattled in the night.

"You can see in the dark," I murmured. "Close your eyes."

I missed her. I missed the things that were gone, but I missed the things that hadn't happened yet even more.

When I started to get cold I stood up, feeling the stiffness from yesterday's long drive, and crossed the street back to the motel. I glanced at the windows of the office. The lights were on, so I decided to go back to the room, collect my things and check out. I figured I wouldn't get back to sleep, so I might as well be awake in my own house.

I made my way through the dark hotel room, past the shapes of desk and dresser to the bathroom. I felt the wall inside the door with one hand, and found the light switch in the usual place. When it snapped, I squinted against the sudden illumination, and then blinked again at what I saw inside. A pair of women's shoes rested on the floor beside the toilet; one of them lay on its side. There were neatly folded clothes on the closed lid, dark blue with a white brassiere and purse on top.

"What the hell?" I said, and then, "Oh, no."

The woman I had met in the parking lot lay naked in the tub. Her eyes were open, and she watched me from underwater. Her dark hair floated around her face, stirred very slightly by an invisible current. I stood stock-still for just a moment, staring at her, and then I bent and hauled her out of the tub. She was dead weight in my arms, and her head lolled, heavy on my shoulder. I knew it was too late even before I laid her out on the tiles.

I knelt, pinched her nose and breathed into her mouth. Her lips were cold and unyielding.

"Breathe, goddamn you," I told her between puffs, but it didn't help.

After a few minutes, I sat back on my heels, spent. None of it was doing her any good. She appeared terribly young, her skin as white against black hair as a bad photograph. I imagined I saw her chest rise and her eyelids flutter, so I started up again. I kept going until I had nothing left, and even imagination failed me.

These were the last kisses she would ever get, but I had to finally give them up. I wished that she had gotten them from someone who loved her, someplace that she dreamed about; not here and not from me. I didn't even know her name.

I stood up. The tiles were pooled with water, my clothes were soaked, and she was finally, irrevocably gone.

"I'm sorry," I told her, for no reason at all. She didn't care about sorry.

I needed to find a telephone to call the police. I worried vaguely that she would get cold, and I knew my own sanity had slipped a notch. Maybe it had slipped a lot of notches. I covered her with a towel, and then a second one, since the hotel bathroom wasn't short of them. Then I left her there alone.

~*~

The lights in the interrogation room buzzed gently against the ceiling. The clock mounted on the wall behind a wire grille said just past last call for breakfast. I didn't imagine I would get any. I had spent the night in the police station, and so far, nobody seemed very satisfied with my version of events.

Rex Raines stared at me from across the table, wearing yesterday's clothes. The collar of his shirt had wilted and his necktie was pulled loose. His round cheeks showed some light stubble. Usually dapper, this made the first time I had seen him in need of a shave. He appeared like the sort of earnest young fellow who moved in next door and would be very sincere trying to sell you an insurance policy. He wasn't any such thing. His pleasant demeanor hid some hard years in the war, and some harder years on the cops.

"Not a suicide," he said. "Certainly not in the usual way. She could have taken too many pills, too much booze and slipped under while she took a bath—or someone could have helped her under. Funny you didn't hear or see anything, if it wasn't you."

"I had a drink," I said, for the hundredth time. "It knocked me out cold. I drove all day, up from Mexico. I woke up in the middle of the night and went for a walk to clear the cobwebs. When I got back to the room, I found her in the bathroom. I didn't see anyone else, before or after."

"Where did you say you walked to?"

"I crossed the street to the beach. I sat on a bench for a little while."

"And she didn't even have to jimmy the lock to get in," he mused. "Or kick the door down."

"I told you, I left the door ajar." I kept my voice patient. "Why don't you think it was a suicide?"

"It will be up to the coroner to decide," he said. "But she had bruises on her arms. Her knees were skinned raw. Every cop in this building thinks I ought to write you up on a murder charge."

"So why don't you do that?" I got instantly angry. "Are you worried about hurting my feelings?"

In a different life, we might have been friends, but we weren't in a different life and we weren't friends. We went back a few years and had an instinctive regard for each other though, and that bought me a little slack from time to time. You didn't last long in my line of work without knowing a friendly face or two on the cops.

"Do you always need to be a wise guy?" he sighed. "Always? What is it with you?"

I didn't have a good answer for that, so I didn't try. I lit a cigarette, my fifth in the last hour. My throat was as raw as my eyes. I figured that outside my nap in the hotel room chair, I had been awake for a full twenty-four hours.

"Tell me again," Raines said. "All of it."

"I saw her outside of the room before I checked in," I repeated. "I never saw her before that. She was hunting for a date, and I wasn't interested. Later, on the job, watching out the window, I fell asleep. You've done the same thing on stakeouts—don't tell me you haven't. When I woke up, I went out to the parking lot to see if my mark's car was parked there. I took a walk across the street to the beach to smoke a cigarette. When I got back to the room, I found her."

"How do you know she wasn't in the bathroom when you left?" he asked. "Did you use it before you went out?"

"I don't know," I admitted. "She could have been. I assume I would have woken up if someone came in."

"Maybe not," he said. "Not if you were passed out. You ever think you drink too much, Crowe?"

I thought that every time I woke up with a hangover, but it was none of his business, so I didn't say anything. He picked up a yellow pencil from the table and tapped it against his teeth.

"You see why a normal, sensible person might have some trouble with this story?" he asked.

"Lucky for me you're not a normal, sensible person," I offered.

He tossed the pencil onto the table and snorted.

"Lucky for you I'm a good cop," he said. "There's enough to your story that doesn't add up to make me believe it."

"Who was she, Raines? No one's telling me a thing. If I'm supposed to have killed her, I'd like to at least know her name."

"Name was Beatrice Stone," he said. "We don't know much about her, yet. Picked up once, about five months ago, on a morals charge. No solid address—she stayed at the Schooner Inn. That was her regular place."

"Across the street from my office," I said.

"Occurred to me you might have bumped into her before last night," he nodded. "We checked the room. Somebody tossed it—maybe related, maybe not. Rooms get burglarized there pretty regular. Doesn't have to be connected."

"What'd they steal? She have anything to her name?"

He shrugged. The Schooner Inn was a six-storey landmark on State Street that lost ground every year to the onslaught of new motor-court hotels like the Sand Castle, springing up beside every highway. It had been a destination once, but it sat blocks from the ocean, and had gotten old and shabby. These days it catered mostly to elderly tourists making pennies stretch, and the fringe trade. If you wanted to find a reefer cigarette, an early-morning drink, or some company for a few hours, it made a good place to start your looking.

Usually, a small group congregated on the sidewalk in front, loiterers and those pausing on their way in or out of the ground floor bar. I rarely glanced across at them when I parked in front of my office building. The window behind my desk faced in that direction, but if I got bored I was more likely to watch the sliver of ocean I could see a couple of blocks down. Even if Beatrice Stone had stayed in the Schooner Inn for years, I would have been unlikely to remember if I had seen her.

"Tell me again how you came to be back in Santa Teresa—and happened to check into a motel just in time to find a broad swimming in your tub."

"Divorce case," I said. "I needed the money. Simple one sitting on my desk from before I left. Guy takes a girl, not his wife, to the Sand Castle every Saturday night. Wife needs some pictures to show to a judge. I didn't have time to take care of it before I left."

"And you checked into the place as soon as you got into town," he said. "Didn't even go home to water your plants."

"I don't have any plants," I said. "It happened to be Saturday when I came back. If I got it done, I'd have a nice check when the bank opened Monday morning. If I went home first, I'd have to wait a week. I needed the check."

"Funny thing to go on a Mexican holiday when you're broke," he said. "Most people save up and take a vacation when they're flush."

I couldn't answer truthfully, so I shrugged.

"I had money when I left," I said. "What fun is a vacation if you don't spend all your money?"

"What did you find to do down there?"

I thought about Annie Kahlo. I thought about the beach that ran opposite the main street of Corazón Rosa, the black sand and blue early mornings. I remembered her face when she woke up, her dark eyes and soft mouth.

"A little fishing," I said. "A lot of tequila. I lost a small bundle at a dog track, and won enough back to have gas money to get home."

"You shouldn't bet," he said. "You don't have a nose for it. Some guys do, some guys don't."

I stubbed my cigarette out and lit another. I needed it like a hole in the head, but there wasn't much else to do. Raines sighed, again.

"So, you're holed up in a room, doing a simple peep job, and some girl you don't know ends up dead in the bathroom. You don't know anything about it, and you want us to believe that just because you say it's so. That about it?"

"I called you, didn't I? If I had killed her, would I have called it in?"

He shuffled the papers on the table between us into a pile, and tapped the edges to make it neat. He nodded at it when he felt satisfied.

"We're going to throw you back for now, Crowe. I told the DA we don't have enough to charge you with murdering the girl. He was half-asleep when I told him. He might feel different when he wakes up, so don't go outside the city limits until you hear from me."

"I appreciate that," I said, and meant it.

"I wouldn't cut you loose if I didn't believe you. The whole thing is just stupid enough and crazy enough to fit your pattern. You're getting into a habit of being in the wrong place at the wrong time, though, even more than you usually are. You want to know what I think?"

I waited. His eyes were slightly bloodshot, and he looked as tired as I felt.

"I think things haven't been the same since the Kahlo broad tried to wipe out half the gangsters in town and got herself killed. I think you were a lot more involved in all of it than anyone ever knew about. You haven't been the same since she died."

"Being in the newspapers is just about a death sentence in my line of work," I said. "So is being on the outs with the cops. How good do you think business has been for me, lately?"

"It's more than that," he said. "You were sweet on her, and you feel responsible. Guilt can eat a guy up. It distracts you, and getting distracted is a good way to get dead."

He stood up and went to the door.

"Someone will be along to sign you out. Like I said, don't go very far—we'll be in touch in the next day or two."

I leaned back in the chair and rubbed my eyes. When I opened them, Raines still stood in the doorway.

"She would have gotten the gas chamber, Crowe. She killed a cop, and the state of California would have killed her in return. It's better you didn't save her. Think about it that way."

He closed the door behind him, very softly.

The Santa Teresa police station was a white stucco affair, across the street from the courthouse and just a few blocks up Figueroa Street from my house. When I came outside, I realized that my car was back in the Sand Castle parking lot, so I went back inside. The sergeant at the desk let me use the telephone to call a taxicab.

I waited for it on the broad flight of steps in front. I watched the gulls on the courthouse lawn, hunting in the grass for things I couldn't see. I still hadn't figured out what they were scrounging for, when the bright yellow car turned the corner and headed toward me.

The Sand Castle didn't look like anything much had happened there the night before. I gave the cab driver a dollar and asked him to wait. Flags snapped in the wind. Early sunbathers were already filling up the beach across the street, and down the strand I could hear the roller coaster making its early rounds.

The same guy lounged behind the registration counter, and I wondered if he ever left. He had traded the baseball game on his radio for Jack Benny, and he laughed to himself at something he heard. I hated to spoil his mood.

"You have my bag," I said. "I imagine you've rented out my room already."

He stood up and came to the counter.

"Didn't think you'd be around to check out," he said. "Congratulations. Got the room key?"

When I said I didn't, he got out a ballpoint pen and a little pad of paper. He licked the tip of the pen as though it was a pencil, and made a note.

"One lost key," he said, and stared up at me. "You left the room in an awful mess. There's damages."

"Didn't hurt the bathroom floor any to get mopped," I said. "Probably overdue."

"Wise guy," he snarled. "I knew it the minute you come in last night. A louse like you checks in, and they're carting a dead streetwalker out before you can turn around. Damages come to five bucks, and fifty cents for the lost key."

Too tired to take the fuss any further, I dealt out the money, leaving my wallet nearly empty. He counted it carefully. I had no doubt it would go straight into his pocket, but that wasn't my problem. When he finished, he reached down and set my suitcase on top of the counter. He initialled the paper with a flourish, ripped the sheet off the pad and offered it to me. I didn't take it.

"I need my car keys," I said. "They were on the bureau."

"Don't know anything about any car keys," he shrugged. "I could ask around. Might cost you a dollar."

I reached across the counter, caught his shirt at the throat and pulled him to me. The mood I was in, he came easily enough. We stared at each other from up close for a few seconds, and then he shifted, got my keys from his trouser pocket and dropped them on the counter. I let him go, and turned to leave.

"She wasn't a bad girl," he said. "The girl you killed."

I stopped with a hand on the door and stared back at him. He seemed to be close to tears. It was the first honest thing he'd shown me.

"I didn't kill anyone," I said. "You knew her?"

"Lotta people knew Bea. She had friends around here. She never bothered anybody."

"That so?" I asked. "I might be back later, to ask you some questions."

"See if I answer any questions," he spat. "I wouldn't give you the time from your own watch."

I let him have that one. I waved the waiting taxi off. The Ford started on the first try, and I took it home. When I got there, I stopped on the sidewalk in front and checked the place over. It had been a while.

I lived in a bungalow, painted a sickly shade of olive green, inside and out. I supposed the previous owner had particularly liked the color, or else had gotten a deal on a trailer load of green paint. Sometimes, when I had a drink too many I got ideas about changing the color to something less gloomy. It became an idea with less appeal when I got sober enough to paint a wall, so it stayed the way it was.

A couple of black walnut trees guarded the place, and kept it in perpetual shade. I left the nuts that dropped from them where they were. The carpet of moldering shells kept any grass from growing, so I had no need of a mower. My home had an abandoned feel, even when I was there.

Annie Kahlo's empty house stood on one side of mine, separated from it by a flowering hedge and a driveway. It looked this morning as it always did. Even though she had been gone for months, the grass stayed clipped, the beds were watered and the windows gleamed. I knew the swimming pool in back would be sparkling and blue. The whole place appeared fresh and clean.

I supposed somebody kept the place up, but I had never seen anyone working there. It just stayed tended and blooming, as though Annie would back her Mercury convertible out of the drive at any moment.

When Annie got officially declared dead, ownership of her place had passed to her mother, Grace Gardiner, who lived on the other side of me, in a white stucco two-story with red awnings. The two women had never acknowledged their relationship as far as I knew, not when Annie had lived here. They had simply treated each other as close friends and neighbors, and it wasn't until after Annie left that I knew they were mother and daughter. The two lovely houses and the lovely women in them bracketed my dumpy bungalow on either side.

The Gardiner's front door swung open, and Grace came out onto the veranda.

"You're home!" she called. "We've been waiting for you!"

I was glad to see her. It would be hard to guess her age, but I figured she had left her seventies behind. A fine, elegant woman, I felt sure she had never been seen beyond her own bedroom door with less than perfect hair, nails, and makeup.

Annie had come by her beauty honestly, even though the two women didn't resemble each other. While the mother reminded me of a silent film actress, comfortable in pearls and silk, her daughter appeared natural in peasant fabric and sandals. Annie's golden skin and dark eyes were a gift from her long-dead Hawaiian father.

Only a couple of people knew that Grace Gardiner had killed the biggest gangster in Santa Teresa, when he had threatened Annie. She had parked her old black Cadillac in front of his nightclub and walked into his office in the back. None of his tough bodyguards had paid her the slightest attention. She exchanged pleasantries with him, and then she had awkwardly pulled a heavy pistol from her purse, aimed it with both hands and shot him in the face.

I didn't put a lot of stock in having friends, and didn't have many of them, but Grace was my friend. I wanted to talk to her, but I wanted a bath and some sleep worse. I gave her a 'later' wave, fished out my keys and went up my front steps.

The lock still stuck, the way it always had. Nothing had fixed itself while I was gone. I jiggled it until it gave up and let me in. The hallway was warm and dry and still, and smelled a little bit like must. I heard a faucet drip, from the kitchen sink in back. I had never gotten around to fixing it, and the unchanging drip-drip had gone on the whole time I had been away. The house had waited for me, nearly motionless, and that comforted me in some strange way.

I took my suitcase into the bedroom and unpacked it. It didn't take long. The clean clothes got put back into the closet and bureau. The dirty got bundled to go to the Chinese laundry on Anacapa Street. When I finished, I glanced around the room. There wasn't much in it, just a bed and bureau on a wooden floor. A lot like me, I thought. Nearly empty, a little dusty, and waiting for something.

I went into the kitchen and fixed myself a short bourbon, with a faucet water chaser. I drank it standing at the kitchen sink. Then I went to the couch in the living room and stretched out on the chesterfield. I watched shadows cross the ceiling, back and forth, until I fell asleep.

-Four-

Hours later, I stood on the next-door veranda. After I rang the bell, I glanced back at the street; the vantage was subtly different than what I saw from my house. It always struck me strange to see a familiar thing from someone else's point of view. Mrs. Gardiner opened the front door, and let me in. I followed her up the hall. Soft music from a phonograph played somewhere in the house.

"It's Mendelssohn," the old woman said. "The Violin Concerto in E minor, if my husband asks you. You confused Mahler with Beethoven once, and he's never gotten over it. You blurt out guesses and then go on with your life, and I'm left to hear about it for weeks."

"I'll be more careful," I promised. "Mendelssohn in E minor, it is."

About halfway up the hall I stopped in front of a painting suspended on the dark panelling. A small bulb beneath the frame lighted it, but it didn't need it. The colors shimmered, unmistakably Annie Kahlo's work.

"This is new?" I asked.

"It's very new. She sent it for my last birthday."

Annie never talked about it, but I knew she had made a lot of money with her art when she was very young. Some of her works had even hung in a museum once, somewhere in Belgium. The building got bombed in the war, and the paintings were lost. Annie mourned them, and had stopped selling her images or showing them publicly.

We stood quietly, and watched the painting. That was the thing about an Annie Kahlo work; you didn't look at it. You watched it. None of them ever held still.

Something about her stuff was recognizable from a thousand yards away, if you knew how to see it. Annie used color in a way you tasted and smelled. She put a light on ordinary things and made you see they weren't ordinary at all. Everything she painted seemed brand new, and looking at them always made me feel funny, like I needed to take a deep breath.

"Tell me what you see," Mrs. Gardiner said.

A snail moved across a rock. The colors were soft, pale purples and greens that seemed almost to breathe. An insistent, soft wind brought bright grass, and the smell of running water. The snail reared its head, looking around. A handsome fellow, with a face like a stallion, it seemed powerfully good, like something you'd ride into a battle. It was just a snail, though. Annie never tried to make things something they weren't. She made you see what they really were.

"I feel like I never saw a snail before," I said. "This is the first time."

"Exactly," Mrs. Gardiner said, happily. "Annie says the things she paints can move on their own. It's all a doorway—to somewhere else. She could teach Monet a thing or two about color, in my opinion."

"It has everything to do with music, and nothing to do with what you see."

We both turned. Dr. Gardiner had come up behind us. He stood, slightly stooped, with his hands behind his back. He gazed at the snail, not at us.

"You hear the colors, like music," he said. "You don't see them."

We looked at the snail, and waited politely for him to explain. He didn't.

"Drinks are ready," he said.

He turned, and Mrs. Gardiner shrugged and gave me a what-can-you-do expression. We followed him to the end of the dim hallway and out into the glass-roofed conservatory at the back of the house. The air felt warm and damp to the point of wet. The heavy odors of greenery and black dirt rode over the perfumes of the potted lilies and orchids. The blossoms were all pink. Pink was the doctor's obsession, and he grew flowers in every shade of pink he could manage.

Mrs. Gardiner took my arm, and spoke into my ear, like a conspirator.

"It's best to let him have the last word," she told me. "He will, anyway, even if you try to resist."

The doctor led us outside, to a table and chairs set up beneath a green-and-white striped umbrella. The drinks trolley ready, he got busy mixing and stirring while I pulled out a chair for Mrs. Gardiner. I knew whatever he served me would be sweet and impossible to identify, and that it would have a lot of gin in it.

When we were seated, I held the glass Dr. Gardiner gave me up to the light. The liquid showed up a sort of chartreuse color today. I tried it. It tasted dreadful, but I knew the gin would compensate eventually, so I choked some of it down.

Mrs. Gardiner held up an arm for me to inspect a large welt on her skin.

"I worked out here yesterday," she said. "I had finished trimming the jacarandas, and was nearly done for the day, when I felt something land on my arm. I glanced down just as it bit me. It had wings that were rotating rapidly, and it flew off before I could get a good look at it."

"You don't say," I said, and meant it.

"It wasn't a bee—I'm sure about that. It could have been some sort of huge horsefly that hasn't been discovered yet, but . . . " She leaned close, for emphasis. "I'm worried about vampire bats. I don't know what they look like in real life, so who's to say?"

I got my reading glasses from my pocket. I put them on, and took her arm to have a closer look. The skin had bruised, with a red welt in the center.

"It bled a lot," she offered. "The whole experience was very painful. Since you're a detective, I felt sure you would know how to identify it."

"I'm no expert," I said, and gave her back her arm. "But, I think a vampire bat would leave two puncture marks, and I see only one. You're probably safe on that account."

"If it was a new kind of fly, it had big teeth—or perhaps one huge tooth," she said. "I scrubbed the wound with carbolic soap, and put alcohol on it. I don't feel sick, at least not yet. There's a lot of Dengue fever going around these days, and that's the last thing I need."

"Bats don't carry Dengue fever," the doctor said. He sounded positive. "It was a fly. I was reading the Sunday paper this morning, and thinking that my vision had gotten blurry, or else the newspaper was printed badly. A fly came right through my glasses and hit me in the eye. I took them off to see how that had been possible, and found one of the lenses missing."

He paused, to give her a significant glare.

"You were with me all morning, and you never said a thing."

"I thought you took the lens out for your own reasons," she said. "If I commented on every strange thing you do that I don't understand, we'd talk about nothing else."

No one paid any attention to me, so I saw the opportunity to refill my drink. I dragged the crystal pitcher over and topped my glass. The sweetened gin wasn't half-bad, after the first couple. When you started to like the taste, you knew you were good and drunk.

"It certainly wasn't the same fly," Mrs. Gardiner finished. "My fly would have taken your eye out and flown off with it."

Husband and wife began to studiously ignore each other, so I gazed around the yard. It was one of the most beautiful places I knew about. There was always a sound of running water. Every time the breeze came up, the canvas umbrella fluttered overhead and a row of shower trees along the back littered the lawn with yellow petals.

A group of five peacocks moved around, commenting quietly to each other about everything they saw. I knew they were Mrs. Gardiner's pride and joy. One of them was pure white.

It was all very restful, and just as my eyes began to drift close, my hostess broke the silence.

"Tell us about you," she said. "Tell us about Mexico—and Annie."

"I got back last night," I said. "I ran into a problem. I hurried the drive back so I could get to a beach motel in time to get some Saturday night adultery photographs—"

"You're a divorce photographer," she interrupted, delighted. "Some people are wedding photographers, and you give the opposite service. You should put that in the business directory, under 'Photographers, Specialty'—you'll be rich, in no time."

I told them about my night. I had no way to know whether the doctor listened, but Mrs. Gardiner's attention stayed rapt. Like her daughter, when she got interested in something, her focus stayed complete.

"You went for a walk in the middle of the night, and returned to your hotel room to find a dead woman bathing in your tub," she marvelled. "What a story! Are you in trouble?"

"I might be," I admitted. "If the coroner says the girl was murdered, I don't have much explanation for things. I don't think she snuck into my hotel room and drowned herself. Somebody helped her, and the obvious person is me."

"I think it's wonderful," she exclaimed, and put her hands together to prove it. "So much more interesting than your usual adultery cases. You must be very happy. Forget what I said about photography—this is what you were born to do."

"It's already been done," the doctor grumbled. "We saw it a couple of years ago. '*Murder My Sweet*', with Dick Powell and Anne Shirley."

He finished his drink, set the glass on the table, and went inside. I could see him through the conservatory windows, examining his pink flowers. Mrs. Gardiner stared after him, appearing puzzled. Then her face cleared.

"*Murder My Sweet* isn't the same at all," she said. "Except that Dick Powell wakes up with a dead body and has to explain it to the police, and you remind me a great deal of Dick Powell. Did I ever tell you that? You are both very ordinary looking. It's a strange quality to find in a movie star."

She put a hand on mine and gave me an earnest look.

"Don't ever see a film with him," she said. "Promise me."

"Don't see a movie with Dick Powell?" I asked, surprised. "I thought you liked his movies."

She took her hand away, offended, and used it to pick up her martini glass. "Of course, I love Dick Powell," she said. "I'm talking about my husband. He analyzes the faults in every film we see. Sometimes he spots a plot weakness and gets so incensed he blurts it out right in the theater. It spoils things for everyone within earshot."

"Is he right?" I asked. "The things he points out?"

"Of course, he's right," she said. "He's absolutely right. That's what makes it so unbearable."

I agreed seeing a movie with the doctor sounded like a bad idea, and promised to never do so, at least not willingly.

"I put little balls of cotton in my ears," she confided. "I can still hear the movie, just not as well—and I can't hear his awful muttering and carrying on, right next to me."

A large tabby cat appeared from a group of ficus trees in the corner of the yard. It made a sinuous path across the grass, spots undulating in the sun. It stared at the peacocks without showing any curiosity, and then disappeared around a corner of the house. I knew it wasn't a house cat at all. It was an ocelot, and it belonged to Annie.

Mrs. Gardiner insisted the large cat never bothered the peacocks. If he did, then she had more peacocks stashed away somewhere and replaced them when they went missing. I wondered if it was wrong to deliberately cover up a crime for an ocelot, and it occurred to me that the gin might be going to my head.

"What are you going to do about the murdered girl?" she asked, returning to the subject of my trouble.

"Nothing, for now. If the police decide I killed her, then things are going to get very complicated."

"No, things are very simple," she corrected. "Do what you always do. Find out the truth about what happened to her, and clear your name."

"This isn't my case," I said. "I don't have a client, and what happened to the young woman isn't really any of my business."

"If you are going to be accused of murdering her, then it's very much your business. You can be your own client. Write yourself a check, and get started."

"Check would bounce," I smiled.

Dr. Gardiner came back outside, and poured himself a fresh drink. He pulled his chair back, so he sat a little bit farther away than before.

"Of course, this is all a message from Destiny," his wife said to me. "You should have stayed in Mexico, much as I would have missed you here. You belong there, and when you came back, bad things began to happen to you."

"I hadn't thought about it quite like that," I said.

"Of course, you hadn't," she said, pleased with herself. "That's why you come to talk to me."

That part was true. I did trust her, and I came here to get her take on things. She was wise, and thought about things from an angle I couldn't. I depended on her, despite the dreadful drinks served by her husband.

"And Annie?" Mrs. Gardiner wondered. "Is she lonely? Is she happy?"

I figured that being lonely was something Annie Kahlo had always done. I didn't know if she even noticed it, anymore.

"Corazón Rosa is very beautiful," I said. "It's hard to find, even if you have a map. The train comes once a week, and leaves you at a tin shed beside the tracks, in the middle of nowhere. It only stops if you ask the conductor in advance. There's a kind of cart track that goes across the desert and up into the hills."

She looked misty, and knocked her drink when she reached for it. I caught it before it spilled, and put it safely into her hands.

"You walk up and up," I said. "When you get to the top, the ocean is all of a sudden spread out before you, as far as you can see. The town sits facing the beach, hidden in a fold in the hills. In the morning, the fishing boats go out. They come back at night, and all the dogs in town get excited. Other than that, it's mostly quiet."

"Is she happy?" she asked, again.

When I thought about Annie Kahlo, I imagined her sitting at a blue-checked tablecloth splashed with sun. I could smell the lemon on a plate in front of her, cut into quarters. She was made from gold, hair and skin. That didn't make sense, and I had no way to explain it out loud, so I didn't try.

"She's fine," I said. "She has a little place on the water. It isn't much more than a couple of rooms with a tiny courtyard, but I don't think she wants more. She paints, and walks on the beach. The locals treat her like she's lived there forever."

"She has a house here," Dr. Gardiner interrupted. "She doesn't need a house in Mexico, too."

I didn't have an answer for that. Annie lived in exile, and she would never come back here, not in this lifetime. It would mean the gas chamber if she did. I glanced at Mrs. Gardiner. She had finished her drink and was pouring another.

"Are you taking care of her house?" I asked him. "I leave my place for a few weeks and it looks abandoned. Her house looks perfect. It makes no sense."

"When something makes no sense, it's almost always to do with love," Mrs. Gardiner offered.

"Those Mexican gardeners—her friends," the doctor said. "They come around once in a while to clip the grass and trim the hedges. I help where I can. I like to take care of the swimming pool."

"It feels like she's still here, out back watering the flowers, or sitting beside the pool with a book."

"She *is* here, she's always here," Mrs. Gardiner said. "Annie takes care of her business long-distance. She loves fiercely. Even if she never comes back, she's always here."

The sun went behind a cloud, and a gust rattled the umbrella and made the shower trees send down yellow petals.

"Some people are like that," she mused. "They aren't like us. They have a foot in another world—they understand strange things. Even when she was a little girl, I knew that a part of her lived somewhere else."

All of Annie lived somewhere else right now, I thought, and that's why I was so miserable. The shower trees rustled their leaves and cried more blossoms. I took another sip of my terrible martini, because I didn't know what else to do.

-Five-

The pebbled glass pane set into my office door had "Crowe Investigations" painted on it in tasteful gold and black letters. I stopped in the hall to admire it before I let myself in. Looking at it made it hard not to take myself seriously, even if nobody else did.

The place needed airing. Nearly a month's mail littered the waiting room floor. I gathered it into a neat pile and took it through into my office. It took me less than a minute to flip through it and satisfy myself none of the envelopes contained a check. I threw the entire stack into the wastebasket, unopened.

There were four dead flies on the windowsill. I got the window open and shooed them out. The phone on my desk rang as I sat down, just as though it had been waiting for me. I stared hard at it, in case it was playing some kind of trick. It rang again, though, so I picked it up. I recognized the voice on the other end, at once.

"He got to you somehow, didn't he?" it said. "The son of a bitch."

"Nobody got to me, Mrs. Highland."

"Then where are my pictures? Where are the photographs I paid you to take?"

"You haven't given me a dime," I reminded her. "I didn't even ask you for a retainer."

I leaned my chair back against the windowsill, and checked the clock on the wall. It had been made to look like Krazy Kat. It rolled its eyes and stuck out its tongue at me, all because it was nine o'clock in the morning.

"That's because you haven't produced anything," she said in a reasonable tone, just as if she made sense. "Why should I pay you any money for doing nothing?"

I hooked the top desk drawer open with a toe. An unopened bottle of Four Roses sat inside, right where I'd left it. I studied it carefully for a moment, and glanced at the clock again. It was probably too early for bourbon.

"I've been out of the country, Mrs. Highland," I sighed. "I left you word before I went, remember? If your husband and his secretary are spending Saturday evenings at the Sand Castle as regularly as you suggest, I'll have your photographs this weekend."

"I don't see why you don't just go to his office," she complained. "I'm sure they spend more time screwing each other than they do working."

I looked at the bottle again, reconsidering. I kept a spare Browning in the locked middle drawer right underneath it.

"That's a good idea," I said. "I can visit his office and sit quietly in the waiting room until they remove their clothes. It should have occurred to me."

"You sound impertinent," she said, too loudly. "Are you being impertinent?"

If I were talking to Mrs. Highland in person, I could use the Browning to shoot her. Maybe her husband would give me a reward. In the end, I said some soothing things and again promised quick results before I hung up. I needed her money.

A small noise came from the outer office. I went around the desk and stuck my head into the waiting room. A woman sat in a chair, looking at one of the old magazines I had put out.

"I didn't think anyone would ever read those," I said. "I scattered them for decoration."

She glanced up at me coolly, through lenses in cat-eye frames. Her face stayed all business.

"I overheard your telephone conversation, Mister Crowe," she said. "I'm sorry, but I couldn't help it. I have to say, you don't inspire much confidence."

"Nothing to be sorry about," I said. "Would you like to come in?"

She went past me and straight to the client's chair across from my desk. A new electric percolator was plugged into the wall. I was proud of it. Some people said they didn't like the way the electricity made the brew taste, but I thought it made swell coffee. Since I had a brought a bag of fresh grinds with me, I set about making some.

"I haven't got any milk," I offered, using my most cheerful voice. "There's fresh sugar, though."

She didn't want small talk, and she jerked her head like a fly had landed on it.

"Fin sent me," she said. "He has a job for you."

"I know that," I said. "He sent me a telegram calling me back from Mexico, and now he's sending you. What makes him think I want a job?"

We looked at each other while the coffee worked. She was tall, even sitting down. Her hair had been pulled back into a bun tight enough to bounce, and she wore a tweed suit. I tried to guess if she'd be better looking with her clothes off. I couldn't decide. I used to be a pretty good judge of that, but since I met Annie my heart didn't seem to be in it any more.

"I don't care if you want a job or not," she said. "I'm bringing you a message."

When the coffee was ready, I found a clean cup and filled it. She shook her head at sugar, so I handed it to her black. She tasted it.

"That's terrible coffee," she said. "Everyone knows the electric percolators are no good."

"I insist on liking it," I said. "I think if you want to be modern, you have to make adjustments."

"Fin told me you were a wise guy," she said. "He says it's incurable, until someone shoots you. He also said you don't believe in anything at all, and that makes you the most trustworthy person he's ever known."

She set the cup on the edge of my desk, and then pushed it away an inch further, as if to underline how much she hated it. She gazed at me. The lenses of her glasses made her grey eyes seem very wide. "Is that true?"

"That I'm trustworthy?" I shrugged. "I don't break rules, as long as they're ones I made up myself. I don't expect anything from other people."

"And you don't believe in anything?"

I thought about Corazón Rosa, and a black sand beach in thin early light, and Annie Kahlo looking out at water that was still dark. I thought about a lemon on a plate, yellow with sun, and her cutting into it with artist's hands and a knife.

"I believe in a couple of things," I said.

She considered me steadily, but I didn't offer to explain. She didn't offer to drink any more of her coffee, either, so it remained a stalemate. She fished a folded piece of paper from her purse, leaned forward and fluttered it into the desk in front of me. Unfolded, it had a place and time written on it. I recognized Fin's elaborate, spidery handwriting:

Santa Teresa Art Museum, front entrance, One A.M.

"He's going to take me to the museum," I said. "Sounds like a swell date. What's this all about?"

"Don't be foolish," she answered. "Do you imagine Fin would tell me that? I meant to bring you a message, and now I've done it."

She snapped her purse closed, stood up and went to the door. I kept my seat.

"I've known Fin for a while," I said. "Never met you, though. Are you a—special friend of his?"

She didn't take any offense at the absurd idea of Fin being tangled up romantically with her. The barest ghost of a smile tugged at the corner of her mouth and was gone. I smiled, too.

"I'm a kind of associate," she said. "I manage the South Seas Room. You'll see me again if he needs you to see me."

"What's your name?" I asked.

"I can't see you ever needing to know that—but it's Chessie," she said. "Chessie Emerson. If you want to know more than that about me, hire a detective."

The outer door closed. Her steps tapped up the hallway and then it got quiet again. I picked up the piece of paper she had given me. It didn't say anything new.

I would never be broke enough to willingly take Fin's money. I owed him though, so I didn't have much choice. I didn't even know what he was, exactly. A criminal, certainly, with his hand in most things that went on in the Santa Teresa darkness, but he had antique ideas about good and evil. He liked to talk about angels and demons, every chance he got.

He drove a gray Packard, and sucked on lozenges that smelled strongly of bitter almond. He said they were medicine for his heart. Someone told me once, in a serious way, he used arsenic; had gotten addicted to the mild hallucinations the poison gave him. Nobody knew exactly what he was involved in or how much he owned, where he lived or when he would turn up. The local gangsters were terrified of him, and the cops didn't know he existed.

I wasn't sure he was human.

The visit from Chessie Emerson surprised me, because Fin had always worked alone, like religion. Maybe she wasn't human, either. I reached across the desk, hooked a thumb in her coffee cup and dragged it over. It was cold, but I leaned back and drank it anyway. I looked out the window and waited for it to be lunchtime.

~*~

My friend Danny López owned a drive-in restaurant on lower Chapala Street. He had opened it a couple of decades ago, before it became popular for people to eat in their cars. I guess he saw the future. Some days I thought everyone but me had an inside track. The tan stucco builring had a big window in front for service, with a gravel parking lot behind it. López was richer than a pharaoh, but he worked at the grill most days.

I ordered myself a couple of hot dogs. The young woman at the window didn't let her black eyes meet mine, and she deftly squirted mustard and piled onions without my asking. She filled a paper cup full of ice and then soda from the fountain, and pushed it across to me with the food. As usual, she wouldn't take my money. As usual, I left two bits on the counter anyway. I knew she had a little girl at home, and that she worked a lot harder than I did.

Red-and-white metal tables were grouped in the shade of a live oak behind the drive-in, and I went to them to wait for López. With the lunch rush over I had the area to myself. I had nearly finished eating when he came out the back door, followed by a tiny Chihuahua that looked more arthritic than his owner. The two of them hobbled over to me and sat down. López struck a match on the tabletop and carefully lit what might have once been a cigar. I smelled the sulfur before the wind took it away.

"You always order the same thing," he said, looking at my hot dog. "*Siempre lo mismo.*"

"Saves me thinking about it," I shrugged. "No point in adding any more decisions to my day."

His smile looked like something that had been dried in the sun.

"I never would have thought of it," he said. "That's why you are a famous detective, and I work at a little taco stand."

"One of the reasons," I agreed.

The little dog bared his teeth at me.

"*Oye, Chiquillo,*" López warned. "*Pórtate bien.*"

The dog ignored him. A low growl started up. His eyes were filmy and his muzzle was grey, but he acted entirely ready to tear my throat out.

"Chiquillo would kill you if he could, *amigo*. That is why God made him so small. Sometimes God protects us from ourselves."

Danny López had come here from Corazón Rosa twenty years ago. He opened his drive-in every morning and stood over the grill every lunch hour alongside his help. He lived poor and drove a truck held together by rust. He was one of the most powerful gangsters in the state, wealthy beyond reason, and probably the most dangerous man I knew. Like Fin, he lived and worked in the shadows. Unlike Fin, he lived under a noble sort of personal code. He served as a kind of protector for the denizens of the barrios, a kind of wrinkled brown Robin Hood. A lot of children went to school with full bellies because López saw to it they did.

He was also the best friend I had. He had saved Annie Kahlo's life, and she lived in Mexico now under his protection. He loved her fiercely, but not as much as I did. Because that was impossible, I didn't hold it against him.

"You don't pay for your meals here," he said. "I do not permit it."

"I appreciate it," I nodded.

"So, you don't need to leave the girl money every time you come here." His voice stayed soft. "I pay her very well."

"I know you do," I said. "It makes me feel good, though. You can't take it with you, right?"

"I think maybe you're wrong about that, *amigo*," he said. "What if you do take it with you?"

Curious, I looked at him and waited.

"What if you have no choice?" he mused. "You wake up on the other side, and you're stuck with everything you bought, everything you stole, everything you had to have in this life? I think you take all of it with you, and that frightens me more than anything I can think of. I wake up some nights, and worry about it."

A blue Plymouth crunched onto the gravel and stopped. A couple of hard cases got out and stood for a minute, looking around. Satisfied, they stretched, threw away cigarettes and headed to the order window. Danny López barely glanced at them, but I knew he watched them carefully. He never missed anything.

"Can you do something for me?" he asked.

I didn't have to nod. He knew the answer. There wasn't much I wouldn't do for him.

"A woman has come to me for help," he said. "She had a brother, much younger than herself, who died. She believes he got murdered, and she has asked me to kill the man responsible."

"I'll help, if I can," I said. "I'm not going to kill him, either."

"I know that." He patted the air to calm me down. "I'm not asking you to kill anyone. It would be a simple thing, but the people involved are not Mexicans. Her father was one of us, a good man, but he died years ago. Her mother was a *gringa* with no connection to our community. You know my policy. I stay inside my own world."

"Why did she come to you?"

"People hear stories about me." He shrugged. "I think it would be a good thing to look into what she says. The man is nothing but a common criminal. If there is truth to her story, it might be a simple matter to arrange that he goes to jail for something else."

"I can do that."

"I will tell her to contact you," he nodded. "If you can help her, then I will arrange payment. She has no money to spend on this, but I do. It's what I can do for her father's memory. I don't think this should take much time away from your detective business."

"What business?" I asked. "I hardly have any business anymore."

Over at the counter, one of the tough guys laughed loudly. López stirred, and puffed at his little cigar. Then he dropped it and put it out with the toe of his *huarache*. The men glanced over at us and then away; they were suddenly aware of us sitting there. They knew who the old man was. After they had paid for their food, they moved back to the Plymouth and got in. As they pulled away, López settled again.

"You were in the newspapers," he shrugged. "Not good for a man whose business is keeping secrets. Things will go back to the way they were, in time. People always forget, if you stay in the shadows long enough."

I finished the last of my hot dog, and crumpled the yellow waxed paper into a ball. I twisted my torso and fired it into a steel trash drum. One-hopper to first base, an easy double play that Pee Wee Reese couldn't have turned any better.

"I should have stuck with baseball," I said.

"You should have stuck with Annie Kahlo." He gave me a sharp look. "You belong in Mexico, with her. You shouldn't have left her there."

"I had to come back—unfinished business." I shrugged. "Now you've added to it."

I watched the parking lot and the traffic going by on

Chapala Street. The sun felt warm but not hot, and a nice breeze gusted. When the stoplight turned red, I got a drift of music from an open car window. I recognized the opening saxophone notes of "I Love You Madly". After a minute the light turned green, and the car left and took the music away with it.

"You should not have come back here," he insisted. "This is not your place anymore."

I held up a hand, in protest. My throat got suddenly tight, but I spoke carefully and kept my voice normal.

"I tried," I said. "You know something? I asked her about staying down there for good. I asked her to marry me."

My eyes were stinging, just a little.

"She didn't answer me, one way or the other," I said. "She just didn't answer—so I came back. I didn't just come here for business. I needed to give her some room, some time to herself. I was going to lose her, if I didn't."

López leaned forward on the bench. His elbows were on his knees, his gaze liquid and dark. His focus stayed absolute. I didn't want to look at him.

"Maybe if you wait a little while, she will tell you," he said. "She moves according to her own time."

I stood up and brushed imaginary crumbs from my jacket. I would have a long walk back to my car.

"Maybe I'd rather not risk hearing the answer," I said. "See you around, Danny."

"I will tell the woman to telephone your office," he called after me. "She has no one to turn to. Help her if you can."

-Six-

A long time after it got dark, I pulled the Ford to a curb at the north end of State Street, at the edge of downtown. The street was a little bit more genteel here than at the ocean end. I parked in front of a bank adorned with phony columns that didn't support anything.

I got my gun from the map compartment and slipped it into the holster under my arm before I stepped out. It wasn't that I didn't trust Fin. In fact, I had never known what to think about him. It was a strange time for a meeting, even by his standards, and my guard stayed up. I pocketed my keys and glanced across the street at the art museum.

Fig branches and drooping willows overhung a broad flight of steps. In the dark, it looked like an artist had drawn the trees in ink and charcoal. They rose all the way up to the arches and pillars of the museum entrance. It was a civilized, pleasant kind of place, even at one o'clock in the morning, and I had it all to myself.

A white stone lion stood at the very top. He kept an eye on the street below, but he didn't seem as though anything that went on down there would bother him very much. When I got there, I gave his cold head a pat.

"The rest of us keep getting older," I told him. "You look better all the time. How do you do it?"

A single electric light burned over the museum door. The blue bulb didn't cast a whole lot of light. I checked the shadows, but didn't see any movement.

"Do you like lions, Mister Crowe?"

The voice came from behind me. I spun around and saw a lone hat-and-coat figure, sitting on a wooden bench at the very edge of the light. It was Fin.

"Don't be bashful," he said. "It isn't your best quality."

I walked over to where he sat. Up close, I caught a whiff of the bitter marzipan that followed him like perfume. He looked up at me, and the light caught his face. It was as gaunt as the rest of him, all aquiline nose and hollowed cheeks. It would have been impossible to guess his age. In fact, when I tried to remember his face just hours after a meeting him, I really couldn't. He wouldn't stick in my mind, and I couldn't tell you if he was fat or thin, good looking or plain, tall or short.

I tried to get a glimpse of him that would stay with me, and as though he sensed it, he shifted slightly. The brim of his hat took all the light and left his face in darkness again.

"I like the museum," he said. "There's nothing inside it that pleases my taste as much as what Miss Kahlo paints, but one makes do. Don't you agree?"

Mention of Annie's name made me uneasy. She knew Fin, and she actually liked him. They shared an odd affection, or at least an understanding, but it still made me nervous when he mentioned her. I didn't trust him. If I ever met the Devil, I figured he would remind me a whole lot of Fin.

"I'm here," I said. "What do you want?"

"I lost a body for you, Mister Crowe," he reminded me. "I arranged for Miss Kahlo to vanish into thin air. I would have done it for her regardless, but she didn't ask me to. You did. That places you in my debt."

I didn't deny it. Annie lived in Mexico under Danny López'

protection, but she wouldn't have made it there without Fin. I owed him, and I paid what I owed.

"I'm not unreasonable," he said. "I didn't set a price, or make any demands. At the time, you offered to help me in return, if I ever needed it. It happens that now I do."

"I'm here," I said, again.

"So you are," he said. "I knew I wouldn't have to persuade you unduly. I'm never wrong about a man's character, though occasionally women mislead me. They are infinitely more complicated, more subtle, more cunning—don't you agree?"

I shrugged. I could fit what I knew about women in my hat and still have room for my head.

"You have involved yourself in another murder," he said. "A sordid scene in a motel bathroom. So unfortunate—such a shame. It's a habit that may one day put you in a place that you cannot escape from."

"That just happened," I said. "How do you know about that?"

He shifted on the bench, and peered up at me. I couldn't tell for sure if he smiled.

"The wind blows, Mr. Crowe. The wind blows and the wind swings. I hear most of what goes on in this city—especially if it concerns me."

"Beatrice Stone concerns you? The coroner hasn't even ruled her death a murder, yet."

"Murder doesn't concern me," he said. "The girl was a common alcoholic who will be missed by nobody at all. She stole something, though, and it didn't get recovered before she died. Someone has asked me to look into it, and in turn, I'm asking you."

"I'm listening."

"Our mutual friend was negotiating the return of the item in question with Miss Stone," he said. "They had not reached an agreed price, but then she got killed. The whereabouts of the item is unknown—it has disappeared, along with her soul."

He extended one hand, and blew into his fingers as though he held a dandelion puff. I could almost swear I saw tiny parachutes floating in the blue light.

"You found her body in a bathtub, and now you can help to find what she stole," he said. "Isn't serendipity delightful?"

"And you have no horse in this race," I said. "You're simply brokering favors—calling in the one I owe you?"

"I like to help people when I can, Mister Crowe. I helped you, remember?"

His shoulders shook, with whatever passed for laughter in Fin's mind.

"What did she steal?" I asked.

"That is not for me to say, Mister Crowe." He shook his head. "In any case, you will hear it from the principals."

He passed me a business card. I couldn't read it in the low light, so I tucked it into my pocket.

"The man in question is expecting you at ten o'clock tomorrow morning," he said. "You have an appointment."

"Why me, Fin?" I asked. "You're certainly—capable. You have more resources than I do. Why not take care of this yourself?"

"Because you can go to places I cannot," he said. "Or will not. We are opposites, but every card, every coin has another side.

That makes you my—friend."

He tasted the strangeness of the word before he went on. He made a strange sound that might have been a laugh.

"My friend," he mused. "Sometimes the darkest, most dangerous corners are filled with angels, not demons. Isn't that how you see yourself, Mister Crowe? As some kind of an angel?"

"Why did you send me a telegram in Mexico, Fin?" I asked. "You sent for me before any of this even happened. The girl was alive when you summoned me. Did you know she would get murdered?"

"Perhaps I am prescient, Mister Crowe," he said. "Or perhaps we only wanted you to expedite the return of the stolen item."

"You hardly needed a private operative for that," I said. "If you had, the telephone directory is full of them. Now there's a dead girl, and this concerns me personally. Is that an accident?"

Neither of us spoke, and after a minute he slipped something from his breast pocket. I had seen the metal pillbox before; the blue light caught at its shiny surface. He slipped a tablet into his mouth. When he spoke again, I could smell the poison on his breath.

"I have no interest in the resolution of your inquiries," he said. "I don't care whether you decide to take the job, or what fee you charge. I have simply agreed to implore you to see the prospective client."

"I'll see your friend, Fin, and listen to what they have to say. I still don't know why you don't take care of this yourself."

"This may involve a kind of magic," he said. "The sort of magic I prefer to stay away from. I am not immune to self-preservation, Mister Crowe, and perhaps not as invulnerable as you think."

He wheezed another of his strange laughs.

"Miss Beatrice Stone chose you," he said. "She found you, to die in your hotel room. Perhaps the favor you will be doing is for her."

I felt an unexpected flash of emotion, like grief and sorrow, all mixed up. It made a bad cocktail.

"I didn't know her," I said. "And I don't know the first thing about magic."

"Perhaps you will get to know her," he said. "You have a strange talent for mixing the personal and intimate into what perhaps should only be business."

He stood up and dusted the shoulders of his suit carefully. It looked odd, as though he tried to brush away the blue light that fell on him from the museum doorway. He touched the brim of his hat, and moved off.

"The wind blows, Mister Crowe, and the wind swings," he said over his shoulder, not looking back. "Fig's a dance."

~*~

Gaynor Glass had its offices in a sand-colored building on De la Vina Street, a block from the bus station. One of the few buildings in Santa Teresa more than three stories high, it was one of those places I had passed countless times and never had occasion to enter. Wide sidewalks, no trees, and not much traffic ran along the street in front of it. Without any of the usual figs or palms, the sun always seemed hotter and brighter along that stretch. Undressed of greenery, the desert's bones showed through.

The lobby had high ceilings, and walls made of concrete, colored to resemble granite. There were a lot of businesses that I had never heard of listed in the glass-fronted directory on the wall. Gaynor Glass took up the whole sixth floor. I checked my reflection in the glass. Satisfied that my summer-weight suit appeared respectable, I headed for the elevator.

The doors opened onto an expanse of marble floor. The reception area doubled as a showroom. The young woman behind a desk jumped in surprise when I stepped out of the elevator. Maybe they didn't get a lot of visitors here. She recovered enough to smile at me, in a practiced sort of way.

"May I help you, sir?" she asked, as though she had rehearsed the line.

"You certainly may," I replied, as though I had rehearsed mine. "My name is Crowe. I have a ten o'clock meeting with Mister Harold Gaynor."

She consulted the large appointment book open on the desk, and looked perplexed. She clearly didn't have her next cue.

"That's Crowe with an 'e' at the end," I said helpfully. "Ten o'clock."

She excused herself, stood up and went offstage. I lit a cigarette and wandered around. The walls of the reception area were shelved, lighted and mirrored. They were stuffed with displays of glassware; vases, drinking glasses, empty bottles of every size and shape, all of it tinted the same shade of dark green. The receptionist trotted back out onto the showroom floor.

"Here you are!" she exclaimed.

She held out a sheet of white paper, and gave me a nice white smile to match.

"Mister Gaynor's private secretary left instructions for you," she said. "He has been called out of town unexpectedly, on business. She herself is in a meeting at the Madagascar Hotel, in Montelindo, and will meet you for a drink or perhaps lunch when she is done. Do you need directions?"

"I know the place," I said. "Should I sit in the lobby with a rose held in my teeth until she finds me?"

"Perhaps the front desk will know who you are," she said. "Miss Lane will likely have you paged."

I counted to ten. It didn't help at all.

"I'm not doing any more running around. When you see Mister Gaynor, sister, tell him that isn't how I operate. He asked to see me, not the other way around. A man named Fin made a ten o'clock appointment here for me, and he won't be pleased to hear nobody had the manners to keep it. Tell Gaynor that, too."

I stopped snarling, and made an effort to put on a more reasonable face. I pulled out one of my business cards and set it on the desk in front of her.

"He can call me on the telephone if he'd still like to see me," I said. "The next appointment we make will be in my office, at a time that's convenient for me."

She stared at me as if I'd pulled a gun on her, and I got startled when a single fat tear rolled down her cheek. Careful of her makeup, she wiped it away with the back of her wrist. She shook a little.

"This isn't my fault," she said. "I just started working here, and so far, everyone is perfectly awful."

I had made her cry. I felt perfectly awful, too, which wasn't unusual for me. I had ruined her day, and now I had the urge to give her a pat on the shoulder. It would have made things worse, so I didn't.

"I didn't mean anything by it," I said. "I mostly talk to rotten characters all day, and it gets so I forget how to talk to decent people."

"Mister Gaynor is a rotten character, and so is Miss Lane," she said, and hitched a breath. "Come to think of it, you all deserve one another."

She immediately became aghast at her own indiscretion. I smiled at her and, after a minute, she tried to smile back. "I need this job," she said.

"Mum's the word," I said. "Just because you work for a person doesn't mean you have to like them. That stays between you and me. Thanks for the warning."

I took the paper from her and read the handwriting on it. I saw nothing she hadn't already said.

"You may enjoy having a drink with Miss Lane," she said. "Most men would. She's very attractive, in a certain sort of way."

"I've given up trying to be like most men," I said. "I don't manage to pull it off."

She gave me a long, cool, speculative look. The tears had gone. She put out her hand and I took it. It was soft and dry.

"I'm Miss Child," she said. "Ann Child."

"That happens to be a name I like quite a lot," I said. "I'm in love with someone named Anne, or at least I'm trying to be."

If she was crushed with disappointment at my unavailability, she made a brave show of hiding it. Since she didn't seem like she would start crying again, I told her to have a pleasant afternoon, and settled my hat on my head. With one hand on the doorknob, I turned back.

"How come all of the glass is green?" I asked. "Doesn't this outfit make any other colors?"

"Oh, no. Gaynor Glass makes all kinds of glass in all kinds of colors—everything you can think of. Mister Gaynor's father started the company years ago, and in the beginning they only made green. It started the fortune, so it's a signature color. It's got a funny name."

"Funny?"

"I know it, but I always forget," she said. "Another thing they make a big deal about here."

She pulled a catalogue from somewhere under the surface of her desk and turned some pages.

"Hau tree," she said. "Spelled 'h-a-u'. They call it Hau Tree Green."

"That's really a kind of tree?" I asked. "I've never heard of it."

She furrowed her brow and stuck the tip of her tongue out.

"It's probably something they made up," she said. "I haven't the slightest idea—about anything."

I laughed and pulled the door open.

"You and me both, sister," I said. "You and me both."

~*~

I took the highway south, to Montelindo. I had a lunch date at the Madagascar Hotel. I arrived early without meaning to, and life seemed grand. The hotel sat swank on an acre or two of green lawn, behind a row of king palms. The valet at the front door sneered at the two bits I gave him and sneered at my Ford like it was a pumpkin. He barked the tires in his hurry to get it out of sight. I tightened my tie before I went up the steps.

The lobby was as cool and hushed as a bank vault. Fans whispered from the high ceiling. A woman in a dark blue dress sat on a sofa beneath a potted tree. Through dark glasses, she studied the magazine in her lap and didn't glance up at me as I passed. She probably wasn't Miss Lane in disguise. I went all the way through, and back outside into the hot sun.

The swimming pool glittered the kind of blue that costs money, and a lot of it. A group of pretty young women splashed water and tossed a beach ball around. They chirped gaily to each other and paid no attention at all to the earnest types walking around the edges showing muscle. The whole scene made me tired just looking at it.

I sat down at a table set into the shade of a stucco arch and gazed around. A bright green gecko made his way up the concrete pillar beside me. He stopped every inch or so to test the air and think about things. I started to tell him we were a lot alike when the waiter interrupted us. I asked for a beer, and said not to bother bringing a glass with it.

"Gin fizz," a woman said from beside me. The waiter nodded and left.

I stood up to pull out a chair. She took her time sitting so I could check the set of spectacular legs. The rest of her wore a pale sundress with hat to match. Her hair had been trapped in careful platinum waves and she had wide blue eyes that looked at me as though I had suggested something outrageous. She was a doll, and she knew it.

"I'm Eleanor Lane," she said, in a sweet voice. "Mister Gaynor's private secretary."

"Of course, you are," I said. "How swell for Mister Gaynor."

She curled a lip, and her voice changed.

"What's that supposed to mean, shamus?" she asked.

The waiter presented the drinks. I tasted my elegant hotel beer. It tasted a lot like the beer everywhere else, which disappointed me. I had never tasted a beer that wasn't wonderful though, so I drank a little more of it.

"I don't like you already," she said.

I shrugged, and looked over at the gecko for some help. He crawled up the pillar and flicked out his tongue at me. Across the table from me, Eleanor Lane stuck out her tongue, too.

"Oh, brother," I said.

She dove into her purse and came up with a brown business envelope, which she slapped onto the glass table and pushed across to me. It looked and sounded as though it had a little weight.

"Half," she said. "Five hundred dollars. You'll get that much again when Mister Gaynor is satisfied with the information you come up with."

"Information about what?" I asked.

"Information about a dead woman named Beatrice Stone," she said. Her voice got a little harder. "Apparently you knew her. We want to know everything about her. We want to know who her friends were, where she went to eat, what time she got up in the morning, her favorite color. Find out where she went to school as a child, what her parents gave her for Christmas at ten years old. Everything."

I picked up the envelope and slit it open. The bills inside smelled fresh from the mint. I didn't need to count them.

"Why do you want to know all that?"

"She stole something from Mister Gaynor's aunt. He wants it back."

"What did she steal?" I asked.

She picked up her gin fizz and drained it. She ran a finger across her upper lip and glanced at the hovering waiter, who scurried off to get her another one. He didn't even glance at my half-full bottle of beer.

"You don't need to know that," she said. "Mister Gaynor isn't hiring you to try to find the item, just to get the information he's asking for."

"I don't take the kinds of jobs where nobody wants to tell me anything."

"You'll take what jobs you can get," she said, and looked prettily at me from under her lashes. "I know all about you. You're washed up in this town. You're lucky to get whatever somebody wants to give you, as long as they're willing to take the risk of reading about their problems in the newspaper."

I had heard enough, so I stood up, and got my wallet from a pocket. I tossed a couple of dollars on the table.

"That should cover the drinks," I said. "Nice talking to you. Tell your boss to find someone else."

She stood up a whole lot faster than she had sat down, and moved in front of me. Up close, she smelled as glossy as she looked; a little like good soap and a lot like expensive perfume. Her teeth were white, her lipstick gleamed, and her eyes were so blue it startled me. She leaned into me, rigid.

"You're going to get me fired," she hissed. "What's wrong with you? Be reasonable."

"I'm willing to be reasonable," I said. "I'm not willing to be insulted."

Her body changed, and a whole lot of soft curves brushed against me as she patted me back and toward my seat.

"Can't a girl tease you?" she pouted. "Why do you take everything so serious?"

I took a step back, and went around her. I stuck the envelope of money into her purse on the way by. The waiter nearly bumped into me, hurrying back with her fresh gin fizz.

"You're going to be sorry about this," Eleanor Lane called after me.

I didn't look back. I felt sorry about almost everything that had happened since I came back to Santa Teresa.

-Seven-

"Coroner's presented his verdict," Rex Raines said. "There will be an inquest, but it's a rubber stamp. You'll say your piece and leave. Nobody's interested."

We stood on my front veranda, because he didn't want to come in. A gaggle of children from the apartment house across from me were playing a game in the street. It seemed to involve a rubber ball and some rocks set down as boundary markers. Any minute now, someone's mother would call down from a window and the game would break up for the night.

"She didn't drown," he said. "She had no water in her lungs. Full of gin and barbiturates, she died before she ever went into your bathtub."

"So, it was definitely murder," I said. "Am I a suspect?"

"Could have been a suicide," he said. "Wash some pills down with booze, run a nice warm bath and drift away. Would have expected to find an empty glass or a medicine bottle laying around, though."

"I only went outside my room for a little while," I said. "No time for anything like that. Somebody dumped her."

"Doesn't matter now," he shrugged. "Nobody's a suspect— not you or anybody else. It's a 'Death by Misadventure'. Coroner's signed off, and the case is closed. She came from Missouri—they found her mother there. She wants to come out here, but she has no money to make any travel arrangements."

A car drifted up the street, and the kids stopped their game and moved to the curb until it had passed.

"You're not going to even investigate this?" I asked.

He gave me a hard look.

"Do you need the facts of life explained to you, Crowe? She was a whore, and a drunk. She lost every straight job she ever tried, either for drinking or stealing. She had to end up in a box, sooner or later. You were a cop—you know how it goes."

I had been a cop, once upon a time. The facts of life made me quit. Nobody cares too much about what happens to the people who get lost, the ones who don't own an automobile or have a bank account.

"Case closed," I said. "Nobody cares."

"Case closed," he agreed.

"Sounds like you checked into it a little," I said. "What was the last straight job she had?"

"She worked the cosmetics counter at Darling's. Pretty enough for the job, but she only lasted a couple of weeks before she got fired. Arrested there twice afterward, for shoplifting. I guess she thought stealing from them made revenge."

"How old was she?" I asked.

He suddenly looked as sad as I felt.

"Only twenty-four," he said. "She came out here to be a movie star. Guess that didn't work out too well."

"What happens to her body, if her mother can't claim her?"

"Santa Teresa County will provide a box," he said. I didn't like his smile. "There won't be any organ music or flowers, I'm afraid, unless you want to send some. Everyone goes in the ground, one way or another. County does the honors if nobody else will."

~*~

I got to my office late the next morning, and spotted the outer door ajar. Bent over, I inspected the jamb, and saw no sign the lock had been jimmied or forced. I got the Browning from my pocket and pointed it at the ceiling. I eased into the waiting room, and caught the sweetish scent of almonds. I put the pistol away.

Fin stood at the window behind my desk, staring out at the street. He evidently saw something that interested him, because he didn't turn around.

"I made coffee," he said. "If you'd like some. I hope you don't mind."

"Make yourself at home," I said. "I see you have a key to the door."

"A key?" He turned around to give me a bewildered look. "Why would I have a key for your door?"

"Skip it," I said.

I took a clean cup off the shelf, ignored the coffee percolator and got the office bottle from my desk drawer and poured myself a short one. I didn't offer the bourbon to Fin. I knew he didn't touch the stuff.

"I asked you to do something for me," he said. "Too much for you?"

His voice stayed mild, but the threat hovered just the same. He sat down in my chair, and I obliged by taking the client chair on the other side of the desk. It was an interesting view. I liked it when I saw familiar things from new angles.

"I dashed all over the city trying," I said. "Your nightclub manager sent me to see you. You sent me to Gaynor Glass to see a man who wasn't there. I chased out to Montelindo to see his personal assistant and pick up a retainer for a case I'm allowed to know nothing about. I think I've chased butterflies long enough already on this one, and it hasn't even started."

"The rich are used to their privacy," he said. "They buy it, with no questions asked. Miss Stone stole a worthless bauble, and they want it back. She didn't have it when she died. They don't want any chance of publicity, and that makes them seem awkward and uncooperative. In truth, they are only shy."

"Her room at the Schooner Inn got tossed before her body even got cold," I said. "That shows Gaynor's money at work."

"Perhaps. She couldn't have sold it, because it had no value. She thought Gaynor should give her money for its return, and with that possibility, she wouldn't have thrown it away. She must have given it to someone—a friend, or a confederate. To that end, you are employed to discover whom she knew and associated with. Is that so difficult?"

"I can't find this thing if nobody will even tell me exactly what it is I'm looking for."

He sighed. It made me think of a damp breeze in a graveyard. Being around Fin made my thoughts turn strange that way.

"I have arranged another meeting for you," he said. "Mister Gaynor will be back in town tomorrow, and will entertain you at his home. I expect he will tell you as much as you absolutely need to know."

I sipped my warm bourbon. It tasted about as good, and bad, as it always did. I saw that Fin wasn't drinking any of the coffee he had made. He had put the fresh pot on just for me, and that made me feel a little bit bad. I would dump it out when he left.

"You don't need me for this," I said. "A big agency could do it faster."

"Oh, but you have an advantage," he said. "There are strange aspects to this case—things that might be in plain sight, but invisible nonetheless. You have the beautiful Miss Kahlo at your side, and her eyes that see what isn't there. A woman who reads numbers and colors, cards and tricks—a woman who has walked through the askew, and seen the questions."

"Annie Kahlo is in Mexico," I said. "She's officially dead. If she were alive, she'd be wanted on—what? A half-dozen murder charges? She isn't coming back here, ever."

"Miss Kahlo is dead," he agreed. "Dead as the proverbial doornail. She burned to death in full view of a dozen policemen, and there is a death certificate filed in the courthouse that says so. She has paid her debt to the great State of California. That makes her quite capable of being invisible, if she needs to be, and she also owes me for that."

"No deal, Fin." I felt outraged. "You can settle what I owe you any way you like, but I won't involve her, even if she's willing."

"As a matter of fact, Miss Kahlo will be arriving at the Santa Teresa station tomorrow evening, at six-and-five. I imagine she'll be tired, and would appreciate your meeting the train. I sent her a telegram. She didn't respond, but I have checked the train schedules carefully and am confident she will arrive in Santa Teresa then. Perhaps I know her better than you do."

I was stunned.

"You called for her? You told her to come?"

He unfolded himself from the chair. Standing, he turned up his collar.

"I told her your life was in danger," he said. "Because it likely will be, knowing you. I sent a telegram to the little seaside village where she stays—you can get a wire to just about anywhere now, in only a few hours. I sent one to you, remember? We live in such a marvelous, modern world."

"You son of a bitch," I said. "You've probably gotten her killed."

"No one tells Miss Kahlo to do anything," he said. "Not even me. Nonetheless, she will be on the train Wednesday evening at six-and-five. Don't keep her waiting, Mister Crowe."

"I have a condition, since you've involved Annie," I said, and took a deep breath to steady my nerves. "Several of them, actually. Nobody is claiming Beatrice Stone's body, so she's going in a pauper's grave. I want you to make travel arrangements for her mother to come out here. I want a headstone, a good one. I want you figure out a church and minister. I want you to go to the funeral and pay your respects."

He didn't laugh. He gave me a long stare with his strangely colorless eyes, and then the slow, sweet smile started. It transformed him, just for a moment.

"That's a splendid idea, Mister Crowe. You continually surprise me, and that's why I like you. I happen to like funerals, too. I will have Miss Emerson make the arrangements, immediately."

"The police will release the body after the inquest, in the next day or two," I said. "They should have the mother's information, if you need help with that."

"Do you think I need help with that, Mister Crowe?"

I didn't answer him, and he went out. My office smelled like bitter almond for the rest of the day.

~*~

Whoever said the rich are just like the rest of us was wrong.

I stood on perfectly raked shells and saw the plastered walls, the banks of leaded windows, and the cement pots of brightly perfect flowers that marched up the steps to the front door. It all smelled strongly of money, and it was all as quiet as death. No one here fought or made love, got sick in the bathroom or scraped burned toast over the kitchen sink. Nobody read the funny papers and sprayed from the nose when they laughed at them. There were no domestic catastrophes, no Italian operas playing on the radio. It wasn't a house for real people.

I walked around to the back of the place and found a garage, big enough for a dozen cars. Built to look like a carriage house, it had a big flagstone courtyard in front of it. Live oaks threw deep shade over everything. A man in shirt and suspenders ran a hose onto a LaSalle limousine. The water arced and splashed onto paint so black it gleamed blue. I walked over to have a gander.

"Twelve cylinders," the man said, as though it explained everything. "They made them better before the war."

"You can say that again," I agreed. "Twelve cylinders is the way to go. I drive an old Ford coupe. Dropped in the twelve from a wrecked Lincoln Zephyr a while back."

He whistled silently. "Goes like a bird?"

"Like a bird."

"You like to drive fast?"

"Not really." I shrugged. "Helps to know I can if I need to."

I fished out my package of smokes and offered it to him. He nodded and went to the spigot to turn the water off. When he came back he thumbed his lighter and held it toward my face. The smell of paraffin got too strong and I waited to let it clear before I spoke.

"Worked here long?" I asked.

He stuck the cigarette in the corner of his mouth and started to wipe the LaSalle with a clean chamois. After a minute, he changed his mind and draped it over a fender. He had a good-natured face, and I saw no reason not to like him.

"Long as I can remember," he said. "I'm the chauffeur for both Mister Gaynor and his mother. Couldn't tell you the last time I drove anyone anywhere. He likes to drive himself—garage here is full of those little English sports jobs from before the war."

I glanced at the closed carriage doors, interested, but he didn't offer to show them to me.

"Old Missus Gaynor never goes anywhere, but she likes to pretend she has places to be any minute, so I split my time between this house and hers, just being ready to do nothing. She lives up the road, in a bigger house than this."

"Bigger than this? Houses come in bigger sizes than this one?"

"Hard to believe, hard to believe." He crossed his heart with a fingertip, to show me it was true. "Her house a whole lot bigger. It's a good job. How about you? Worked here long?"

"Who says I work here?"

"Maybe you don't, and maybe you do," he said. "You wouldn't be back here talking to me if you didn't, one way or another. You got a name, Mister?"

"Crowe," I said. "You can call me Nate if you like. What's your name?"

"I'm Jackie's brother," he said. "You like baseball?"

"I follow it as much as the next fellow," I said. "I check the box scores."

"Well then, you know who Jackie is, don't you? I'm Jackie's brother."

"You're Jackie Robinson's brother?"

He put his cigarette out carefully on the wet stone and carried the butt over to drop it in a tin can set just inside the garage door. When he came back he peered at me, his good nature suspended.

"You think I'm making it up," he said. "You don't believe me."

"I believe you," I said. "Why wouldn't I? That doesn't tell me your name, though.'

"My name is Herb, but tomorrow you won't remember that. You'll only remember you met Jackie's brother. There's no point in fighting a thing like that, so I don't. It's what I call myself now— 'Jackie's brother'. Why be called something different than what you are?"

He picked up his chamois again and started to slap at the paintwork in a desultory way.

"Makes sense," I offered.

"Damn right," he said. "World be a simpler place if everybody just be called by what they really are."

I wondered what I would be called, if I were called what I really was. I occurred to me I didn't want to know, and I didn't want to take the chance he might tell me. I said goodbye and left him there to his business.

I went back up the side of the house to the wide steps. Once I had climbed them, I pulled at the bell. A short, squat number in a black maid's outfit kept me standing in the doorway while she checked my business card, front and back. She took so long I started to get curious about what had been printed on it; maybe there was more than I remembered. When she had finished reading it, she swung the door open and stood aside. She went off somewhere with the card held at arm's length and left me standing in the vestibule.

The room was nothing special, no bigger than a smallish big city train station. It had high ceilings, gold walls and the statue of a woman without any clothes on in the middle of it. I walked over to get a better look at her, but she glared at me with eyes like hard-boiled eggs and changed my mind. No one else seemed to be around, so I found a sofa set into a little nook and sat down to wait.

After a while, I heard a door open and close somewhere out of sight and heels tip-tapped across the marble floor. Eleanor Lane came into view. She wore a little coral-colored suit today, with some white showing at the throat. She went all the way to the front door without noticing me sitting there and stopped in front of it. With a flourish like a magic trick, she produced a compact case and got busy in the tiny mirror, touching up lipstick and patting her platinum hair into place.

"Finished with another hard day's work?" I asked. "Or are you getting delectable just for me?"

She jumped a little and looked over at me. Her eyes narrowed.

"Have I ever mentioned that I hate you?" she wondered. "I really do. Who let you in here anyway?"

"I let myself in, sister," I said. "Why not? I was out back talking to the chauffeur. We're friends now. He's Jackie's brother, you know. It must annoy the hell out of you to work with someone so famous."

She put her makeup away and curled a lip at me.

"I have no idea what you're talking about, and don't call me sister."

She checked the jeweled watch on her slender wrist and pursed her mouth as though she decided something. Crossing the room briskly, she slid back a panel in the wall to reveal a hidden bar. She got busy, and then she came back and handed me a heavy cut-glass tumbler brimming with amber liquid.

"Let's not quarrel," she said, in a different tone. "You're very early, you know. Besides, Mister Gaynor is taking a telephone call right now, long distance. You may as well have a drink while you wait. I'll be back to get you in a little while."

When she had gone, I sipped at the glass of Scotch whiskey. She hadn't brought any ice with it. I didn't care for Scotch, but it seemed rude to waste it. I nibbled at it bravely while I wandered the room and looked around. There were a lot of paintings on the walls that appeared as though real painters had done them, and a vase full of cut flowers stood on every flat surface that would hold one. I pinched and sniffed a yellow petal. The flowers were real, too, and I wondered why anyone would bother.

After a half-hour, Miss Lane came back and took my empty glass without a word. She led me up a long hallway lined with closed doors. She stopped in front of one of them and tapped on it twice. She turned to me and laid a warm hand on my cheek, her blue eyes were inches from mine. Her voice was sweet and humid, with lips that matched. "I hope Mister Gaynor doesn't catch the liquor on your breath," she murmured. "He detests it. He'll fire you on the spot if he smells it."

I laughed at her. I couldn't help it. "It would be a shame," I said. "In that case, thanks for the drink."

"It would be a shame," she agreed. "I'd have to look in the telephone directory under 'cheap gumshoes' to line up your replacement. It would probably take me at least three seconds to find someone as competent as you."

She cracked the door open, put her head in and spoke to someone out of sight.

"Mister Crowe has just arrived, Mister Gaynor," she said. "He's quite late, I'm afraid. Shall I send him in?"

An unintelligible reply came from inside, and then Eleanor Lane turned back to face me. She stood on tiptoe and gave me a soft, lingering kiss on the cheek. When she was done, her perfume and her smile stayed behind on my skin. Her blue eyes were warm and intimate.

"See you around, peeper," she said. "Nice knowing you."

-Eight-

The room had been done up like an English library in some fancy decorator's imagination. Any spaces that weren't filled with the kind of books nobody had ever read were colored dark maroon or else covered in leather. Gaynor stood with his back to me at a bank of tall windows, gazing at what his money had bought.

"Come in, Crowe," he said. "You're three-quarters of an hour late. I suppose punctuality doesn't count for much in your line of work."

He didn't bother turning around to look at me. He appeared the kind of man accustomed to giving orders and having them obeyed. He expected to be admired, and used manipulation for love. I had met his type before. He made people afraid of his money, and he had gotten his own way for so long it had driven him crazy.

"I'm confused," he said. "My employees don't usually call meetings so I can explain myself to them."

"I'm not anyone's employee," I said. "And I don't work without some slight idea of what I'm working on."

"I was advised to hire you," he said. "I did so, even though I don't have much respect for your kind. Your private detective work seems to me a kind of make-believe—as much a profession as illustrating children's books or selling ice cream at the beach. It isn't something a serious man does."

"I've tried to be a serious man," I said. "It didn't take."

He turned around, and his face turned furious. The rage got held back with great effort. He had real craziness in his eyes, the kind of madness that runs up the street laughing wildly and throwing handfuls of confetti before it starts killing. He put up a civilized façade, but when he went home at night and took off necktie and mask, poured a drink and put his feet up, I thought he was probably a very dangerous character indeed. I wouldn't want to be his dog.

"The first thing I asked you to do, you refused," he said. "You disrespected my secretary, which means you disrespected me. I won't tolerate it."

I didn't much care about what he tolerated. Most people get trained to respond in a certain way to the kind of authority that is assured by its simple existence. The more lunatic it is, the greater its weight, which is why madmen run countries. I wasn't brave. I was just too broken inside to pay attention to any of it.

"Your ticket's already halfway cancelled in this town," he said. "Do you want me to cancel the rest of it for you? Would you like to never work in this city again—or worse?"

"That's a threat?"

"I don't make threats," he sneered. "I just pick up the telephone and things get done."

I thought about Annie, and Corazón Rosa.

"I don't much care," I said, truthfully. "It would be a kind of relief, really."

He stared at me for a long minute. I stared back at him. Maybe it was the Scotch, but I felt exhausted. I was tired of all of it, the late nights and secrets, the lies and dirty little motives. I was tired of people in masks who never stopped talking about themselves.

"Make the call," I said. "I didn't take a nickel from you, so you can go to hell. Do whatever you like."

I had the door open and one foot in the hallway, when he took an audible breath and spoke from behind me. "Wait," he said.

A different tone in his voice stopped me, and turned me back around to face him.

He looked close to tears. They seemed genuine, and I wondered if I had misjudged him. He was like a balloon with all the air gone from it. Maybe what I had taken for cruelty was distress, or fear. Maybe the authority was a mask he put on, just like any other mask. Mostly, I needed his check, so I took my hand from the doorknob.

"I don't really have a choice in this," he said. "The whole thing is embarrassing, frankly."

"You don't strike me as a man that embarrasses easily, or about much of anything."

"I'm not," he said, and a little of his assurance crept back in. "I'm not embarrassed for myself. Sit down. Let me get you a drink."

"I didn't think you were a drinking man," I said.

He crossed the room from the window and slid aside a wall panel to reveal an impressive wet bar. I nodded at the offer of bourbon, and he got busy with glasses and ice tongs.

"Why do you say that?" he asked, surprised. "That I don't seem like a drinking man?"

"No particular reason," I said, and mentally scored a point for Eleanor Lane.

"I know all about you, Crowe," he said, handing off my drink. He sat down behind his desk, ready to put the conversation back on a footing he liked. "You got yourself in a mess a little while back. You're lucky they didn't pull your license. Working for me could be your ticket back to respectability."

"I'm not in a respectable profession. You said so yourself."

"My family suffered a theft," he said. "We identified the thief. Beatrice Stone was employed as my mother's personal assistant, and pocketed the item when she got fired. We made every attempt to recover what she stole without embarrassment for any of the parties involved. She was offered suitable reward for its return, and she refused to cooperate."

"Have you called the police?"

"My family does not call the police in a case like this," he said. "Nor do we call the newspapers and ask them to print our stories on the front page."

"Point taken," I said. "But you're asking me to recover something without telling me exactly what it is I'm after. That's foolishness."

"You misunderstand. I'm not asking you to find anything. I have the means to do that myself, once I have a sense of where to look. I have a firm who will do the finding."

"Why involve me? Why pay twice?"

"You have local contacts," he said, shortly. "You know the underbelly of this city. She didn't move in polite circles. My men have no idea where to start, so they will go where you point them."

"Thanks for the compliment," I said. "Underbelly."

He sighed deeply. "Beatrice Stone put our property somewhere for safekeeping. The police didn't find it in her effects when she died."

"I'm sure you know that for a fact," I commented. "I'm sure you got an inventory of whatever she left behind."

"Of course, I did," he said. "I've done a great deal for this city, as did my father before me. Should I apologize because the police are willing to assist me in ways beyond what might be available to the general public?"

"Why did you fire her?"

"That's confidential," he said. "Surely in your profession you appreciate the need for privacy."

"In my profession, there's no such thing," I said. "I'm not a blabbermouth. I wouldn't stay in business, or even alive very long if I were. That doesn't change the fact I need to know just about everything there is to know about a thing. Confidentiality is the essence of what I do. If you want results, you have to trust me."

"All right," he said, pondering. "I'll tell you all of it. I'll tell you why she got fired."

Then he thought about things for so long that I thought maybe his brain had locked up. Finally, he gave himself a visible shake and looked me in the eye.

"Before we go any further, I want you to take a check," he said. "I'm about to tell you some things I'd prefer not to tell anyone. I sent Miss Lane with cash, because I thought you'd rather have that. At this point, I want a cancelled check with your signature on the back of it."

I nodded, and he got a leather-bound book of checks from the drawer. I had never seen a millionaire's checkbook before, and I didn't get let down. It appeared as large a plantation ledger. He wrote carefully with a fountain pen, signed with an economical little flourish and tore it free. He shook the ink dry before he handed it across the desk to me, and waited until it got folded into my wallet before he spoke again.

"Beatrice Stone was a degenerate," he said. "A degenerate in just about every way you can think of. You'd be surprised."

"I can think of a lot of ways," I said. "Very few of them would surprise me. Give me an example."

"She was a prostitute," he said. "That much is common knowledge. Surely you don't need more than that."

"I know some prostitutes," I said, mildly. "Some of them are entirely decent people, to my mind. A lot more decent than some of the respectable people I've met. I assume she didn't do any business while she was in your mother's employ."

"You have a strange way of seeing things," he said, and glanced at me sharply. "I'm not sure I like it very much."

"Miss Lane told me the same thing just now," I said. "It ruined my day. Why did your mother fire Beatrice Stone?"

"She drank, for one thing," he said. "She kept bottles of vodka and gin in her room. My mother knew about it, and felt inclined to overlook it, as long as she did her job."

"Why was she fired?" I repeated, getting impatient with the whole thing.

"She had impulses that weren't natural," he said. His face reddened. "There was talk in the house that Miss Stone behaved inappropriately with one of the maids. My mother arranged to have them watched. They were discovered together—disrobed. Of course, Miss Stone was dismissed. My mother felt the maid had been coerced, and allowed her to stay."

I felt a jolt of sadness. Beatrice Stone had been alone in more ways than I had thought. I remembered the quick look of hurt on her face when I had turned her down. I had pawned her off with a few dollars. If I could have the moment back, I would have taken her to dinner with me. I would have told her I thought she was swell.

"I don't like you very much, either," I said. "You, or your mother. Tell me what Miss Stone stole on her way out the door."

"Most of my employees don't like me," he said. "I don't encourage them to, and your feelings are immaterial to me. She stole a glass bauble that belonged to my aunt."

He opened a drawer and slid a colorized photograph across to me. I picked it up, and sat back in my chair to inspect it. The image showed a glossy sphere, against a neutral background.

"I have photographs taken of everything I collect, for insurance," he said. "My father acquired this years ago. Its value is negligible, but there is some."

"A glass ball?" I asked.

"Egyptian glass," he nodded. "Very old. It's about half the size of an English billiard ball."

"What is it for?"

"I have no idea." He lifted his shoulders and spread his hands, to underline that he didn't know. "A decoration of some kind. All I know is that it's Egyptian, and ancient. We have never had it appraised for origin or value, because as soon as my father got it, my aunt adopted it for herself."

On the desktop, the smooth figure of an insect crouched, a tiny statue. It had a faint blue-green shine and appeared to be very old. There were faint black markings on its back; whatever paint had been used had faded badly. Gaynor probably used it as a paperweight. He saw me looking at it.

"A scarab," Gaynor said. "A dung beetle, also Egyptian glass. They were amulets used to protect the dead. My family doesn't just make glass—we love glass, the older the better. Egyptian glass is the oldest there is, and I've added over the years to my father's collection."

"I had heard that the Egyptian government had begun to crack down on these souvenirs being exported out of their country."

"If you know the right people, and you're willing to pay the price, those obstacles aren't as tricky as you might imagine."

I suddenly had a pretty good idea of what made his association with Fin. The lucrative sale of stolen antiquities would be right up Fin's alley. I decided I had no reason to ask Gaynor about it. I tapped the photograph on the desk.

"This glass ball came from the same sort of place?" I asked. "Like maybe a mummy's tomb? It looks like an oversized cat-eye marble."

"Possibly." He shrugged again. "Again, I don't believe it has any great value. It is of great interest because of my aunt's attachment. It does resemble an eye, which is why she likes it so much, even though she can't see it. I believed I had recovered it from Miss Stone, but it's still missing."

This was going too fast for me.

"What do you mean, she can't see it? And you thought you got it back?"

"I paid Miss Stone a thousand dollars up front for its return," he said. "I felt reluctant, but willing, to do that to avoid going to the police. She held it back. Perhaps I made too easy a victim. She said that had been a deposit, and asked for another ten thousand dollars. We were—negotiating that when she died."

"A death you had nothing to do with," I offered.

"Of course not," he snapped. "What kind of a man do you think I am? I would have paid the ten thousand, if it came to it, to keep my aunt happy."

"The cops say her room at the Schooner Inn got tossed," I said. "Probably right after she got killed. I'm assuming that was you, or your employees, hunting for your property."

"I assure you it wasn't." He managed to seem offended. "If I had such people in my employ, I wouldn't be talking to you, would I?"

He had a point. I drained the last of my drink, and set the glass on the desk. Between the scotch and the bourbon, it had been one hell of a party.

"Why did you say your aunt couldn't see the glass ball?"

"She's blind, Crowe," he said. "She has been since she was young. A fever took her sight. She's always lived with us. She and my mother are quite close—nearly inseparable."

He shot a cuff and made a show of checking his wristwatch. He seemed to make up his mind about something.

"I think my mother would be of more help to you from this point," he said. "Can you arrange to visit her at the family estate?"

"This isn't the family estate?" I wondered.

"This is just a house, Mister Crowe. My father didn't build this. In time, when my mother passes, I'll sell it and move back to the home I grew up in."

If this was just a place for him to flop, the estate must be some palace. I managed to keep from whistling in admiration.

"Miss Stone was my mother's personal assistant, and so my mother knew her best," he said. "I'll arrange an appointment for you. I'll trust you not to dwell on Miss Stone's indiscretions. The subject upsets my mother greatly."

I pinched a finger and thumb together and zipped my lip. He gave a quick nod, reassured.

"Keep the photograph," he said. "It may be useful to you, and I have a copy. I'll have my private secretary call your office with details on meeting my mother, once she's made them."

"Oh good," I said. "Eleanor Lane and I have gotten to be friends already. How much does she know about this affair?"

"She's my private secretary, Crowe." He seemed a little put out. "She knows about all of my business. That's what she's for. If she didn't have my compete trust, she wouldn't have the position."

"That's swell," I said. "Don't call her to let me out. I want to make it to my car in one piece."

I left him appearing slightly puzzled. Before I tucked the photograph into my breast pocket, I glanced at it again. It didn't look like a glass ball, at all. It looked like an eye.

~*~

The *California Dreamland Limited* was late getting into the Santa Teresa station. When I asked, a reluctant ticket seller barked at me that there had been track trouble in Los Angeles, and wondered to himself why people didn't listen to the announcements over the loudspeakers. The train was expected a few minutes after eight o'clock. I felt bad about the delay for Annie Kahlo's sake. She would have spent more than three full days on the train from Corazón Rosa, leaving only a day or two after I had. North of the border the trains were more comfortable than they were in Mexico, but even in a Pullman coach, the added hours must have been miserable.

I went and found a plate of pork chops, string beans and fried potatoes at a place I knew on Ortega, and then I killed another hour with coffee and a newspaper. When the clock said it was time, I went back to the station.

The building was grand, outsized for the small city. A latticework of pipes and beams and girders rose in delicate disarray to an acre of glass-paned roof that held back the night sky. As I went down the stairs to the platform I felt like I made my way down a spider web. Below me, the massive train still shuddered on its rails, bereft at the loss of motion. Arrogant and black, the locomotive breathed clouds of steam. They rose and drifted, were caught by the spotlights and turned lavender and green before they faded away.

The bottom of the stairs showed a jumble of moving faces. I got jostled by voices and the smells of perfume and clothes and tobacco smoke. I tried to keep one hand close to the gun in my pocket. I would have a hell of a time if trouble started.

I made my way through the people, searching. All at once the crowd shifted, and Annie was simply there. She stood next to a pillar, half-turned away from me, gazing at something else. She had dressed like Corazón Rosa, a peasant in unbleached muslin. It covered her head and fell away loose to her calves. She wore plain huaraches on her feet and carried a cloth bag over one shoulder.

Somehow, she faded the perfumed and high-heeled women around her to vague pastels.

She turned my way, gold hair and skin gentle against the rough muslin, dark almond-shaped eyes narrowed. I saw the old woman she would be and the little girl that she had been. They were both there at the same time, and for just that instant the world made a kind of lovely sense to me.

"They're watching," she said, when I got close enough to hear. "They followed you here. Don't act like you even notice me."

I obliged her. I turned away and checked my watch, then scanned the crowd like I expected someone else. I didn't see anyone who appeared to be tracking us. Annie saw ghosts, though, and I believed in her. More than once, her phantoms had turned out to be real.

"Meet me on the boardwalk," she said from behind me. "Give it a couple of hours."

Everyone around us was busy with suitcases and greetings, shouting to be heard over the general hubbub.

"Where on the boardwalk?" I called softly, over my shoulder. "How will you get there?"

Annie didn't answer, and I looked back to repeat myself. She had vanished.

-Nine-

State Street was mostly deserted. The few people I saw in lighted bar windows seemed like department store mannequins. My car followed its headlights down to Cabrillo and then along the ocean. I left it in the parking lot of a seafood joint that was closed, and crossed the empty street to the beach.

I saw her from a long way off. It could have been anyone, a slender figure standing at the rail and gazing out at the night water, but I knew it was Annie. She stood on the boardwalk, underneath the cone of light from a hooded bulb. I walked toward her, but I didn't hurry. I wanted to look at her for a little while.

When I got close enough, she turned to face me. Her kiss hello made the barest brush.

"Am I what you expected?" she asked.

"You're you," I said. "You're never anything I expect. I haven't seen you in a few days, but it seems like years."

I pulled her in and murmured into her ear.

"There are a hundred people in this city who would shoot you on sight. I don't want you dead."

She held me back and looked at me.

"Would that make me any different?" she asked. "I am dead. I'm a ghost. No one is hunting me—if they saw me on the street, they'd look right through me. It's just human nature, and I don't have to do anything else to make myself invisible."

Her face would never make it into a cigarette or liquor advertisement. When she occasionally bothered with lipstick and silk stockings, it was masquerade. She would always cause a faint flutter of panic whenever she walked into a beauty parlor, and no hair stylist would know exactly what to do with her.

She was the most beautiful woman I had ever seen, and the ancient queens would have understood her perfectly.

Nefertiti following a torch down a long corridor, Cleopatra trailing fingers in the warm Nile and watching green reflections in the water, Helen on a night-time balcony gazing across a vast expanse of sand and missing home—they were so utterly alone, but such a deep part of everything that colors and tastes and smells around them turned bright and rich. Secret sisters, they had eyes and faces that absorbed light and gave back a cloud of bats in a night sky, a light at the top of a dark building, a smooth edge of waterfall in the moment before it slid and crashed.

"Have you eaten?" I asked.

She shook her head, no.

"I'll take you somewhere," I said. "There ought to be something open on the boulevard."

She shook her head again, and took my arm. She pointed at the stairs leading down to the beach. I let her lead me. Our steps sounded hollow on the boards going down, and then were silent when we landed on the sand. It was as if we'd passed though a barrier.

The smell of the ocean got stronger, the surf sounded loud, and the darkness felt wet and vital. I took off my shoes because she did, and the sand was cold. The feel of it on my bare feet made everything seem more real.

I followed her up the beach. I glanced back once, at the space under the boardwalk. I sensed something squatting among the pilings, watching us. It was nothing more than a black spot in the blackness, but I thought it shifted when I looked at it. My hand went to my pocket, but felt no gun. I had left it in the car. No help for it, so I shrugged off the feeling and hurried a little to catch up to Annie.

She sat down at the base of the seawall, and I sat beside her. The concrete rubbed rough against my back. We faced the invisible night-time ocean. When she spoke, it was delicious. Her voice sounded better than any movie star; a tropical breath that made the sound of the cold surf different. The sand beneath me felt as though it were melting; it was as soft and warm as if it were in the sun.

"What's the earliest thing you can remember?" she asked me. "The very first thing?"

As usual, small talk got lost with Annie. There were no pleasantries, no exchanges of recipes, no sports chatter, not even the smallest concessions to convention. It was as though she lived on a distant world, and when she visited here had neither inclination to dabble in small scurryings of gossip nor time for linear conversations. Almost everyone thought she was crazy. I knew different.

"A birthday party," I said, thinking about it. "I turned three years old. My mother baked me a cake, and she had found a way to tint the icing green. She acted happy about that. I can almost hear her voice."

The moon glow was everywhere, like pale ice cream. I heard music, the long-ago radio playing in my mother's kitchen. Annie scared me sometimes, just a little.

"Of course, you can hear her voice," Annie said. "If you listen hard enough, you can hear everything she's saying. You're in the kitchen? You can hear the radio on in the living room, cars on the street, bees in the bush outside the window."

"You can read my mind?" I smiled at her, and felt her smile back in the dark.

At first, the sea appeared nothing but black. The waves rolled onto the beach, white and phosphorescent, coming from nowhere. Like ghosts, they landed and spread and disappeared, and no matter how many times it happened it startled me a little bit each time.

"People don't believe me if I tell them that," I said. "They say it isn't normal to have memories that early, and I must be imagining it. Of course, I'm not the sort of fellow who tells people my memories very often."

"No—you're not that sort of a man, are you?" She laughed. "At least not until now, with me."

"How about you?" I asked. "What's your earliest memory?"

"You can remember before your third birthday," she said, as though she hadn't heard my question. "If you can remember all the way back to the beginning, and then you can remember before that. When you get back before the beginning, then you'll know where you go when you die."

"Makes sense," I said, because it did, at least at that moment.

After a little while, my eyes adjusted. The moon sent enough light through the cloud cover that I could see the waves. There were tiny sparks out on the water, coming and going, never in the same place. I could make out Annie's face, turned toward me.

"I remember before the beginning," she said. "My earliest memory is of a river. The water was green, and animals made of stone came down to it to drink. I had a piece of glass, and I took it with me when I went into the river for my bath. When I held it under the surface, it changed color."

Something burst up from the sand with a strangled cry. It flew over our heads with a sound like laundry flapping on the line, a bare glimpse of paleness in the black air, and went out to sea. It was a seabird, or a couple of them.

"What else?" I asked, when my heart slowed down. "What else do you remember?"

"I'm still working on it," she said. "That's part of what you're for."

I watched the beach, to see if I could spot whatever had startled the birds. Whatever it had been stayed hidden in the dark.

"What are you afraid of?" she asked, changing the subject again.

"Not much," I said.

"I'm always afraid," she said. "Of all of it."

"You don't seem like you're scared of anything."

"I am, though. Tell me what you're afraid of—there has to be something."

Her look became palpable, dark and heavy. I felt the weight of it, even in the low light, and it made me breathless. Another of the waves rolled in and spread out, and I thought about telling her they made me uneasy. Whatever crouched under the boardwalk made me uneasy, too, but uneasy wasn't the same as afraid, so I kept those things to myself. I struggled for words.

"It's all different now—since you," I started.

She sat quietly and waited. I shifted a little against the wall, so my shoulder touched hers. I felt glad when she didn't move away.

"I thought I was okay, but I wasn't," I said. "I didn't know any better. It's different now, with you around. It played like a silent movie, and now—there are colors. I don't want it to be like before you came, ever again."

She leaned into me, just barely.

"I'm afraid of losing that," I said. "It's the only thing I'm afraid of."

We sat very quietly for a long time, and then I sensed her nod. I nodded, too, relieved. I closed my eyes.

"Don't die first," she whispered. "Promise me."

When I opened them, she had gone. I must have gone to sleep for a little while, because the moon had come out, and the beach looked as bright as noon. The sea sparkled purple and white. I touched the sand where she had been sitting. It felt cold, and so did I.

I stood up and brushed myself off. I didn't see my shoes, and then I did. I picked them up and started walking, to wherever it was I was going.

~*~

The Ford waited quietly in the restaurant parking lot. I didn't see another set of headlights the whole way home. When I got to Figueroa Street, I put the car to bed at the front curb, and started up the sidewalk.

Next door, the Gardiner's house showed a dim light in one upstairs window. I had an idea that the old couple didn't sleep much. On the other side, Annie Kahlo's windows were black. If she had returned to her house, she was keeping a low profile. Some nights, the flowering hedge between her house and mine smelled nice in the dark, but tonight I smelled only the faint odor of sleeping city.

I wondered where she was dreaming tonight.

I wondered if I had any chance of keeping her safe, and why she wouldn't marry me, and if I had gotten too old to marry anyone in the first place. I wondered who had killed Beatrice Stone, and if the Boston Braves could turn the corner this year. I wondered what made people act the way they did. I wondered a lot of things.

Inside the front door, I switched on a light. My living room appeared as empty as it always did. One of these days, I would hang a picture or two. There were a lot of naked walls in the bedroom as well, so maybe I would need a lot of pictures. I emptied my pockets onto the dresser, and left my gun on the small table beside the bed.

I took a tepid shower, and the faucets squeaked louder than usual when I turned them off. The noise echoed from the tiles. I got my threadbare robe off the hook, belted it, and went out to the kitchen. A bottle of Kentucky Cream sat doing nothing much in the cabinet over the sink, so I got it down and splashed one of the jelly jars that I saved for special occasions.

Back in the living room, I flipped through cardboard record sleeves until I found the one I wanted. When the needle dropped and started to hiss, I left the record player behind and went to sit at the kitchen table. Charlie Parker's saxophone followed me, and began to nibble at the opening bars of '*I Love You Madly*'.

After I lit a cigarette, I tried some bourbon. I didn't much like Kentucky Cream. I thought it tried too hard to taste expensive, and that's why I had a half-bottle wasting space on the shelf. It seemed swell tonight though, so I poured myself another inch. When the record finished, I didn't get up to change it; enough of Bird's saxophone lingered I didn't need to.

I felt homesick. It made no sense, since I was at home.

Annie's house showed through the kitchen window. It was still dark, but I watched it for a while to see if anything changed. Nothing did, so when the bottle was as empty as I felt, I got up and went to bed.

~*~

After standing at my kitchen drain board through three cups of coffee, I left the Ford at the curb and walked to the office early the next morning. I just wanted to feel like I was going somewhere and knew what I was doing. The streetlights on Figueroa Street were still on. The windows in the houses on either side of mine were dark. The Gardiners were still asleep; if Annie had stayed in her house last night, she still slept too. They didn't have important things to do, like I pretended to.

If I had slept at all, I didn't remember it. There had been too much bourbon at the kitchen table. I worried so much about

Annie I could barely breathe. I would need a ledger to list the people in town who would line up to kill her if they didn't think she had already died. She didn't seem to understand the risk, and that scared me. She didn't care, and that scared me more.

I heard the telephone in my office ringing from out in the hall. I got the door unlocked and glanced at the Krazy Kat clock on the wall as I picked it up. It said barely six o'clock. The woman on the other end sounded out of breath. I couldn't tell if she was young or old.

"Are you the detective?" she asked. When I agreed, she pressed me further. "Are you open for business? You're not with the cops, are you? Why don't you answer your telephone?"

When we established that I wasn't part of the police department and therefore wouldn't be at my desk around the clock to answer calls, she told me that Danny López had told her to telephone me.

"What's your name?" I asked.

"I'm not going to tell you," she said. "The thin man said he would kill me if I stirred up any trouble for him."

"The thin man?" I wondered.

"If you cause him problems like I want you to, he won't know that I'm involved if you don't even know my name."

I thought about the logic of that, and decided there wasn't any. I tried to think through a headful of last night's bourbon, though, so maybe it was me. In any event, I was working for Danny López. I decided I didn't have to have her name, at least for now.

"What can I help you with?" I said. "You can't keep that a secret, too, or I can't help at all."

"Of course not." She sounded surprised. "I want you to kill someone, but Mister López said you don't do that. He said I should talk to you, anyway. A man named Joey O'Meany killed my brother, and got away with it. My brother's name was Allen, with an 'e', and he was only fourteen."

I knew Joey O'Meany to see around town. They called him 'the thin man'. He was a jittery hophead who had once pulled trigger for Sal Cleveland. He had a reputation for being unnecessarily vicious, and I didn't mind causing him some trouble if I would get paid for it. I had no idea who he might be working for now, but I understood why Danny López couldn't directly involve himself. It might start a war.

"When did this happen?" I asked.

"Almost two months ago. I didn't do anything before because I thought it had been an accident. Then I heard it wasn't. He got murdered."

"What did the police say about your brother's death?"

"They said he drowned," she said. "He did drown, but the thin man forced him to. I wouldn't know that, but he bragged to a friend of mine about killing him, like a joke. My friend came and told me."

"It might be better if we discuss this in person," I said. "Can you come to my office?"

"Oh, no, I'm not coming to your office," she said. "He drinks at the South Seas Room. I went to see him there, and have it out with him. He laughed at me and said he would kill me, too, if he heard I was stirring up any trouble for him."

"He won't hear it from me," I said.

"There's a new Barbara Stanwyck movie, *The Other Love*, playing at the New Linear," she said. "David Niven is in it. I always feel like most Englishmen are a little bit flit, but that's no reason not to see the movie."

"Not in my book," I agreed. I had no idea what she was talking about.

"I'll meet you at the seven o'clock show," she said. "Buy your ticket and meet me inside. I don't want to be seen with you."

"You're not the first woman who has felt that way about me," I reassured her. "How will I know you?"

"I'll wear a red dress."

"That should narrow things down enough," I said. "I'll see you this evening."

As soon as I put the receiver back in the cradle, the telephone started ringing again. Not even seven o'clock, and business was booming. Maybe this was why Pinkerton's never slept.

"Want coffee?" Annie asked. She sounded happy and excited. "I'll pick you up downstairs."

"What made you think I would be here, at this hour?" I asked. She didn't answer, and I took the question back. "Give me long enough to put my hat on, and I'll be down."

This early, and I already had two dates lined up. Maybe I should stay open around the clock. Pinkerton's was definitely on to something.

Downstairs, I stood on the curb and waited. The sun was up, barely, and the buildings on Chapala threw long shadows onto the empty street. The coming day murmured, the soft sounds of gulls and far-off traffic. A block away, a truck snorted and ground a gear as it moved off, and then it got quiet again.

A man sat on the sidewalk, leaned up in the doorway of a bar. He slept with his head on his knees. I could see a small smear of dried blood on his cheek. He wore blue jeans, a western shirt and no shoes. One of his black socks had been pulled halfway off his foot. I figured his boots must have been pretty good if someone wanted them enough to take them off. A straw hat lay on the cement nearby, crushed flat.

Looking at him, I tasted my own mouth, bourbon under the mouthwash. I felt the darkness of all the nights-before, the passing of time, and the guilt. I stood a thousand or two miles away from the place I had been born in, and I wondered why the loss of that seemed to matter so much sometimes. The air moved against my face, fresh enough to hurt. It carried the smells of ocean and tar on the coolness of the night before. It mocked me. My necktie felt too tight, and I loosened it a little.

A car turned the corner and pulled over in front of me, pointed the wrong way. It was a two-tone Mercury convertible, aqua over green, light over dark. The folded-down top showed off a vanilla-crème interior. It was an exact replica of the car Annie had allegedly died in.

"Brand spanking new," I commented. "You're supposed to be dead, Annie. You think it's a good idea to drive a car the same as the one that went up in flames, with you inside it? Have you thought about that?"

The convertible gleamed, so mint that a dealer's number still stuck to the lower corner of the windshield. I peeled it off and stuck it into my pocket.

"I paid cash for it," she smiled. "They opened early, just for me. People will bend a lot of rules if you're paying cash. I loved that car—and now I love this one."

The sun glinted off her dark glasses as she took them off. The skin on her bare arms and face was honeyed, and her eyes were dark and happy. I caught the scent of her, warm and clean, and from nowhere felt a flash of anger.

"Someone is going to recognize you," I said. "This town has two kinds of people—the kind who want you in jail, and the kind who think jail would be too good for you. If you don't start acting like all of this is real, you're going to get both of us killed."

The door unlatched and I stepped back as it swung open and she got out of the car. She brushed by me without looking and went to the man sitting in the doorway. She squatted on her heels and spoke to him. After a minute he stirred, and she took both of his hands and helped him up. He propped himself against the wall, unsteady, and stared at his feet. With one arm around his waist, Annie murmured into his ear, too low for me to hear.

She bent and picked up his hat from the sidewalk. The man watched her blankly as she turned it in her hands, straightening it. She put it on his head and touched his chin, turning his face to adjust the set of the brim. After a minute or two he nodded at her, collected himself, and moved off.

Annie stood and watched him shamble up the street in his stocking feet. When he had turned at the corner and gone from sight, she came back to the car. She didn't look at me as she got in and closed the door. She started the engine and sat with both of her hands on the steering wheel.

"I'll never be real," she said. "Are you coming?"

I went around to the passenger side, and got in.

"I'd follow you anywhere," I said, and meant it.

-Ten-

"You need to eat something."

Annie sat across the table from me. The restaurant had been a Polynesian Tiki bar before the war. Later, it got sold to somebody who served breakfast and lunch, and had no interest in spending money to redecorate. The Tiki booths, bamboo walls, and colored lights had all stayed behind when the bar closed. At eight o'clock in the morning, it looked like a bad dream. Annie liked the place.

A man in an apron came to the table, and I asked him for toast and eggs. Annie just wanted coffee.

"You tell me to eat, but you're just having coffee?" I asked.

"I didn't sit at my kitchen table drinking bourbon for most of the night," she said. "Not that I went to bed, mind you."

I didn't ask how she knew. Annie knew things in her own way, and I felt used to having my mind read by her.

"So, our job..." she started.

"My job," I interrupted. "You're in enough danger, being here in Santa Teresa, at all. I won't expose you to more. What exactly did Fin say in his telegram, to get you to come back here?"

"He said you needed my help," she said, unperturbed. "Let me see the photograph of the eye, please."

I got the photo Gaynor had given me from my jacket pocket and handed it across to her. There was no point in trying to convince her to stay out of it.

"The job is to get to know Beatrice Stone," I said. "We need to get a sense of her routine, her friends if she had any, her personality—to give Gaynor some idea of where she may have left the glass ball."

She considered the photograph in her hand. Her concentration became so complete it felt like gravity.

"It's definitely an eye," she said. "In fact, it reminds me of something. I can't quite put my finger on it, but I will, in time. Why don't you just locate the missing eye and get it back? That's what the man is after."

"He doesn't want me to," I said. "I'm not trying to do any more than I have to. He'll have an agency take over once I get him some ideas about where he might look. She lived a transient life, and he has nowhere to even start. None of the markers of a normal life are there."

"Which also means he doesn't want you checking too closely into what's being recovered," she said. "He paid a great deal of money to get it back, and he became willing to pay ten times the amount when she reneged and asked for more."

"Which gave him ten times the reason to kill her. Maybe he didn't take to being double-crossed."

"He didn't kill her." Annie shook her head, definite. "He wouldn't have risked exactly what happened—that the eye went missing. He might have been unhappy, but he would have paid her. Someone else killed her."

"You've got that figured out?" I smiled.

"Two and two can add up to all sorts of things," she said. "But yes."

The waiter brought my eggs. The smell of them didn't agree with me, but Annie was right. I needed to eat something, so I shook out my napkin and picked up the fork. Across from me, she measured and stirred cream and sugar into her coffee. It always became a careful ritual with her, as though she mixed a potion.

"The glass eye is worth a lot more than anyone is admitting," Annie said. "That will be the key to this whole thing. Why would Beatrice Stone take one thousand for it, and then not deliver? What did she find out, that made her want ten thousand more?"

"She got greedy," I suggested. "She didn't expect Gaynor to be such an easy mark."

"I don't think so." Annie shook her head. "Beatrice found something out—something that changed the stakes."

"I'm going to see Gaynor's mother at her estate in Montelindo tomorrow," I said. "Want to come along?"

"I wouldn't miss it," she said. "What else are we hoping to find out?"

"Fin sent me a wire days before Beatrice Stone got killed," I said. "She hadn't died yet, and Gaynor was still dickering the ransom to get it back, even if it didn't make him very happy. No case existed when I got on the train—so why did Fin send for me?"

The man in the apron came around take my plate. He licked his pencil stub and added things up before he slapped the tab down in front of me.

"They knew the whereabouts of the glass eye," I said. "The girl didn't hide. They could have paid, or they could have taken it by force. There was nothing they needed me for."

"Fin knows things," Annie said. "There's no use wondering about that part. He'll never tell you. We have to find out who has the eye now, or is hunting for it. We have to find out what the eye really is. When we know that, we'll know who killed Beatrice Stone."

"So, someone else wanted the glass bauble, enough to kill for it. Again, it can't have been just an old lady's worthless keepsake."

Annie had finished her coffee. She stood up.

"What about the police?" she asked. "Are they going to be in the way?"

"There's going to be an inquest in the next day or so," I said. "It's a formality. They don't care what happened to a girl like Bea Stone. She had it coming, as far as they are concerned."

I turned the check over to look at it, and got some coins out.

"I wouldn't mind if we found out who killed her," I said. "As long as we're poking around."

Annie put her hand over mine. "You care about her, don't you?" she asked. "You care more about justice for her than finding the glass eye for these rich people."

"I think she was alone," I said. "I think she was as alone as anyone I've ever heard about."

"She has us now," Annie said. "So, I care about her, too. In the end, a person could do a whole lot worse than that."

~*~

The lobby of the Schooner Inn stayed busy, echoing with the comings-and-goings of people who saw an entirely different Santa Teresa than the tourists did. The expansive front desk had been boarded up, from countertop to ceiling, leaving only a grated window, like a bank teller's cage. The clerk behind it seemed happy to take five dollars to tell me that Beatrice Stone lived, most of the time, in room 303. It took another five to get the use of a key to get in.

"Cops said not to let anyone in," she said. "Room's paid through the end of the week. There's a relative coming to collect her things."

"Her mother is in town," I confirmed. "I don't expect there's anything worth collecting, though. Did a man named Fin pay the bill?"

"I don't know anything about anything," she said. "I need the key back in fifteen minutes."

"You took five bucks from me," I protested. "That should buy me a week."

"Any other room in the place, it buys you three nights. This one, fifteen minutes. You want a different room instead?"

The elevator had been barricaded. 'Temporarily Out of Service' meant broken forever. I found the stairs. A man and woman were asleep on the second floor landing. Neither of them stirred when I stepped over them. On the third floor, I used the passkey to let myself into 303. It was dim inside, and smelled like dust. Instead of using the light switch, I crossed to the single window and pulled a curtain open.

If the room had been tossed, somebody had cleaned it up afterward. The bed had been made and nothing appeared out of order. The closet held three dresses and two pairs of shoes, one of them with a broken heel. Two of the dresser drawers were empty; the third held a jumble of underthings and a snapshot of a young, dark-haired woman sitting cross-legged on the deck of a boat. It wasn't Beatrice.

A collection of glass curios covered the dresser top, most of them animal figurines, tigers and horses and dogs. The largest of them depicted two children holding hands. I looked them over carefully. I found no glass eye, not that I expected to.

I picked the closest figurine up and held it to the light from the window. A small elephant, to my eye it appeared to be plain glass, not any kind of crystal. The collection was probably worthless, but likely the only thing approaching earthly treasure Bea had owned. A noise made me glance up.

An old man stood in the open doorway, his fists balled. "What are you doing in here?" he demanded.

"I could ask you the same thing," I said, keeping my voice mild.

"Put up your dukes," he growled, and put up his, to show he was serious. I put my own hands up, showing the palms in surrender.

"Easy, friend," I said. "I'm not here to rob the place. I'm a private investigator. Lady who stayed here got killed, and I'm looking into it. If you're a friend of hers, we're on the same side."

"How do I know that?" he snarled, and I got my wallet out to show him the photostat of my license. It didn't prove anything, but he calmed down quickly and put out a hand. I shook it.

"What's your name, friend?" I asked.

"Charles Martellus. I live across the hall."

"You knew Beatrice Stone pretty well?"

"We were friends," he shrugged. "I'd give her a drink once in a while when she needed one."

"How often was that?"

"Not often. She bought her own, but she didn't have a regular business, with a payday. If she got sick, or the calendar made it a time of month she couldn't work, things could get tight. Sometimes she fell behind on the rent a little, and would disappear until she had the money. They weren't going to kick her out. It wouldn't make sense, since she always paid up and didn't damage anything. It frightened her when they knocked on her door, though, so she slept on the beach until things got better."

"So, you knew her pretty well, then."

"In most ways she felt like a daughter to me, except . . ."

He got silent for so long, I decided to help him out. "You got close with her once in a while? Closer than you would if she had really been your daughter?"

"My wife has been dead for years," he said. "I get lonely, like everyone else."

"Like everyone else," I agreed.

"Beatrice was generous." He thought about it. "I don't think she found any pleasure in it, except for being held at the end, and having her hair stroked. I think it comforted her. I hope so."

I found nothing strange in his story, and not much I hadn't seen. "I'm not a good person, but she was," he said. "I think it's important you understand that."

I didn't have anything to offer, so I didn't try. "I need to ask you something. Did Miss Stone leave anything with you for safekeeping?"

His face got instantly suspicious. "I won't lie to you," I told him. "Something pretty valuable is missing— a small piece of glass, like the ones on the dresser. I won't try to explain my motive for asking, but you should know some pretty rough characters are hunting for it."

"That don't frighten me," he said. "I don't scare easy."

"I'm sure you don't, but just now I reached into my pocket to get my wallet. If I had pulled out a gun instead, I would have had six bullets in you, before you took your last breath. You're plenty brave, but you need to see sense, too."

He rubbed the stubble on his chin while he considered it, and gave me a reluctant nod.

"She didn't leave anything with me, and I would have been the one," he said. "She knows I would have kept it safe for her. Is that why someone broke into her room?"

"I expect so. Somebody searching for it."

"Makes sense." He nodded again. "I'm the one called the cops. I heard a commotion through the walls, like someone throwing things. That's nothing new around here, but you stay here long enough, you get to know the sounds the building makes. I thought it came from Bea's room. It was still empty. The cops hadn't let them clean and rent it, yet."

"Did you see anyone?"

"I stuck my head out the door," he nodded. "I saw a woman in the hallway. I'm pretty sure she had just finished closing Bea's door. She stared me up and down, bold as can be. She didn't care I saw her."

"A woman?" It surprised me. "Can you describe her?"

He looked embarrassed. "I was drunk. I'm a little fuzzy sometimes, when I've had more than two or three. I know she was good-looking—and she wore a tan raincoat, belted tight. I think her hair was black or brown—I'd remember blonde. Better than average figure. I remember that, because it wasn't raining and struck me odd."

"Anything else? Hair color? Eye color? How old?"

"Not old, but I can't remember anything else except good-looking and wore a raincoat." He appeared hopeful. "Maybe if you put her in a line-up, it would jog my memory. That happens sometimes."

"I'm not the police, Mister Martellus. I don't put people in line-ups, I'm afraid. The room's in apple pie order—I expected shambles. You clean it up?"

He nodded. "I told you I was her friend. She meant something to me. What exactly is it people think she had? What is everyone looking for?"

"I can't tell you that, at least not now." I shook my head. "I'm sorry you had to lose her. When I get this straightened out, I'll come back and tell you all about it. In the meantime, you might want to keep your head down. If anyone asks you about her, don't volunteer much. You don't want the wrong people to think you're hiding something."

"The wrong people would be sorry they ever met me."

"I'm sure you're a tough cookie, but there's always somebody who's tougher. Getting hurt won't bring her back."

"She got hurt badly in her life," he went on. "I don't know what bothered her, but she had a lot of hurt, something she wasn't going to get over. It made her drink, and sometimes she could get out of order, but she was a good person. She deserved better than she got."

I gave him one of my cards, and told him to telephone me if he thought of something and felt like talking about it. He stared fixedly at the glass elephant in my hand, so I put the figurine back with the others. I thanked him for his time, and he nodded. He followed me out, and watched me while I locked the door.

"One thing about that woman, Mister Crowe," he said. "She made me nervous. Something about her eyes frightened me. She shouldn't have looked at me so bold, after she had just broken into a dead girl's room. There was something crazy about her."

"If you remember anything else about her, my office is right across the street."

He promised to find me, if he did. I glanced back from the top of the stairs, and saw him still at Bea's door, a sentinel at his post.

~*~

I like the twilight. I always have. I don't mind standing around and looking at it. When the light is almost gone, the air has its real color, its true color. The dying day gentles rose and purple into lavender and gray. Blues are soft behind the red glow of passing cars. It's always intense, like music coming from somewhere, and no matter how many times I see it, there's always the sweetness of maybe being the very last time.

The sky showed dark silver mixed with green, because it was drizzling, and the street started to shine. The warm green air meant it would rain all night. Twice, I waved on taxicabs that pulled to the curb in front of me. Like a lot of things, when you wanted one, they were never around.

I kept dry under the big marquee in front of the New Linear Theater. The lights were on, and they reflected from the wet pavement. The next show wouldn't start for another hour, so I had only a man in the glass ticket booth for company. He stood up and stared out from his aquarium occasionally, keeping a sharp eye on things.

A woman in a red dress came around the corner, moving well on her high heels. She stopped under the awning and shook her umbrella off before she glanced at me.

"You're Crowe? What are you doing out here? You were supposed to meet me inside—that's what I told you."

"I've seen the movie," I answered. "Don't want to see it again. Never cared much for Barbara Stanwyck, anyway."

She moved over to stand close to me. Another yellow hack squealed its wet brakes pulling up to the curb. It waited for us, and I leaned down to wave the driver on.

"I heard you were a character," she said. "Don't try real hard, on my account."

She had red lips, and dark hair that went well with her dress. Under the makeup, her cheeks were lightly pocked with the scars of old blemishes. She smelled like springtime somewhere, and looked entirely ready to be kissed.

"No thanks," I murmured. "I've seen that movie, too."

"Beg your pardon?"

"Talking to myself," I said. "You have something for me?"

"I told you my brother got murdered," she said. "The man

who killed him, Joey O'Meany, is going to get away with it."

"What makes you think so?"

I offered her a cigarette and lit it for her. She tucked it into a corner of her mouth, and handed me her purse to hold while she stripped off her dark blue gloves, one by one, hooking a thumb at each wrist. The ritual was curiously feminine, but not enough to change my mind about the movie.

"He told people about it," she said. "You know the reservoir at Rocas Perdidas?"

"I've been there."

It was a place I liked, a desert canyon that had been dammed and flooded before the war. You twisted down an arroyo highway, and then around a bend came a sudden explosion of blue water and green leaves.

"At the south end, there are concrete walls to keep the water in," she said. "Like a strange swimming pool, but it's about a five foot drop from the top of the wall to the surface."

"I know the spot," I nodded.

"Kids swim there sometimes. It's tricky to get back out after you jump in—there's only a rusty iron ladder set into the concrete in one corner."

"It's a dangerous place to go swimming," I agreed.

"The thin man takes cats there," she said. "Strays he gets from the pound. He throws them in and watches them drown. They can't get out."

"Nice hobby," I said. "I can't wait to meet him."

"One day, he had just dropped a cat into the water. My brother was at the reservoir, goofing around. He saw and yelled at him to stop. The man just laughed. The boy did the only thing he could, and jumped in the water to save the cat."

"Couldn't have been an easy thing to do," I said. "Cat wouldn't much like being saved."

"How would I know what cats like?" she shrugged, annoyed. "The kid got the cat and swam back to the ladder. The man stood at the top and showed him a gun and told him to get off the ladder or he'd shoot him. He wouldn't let him get out of the water, and he got tired and drowned. The man watched him die, and then he watched the cat drown, too."

Another yellow taxi pulled to the curb and stopped. It seemed my night for them. I waved the driver on.

"My brother was younger than me," she said. "My parents had him late, when I had nearly grown. They expected I would take care of him, and I mean to do just that, even if it's too late. I'm going to see Joey O'Meany dead for what he did."

"How did you hear this story?" I asked. "If nobody saw it, how do you know what happened to your brother?"

"He tells lots of people the story," she said. "Like it's a funny joke. It makes people afraid. The kid was a lot younger than me—the only family I had. I should have looked out for him."

"I know the feeling."

She shook her head, like a fly had landed. She didn't much like remembering or talking about it.

"You won't see a movie with me?" she asked.

I shook my head, no, and gazed out at the street. "That's all you have?"

"Isn't it enough?" she snapped. "He drinks at the South

Seas Room. I went to see him there, and he didn't deny it. He just threatened to kill me, too."

"Maybe I'll drop in on him," I said. "See what he has to say for himself."

"You'll find him there most nights, eating dinner at a corner table. You won't miss him. He's a thin, ugly-looking man—very, very thin. He's always hungry, and he never stops eating. He always has more than one dinner."

"Elegant," I murmured.

She gave me a sharp glance.

"You don't understand," she said. "He never stops eating, but he stays thin. They say when he turns sideways, you see can't him at all. He disappears. He's always hungry, and people are afraid of him. You ought to kill him, not talk to him."

I had no answer for that. I was too tired to be afraid of much, these days. It was getting dark, raining harder now. Things were getting blurred, and the cars splashed through the puddles of their own lights. We stood and watched it all for a little while; neither of us seemed to be in any kind of hurry.

"Do you want me to flag you a cab?" I asked. "I seem to have the knack of it tonight."

Already headed to the ticket window, she stopped and gave me a long look over her shoulder. Her eyes were full of broken promises and lost chances.

"Stick it in your hat," she said. "I haven't seen the movie. Do you think I picked this place just so I could meet you?"

I lit a cigarette and watched her at the ticket window. She wasn't hard to look at. She came back over after she had paid, not ready to give up.

"You won't see one lousy movie with me?" she asked, again. She was persistent, but I was, too. I shook my head again, and watched the street.

"What's her name?" she asked, and waited.

"Annie," I finally said, because I had no good reason not to. "Annie Kahlo."

"Would she care so much?"

She watched my face, and I kept no expression on it and watched the rain. I had nowhere to be, and no reason to run away.

"I don't know if she'd care so much," I said. "Maybe she wouldn't care at all. I would, though."

Another taxi paused hopefully at the curb, and I signaled this one to wait. The rain hit me hard as soon as I stepped out from under the marquee. I was surprised by how warm it was. I caught the door of the cab and got in. I saw through the glass that the woman had followed me, so I rolled the window down. Her umbrella was up, but her face was wet.

"If you won't take me to a lousy movie, will you at least kill the bastard for me?" she asked. "Will you at least do that?"

I couldn't think of a good answer for her. Matter of fact, I couldn't think of any kind of answer. I tapped the back of the seat so the driver would go.

Part Two

Jackal Eyes, Cat's Eye

-Eleven-

Saturday, September 6, 1947
Santa Teresa, California

    Beatrice Stone walked southwest on Cabrillo. Hotel steps lined the sidewalk, facing the beach and ocean on the other side of the boulevard. The night air blew soft, the essentially southern California kind of breeze produced by mixing desert and sea. The sun had slipped down, and the hotel marquees glowed gently.

    A doorman frowned at her, so she looked both ways and crossed the street during a pause in traffic. Walking on the hotel side made her feel as though she was working, but the beachside felt like freedom. Thanks to the five-dollar bill the stranger had given her, she had the night off. She had taken it to a package store and picked up a fifth of orange gin. Most of the five remained, and the night felt warm and infinitely full of promise.

    She thought about the man. His name was Crowe, he said, like the bird but with an 'e'. He had turned her down, but given her money anyway.

    "Get yourself a bath and some dinner," he had said. "It will have to be without me, though."

    Then he stood beside his suitcase and watched her walk away. She had felt his eyes.

    He had been quiet and ordinary, not the kind of man you'd glance at twice—except for those eyes. They were tired and sad, like a priest's eyes that had seen too much and knew more than they should. They were entirely kind, without holding any hope, like candles in a dark church. Bea thought that he must be an extraordinarily dangerous man.

The pavement bordering the sand was dark, lit only every hundred feet by electric bulbs on poles. A wrought iron bench sat beneath each of the lights. Beatrice paused in the shadows. With one hand in her purse, she slipped her bottle from its paper bag with the ease of slipping clothes from a familiar lover. The label said, 'Gibson's'. She unscrewed the metal cap, and with a single look over her shoulder brought the bottle to her lips.

"It's no good unless you really mean it," she thought. "You have to make it count."

She took a long, five-swallow pull. The gin hit her painfully in the throat and stomach, nearly making her gag. She forced a shallow breath and waited for the clenching to pass. Her belly relaxed. The heat travelled down her arms to her fingertips, and she felt her headache begin to loosen its grip and slide away. The enchantment began.

"Orange gin doesn't taste like oranges," she said out loud, and giggled. "It tastes like orange perfume."

She took one more pull, for good luck, and to make sure of things, and then she capped the bottle and slipped it back into her purse. She walked toward the beach amusement park, a half-mile away. The colored lights were just coming on. She would find a place in the dark to sit and drink and watch them, twirling and twinkling, until she fell asleep.

The rent on the room she kept at the Schooner Inn was a week overdue. It had happened before. They wouldn't put her out yet, but it seemed best to avoid a confrontation and steer clear of the front desk until she had some cash. She didn't mind spending a night or two with a friend, or even under the stars. Her blue dress would weather a day or two and still look acceptable.

A solitary figure sat on the next iron bench up the path. The beach area was otherwise deserted now, and Bea tensed as she approached. She had her heart set on a free night, and she didn't want to fend off advances. She had made a living from strange men in strange places for months now, long enough she had gotten used to being afraid and hardly noticed it any more. There was something odd about this person, though.

As she got close, the figure rose gracefully from the bench and stood on the path. It wasn't a man, at all, but a woman. She had a beautiful figure, and she stood deliberately in the light so Bea could look at her. She was slim, but her curves were generous. Strange for the beach, she had dressed for a party, in a strapless dress and heels. Even stranger, she peeked out from behind a sequined eye mask. A bouquet of black and white feathers had been attached to the corner by her left eye. The plumed masquerade sprayed outward, caught the light and then disappeared into her careful blonde hair.

Hipshot, the woman blocked Bea's way. As graceful as a mime, as elaborate as a maître d'hôtel, she gestured to the empty bench.

"Come sit with me," she said.

Her voice sounded peculiar; it grated and seemed somehow childish, like a small girl with a sore throat.

"Come sit with me," the woman said, again. "Let's have a drink together."

She pulled a handkerchief from her bosom and made a show of wiping and dusting the seat of the bench. After she considered it carefully and decided it would do, took Bea's hand and indicated that she should sit. Her costume was fabulous, like something a film star would wear, and Bea felt embarrassed by her own second-day-worn blue dress. When they were seated, the woman shifted to face her.

"Give me a drink, please," she said, in her awful, little-girl voice.

Bea felt a little reluctance, but she opened her purse and handed over the bottle of orange gin. The blonde woman took a dainty sip, and made a show of thoroughly wiping the neck of the bottle with her handkerchief before she handed it back. She fitted a cigarette into a long holder and lit it. Bea wondered idly if too many cigarettes had left her voice ruined.

"You drink, too," the woman said. "It's no fun drinking alone. When this is done, I'll buy us another bottle of expensive stuff. Perhaps something you've always wanted to try, and haven't yet."

Bea brightened at the secured prospect of enough booze for the night. After she had taken a drink, she offered the bottle back. The woman shook her head and leaned close, as intimate as if they had known one another for years. The light sparkled from the sequins on her mask.

"You stole something," the woman said. "I want it back."

There were familiar stirrings, of guilt and bad dreams. The woman stared at her as though she knew—everything. Bea became instantly afraid. She looked longingly at the concrete path, but the woman had a hand on her bottle and she wasn't going to leave without it.

"I didn't steal anything," Bea said. "I don't know what

you're talking about."

"Yes, you did," the woman said, and kissed her carefully on the mouth. "And yes, you do."

She leaned in close, and kissed her again, and again. They were soft kisses, on cheeks and brow, not what Bea was used to. She didn't kiss the men who dated her, and didn't allow them to kiss her. Part of her felt uncomfortable, but another part of her had known no affection in many months. That part of her had been starved, and she allowed the kisses to go on, and began to respond to them. She kissed the woman back.

"You stole something made of glass, you bad girl," the woman murmured. "Didn't you? You tell momma where you put the glass eye."

The woman's eyes peered out from the holes in the mask. She was very pretty and didn't seem so strange any more, and Bea found herself wanting very badly to please her, to confide in her.

"I took it, but I had to get rid of it," she confessed. "It got to be too much trouble, and I couldn't keep it. I wouldn't give it back, though. I wouldn't give them the satisfaction."

Bea closed her eyes. While the woman kissed her lids, bare brushes of lips, she told her almost everything. She told her about stealing the glass curio out of spite, without understanding what it was. She told her about the strange things happening, the people who followed her, letters in the mail with nothing written on them, the bumps in the night.

"So, I hid it," she said. "I hid it right out in the open, where it won't ever be found. They'll look right at it, and not see it."

"How clever you are!" the woman exclaimed. "What a

lovely, clever girl. Tell me where you put it."

She put her mouth to Bea's ear. Her breath felt warm and slightly damp.

"Tell me where you put it, and I'll kiss you again," the woman whispered. "Tell me and I'll kiss you to death."

Bea felt light fingers on her jaw, and as her face got turned, she closed her eyes again. She smelled the night, the beach, drying kelp and the slightly poisonous odor of a dead fish or crab somewhere nearby. Lips pressed against hers, and she instinctively opened her mouth.

"Why not?" she thought. Nobody had loved her for a long time, and it seemed likely no one ever would again. "Why not?"

As the woman's tongue found and caressed hers, the odor of fish and rot intensified. Bea resented the sensory interruption. Her first real kiss in such a long time, peculiar as it was, and something on the dark beach had to go and stink. The woman's fingers were moving, stroking, and Bea sighed and leaned back against the bench.

"Tell me where you put it."

The hands on her shoulders grasped harder. The kiss started to feel rough, invasive, and the smell of rot got stronger. Fondles felt like pinches. Bea had a sudden image of graves, decades old and opened in dim light. It became stronger than just thought, and she suddenly knew she was going to die. The idea got urgent, clear and absolutely certain. She stood up from the bench, meaning to run. The concrete walk tilted and whirled up to meet her.

She landed on hands and knees, felt the burn and knew her stockings were ruined. Her teeth ached, and she tasted blood in her mouth. Nothing was right, and something was terribly wrong.

"Did you put something in my gin?" she screamed. "You did, didn't you?"

The woman stood over her.

"Tell me where you put it," she hissed.

"What's going on here?" a man's voice said from behind her.

Bea had the hope that it might be the man from the parking lot, come to save her. Looking up over her shoulder, she saw someone different. She knew the man. He had been a friend, a long time ago, and she felt the flood of relief. She tried to say his name, but found his hand clamped firmly over her mouth. It was a warm hand, and she decided not to fight it.

"The bitch put a mickey in my bottle," she thought, with the idea if she thought it loud enough he would hear her.

He caught her elbow with his other hand, and helped her up. She knew that he was strong. On her feet, she realized her balance had entirely gone. The poison in the gin worked through her blood, faster than she would have thought possible. The man was gentle, but insisted that she walk.

"Got a room for you across the street," he said. "Gonna take care of you, now."

She leaned into him, feeling his hand on her face, and the warmth of his body through his suit coat. They began to move slowly toward the street. Bea wanted to help him save her, but consciousness was leaving and her legs were traitorous. As she felt herself begin to slip down the man's side, someone caught her other elbow supported it.

She glanced over gratefully, straight into the horror of the woman's smile. She took the sparkles on the mask with her, down into the darkness.

-Twelve-

There was baseball on the radio; an east coast game. The Giants were in Brooklyn. From thousands of miles away, I listened to the sounds of a whole stadium full of people that I would never see and never meet. It made me sad. Nothing ever seems to last, except as recollection.

I moved around the kitchen, swiping at things absently with a damp rag. Annie Kahlo sat at the table, watching me. A puddle of muted sun lay on the tablecloth, and she turned a spoon this way and that in it, undecided about which way it should point. The coffee in her cup had tiny white curdles floating on the surface.

"It's been hard," I said. "With you not around."

"I'm here now."

The warm afternoon was faded, sepia as a dream, and I saw it through the clouded eyes of the old man I would be someday. An electric fan rattled and moved the air, back and forth. The breeze caught her smile; it tore gently at me as it went by.

They say you can only miss the past, but that isn't true. Sometimes you miss the things that haven't happened yet.

"For good and always," she said softly, as though she could read my mind.

~*~

Fin kept his word and threw Beatrice Stone one hell of a send-off. Her funeral got staged in the Episcopal Church on State Street, not far from the art museum. I had been to the Catholic cathedral in Santa Teresa, an Old Spanish mission with white mud walls and a red tile roof, shaded by king palms. The Episcopalians were having none of that. They were quartered in a stern pile of granite that appeared to have been flown by magic, straight over from England.

The black hearse had already parked in front, handy to the long flight of stone steps. I felt bad for the pallbearers; there were a lot of stairs. The steps were lined with red geraniums that didn't look like they were enjoying the heat. Annie and I took the Gardiners by the elbows for the trip up. The huge front doors were propped open, and a ghoulish type in a black morning coat stood just inside. He hissed a greeting and told us to sit wherever we liked. Since the church gaped completely empty, it gave us a lot of seats to choose from.

The interior was warm and hushed, the way only churches on a weekday mid-morning can be. Colored light floated down from the windows and mixed with the sweet smell of beeswax, flowers and clean dust. A small noise from the organ loft above us made me jump.

The dark coffin had been placed in front of the altar. It appeared to be mahogany, but a blanket of pale roses made it hard to be sure. There were massed banks of lilies and carnations displayed on either side of it, a flood of white blossoms that must have emptied every florist shop in Santa Teresa. Beatrice Stone might have been a common streetwalker, but Fin was sending her out like a queen.

Behind us, the organ pipes wheezed softly into life, a sound that swelled into a melody too big for the empty church. Annie squeezed my hand, hard.

"Don't ever let this happen to me," she murmured. "Promise."

"You already had your funeral," I reminded her. "Neither of us went to it."

She looked at me, unsmiling, from behind the veil pinned to her hat. The dark gauze didn't lessen her eyes. She looked beautiful in black, but Annie belonged in sandals and unbleached muslin, with colors braided into her hair. Seeing her in dress and heels always made me a little bit sad. It was a little bit like meeting a mermaid who had been granted legs.

"You can't have another funeral for at least fifty years," I said. "I'm sorry."

"Promise me," she said, again. "And promise me you won't die first."

I thought about Corazón Rosa. A cemetery lay on the edge of town, built into a hillside. They did it different in Mexico, and it was a lovely place. The graves were tucked here and there under the roots of huge trees, and the wandering paths and stairways were marked by a carnival of cement statues. The dead had their own city, littered with wildflowers and balloons and faded photographs. In the daytime, they slept in the warm shade and bothered nobody at all. At night, they trailed sparkles, dancing to unheard music. You could see them move, if you looked hard enough.

"I promise," I said. "When the time comes, it won't be like this."

"Don't die first," she reminded me.

Fin appeared at my elbow. Annie gave him a kiss without saying anything, and then took the old couple away toward the front, to sit down.

"Do you like churches, Mister Crowe?" he asked.

I didn't figure it was really a question, so I didn't answer.

"I like churches," he nodded, as if I had. "They are perhaps the place I feel most at home. Does that surprise you? Every card has two sides, as does every coin, remember."

He hadn't removed his fedora, church or not, and the face below the brim comprised the usual assortment of parts that didn't quite ever make up a whole you could remember. I had known Fin a long time, and I couldn't have picked his face out of a photo line-up if my life depended on it. Whether midnight or broad daylight, you were left with a vague memory of pointed chin, hollow cheeks and shadow. The only thing that marked him was the sweet smell of poison that hung around him in a cloud.

"You see the heart of things," he said. "You see the heart of things, and it bewilders you. It might just be your best quality."

The organ music swelled into a thundering crescendo. Whoever Fin had paid to play it took the job seriously. I took it as a good reason to excuse myself from the rambling conversation with Fin, and looked around for Annie. She sat with the Gardiners at the front of the church, close to the coffin. I noticed a dark-haired young woman sitting by herself, about halfway up. She didn't glance at me as I went past.

Annie and I sat in the front pew, nearly close enough to touch the coffin if we'd wanted to and close enough to be overwhelmed by the smell of carnations. When the minister made an appearance, the organ music faded and I figured we were ready to start. I checked over my shoulder. Fin sat with a tired-looking woman I figured for Bea's mother, about halfway back and across the aisle from the young dark-haired woman.

"It makes me sad that her mother isn't up in front," Annie murmured. "She's ashamed."

"I don't think her mother knows any thing about her life here," I said. "I don't think they stayed in touch."

"Mothers know everything."

At the very back, in the shadow of the organist, I spotted Herb Robinson, the Gaynor's chauffeur. He stood alone, with his hat in his hands.

The minister began, and raced through the various speeches and incantations as quickly as humanly possible. I wondered if he wanted the fallen woman out of his church. In fairness, it might have been Fin who made him nervous. Fin kept his business away from the sunlight, but he was paying the freight and a few minutes alone with him would instinctively scare the hell out of most people.

There was no eulogy. At the end, the rented pallbearers hurried the coffin down the steps and into the waiting hearse. We all went to our cars and waited while they loaded some of the flowers, and then the small gaggle of cars followed the black wagon to the cemetery. Fin's gray Packard stood in front of us. Bea's mother sat in the passenger seat.

The cemetery had once been outside the city, but the city had grown around it and surrounded it with houses. We got out and I stood beside Annie in the sun. I gazed at the houses and wondered what it would be like to see a forest of tombstones, an army of marble angels every time you looked out your kitchen window. I supposed you just got used to it, like everything else. Fin brought Bea's mother to us while we waited for the funeral home folks to unload. She wore a pillbox hat. She ignored Annie and gave me her hand.

"I'm from Missouri," she said, by way of introduction. "I flew here on a Constellation. Mister Fin sent me a ticket. He's taken wonderful care of me."

I told her I had grown up in St. Louis, and she shook her head vehemently.

"Too big for me," she said. "Not my kind of place at all. Mister Fin told me you were a friend of Beatrice. Are you in the movies?"

"I didn't know her for very long," I said, truthfully. "I liked her fine, though. I'm not in the movies."

"I didn't mean you were actually in the movies. You aren't the type—I thought you might be a director or a cameraman." She shook her head again, this time sadly. "Beatrice was going to be a star. She had a certain quality, didn't she? I know she would have made it big."

I agreed, and we made a little bit of the awkward conversation that strangers make in cemeteries. Annie watched us and offered nothing. She didn't believe in small talk. Eventually, the woman wandered off to find Fin and we got ready to leave. The young woman who had been sitting alone in the church approached us. Dark-haired and slim, she wore glasses with blue frames. I recognized her as the woman in the framed photograph I had seen in Bea's room at the Schooner Inn, although she hadn't been wearing her glasses when the photographer snapped her sitting on the deck of a boat.

"Are you the man that found Bea?" she asked. "The private detective? My name is Miss Rice. I need to talk with you—alone."

Her body language seemed somehow defensive. She looked pointedly at Annie, and then at the Gardiners, who were watching the gravediggers approach the hole and paying no attention to us.

"Have you a car here?" Annie asked. "Perhaps Mister Crowe could ride back to town with you."

The woman hesitated and then nodded, so I kissed Annie's cheek and told her I would see her later. I kissed Mrs. Gardiner on the cheek, too. The doctor appeared slightly alarmed. He gave me an almost imperceptible shake of the head, so I skipped the kiss and gave him a small wave instead.

I followed Miss Rice to her little sand-colored Hillman Minx, an English car made before the war. It seemed to be in pretty good shape.

"It isn't much," she said. "The chauffeur keeps it running for me."

"Herb Robinson?" I said. "We've met. He's Jackie's brother."

She looked surprised. "I didn't think many people knew that."

"I thought everybody did."

"He's proud of his brother and ashamed of himself," she said. "He's very kind to me. Sometimes, I don't know how I'd manage without his help. It isn't easy for anyone—being alone."

I agreed it wasn't. The car started on the first try, and ran smoothly.

"Where should we go?" She seemed suddenly nervous, alone in the car with me.

"We can talk right here, if you'd like."

That seemed to relax her, and she nodded and shut the engine off. With some gentle nudging, she told me her first name was Wanda. She had worked for the Gaynor family as a live-in maid for about four years, six months of that with Beatrice Stone. She didn't have much understanding of what Bea's duties as personal secretary had involved, but the position didn't get filled again after she left. Bea hadn't much liked California, and had talked often about going home to Missouri.

"Her mother seems to think she starred in the movies out here," I said.

"That's what she came here for," she nodded. "She was beautiful, but so are a lot of other girls. In the beginning, she sent photos out to talent agencies, but I don't think anybody ever called her. She had a job at Darling's on the cosmetic counter, before she came to work for the Gaynors instead."

"What are the Gaynors like to work for?"

"It's easy enough, I suppose." She gave me a long look, as she considered it. "Just the two of them. How much help do two old women need? The cook, myself, a secretary, and the chauffeur part-time. He drives for the son, as well. Gardeners, but they never come inside. Some people have more money than they need."

"Was Bea an acceptable employee?"

"She did her job," she nodded. "She knew what she was doing. She drank a little, but not so it interfered with her duties."

"Not enough to cause her to be fired?"

"Why don't you say what's on your mind?" she snapped. "We were very close. Bea and I were about as close as two people can get."

I was taken aback. I hadn't been trying to get at anything in particular. She shifted slightly, to see me more directly. Her eyes were very large behind the lenses of her glasses.

"I'm sure that disgusts you."

Only the hearse remained. The funeral parlor people stared at us incuriously before they got in the front, one on each side. Blue smoke puffed from the exhaust and the black wagon moved off.

"I mind my own business, unless someone is paying me not to," I said, carefully. "I rarely form opinions of people."

"Explain that to me," she said. "I'd like to hear it."

Her voice stayed steady. I took a breath; I didn't much want to have this conversation.

"I stopped deciding a long time ago what other people should do. I have enough trouble figuring my own self out. I wish I could claim some virtue in that—but mostly I think I'm just tired. Maybe I've seen too much."

"You're part of the problem, though." Her voice rose into a challenge. "All men are."

I was suddenly tired of her, or maybe tired of the whole thing. In front of us, the Gardiners were settled into their Cadillac. Annie stood at the open door, looking back at me before she got in.

"I don't doubt or deny that, sister," I said. "Not for a minute. I'd like to find out who killed your friend, though. Nobody's paying me to do it. If you think you have something that night help, tell me. Otherwise, I can get out before my ride leaves and I have to walk back to town."

She stared at me, and I stared right back. After thirty seconds, something melted or broke and she looked out the window and hitched a breath. The shudder in it was genuine. "She's dead because of me."

Outside, the gravediggers walked toward the hole. One of them glanced our way before they got busy filling it in. I waved good-bye to Annie, and the Cadillac drove off slowly.

"She took something from the Gaynors," Wanda said. "She stole something from the room when Mrs. Gaynor fired her. She slipped it into the pocket of her dress. She wanted some money to give it back."

"I know about the glass eye," I said. "Since we both know, there's no sense in talking circles around it."

"She planned to return it, but something changed her mind. She decided they deserved to pay more. When the people started to scare her, she asked me to find a place to keep it. She had nowhere to hide it. I told her I wouldn't."

"What do you mean?" I asked. "What people started to scare her?"

"She didn't know them," she said. "Two men in a black sedan that looked like a police car. Obviously the Gaynors sent them. First, they followed her everywhere—she thought they were the police, because they seemed like policemen. They searched her room when she went out. One night they cornered her and searched her pockets. Then they—raped her."

Her glare became utterly defiant, and I could see the glint of tears.

"I suppose you think that isn't important," she said. "What does it matter if a woman who sells herself to strangers gets raped?"

"I think it matters," I said. I stayed quiet for a moment, because I had never really thought about such a thing. I remembered the woman in front of the Sand Castle, beautiful under the wear-and-tear and the booze. I remembered the look of hurt on her face when I had turned her down, and I felt a vague stab of guilt and the beginnings of anger. "I think it matters a lot. You have nothing else on these characters? Did she describe them to you?"

"Just two men," she shrugged. "Two men who looked like cops, in a black car. I met Bea once, downtown, and they rolled by. Bea pointed them out, staring at us. They seemed like police."

"I'll check into it," I promised. "Do you have any idea where she might have left the glass eye?"

She shook her head, and I saw she was crying. I stopped the impulse to touch her shoulder. I had a sense it wouldn't give her any comfort.

"I wouldn't get involved." Her voice got strangled. "She had no other friends, and her room wasn't safe. If she hid it, it was in plain sight—someplace public, so she could get it back when she needed it. I can't imagine where that could be—where you'd find a public place safe enough you could be sure nobody would come along and steal it."

"If there's any logic to it, I'll figure it out," I said. "I need the time to think."

"That old woman really believes the eye makes her see," she said. "It cures her blindness when she holds it in her hand.

They won't stop at anything to get it back. This is more dangerous than you think."

Wanda stared at me for a long moment, both of her hands on the steering wheel. She appeared to have cried herself out, and appeared ready to leave. Her voice went flat.

"She planned to give me some of the money," she said. "She wanted to get me away from that house and give me a fresh start. I would have left with her. It's what she hoped for, but I didn't tell her my answer was going to be 'yes'. I let her wonder. Some friend I turned out to be."

"You know something?" My hand rested on the door handle. "I think she had a pretty terrific friend. I'll take care of her from here."

"Thank you," she said. "Maybe she did. Not a good enough friend to save her, but maybe she did."

"I'll let you know how I resolve this," I said.

She stared at me some more. "You think you're going to fix this?"

"I usually do," I said. "One way or another."

I could see she didn't believe me. I could also see that she probably didn't like me, and I had no real reason to fault her for it. I told her a walk back to town would probably do me good.

"Beatrice was sad," she said. "She was a sad person. I wish I had made her happy."

I had no good response for that, so I didn't try. I got out of her little car and watched her drive slowly away along the winding lane between headstones. The gravediggers had finished their job and disappeared. As far as I could tell, I was alone in the cemetery.

I looked at the small mound of dirt that marked the end of Beatrice Stone.

"Just you and me now," I told her.

-Thirteen-

Danny López and I sat on a bench in the sun. We watched the blue-and-gold beach.

"If we want to get shot," I said. "Sitting out in the open like this is as good a way as any."

"Probably." The old gangster didn't look as though it bothered him much.

"Nice day for it, if it happens," I said. "We could find a worse place to do it."

"This is pleasant," he agreed. "I will tell you something, *amigo*. There's a lot more fuss when you come here than when you leave."

I got up and bought two papers cup of vanilla ice cream from a truck parked in the shade. I took them back to the bench and handed one to the old man before I sat down. It came with a little wooden paddle. He held his up to examine it, like he wasn't sure what it was for.

"What is this?" he asked.

"It's a spoon," I said. "Use your imagination."

He stared at it for a moment longer, and then he shrugged and used it to try his ice cream.

"Life is nothing but a long series of goodbyes," he said. "I say mine to the world every morning when I wake up. That way I'm ready, and then I don't have to worry about it for the rest of the day."

"Seems sensible," I agreed.

The ice cream was cold and sweet and perfect. I didn't think there was any way to beat the taste of vanilla when it came right down to it, and the wooden flavor of the spoon went with it just right.

"We are all guilty of secretly believing that the world ends when we die," he said. "How could it go on without us?"

A black dog came off the sand. He was wet from playing in the surf, and he shook himself off as soon as he got close enough to get us wet, too. I didn't mind. He sat down and gazed at me happily, as if he was waiting for something.

"The world doesn't end when we do, though," López said. "It keeps going, and it takes us with it. We leave the theater, but the movie plays, with us still in it. The good things and the bad things we do live on in other people—in the lives we have changed. Our kindness and our sins don't die. They grow and grow, even after we're gone."

He smiled at me and wiped a dab of pale ice cream from his moustache with the back of one hand.

"We don't get to see the end of our movies, *amigo*." He laughed. "We don't ever know how we turn out. Imagine that."

I held out the cup for the dog so he could finish the last of my ice cream. When it was all gone he ran off to play in the ocean again, without looking back.

"I met with the woman you referred to me," I said. "She told me Joey O'Meany killed her brother. She wouldn't give me her name, or much of anything else—just that her brother's name was Allen, with an 'e'. Hard to start running things down if I don't even know the player names."

"Her name is Florence Nickerson," he said. His face wrinkled into something that might have been a smile. "She wants to stay in the shadows, like all of us."

"Brother had the same last name?" I asked. "Allen Nickerson?"

He nodded. "I'm not asking you to resolve anything, *amigo*. Make her feel better, if you can. Make her feel like someone cares enough to do something. You're not going to do anything about Joey O'Meany. The thin man will annoy the wrong person and get himself killed one of these days."

"If I satisfy myself that he killed a kid, I'll figure out a way to do something about it."

"Be careful," he said. "Don't take him lightly. He's completely *loco*, and that makes him dangerous. This business is pleasure to men like him, and you cannot predict how they will react to anything. In any event, if you convince this woman someone cares about her and her brother, then the world will be set right. Just make her feel as if she is not invisible, and then send me a bill."

"I'll get her some real justice, if I can."

"He is a *psicópata*, a . . ." He looked to me for help.

"Psychopath."

"Yes, one of my favorite words, and I can never remember the English. Psychopath. Examine him from a distance. He would enjoy killing you, I think."

Somebody nearby had an automobile radio playing. The soft sound of it disappeared every time the breeze rattled the palm fronds over our heads. Out on the sand, a gull found something and flew off with it. There was a flurry of white wings and a dozen more gave chase, in case anything got dropped.

"I thought you were going to stay in the shadows, *amigo*," he said. "I heard you were involved in another murder. A girl killed in a motel at the beach."

As far as I knew, the murder of a streetwalker hadn't been worth even a line of newsprint, but that didn't mean López wouldn't know about it. He had an ear to the ground in every block of the city. I figured we weren't far from the spot where Beatrice Stone had been killed. I wondered if her ghost still hung around. The idea made me sad. I hoped she had gone somewhere else and had something better to do.

"I found the body, and by coincidence I'm still involved," I said. "I've been hired to find something she stole before she died." I told him about the glass eye. I didn't talk about my cases, but it seemed like everyone knew more about what Beatrice had stolen than I did, and anyway, Danny had been born with a closed mouth. I trusted him completely.

"Girl found dead in your motel room, and now you're working a case that involves her?" He raised an eyebrow. "*Que coincidencia*—you don't smell something funny?"

"Of course, I do, but I need the job. If I find out what happened to the item she stole, I might find out who killed her. She was being chased before she died."

I told López about the two men who had followed, searched and eventually molested Beatrice Stone.

"Rape crosses the line," I said. "Makes it personal, somehow."

"It does," he agreed. "Something like that would offend a man like you, down to his soul. It offends me. Sounds like cops—a couple of cops."

I glanced at him, surprised. "That's how they were described to me, as looking like cops. Gaynor swears the police aren't involved, though. What makes you think so?"

"Ask any working girl about the man who takes what she sells, for free," he said. "She'll tell you it's the neighborhood cops. Criminals tend to understand the business and respect it. It's a living, like everything else. Cops don't respect it. They treat it like it has no value, just there for the taking."

He was still working on his ice cream. He wasn't as adept with the wooden spoon as I had been, and he didn't have a dog to help him.

"Another thing," he said. "When someone gets described as a cop, he usually is. It's an appearance you earn, and it doesn't wash off easy. You were a cop, and you still look like one."

"If it had been Santa Teresa buttons, somebody would know them. Somebody would have said something."

"Private," he suggested. "Like you. Most of them start out as cops, and never lose the swagger, never lose the attitude."

"Who the hell would they be working for?" I wondered. "If it was Gaynor, he wouldn't be wasting his money on me."

"What is this glass eye really worth?"

There were no answers for that, but I had an idea where I might start checking.

"I have another question," López said. "Why did you not come to me about the dead woman right away? Why endure trouble with the police? I might have helped you with this, had you asked."

"I bother you enough, don't I? Annie lives in your house in Corazón Rosa. You've kept her safe."

"She bought the house from me," he said, and patted my hand. "It is hers, now—her home, and perhaps one day, yours. Anyway, I would help her a thousand times, gladly. And you."

Danny and I didn't have anything else to say to each other, and neither of us talked when we didn't need to. We sat together and watched the beach instead.

~*~

When I took the elevator to the sixth floor of the sand-colored building on De la Vina Street and entered Gaynor Glass, Ann Child wasn't at her reception post. I wondered if they had fired her for being human. The kitten sitting in her chair stared at me blankly when I asked if she was new. She took my card and read it off into her telephone. After she hung up, she crooked a finger and led me past the display cases of glass and then up a carpeted hallway. She showed me in to see Harold Gaynor without getting playful, which disappointed me.

His office looked a lot like the one he kept at his house, with a lot of leather, and books for decoration. A row of windows framed with velvet drapes overlooked the street. Gaynor didn't appear surprised to see me.

"You have something for me, Crowe?"

"I have a question," I said. "Who are the clowns in the black car?"

He raised one eyebrow. "I'm sure I don't know what you're talking about."

"They raped her," I snarled. "That much I know for sure. I have a good idea they killed her, too, and I intend to find out for certain. This is personal, now."

His complexion seemed to change its mind between turning red and deathly pale, so it settled for half-and-half. His cheeks were livid.

"I haven't the slightest knowledge about anyone being— raped," he said.

If he wasn't genuinely shocked, he did a good impression of it.

"You can probably give me a good guess," I said. "Let me pretend like I believe you, and I'll give you a description. Two men that looked a lot like plainclothes cops followed Beatrice Stone around, trying to intimidate her."

"Maybe it was the police, on an unrelated matter," he said. "Miss Stone didn't lead an upstanding life. As I told you, besides stealing from us, she had a generally degenerate lifestyle. I can only imagine what other kinds of trouble she was in."

"I was a cop once," I reminded him. "Plainclothes detectives don't waste weeks following around streetwalkers and petty thieves, as a rule. They also don't drive around in black sedans that look like police radio cars. It defeats the purpose of working incognito."

"What's your point, Crowe?"

"They were private operatives, which means someone hired them. Since they were trying to shake loose the glass eye she held, that someone was you. Nobody else has an interest in this."

"If I hired anyone, they came from an agency," he said. "I bear no responsibility for its employees. That's hypothetical, of course, since I'm not saying I hired anyone in the first place."

He got a cigarette from a small box on his desk full of them. He didn't offer me one. When he had it lit, he blew out smoke and went to the window.

"Why would I have hired you, if I already had someone working on this?"

"You as much as told me you did. You said you needed me to turn over the underbelly of Santa Teresa so they would know where to hunt."

He was clearly at a loss.

"So, I hired the Parklane Agency in Los Angeles," he said. I knew them. They were a big outfit, not above getting dirty if the money was right. "We've used them before, when competitors have pulled dirty tricks. I deal with their office, not their detectives. I wouldn't have the slightest idea if the men you're describing work for them or not."

"So, get them on the phone and find out."

"Get them on the phone and start making wild accusations about men in a black car? They would end our association immediately. If the men you're talking about belong to them, they'll be withdrawn from the case and you'll never find anything out about them."

He was right. I sat and fumed.

"I would never countenance anything like what you're describing," he said. "If I had violent intentions toward Miss Stone, I certainly have the means to use them. I would have had the eye back in my possession in no time at all. In fact, I gave her a thousand dollars to return it, and even when she reneged on our deal I remained open to negotiating her new price."

His bewilderment began to turn to outrage. His voice rose, and he pointed a finger at me. It shook, ever so slightly. "I told you before, I never called the police," he said. "She had my stolen property in her possession. How long after I picked up the phone would it have taken to have her behind bars and my mother's glass returned to her? Why do you think I didn't do that?"

I got out a cigarette of my own, to buy a few seconds for me to think. Upset people tended to say more than they intended to, and I didn't want to waste the opportunity. "Maybe you had your own good reasons," I said. "Maybe the eye was a stolen artifact in the first place, and you didn't want to draw attention to it."

"What nonsense!" he sputtered. "My family is a pillar of society in Santa Teresa. How dare you imply we would involve ourselves in a crime?"

"In my experience, pillars of society generally get to be pillars by committing lots of crimes. I wouldn't hold it against you."

He crossed the room toward the door, clearly meaning to toss me out. Halfway there, he seemed to think the better of it and went to the window instead. I smoked my cigarette and gave him time to simmer down as he watched the traffic on Chapala Street, below him.

"I felt sorry for her," he said, so soft as to be almost inaudible. "That's the truth of it. I felt sorry for her."

Whether it was true or not, I had nothing to add to it, so I let myself out.

~*~

The Camel Diner had been open on the corner of Garden and Anapamu Streets since before most of its patrons were born. I could never remember its real name. Most people didn't know it had ever been called anything else. At some point the sign over the front door had been taken down, maybe to freshen the paint, and they had never gotten around to putting it back up. The only identifier it had was the Camel cigarette advertisement nailed beside the entrance. The painted tin had turned mostly to rust, but enough remained to give the place a name.

The restaurant didn't fit the neighborhood, but the neighborhood probably didn't notice it there any more. It sat well off the main drag, a run-down little place in an area of nice, respectable homes, shaded by a lot of monkeypod and shower trees that carpeted the sidewalks with their flowers in the fall. The monkeypods didn't belong here any more than the restaurant did. They had been brought here from the South Pacific and planted. Somehow, they had survived and grown old. I knew how they must feel, and I usually patted a trunk or two as I passed by.

The diner served decent food, better-than-decent coffee, and I could almost always get a booth where I could watch the door. I saw enough strange things and strange people in my life to make me allergic to any craving for change or excitement. On nights when I couldn't find anything in the icebox, or just got tired of myself, I walked the couple blocks for an hour of familiar company that didn't speak to me.

The waitress came over to the table, bringing a cloud of

Beechnut chewing gum with her.

"You're in early," she said. "Don't usually see you in here before midnight. You sleeping these days?"

"We never sleep," I said. "I'm sure you must have heard that."

Roxanne was a blowsy redhead from New York. Her husband drove a Greyhound bus up to San Francisco and back three times a week. She swore they were going to pack everything up and move home, back to New York City. She had been swearing it for a while now, with no eastward progress I could see.

I liked Roxanne, maybe because I liked people who had dreams. It seemed to give them a certain kind of energy other people didn't have. I didn't know what happened to them if any of the dreams came true. Maybe they faded away and turned into ghosts. Dreams weren't a table I played at very often though, so I didn't wonder about it too much.

"You're thinking of Pinkerton's," she said. "Is that your dream? A big detective agency someday?"

It startled me a little, her reading my thoughts. "My dream would be leaving this racket," I told her. "Walking on the beach with a dog every morning."

"That's a good dream." Her face got sympathetic. "Have the meatloaf."

So, I had a late, solitary dinner of meatloaf, peas, and mashed potatoes. After I washed it down with a couple of cups of coffee, I walked myself home through the puddles of streetlight on the sidewalk. The houses on either side of mine were dark. The Gardiners were probably in bed. There was no telling where Annie had gone. I picked up the newspaper off the mat as I fumbled out my keys.

I spread the paper out on the kitchen sideboard and glanced at the headlines while I made a drink of Four Roses and a splash of water from the faucet. When it was ready, I picked up the sports page to take with me to the living room. The house seemed too quiet, and I thought about breaking the silence by putting something on the phonograph. Someone beat me to it.

The opening saxophone notes of 'I Love You Madly' floated down the hall.

Beatrice Stone sat in my usual chair, gazing out the front window. Something outside the dark glass had her complete attention. Her face stayed composed and lovely. She wore blue pumps, and her navy dress had been set off with a strand of pearls. The skin on her cheeks was slightly discolored and her bare arms showed faint scrapes and bruising, but her hair was clean and arranged becomingly. Overall, she looked a lot less dead than the last time I had seen her.

Her hands were closed into small fists in her lap. Without looking at me, she brought the right one up and opened it. A small glass orb sat in the middle of her palm. While I watched, she let it slide off onto the floor. It hit the wood and bounced once, then clattered as it rolled to a stop at my feet.

"You're dead," I said, and felt stupid for saying it.

The room felt silent, even with the record playing. I had it on good authority she wasn't breathing any more, since I had seen the coroner's certificate. I suspected I wasn't either.

"What do you want?" I asked. The voice in my ears sounded like someone else.

She didn't look away from the window. I set my drink carefully on an end table, careful not to spill any, and left the room. I went up the hall to my bedroom. Without undressing, I got into bed and pulled the sheet over me. The shadows moving on the dark ceiling didn't tell me a thing. After a few minutes, the idea of sleep became absurd, so I got back up to confront my imagination.

The ghost still sat in my living room. From the hall, I could see her crossed ankles and blue shoes in the pool of lamplight on the rug. She hadn't moved. I walked past the entry and let myself out the front door. I could feel her eyes on me all the way down the sidewalk.

The house next door was completely dark, but Annie pulled the front door open moments after my first knock. Her long hair fell loose, down on the shoulders of her striped cotton pajamas. She watched my face as she shrugged into a robe.

"Beatrice Stone is sitting in my living room," I said. "She's in my chair, listening to a phonograph record. I don't know what to do."

Annie thought about it and nodded, as if it all made perfect sense. "You probably don't need to do anything, unless she's careless and scratches your record."

"Well, she's dead," I said. "We went to her funeral, remember? Either I'm crazy, or she must be a ghost."

She watched the sidewalk. Even in the dim streetlight, her eyes were luminous. Her smile broke slowly and took my breath, just like it always did. She tightened the belt on her robe.

"Naturally, she's a ghost," she said. "That has nothing to do with your being crazy. I'll go talk to her."

I followed her across the dark lawn and up the steps to my door. The chair in the living room was empty. I saw no glass eye on the bare floorboards. I got down on hands and knees to see if it had rolled under a table or chair. I saw nothing but cobwebby gatherings of dust.

"She was here," I muttered. "I didn't just catch a passing glimpse. I stood and looked at her. I even spoke to her."

"She didn't speak to you?" Annie asked, and went to sit in the chair Beatrice had occupied. She leaned her head back and closed her eyes. "You have to save her this time," she said.

"What do you mean? She's dead."

"You weren't able to save her in the hotel bathroom," she said. "She knows what's happening to you. She knows it's tearing you apart inside. She's giving you another chance."

"I heard the glass eye when it hit the floor and bounced," I said. "It was real."

"Of course, it was real." She shook her head, a little impatient. "Why would you think it wasn't real?"

She stood still, for thirty seconds or so, staring at the empty chair. Then she gave herself a nearly imperceptible shake and reached for my hand.

"You shouldn't stay here tonight," she murmured.

I kept my hand in hers while I locked up my front door with the other. We held hands crossing our dark lawns to her steps. I still had hers in mine as we went up her hallway without turning on a light, through half-seen paintings and fresh flowers in the dark, the fragrance of citrus and clean, cool running water. She stopped at her bedroom door and turned toward me. In a single fluid motion, she raised hands over her head and her white cotton shift puddled on the floor at her feet.

"Sanctuary," she said, and opened the door.

-Fourteen-

In the morning, I went to see Harold Gaynor's mother. Annie rode with me.

"We're going to see two women," I said. "They share the same last name and live in the same house, but they aren't sisters. One is Gaynor's mother, and the other is his aunt. They're unusually close, I gather. Been together a long time."

Chin propped on elbow, Annie watched the scenery passing her open window and gave no indication she heard a word I said. I knew her concentration was absolute, though.

"It's the aunt who's blind," I continued. "Beatrice Stone stole the glass marble from her when she got fired."

"Not marble—eye." Annie murmured a correction, without looking at me.

"Apparently, the blind woman believed it was an eye," I agreed. "I've started to think of it that way myself. She claims her eyesight gets restored when she holds it in her hand. I can see why she'd be upset at losing it, if she believed that. These women are upper crust, though. They didn't kill Bea."

"They didn't?"

I glanced over at her, surprised. Her tone hadn't changed, and I didn't know if she had really asked a question. She didn't generally make small talk, though. We were at a stoplight, and she gazed at an elderly woman who crossed the street with a mallard duck tucked under her arm. They reached the corner and paused. The woman settled the duck more comfortably, and appeared to be scolding it. I saw a lot of strange things, most of them when I was with Annie.

"It's a stretch to think two older women, one of them blind, could have wrestled Beatrice Stone into the bathtub in my hotel room. I'll keep an open mind, though."

"What are we doing here?"

"I'm here because Gaynor paid Beatrice a thousand bucks to return the eye. She had second thoughts, and raised the price. She kept the thousand, which was bound to make people mad. She got killed in the middle of negotiating, and the eye is missing. I'm supposed to get background on her movements before she died—a sense of where she might have stashed it. You're here because Fin sent you a telegram, which lied and said I needed you here."

"I know all that," she said. "And of course, you need me here. We're really here to get some answers for Beatrice Stone. Finding the eye is just a means to that end."

"Since Harold Gaynor ostensibly had a motive for killing her, he probably won't mind if we find out who did."

The address was tucked into a hillside just outside the Montelindo town limits. I nearly drove by the entrance, a couple of high gates set into a stucco-plastered wall topped with broken glass. I backed up and turned in. A stone lion sat on his pedestal and watched me as I got out of the car and crossed to a call box. The heat didn't seem to be bothering him any.

I pressed the buzzer, and glanced back at the car. From the passenger seat, Annie watched me with about the same expression as the lion. She had insisted on keeping me company when I visited the Gaynor estate. I didn't really see the point, but truthfully the night before had been something special and I wasn't quite ready to spend time apart from her yet.

"Miss Kahlo and Mister Crowe," I said, when the speaker squawked. "We're expected."

Nobody answered, but a servomechanism hummed and the gates parted. I got back in and steered the car through them, and then up a curve of winding drive. No house had come into sight, not yet. The grounds were lush, green and clipped; everywhere were flowerbeds, white statues and fountains. It seemed about as far away from California as you could get without using an ocean liner.

"This is an estate," I told Annie. "The son, Harold lives a little way down the road in a mere mansion, which isn't the same at all. It seems like we're in England. If they had tropical plants there, this is what it would look like."

"A lazy English," she said. "With specific affectation."

The brakes on the Mercury chirped as I pulled over and tucked it tight against a stand of giant ferns. Out of sight of any watching eyes, I opened the map compartment, got the Browning out and checked it. When it was stowed in my jacket pocket, I released the brake and got ready to drive on.

"Wait—wait." Annie said, a hand on my arm. "The sisters are in their eighties. Are you planning to shoot them?"

"I told you they aren't sisters, and being old doesn't mean they aren't dangerous," I said. "Hatpins, occult spells, needles—who knows? They probably have spiders and poisonous orchids. Aren't you afraid of dying?"

"They are sisters," she said. "I see them—they're sisters in a way you may not understand. A gun won't do you any good against the sisters. I'm usually not so direct with you, because I know it takes you time to think—but sometimes you need pointing in the right direction. Here goes."

She took an audible breath.

"Mayonnaise, ocelot, tomato, orange, raspberry, drawer—can you remember that? Magic words, when the time comes."

I didn't know what she was talking about, but I almost never did at first. I made a living by listening and having a good memory, though.

"Mayonnaise, ocelot, tomato, orange, raspberry, drawer," I repeated.

"Very good!" She pressed her hands together and smiled indulgently at me. "That's what you'll need. You'll see—later."

"Aren't you afraid of dying?" I persisted.

Her head tilted, thinking about it. She patted down my face with her dark eyes, measuring the question. I knew she saw and understood things about me I didn't even suspect.

"I'm a bit afraid of airports," she said, a little reluctant. "I'm afraid of the smells and noises; the crowds and the announcements over the loudspeakers. I'm afraid of early mornings and the late-at-nights—the bright lights and hurry, hurry, hurry. I'm afraid of losing my luggage and my tickets. I'm afraid of the people I see from the corners of my eyes. They might be following me."

Her face became grave, behind the hat veil. She rolled down her window all the way; to let the fern fronds come inside the car. They brought their cool shade in, and their intensely green smell. "When I walk out onto the tarmac, I'm afraid of the clouds hanging over the runway—low and black and flickering lightning.

I'm afraid of the wind—damp and gusting. The plane is huge and loud. The stairs are too close to the propellers. I look back over my shoulder at the place I'm leaving, and I know I'm never coming back. I'm afraid nobody will miss me or even remember me—and most of all, I'm afraid it will hurt."

Her smile came, sudden and wonderful. "I'm not afraid of flying, though," she said. "Not of flying, and not of the place I'm going to land. So, I'm not afraid where it matters—I'm scared of getting there, but not scared of being there. Does that make sense?"

We sat, looking at each other. I noticed again, for about the seven-millionth time, how beautiful she was. Being with her was like remembering how to breathe, every single time.

"Mayonnaise, ocelot, tomato, orange, raspberry, drawer," I said. "It makes sense."

"There's more," she said. "There's always going to be more."

I nodded, let the clutch in, and drove on. The house appeared like something lifted from an old novel, covered in gray stone and dark ivy. Herb Robinson abandoned the black LaSalle parked further along the circle of gravel in front of the steps, and met us when we got out.

"Good to see you again, suh," he said. "You going to be working for the sisters, too?"

"I'm working for Harold Gaynor," I said. "Not his mother. I'm just here to get some background information."

"Same family, same thing," he shrugged.

I stopped halfway up the steps, struck by something.

"Sisters?" I asked. "You call them sisters, too?"

He shrugged again. His expression hid something. "Miss Olive and Miss Chamomile been so close, together so long, they call themselves secret sisters. They have the same last name. Guess we all think of them that way, too."

I decided not to press him, and followed Annie up the steps. The big front door got pulled open before I had a chance to ring the bell. Wanda Rice stood in front of us, wearing a black-and-white maid's uniform. Her eyes gave no indication she had ever met me before. Annie and I followed her into the house. We crossed through a great hall that seemed oddly and eerily familiar, until I realized Harold Gaynor must have modelled his Montelindo mansion on this one.

His mother's house showed a patina of age, though, and something like faint grime. The air carried a faint odor of standing water. Wanda led us past a grand staircase, grim portraits of dead and forgotten California robber barons, all the way to the back of the house. She left us at the door of the conservatory.

Annie stepped in and looked up, and I followed her gaze to the dirty glass panes that formed the ceiling. The conservatory was really nothing more than a huge glass greenhouse slouched up against the side of the house. It had been filled with pots of spider plants, hundreds of them. They were hung from the ceiling, suspended on lattices and standing in pots on every surface that would hold them. Some of them were yellow and dead, but most seemed obscenely healthy, bursting with green.

Groups of furniture stood here and there, arranged as if they had simply been dumped and forgotten, most of it made of wicker that appeared rotten. Unlike her son, with his affection for gleaming marble and rich leather, she either had no pretensions or felt herself above what anyone thought. The room was shabby to the point of looking as if it had been left derelict for years. The conservatory made a curious contrast with the grounds; the rank vegetation and decayed wicker nothing like the lush, clipped lawn outside. With enough money, you didn't need to make any sense.

Two women sat behind a large table at the far end of the room. I felt the weight of their gaze. I glanced at Annie; her face had the vacant composure that told me she had gone invisible in her own mind.

"Mrs. Gaynor?" I offered. "Nate Crowe, and my— associate, Anne Kahlo."

"I know who you are," one of them said. She smacked her lips audibly.

I walked toward the women, spider-plants brushing my shoulders. I didn't check to see if Annie followed. She would do as she pleased.

The one who spoke had a face as hard as the blunt end of a hatchet, and a voice that matched. She had been a looker, once. She still held onto something that could be called handsome, although she seemed to have put any feminine airs and graces behind her.

"I am Olive Gaynor," she said. "This is Chamomile. You should have been here before now. You must not be much of a detective."

She poured ruby liquid into crystal, managing to only spill a little. When she had the stopper safely back in the decanter, she picked up the glass and gobbled most of it down.

"This is my medicine," she said. "I have an incurable condition."

"Cheers," I said. "Is that port or sherry? I get them mixed

up."

She glared at me over the top of the hand she used to wipe her mouth with. When she took it away from her face, I saw she had smeared her lipstick. It gave her a sardonic look that suited her. "You're staring at me as though I should offer you a glass, Mister Crowe," she said. "This is real medicine, not a social remedy. We are here to talk business. By all accounts, you drink too much as it is."

I thought about taking out my gun and shooting her. I glanced at Annie. I knew that she read my mind, and I got a disapproving eye back, so I left the gun in my pocket. Mrs. Gaynor got back to her medicine, and once through it seemed restored enough to get down to whatever bothered her.

"She's blind," she said, indicating the woman beside her. "It isn't her fault."

The second woman sat in a wicker wheelchair. Olive Gaynor was slender, and appeared to be well within the limits of middle age. Chamomile Gaynor was plump, and ageless. She might have been twenty years old, or a hundred-twenty. She wore a lavender-colored dress and a straw hat, lacquered black and woven into coils that looked like braids. The veil hung from the brim was black, too, and hid her face. It all gathered at her neck, like beekeeper's netting, and gave the curious impression that she had no head. I waited to see what she had to say.

"She doesn't talk," Olive said. "I speak for her."

A small, domed birdcage, painted gold, sat on the table. The blind woman reached out and touched it with a hand like a soft claw. Behind the wire bars, a little sparrow sat motionless, with feathers puffed up. There appeared to be something wrong with it.

"The bird is blind, too," she said. "Chamomile likes to have a blind pet to keep her company. When it's done quickly, with a very hot needle, the bird hardly notices."

I felt a creeping horror.

"You blinded the bird deliberately?" I asked.

"Of course!" she laughed gaily. She suddenly sounded like a young girl. "Do you think I can walk outside and just pluck a blind bird from a tree whenever I want to?"

The colors in the room went all wrong. A low buzzing sound filled the air. I couldn't tell where it came from, but it made me feel a little bit sick. I glanced over at Annie. She had a funny look on her face, one I recognized. Olive Gaynor caught it as well.

"Why are you looking like that?" she snapped at her. "You look ill. Are you ill?"

Annie could be dangerous as hell, and I almost felt a little bit sorry for the women across from us. They had bought themselves some trouble, our employers or not.

"There's a reason to be ill, presently," Annie said. Her voice got quiet. "I happen to like birds."

I thought about putting a hand on her arm, and changed my mind.

She was sweet and dark and strange, and most comfortable moving at night. She didn't try to make sense when she talked, and she didn't mind if people thought she was crazy. What you didn't see right away was that she shone full of clean light, from top to toe. She walked around in the middle of a rainbow, and if there was such a thing as angels, maybe she was one. Children and dogs knew it immediately. She had a streak of something so good you couldn't look straight at it. I didn't believe in much, but I believed in her.

"Why exactly are you here?" Mrs. Gaynor asked, oblivious. "My son didn't give a very good explanation."

I chose my words carefully. "Your son has employed me, in a limited way, to find out as much of Beatrice Stone's background as I can. The hope is that it may shed some light on where the missing glass eye is. It may also lead to some information on her killer."

"If you're a detective, why don't you just find it?"

"It's my understanding a Los Angeles agency has tried. They've checked in all the places that make sense. Sometimes the direct route doesn't work. I have local contacts, and might have some luck with another approach. She might have had a friend she trusted to hold it for her."

"Surely, they would have thought of that," she snorted. "Obviously she handed it off to a confederate."

"Miss Stone didn't live an entirely conventional life," I said. "Finding out who her friends were might not be as simple as it would be with some people. That's where I may be able to help."

"In so many words, you're a degenerate, like she was. You know other degenerates who might have associated themselves with her."

"In so many words," I agreed.

The blind woman lifted a hand feebly toward me, and began to make soft mewling sounds. I didn't know if they were meant to be words. Olive Gaynor held up one finger and cocked her head. After a moment, she nodded, satisfied with something, and addressed me.

"She can't see," she said. "She needs her eye. She wants it back, and she says for you to get it for her."

The other woman cooed again, and reached for me. She wanted me to take her hand. I felt repulsed in some way I couldn't explain, and did no such thing. I glanced at Annie. Her face got furious.

"She has a lot of faith in you," Olive said. "I can't account for that, because I certainly don't."

I glanced at Annie. She stared fixedly at the sparrow in its cage, with an expression I didn't much like. I touched her elbow. Without shifting her gaze away from the bird, she slipped her hand absently into mine.

"Thanks for your time," I told Olive Gaynor. She stayed busy with her decanter and paid no attention. I led Annie through the maze of spider plants and into the great hallway. We didn't see Wanda Rice or Herb Robinson or anyone else on our way out to the car, but the gate at the end of the drive slid open as we approached, as if the house couldn't wait to be rid of us.

-Fifteen-

Five o'clock came and went, but I stayed at the office. I didn't do any work. I just didn't feel like I had any place I wanted to be. I got the bottle of bourbon from the top drawer of my desk and treated myself to a snort.

I pulled the telephone over and caught Rex Raines still at the station.

"A kid named Allen Nickerson, drowned at the Rocas Perdidas reservoir a couple weeks ago," I said, by way of hello. "Know anything about it?"

"Should I?"

"I'm not sure," I said. "I think it got tagged as accidental. Client of mine says it might be murder. Can you take a look at it?"

"Of course," he said. "There's nothing at all going on here, but fighting crime and guarding public safety. I just sit here dozing, hoping you'll call me with another one of your wild goose chases."

"Can you pull the file?"

"Give me a day or two." He sighed, loud enough to be sure I'd hear it over the telephone line. "Speaking of wild goose chases, have you given up on the woman in your bath tub?"

"I have it on pretty good authority that Harold Gaynor didn't just hire me. He hired Parklane first. L.A. agency—you familiar?" He confirmed it, so I went on. "A couple of their boys are in town. They got rough with Beatrice Stone, and someone told me they raped her. Rape makes it a lot more likely they would have murdered her later. Her death wasn't a misadventure."

"Well, if someone told you that, let me get my hat. If you have the bad guy's address, I'll write it down, and run right out and arrest them."

"I'm not in the mood for wisecracks."

"That makes for a nice change," he said. "Do you have any idea how enthusiastic the D.A. would be about filing a rape charge, with a dead streetwalker as the complaining party? Do you think we sit around here bored stiff, hoping you'll call us with something entertaining?"

I put the phone back in the cradle, without saying goodbye.

The lights were off. I sat with my feet on the desk, a glass of bourbon balanced on my chest, and watched daylight leave the sky. I wasn't doing much about drinking it. My gun waited patiently on the blotter beside my shoes, in case of company. I leaned back in the chair and looked out my office window. I felt pretty sure it would rain. There had been clouds over the Channel all afternoon.

Meeting the Gaynor women had disturbed me more than I wanted to think about. I didn't like Harold, and I liked his mother and aunt a whole lot less. I didn't get paid to like the people I worked for, and I seldom gave it any thought. I couldn't shake the idea that I had signed up on the wrong side. I felt like I worked for Beatrice Stone, which made no sense. She didn't care.

I heard the outer office door open, and I picked up the Browning and held it out of sight. Footsteps crossed the waiting room, and Annie followed them in. She sat down across from me, and I put the gun back on the desk.

"Of course, she cares," she said. "That's why she visited you in your living room."

I had passed the point of being surprised by her occasional inclination to read my thoughts. I didn't know if she was a psychic, or just an intuitive who knew me better than I knew myself.

Outside, lightning flashed once, almost invisible in the neon outside the window. The rain poured down. The storm had gotten lost out at sea and finally come ashore to crash against Santa Teresa's mountains. I leaned forward and snapped on the lamp. Annie gazed at me from across the desk. I pointed at the bottle.

"Drink?" I offered. She shook her head and I turned the light back out.

"What are we going to do about all this?" she asked.

"I don't know. We have to wait. Bad things don't make you wait long, as a rule."

"When we find the eye, you can't give it back," she said. "It doesn't belong to them."

"Who does it belong to?"

She ignored the question. "I like storms," she said. "The rain makes me safe—invisible. I feel like I can fly when it's windy."

I leaned back again. Outside the glass, the city got washed shiny black, and the wet streets reflected neon blues and pinks. Across the street, the Schooner Inn bar was lit up, but I figured it was mostly empty. Desert people didn't know what to do in weather like this, and they stayed hidden.

"You think I'm crazy, don't you?" Her voice was soft. "Everyone does."

I sipped a little bourbon and thought about it. "People wear masks," I said. "Me, too. We put on a different mask, depending on the time of day and the situation and who we're talking to. We slip them on and off, easy as pie. Everyone is hiding, and they don't even know they are. It makes me—lonely."

I could see the shine of her eyes in the dark.

"The masks remind me that everyone is going to die alone," I said. "Especially me. You don't have a mask, though. You don't own one, or even know how they work. I see you, and you have no idea what that does to me."

The rain wasn't letting up at all. The streets might flood tonight. Tomorrow the air would be impossibly clean and blue, and the desert would come alive for a little while. The ocean would sparkle; the orange and avocado groves would glisten, and it would all smell like perfume. Tonight, though, everything seemed as wet and dark as the end of the world.

"I see you," she said. "I see you, too."

My eyes felt funny, like the start of tears. It was probably just the booze. I took a breath and blew them away.

"I know you do," I said. "And if you see me—how could you be crazy? How could I think you're crazy?"

"Don't die first," she said. "Promise me."

"I can't promise that," I said. "Nobody could. One of us has to go first, and leave the other behind, at least for a little while."

"I don't want to be left behind, alone."

I thought about that. I had nothing to lose by dying, but I didn't want to stick around living if she wasn't around, either. I wondered if I could love her enough to make a promise like that, and keep it. I decided to keep my mouth shut and say nothing at all.

"All right," I said instead. "I promise."

We sat for a little while in my dark office. When I had finished my drink, I set the empty glass on the nearest desk corner, and the neither of us moved until the rain stopped. Then Annie got up, and let herself out.

~*~

I looked for Joey O'Meaney the next couple of nights at the Hi-lo Club, but he didn't show. The regulars didn't know where he had gotten to, or if they did, they weren't telling me. Finally, one of the women who patrolled the alley behind the place told me that the thin man had run into a little good luck. One of his jobs had paid off, and when he was flush he liked to drink at the old Starlite Lounge in Montelindo.

It wasn't a joint I cared for much, a sort of phoney place I liked to avoid. Also, I had caused some trouble there, and while I had caused trouble in a lot of places, this had some sentimental bad memories for me. More importantly, Fin was probably the invisible owner, a silent partner, and I mixed with Fin's business more than I wanted to these days. In the end, I didn't want to wait for O'Meaney to get broke again and come back to the Hi-lo, so on a nice twilit evening I got my hack off the curb and headed to Montelindo.

Only a fifteen-mile drive down the coast highway separated downtown from the nightclub, but it had been a while since I had blown the charcoal off the engine valves, so I put my right foot down hard. I drove a 1940 Ford, as black and plain as a lunch bucket. It had seen a lot of miles, and looked it. I knew a mechanic from Mexico City, introduced to me by Danny López, who took exceptional care of it. He knew a lot of tricks, and the sedan wasn't what it seemed.

A year ago, some rich fool had piled a brand-new Lincoln Zephyr into a stand of trees on Las Palmas. He survived, but the car didn't. The wreck had found its way to my mechanic, and the twelve-cylinder motor had found a new home under my hood. With modified shocks and springs and a heavy-duty steering box, the old Ford flew like a bird. Sometimes, I needed it to. Tonight, I enjoyed the feel of it, the way I always did at speed. Too soon, I came to the turnoff that led to my destination. It took me past the golden spun-sugar pile of the Montelindo Hotel and then the entrance to the nightclub.

They had changed the name, and it wasn't the Star-lite Lounge any more. Now they called it the 'South Seas Room'. The outside floodlights were green instead of blue, but everything that went on inside stayed the same. The drinks were still strong, there were the same pretty girls and even prettier boys at the bar, and it all came with premium prices. It promised some fun and a little danger, but if you wanted to buy some truly unusual company, a little reefer, or a cold gun, you were better off sticking with the Hi-lo Club.

The gravel parking area stood neatly raked and just about empty. I left my car beside an egg-crème LaSalle saloon so it didn't get lonely, and crossed the lot to the big front door. An oily type with too many muscles sat on a stool under the portico. He wore a white shirt and tie, and didn't appear as though he enjoyed it. I saw the bulge of what must have been naval artillery under his suit coat, buttoned up tight, so he couldn't get to the gun fast if he needed to.

"Not very busy tonight," I remarked, pleasantly.

He gave me a look, moving his eyes without turning his head. His mouth clenched into something that made me wonder if he was smiling. I decided he wasn't.

"Not even dark yet," he answered. "You thinking about buying the place?"

"Is Fin selling it?" If the name meant anything to him, he didn't react, but I had more of his attention. I slipped a five-dollar bill from my wallet, and folded it once lengthwise, so he could see it. "I'm looking for a guy named Joey O'Meaney. Know who he is?"

"The thin man?" he asked, and pawed the money from my fingers. He was clumsy, and I felt a little sorry for him. Even if he unbuttoned his coat, a child wearing mittens could shoot him a dozen times before he got his pistol free. "Everybody knows him."

"I don't. Care to point him out for me?"

Inside, we paused to let our eyes adjust. The old Star-lite had done its best to be elegant, but this tried for something else. Now it had a lot of fake grass thatching and bamboo plastered on it, and lights tinted pink and green. A tired-looking trio went through the motions on the small stage. My new friend pointed at the farthest corner.

"There's your man," he said. "Sitting by himself."

Joey O'Meaney sat at a tiny table mostly covered by a big plate of pale spaghetti. He stayed busy shovelling it in, and barely glanced up when I pulled a flimsy cane chair up and sat down.

"Mind if I join you?"

"Suit yourself," he said, without bothering to swallow first. "You like clam sauce?"

I hoped he wasn't offering me any of his. A waitress in a pair of short pants that didn't go with the bar's Pacific theme hovered over me. I ordered a bourbon and water to make her go away.

"Bourbon and branch," she nodded.

I figured the branch came straight from the faucet, but saw no point in making a scene about it, so I nodded back. I turned my attention to the thin man. He lived up to his billing. He wore an expensive suit that looked like he didn't bother hanging it up when he got home. Even sitting down, I could tell he went over six feet tall, and I figured him for about a hundred and thirty pounds once he had tossed his clothes on the floor. Lank hair that needed a wash kept falling in his eyes as he ate, and he absently brushed it back every few seconds, like he was used to it.

"Came to talk to you about a kid named Allen Nickerson," I said.

"I don't know him," he said. "I already told you people that."

"I'm not a cop."

He sat back and picked a butt from the smoldering ashtray beside his plate. After he got it going, he squinted at me through the smoke.

"What's your name?"

"Crowe. I'm a private license."

"I heard about you," he said. "You got mixed up in monkey business earlier in the year, when the cop got killed. Heard you're either dirty, or stupid. What do you want?"

"I heard about you, too," I said. "I heard you have a hobby. You like to take stray cats to the reservoir at Rocas Perdidas and drop them into the water. Have a little picnic while you watch them drown. Tell me—does it take a while for a cat to drown?"

He took a long draw on his butt and smiled at me. His teeth needed work. "Sometimes. Some of them swim better than others."

I felt a familiar rage start in my guts, a deep burn that always felt like the color red. I could abide a lot of things, but cruelty to animals started up an engine inside of me that I didn't like. I touched the Browning in my pocket. I didn't realize I did it until I saw O'Meaney's eyes widen.

"I'm doing a public good," he said. "They gas them anyway. What's the difference?"

"I hear that a kid named Allen Nickerson tried to save a drowning cat," I said. "He must have been a good kid. Brave, but maybe not a good swimmer. You showed him a gun and wouldn't let him near the ladder. Watched him get worn out and go under."

"Prove it," he said. "The cops heard that gossip, too. Do I look like I'm in jail?"

His confidence came back. He put the cigarette in the ashtray and got busy with his plate again, mopping up clam sauce with a piece of bread.

"I'm not a cop, so I don't have to prove anything, except to my own satisfaction. I'm fairly satisfied."

The waitress dropped off the drink I had ordered. I gave her a dollar and left the bourbon where it was. The thin man watched her rear end move in the tight shorts as she walked away, with the same attention he had given to his spaghetti and clams. I didn't care for the look, and found myself wondering if he had an appetite for more than just cats.

"You're a loser, Crowe," he said. "I'm connected in this town, in case you hadn't stumbled on that. You got mixed up with some crazy broad, got a cop killed. You're finished here. You aren't worth this conversation. Tell you what—get up and leave, never bother me again, and I'll pretend we never had it."

"I got what I came for." I stood up. "Someone told me a story. I just wanted to see what my instincts told me about you."

I started to leave my drink untouched, but changed my mind. I needed it, to wash away the taste of him. I downed it in a go, and set the glass down.

"Got a problem with booze?" He smiled up at me. "Can't recall if I heard anything about that, but it fits."

I settled my hat and headed for the door, back through the green light and Polynesian music. The tired horn player caught my eye as I passed the stage. His expression didn't change. When I had a hand on the front door I heard my name called, loud enough to get above the music. Chessie Emerson, Fin's associate, walked toward me, just as cool and tall as I remembered her. It took me a minute to place her, because she had let her hair down from its tight bun, lost the glasses and tweed suit. She wore something shimmery, and when she got close, just enough good perfume.

"Fancy meeting you here," I said. "Coincidence?"

"I'm general manager of the South Seas Room," she said. "I'm often here. Can we talk a moment?"

I held the door for her, and we stood on the front steps, away from the smoke and music. I couldn't see the ocean in the dark, but I could smell it.

"Fin offered me the position here, last summer," I said. "I wouldn't work for him."

"No, you wouldn't. He told me. He tried to help you after your trouble. Give you a place to land."

I shrugged. "I always land, one way or another."

"How is the business with the Gaynor's missing item proceeding? Are you approaching a conclusion?"

"I'm not sure I've even found a beginning," I said. "I don't even know what I'm looking for, or if I'm supposed to be looking for it at all. Gaynor says he has his own men hunting for the glass, and he only wants me to scare up background on Beatrice Stone, to give them an idea where to check. By the time I find out one, I will have found the other. As for the missing piece—it's either a worthless bauble or a valuable piece of ancient Egyptian glass. That's a short list of all the things I don't know."

She turned toward me. Her eyes glinted green in the spotlights.

"I think it's safe to say the item is very valuable." Her voice got cool. "Common sense should tell you that. Nobody would go to this kind of trouble over a curio."

"Gaynor says his aunt believes it really is an eye, and her blindness is relieved when she holds it. That's what makes it important."

"The ravings of an old woman." She waved the idea away like smoke. "Do you imagine there would be all this fuss and expense over a blind crone's toy? The glass eye is valuable in its own right—perhaps priceless."

"And is it Egyptian?" I asked. "Is Fin selling artifacts to the Gaynors? Plundered stuff, like from pyramids? Isn't that illegal?"

"The Gaynors have collected Egyptian glass for years. Fin is in various businesses, and he may have acquired items on the family's behalf from time to time." Her smile came, indulging me. "I wouldn't know, or care, about legal or illegal."

"Why would Gaynor negotiate the return?" I asked. "If the glass eye she held was priceless, and she wanted a few thousand, why risk all the fuss? Even if she got killed later, as punishment, why would anyone risk killing her before it had been safely returned?"

"That's why they hired you—to find those answers. Isn't it?"

"I still don't understand Fin's interest in this. Where does he fit in?"

"Fin seldom explains himself," she said. "Even to me—so I can't answer that. I have another reason for speaking with you tonight."

She watched the blackness beyond the parking lot. If anything moved on the beach, I couldn't see it.

"You came tonight to see the thin man," she said. "We expected you would."

Her eyes crawled over my face. It made a strange sensation, and I had the same feeling I sometimes got when I was around Fin, of something that had never been quite human or at least forgotten what being human was like. It didn't threaten, although I sensed a capacity for evil. It held amusement, and incurious curiosity.

"The thin man is useful locally," she said. "He willingly does things most will not, and that has earned him a certain place—gained him an occasional immunity. Fin wishes you to know that he does not extend any blessing or protection to this man. Handle your business with him as you see fit."

"Fin doesn't like him?" I guessed.

"Fin likes or dislikes very few people," she shrugged. "He likes you."

She turned to go back inside, and paused with one hand on the door to glance back over her shoulder.

"He also likes me," she said. "And I'm very fond of cats. Cats are probably my favorite thing. I don't like people who hurt them."

She winked at me, and disappeared inside.

-Sixteen-

"Always a good girl," Mrs. Stone told me. "I never had a bit of trouble with her. Did you like her?"

"I only met her once," I reminded her, truthfully. "I liked her fine."

We sat in the main dining room of the Montelindo Hotel. Fin had kept his word, and put Bea's mother up in style. I wondered if this had become an adventure for her, perhaps the best vacation she ever had, and if the grief over her daughter's death would crash all the harder when she got back to her own house in St. Louis. I wondered if the years Bea had been gone had prepared her for the emptiness on the way. I had never had a child, but I knew about loss, and the way it poisoned things.

The booths were red, the walls pale green, with a lot of oak trim showing here and there. Silverware clinked gently against crockery, and light caught the edges of crystal and cut glass. I smelled the pleasant odors of polite food. The joint catered to people who came from somewhere else and wanted to be reminded of it. It wasn't the kind of place I came from, so it wasn't the kind of place I often went to.

We had tea, poured into delicate white china cups. I tried mine, and didn't like it. I dropped in a couple of sugar cubes, careful not to break the cup. I tasted it again, to see if it helped. It didn't. It still tasted like soap, only now it was sweet. Sweet things often fooled me, but even sweet could only go so far. I put the cup gently back onto its saucer and left it alone.

Annie and I sat across from Fin and Bea's mother, the four

of us at a table set for six. I looked at them; Annie looked at nothing at all. Her face remained composed, nearly serene, and her eyes were luminous. She filled the room, the way she always did.

I fingered the heavy edge of linen that hung beneath the table and took a breath.

"What else can you tell me about her?"

Mrs. Stone seemed surprised by the question. "She was just a normal girl," she said. "Normal in every way. Why are you asking me this?"

Fin set his teacup into its saucer, carefully, and moved a spoon until it lined up more to his liking. He looked splendid, in pale seersucker. I watched the light catch at a ruby on his little finger. When things were dainty enough to suit him, he gazed at her steadily.

"Mister Crowe and the wonderful Miss Kahlo have been engaged to investigate the circumstances around your daughter's death, my dear."

"She had an accident." Surprise turned to confusion. "She drowned."

"Of course, she did," Fin reassured her. "We all just want to be sure there was nothing untoward. She was discovered in a stranger's hotel room, after all."

"Beatrice would have been a famous actress," Mrs. Stone told me earnestly. "She was well on her way. She would never have risked her career by being in a strange hotel room, unless she had a perfectly good reason. You know how Hollywood gossips. Anyway, we are Catholics, and you can be sure she wouldn't risk a state of sin. The nuns taught her better than that."

Fin coughed delicately. "As a matter of fact, it was Mister

Crowe's hotel room, and his bathtub."

The woman's eyes went perfectly round, and she placed a gloved hand on my wrist. "If it was your room, then you must know what she was doing there."

"As a matter of fact, I don't," I said. "I *can* tell you nothing unseemly went on. I wouldn't risk being in a state of sin either."

Annie kicked me under the table, hard. I struggled to keep my face straight.

"It may be a little bit late in your life to worry about sin, Mister Crowe," Fin commented. "Quite late, perhaps."

"I'm not interested in sin," Annie interrupted, focusing her attention on the older woman. "Sin is an invention. Evil isn't. Your daughter came across something and someone evil. When we understand what the something is, we'll find the someone."

"What are you getting at?" the woman stammered. "My daughter had an accident. You are speaking as though someone— harmed her."

"That isn't what Miss Kahlo means," Fin said. "Not at all."

"It's exactly what I mean," Annie snapped, glaring at him. "Why are we pretending something else?"

Fin shifted his attention to her. He had a face that would be right at home with grieving statues and candles flickering in catacombs, but I saw something more in his eyes. He looked as though he had seen things no one else would be able to talk about, and found them quietly amusing. He gazed at Annie for a long moment, and then nodded almost imperceptibly. He sat back in his chair and watched her.

"Your daughter got murdered," Annie said. "Someone killed her. It was not an accident."

"She couldn't have been murdered," Mrs. Stone cried. She turned in her seat, rummaged in a large purse, and came up with a photograph that she passed across the table. Annie looked at it for a few moments, and then passed it to me. A very young Beatrice Stone, ten or twelve years old, smiled at me from a portrait that appeared to have been removed from a frame.

"My Bea was a good girl," her mother insisted. "Does she look like a person that would get herself murdered?"

"Nobody thinks it could happen to them," Annie said. "She crossed paths with someone quite evil. This developed over a period of time. Did she write you letters?"

"How could my daughter cross paths with evil? I just told you, she was a Catholic."

"Evil stands behind the door when you walk into an empty house," Annie said. "It giggles secret laughs that make no sense, and peeks sideways at you so you feel all alone in a room full of people. Wicked wakes you up in a bed you didn't fall asleep in. It's the figure you can't quite make out under a streetlight, and it's a fast-rushing thing you can't stop."

I loved her voice. It sounded like quiet music, mesmerizing, straight off the silver screen. I could listen to her all day and not get tired. If she read me hours of recipes from a cook-book, I would ask for more.

"When you're walking at night, wicked rides past on a bicycle, with a rope over its shoulder," she said. "It tells you it's searching for a lost dog, but you know it's a lie."

"I think you are the strangest woman I've ever met," Mrs. Stone said. "I'm sorry to say I don't like you much, at all."

Fin pushed his tea away and ordered whiskey from a

passing waiter. He looked at me, and I shrugged and asked for the same. Annie shook her head, a movement so slight as to be almost invisible. Mrs. Stone ignored the offer. We waited in silence until the drinks came. Fin made half of his disappear, and set it down with a hand that shook a little. Red blotches bloomed on his cheeks. The glass made a small wet patch on the tablecloth.

"Miss Kahlo is trying to find out if you talked with your daughter very much," I said. "Did she write to you? Telephone you?"

"She lived on the West Coast. Do you have any idea how much it would cost to telephone St. Louis? Anyway, I don't have one. I go next door to the neighbors if I need to make a telephone call, which I never do. Mister Fin called me there, to give me the terrible news about Beatrice."

She stopped, perplexed by a sudden thought, and turned to him.

"How did you find the number, anyway? How could you have known who to call?" He spread his hands modestly, and didn't answer. I hoped he would never share his methods with this poor woman; the world puzzled her enough. I tried a little of my whiskey. It was excellent, and I figured it might avert the headache the woman kept trying to give me.

"Did you exchange letters?" I prompted. "Did your daughter at least let you know how she was?"

"Of course, we did. She had put her acting career on hold, just for a little while. Her job went wonderfully, and she had met someone she felt sweet on. She said she had finally met the right person. I told her she ought to forget about acting and just get married, if he was the right fellow."

Annie and I exchanged a glance. "Did she mention this person by name?" I asked.

"No, she didn't. Beatrice could be very secretive, even as a small girl. I'm sure she found a fine young man." She suddenly arranged herself, and retrieved her purse. "I'm not feeling well. I'm going up to my room to lie down. Will I see you at dinner, Mister Fin?"

He nodded, and she left in a swirl of rusting floral fabric.

"A fine young man," I commented. "If she thinks so, then I doubt she knows anything else about her daughter."

"Do explain," Fin said. He leaned forward, interested. I struggled with how much to say, and what part of this constituted his business. Fin had paid for Bea's funeral, and took considerate care of her mother. On the other hand, I didn't feel clear on his connection to my employers, or the glass eye. In the end, I shrugged inwardly. Fin had a way of making everything his business.

"Beatrice Stone might have met the right person, but it wasn't a man," I said. "She had relations with the Gaynor housekeeper, a woman named Wanda Rice."

"Relations," Annie murmured, as though it was a word she hadn't heard before.

"How remarkable," Fin said. "The wind blows and the wind swings, doesn't it, Mister Crowe? Tell me, do you see that as evil? So many people do."

"I don't think anything about it one way or the other," I said. "I think you and I have both seen enough real evil to know it doesn't qualify, don't you?"

"I'm interested in evil," Fin said, ignoring my question. "It doesn't do what people imagine it does. It doesn't hide in the shadows. It doesn't stand behind doors in dark houses. It doesn't jump. Wicked feels gently around the edges of things—it pats and caresses with soft fingers."

He drank a little more of his whiskey, and patted his lips with a linen napkin.

"It sits in the sun like a fat toad, in plain sight," he said. "It's happy to see you. It wears a mask that smiles and asks after your mother. When you say she's not well, the mask cries. It can't be hurt, because it believes in absolutely nothing. Miss Stone and her friend weren't evil, but they attracted something evil to them, and now you stand in their stead, provoking that same evil on their behalf. You have no chance against it. I like you, but you're an incurable fool."

I took a breath. He held up a hand to stop me.

"The wind blows and the wind swings, Mister Crowe," he said. "Through sanatoriums and empty bedrooms and bare trees, it blows and swings, blows and swings. You've never understood it, and that will be what ends you."

"Maybe I'm a naturally lucky person," I offered. "I've survived so far."

Annie watched us, her eyes moving back and forth between our faces.

"You're a child," Fin said. "Underneath your sneer, the gun and your bottle, you believe in angels. Beneath your exhaustion, you believe and you hope—and that hope makes you helpless. You can't shake your own belief in what isn't real."

Annie spoke up.

"I believe in what isn't real," she said. "Am I a fool?"

Fin shifted his attention to her. He sat back in his chair.

"You are different, Miss Kahlo," he said. "You are made of a fundamental magic. The world only reluctantly mixes its business with yours."

"I believe in numbers and colors," she said. "I believe what the cards tell me. I believe in stars and sand. I believe in letters. Most of the time, I believe in the dark. I believe in what waits for me."

"Quite so…" he murmured.

"That might mean I'm crazy, but never a fool," she said. Her voice dropped. There were spots of color on her cheeks now, rose under honey. "I'm not a fool, and I'm not afraid of your wind. It can blow and swing all it likes."

"I believe in you," I said.

She paused, and glanced over at me. She gave a tiny shrug. The corners of her mouth twitched, and then she tilted her head and surrendered. Her smile was breathtaking.

"Yes," she said. "You do, don't you?"

"How do you progress on the case, in other respects?" Fin asked. "Do you draw closer to the missing eye? Do you have any clues as to where Miss Stone might have hidden it?"

"More questions than answers," I admitted. "She doesn't seem to have had any friends, or reliable contacts—nobody logical that she would have trusted it with."

"A logical result of her lifestyle," he agreed. "People in her position rarely form close ties with anyone. What about her— friend, the housekeeper?"

"Wanda Rice told me Bea asked her to hold it, and she

refused. She feels a great deal of guilt over it."

Fin drained his drink, set the glass down carefully, and leaned back in his chair. He gazed at Annie.

"Something doesn't fit," he said. "Something fundamental, and primary. Do you see it, Miss Kahlo? Do you see the puzzle piece that doesn't fit?"

Annie watched something on the ceiling, and didn't answer. Her mouth twitched.

"Of course, you do," he answered his own question. "Miss Wanda Rice doesn't fit, in so many respects."

He gazed at me meaningfully, and I figured he had known about Bea's affair with the housekeeper all along. Fin knew everything about everything, as a rule, even if he didn't say so.

"If the two women were romantically tangled, why did Miss Rice allow her lover to descend into a life of sleazy hotels and the marketing of herself to strange men? Why did she remain employed by the Gaynors, who were causing so much misery to her—beloved?"

"Good question. What do you think?"

"I don't think that's how one treats a beloved person," he remarked. "Not that I would know the first thing about it. How could she allow Miss Stone to sink deeper into the bottle and the streets, without trying to save her? You must wonder about that, Mister Crowe. You like to save people, after all."

"You have a point, I'm sure." I got impatient. Fin liked to put flowers on every grave he came across, and it could get tiresome.

"Only the point that it brings me to another question," he said. "Beatrice Stone got fired for her drinking, and for her dalliance with the maid. She stole a treasure on her way out the door, and played a game of ransom, ultimately not returning it. Why did the maid keep her position? Why did Miss Rice stay in that house, stay in that job? Why didn't she get fired, too?"

"Maybe she did a good job," I offered. "And maybe she stayed because she had no other job to go to. She and Olive Gaynor reached a truce. What's your interest in this, Fin? I thought you brokered my hiring because you owed the Gaynors a favor."

"Certainly," he agreed. "And I don't like to owe favors. I also have an interest in the glass eye. It's Egyptian, priceless, and I don't like to think it might be rolling around at the bottom of a storm sewer. I sold it to the senior Gaynor, long ago, not realizing its value. I would have kept it for myself if I had."

Fin slipped a filigreed silver case from his breast pocket. Small and flat, the etched design on the metal had worn nearly to invisibility. He released a tiny catch, extracted a small white pill and slipped it under his tongue. He glanced at Annie. She shook her head, as if he'd offered her one.

"I think there's more to Miss Rice than you have acknowledged," he said. "The French have a saying…"

"*Cherchez la femme,*" Annie murmured.

"*Cherchez la femme!*" Fin was delighted, and beamed at her like a prize pupil. "*Cherchez la femme,* Mister Crowe."

~*~

The next morning, I had nothing lined up before lunchtime. Restless, I decided to take a drive to the Rocas Perdidas reservoir. I didn't think viewing the scene of cat killings would help much, but seeing some greenery might do me some good. Doing anything was better than doing nothing, even if the results were about the same.

The reservoir lay at the end of a hard two-mile drive up one of the canyons behind Santa Teresa. I got off the coast highway at Carpenter Beach, took the beach frontage road and then a fire road up into the hills. It got better maintained than most of them, but still not much more than a gravel track. It clung to the arroyos, and a slide in a couple of places meant a three hundred-foot drop. For a kid that wanted to go swimming, it meant a hell of a bicycle ride.

I left the car in a turnaround and walked the path downhill to the dam. It was one of the clear California mornings that felt like how they advertised Paradise. The air felt soft in my lungs, and the reservoir allowed green vegetation that had no business growing in the desert.

Iron handrails, painted green, stretched across the concrete top of the dam, so you could walk across to the other side if you had business there. I didn't. A long drop fell to the greenish water on one side, and a much longer plummet to a rocky arroyo on the other. Rising from the water's surface, a rusty set of handholds made a ladder back to the top. Kids jumped from the dam and climbed back up, just to do it again.

A dog nosed its way out of the brush, a female, brown-and-white Boxer. She wore a leather collar and looked cared-for. I figured her owner must be hiking in the area, but I didn't see anyone. She seemed like a peaceable dog, and when she wandered over I gave her a scratch behind the ears. She stood beside me and looked down at the water.

Once you were in, the ladder presented the only way out. A

fly couldn't climb the canyon walls that bordered this end of the reservoir. I could see how it would go for the cats that the thin man tossed in. They would swim until they couldn't anymore. It would work the same for a young boy at gunpoint.

The currents would be fierce when they opened the sluices, but right now the water was still and green. I could imagine strange things moving beneath the surface. I resisted the urge to kick my shoes off and jump into the coolness, and join them. I sat down on the warm cement, instead. The dog sat down beside me.

I found it easy to imagine Allen Nickerson here, enjoying a hot day. It wasn't so easy to imagine him struggling at the ladder on the far wall, held away from it by the threat of a gun. It seemed a shame, someone so young, but I supposed it was a shame for old people, too.

"Do dogs worry about things like this?" I asked the Boxer.

She didn't have anything to say about it, but I had a feeling she understood, and thought I was a nice kind of fool. "We all leave someday, I guess," I told her. "Every one of us. Not a thing to do about it—no point in fussing too much."

A woman in a red sweater stepped from the trees and whistled. The dog bounded away, to her. We gave each other a friendly wave, and woman and dog walked out of sight. I watched the water for a little while longer. With the dog gone, it got lonely. After a little while, I brushed myself off and went back to the Ford.

-Seventeen-

Highland kept his office on upper De La Vina Street, not far from the hospital. I knew he had done pretty well for himself selling life insurance policies, but I didn't know if that was why he kept an office so close to the morgue. I didn't get paid to chase such things, so I decided to stop wondering about it.

I had my Ford parked across the street, with me parked behind the wheel. I watched the insurance office because I didn't want to wait for Highland and his secretary to keep their next weekend appointment at the Sand Castle Motel. If I stayed honest with myself, I really didn't want to see the place again. Beatrice Stone, or whoever had been sitting in my living room chair, had rattled me. I didn't need to stir up the memories.

The building had been plastered tan to seem like adobe, and the front door presented one in a series set beneath an arched colonnade. It was all very cool, chic, and modern looking. Venetian blinds kept casual passers-by from seeing whatever insurance business might be going on inside. Regardless, if anyone stirred from it, I had them dead to rights.

Lunchtime came, and nobody had gone in or out of the place in a couple of hours. I just about considered giving up and going to find something to eat, when the door opened and Highland came out. I recognized him from a photograph his wife had showed me. A woman came out behind him, and stood to one side as he fumbled a set of keys and got the door locked.

His photograph hadn't done him justice. He was a dandy. If I had expected a pasty-faced, balding pencil-pusher, he wasn't it. He wore a pale seersucker suit with a pink tie. Before he settled a straw hat with a pink band on his head, I noticed he wore his blond hair a little bit longer than conventional. He carried himself like a guy who had the world in his back pocket. I knew better.

I had no reason to know that the woman beside him was his secretary, but I had no doubt about it. Even from across the street, she telegraphed her adoration. She kept her body turned toward him. He talked to her as he worked the door lock, and her focus stayed absolute. A couple of inches taller than him, she leaned down to catch every word.

She wore a dark blue sailor dress that hung on her awkwardly. A figure like hers would make everything too big. She wore her hair in an updo, which made her appear even taller. A pair of glasses with oversized frames didn't do her chin any favors. A lot younger than Highland, she looked like she just emerged into the world from some small women's college. I didn't figure her for Highland's type, but I had given up on guessing at things like that a long time ago.

The two of them grabbed hands and moved off. At the end of the colonnade, they turned the corner, out of sight. I started up the Ford while I waited. After a minute or so, a beige Cadillac nosed out from the driveway and passed me. It was a good-looking automobile, with whitewall tires and a red interior. The roof had been lowered, and behind the wheel, Highland sported a pair of black sunglasses. He looked like a minor movie star.

I followed them up Pueblo Street, relieved when they pulled to the curb in front of a delicatessen. I knew the place had good pastrami, and I felt famished. Since they didn't know me, they had no reason to hide. I followed them inside. The dim interior smelled of spices and olive oil. I stood behind them at the sandwich counter.

Up close, they were an even more unlikely couple. If he had been a little bit taller, he might have made it into the picture business. His tan was even, his teeth were even, and his blond hair was carefully barbered. His seersucker stayed as crisp as if he had put it on ten minutes ago. Beside him, she seemed drab and lanky and rumpled. She had the kind of hair that would do exactly as it pleased, no matter what a beauty parlor did. Her spectacles were too big, and her chin faded to nothing. She would never dance without stepping on her partner's feet.

She rummaged in her purse. As if to prove her clumsiness, she pulled her hand out and scattered a few coins onto the wood floor. As I bent to pick them up for her, she bent too, and bumped her head smartly into mine. I looked up into her face. She rubbed the top of her head. Her eyes were turquoise, beautiful, and welling tears.

"Oh, I'm so sorry," she blurted. "I'm hopeless."

"You're not hopeless at all. I might have warned you before I dove for your money."

"How completely kind you are," she murmured, and accepted her coins. Her voice was as soft and gorgeous as her eyes, seasoned with the Midwest.

"Chicago?" I wondered.

"I'm from Chicago!" She put a hand on my arm. "Is it that obvious? Are you from Chicago, too?"

"St. Louis, originally," I said. "A lifetime ago."

"Do you miss it? Do you get homesick?"

"I don't think so," I said. "I've been here a long time."

She turned away from me, to Highland in front of her at the counter. She caught at his sleeve. "Darling, this wonderful man is from St. Louis." He glanced over his shoulder at me, friendly but not really interested. We nodded at each other. He returned to ordering food, and the woman turned her attention back to me.

"The sandwiches here are wonderful, aren't they? And the park on Marina is so close by—it's the recipe for a perfect picnic."

She was as sweet and wholesome as springtime.

"Exactly!" I exclaimed, feigning surprise. "That's where I go, every time the weather is perfect."

"This is southern California," she laughed. "You must do it every day, since the weather is nearly always perfect."

I followed Highland's Cadillac along the long sweep of Marina Drive and parked behind it when it stopped. I took my sandwich to a picnic table a little way away from theirs. The woman waved brightly as I passed.

It made for a nice picnic, with the green grass and the ocean in the distance. They seemed to be sharing tastes of each other's food, and they were getting more from each other than the food. It all made a perfect lunch, and when they kissed I had my camera ready. I had experience, and had gotten good at using it from behind a newspaper. When the photographs I took were developed, the two lovebirds would be ruined.

I also had a lot of experience with disliking myself, and by the time I tossed my sandwich in a waste bin, put the car in gear and drove away, I had reached a new level of it.

~*~

Annie sat in a pool of yellow light and moved her hands

through the pile of books in front of her. Some of them appeared very old. This late, we had the whole upstairs part of the library to ourselves. Pillars rose up to where night showed in the small windows high over our heads. Aisles of shelves radiated out from the group of tables and disappeared into dimness. From it came a constant tiny shifting, and a sense of rustling movement in the shadows. I peered into the rows, trying to make sense of it.

"It's the books," Annie whispered, as if she could read my mind. "When it's perfectly still, you can hear them. They move by themselves."

She went back to turning pages, and I went a little way away to give her some space. The murmurs from the stacks rose and fell. If the books were making the sounds, it unsettled me. I touched the gun in my coat pocket without realizing that I did it.

I heard footsteps on the marble stairs, and after a minute a librarian appeared in the arched entrance. She crossed to where I stood, a young woman who worked hard at being old. A pair of tortoiseshell spectacles hung on a chain rested on her bosom; the tiny glass beads glinted in the low light. Her hair had been pulled back tight into a painful-looking bun.

"We're closing in fifteen minutes," she said. "You need to start getting ready to leave."

Her breath smelled a little bit sour. I tried for a snappy comeback, but nothing came to mind, so I settled for a nod. She stared at me, vaguely disapproving.

"Fifteen minutes," she hissed again, in case I hadn't been paying attention.

I trailed behind her as she crossed to where Annie sat. After she had bent and whispered, the woman glanced over her shoulder at me once and left. Her sensible heels clicked on the stone floor. I could hear them going down the stairs after she went out of sight. Annie tapped the book open in front of her with her index finger.

"Here's the missing eye," she said. "It belongs to the figure of Anput, who guards the door of a queen named Nitocris. Her pyramid is at Saqqara. They discovered it about twenty years ago, and found looters had been there first."

I peeked over Annie's shoulder, at a lithographic image of a large animal. One of its eye sockets was an empty black hole.

"Egyptian?" I asked. "What is that, a jackal?"

"She isn't a quite a jackal," Annie said. "She's more of a dog. Even that isn't quite right, but that's what we see when we look at her. Our minds can't translate her, really. Isn't she beautiful?"

I looked closer. The figure stood on its hind legs. It had a long black snout and large pointed ears. Its remaining eye appeared enormous. It was a dog-jackal, if Annie said it was, but the body looked feminine, long-legged and sensual. It stood beside an opening, a doorway set into a stone wall.

"Why is the eye missing?"

"Tomb robbers grabbed what they could," she said. "The Sixth Dynasty pyramids are mostly rubble, and it would have been dangerous even moving around in one. There's no way they could have dragged the statue out, so they settled for prying out an eye. Anput does more than guard tombs. She weighs hearts."

"She does?"

"Absolutely," she nodded. "The weight of your heart determines whether you can cross the river, to leave here when you die."

She caught my lapel and pulled me down into a brief kiss. She tasted like cloves and cinnamon.

"Your heart is fine," she said. "I've already weighed it."

Annie touched the image with a fingertip, tracing the form. "Anput is female, so she's trusted to guard the sleeping places of the great queens. She keeps them safe. They placed a statue of her at doorways as a warning that the bedrooms were sacred, and not to be touched."

"Bedrooms?"

"Of course, bedrooms," she said. "That's where you sleep, right? These bedrooms were deep inside pyramids, but that's what they were. When the queens died, they put them to bed so they could leave. They dreamed, and crossed the river on their dreams."

"You seem to know a lot about Egypt," I said. "I had no idea."

"I do. When I was young, I used to dream about Egyptian queens. It seemed more like remembering than dreaming. It made my mother very worried about me. Perhaps I dreamed that I was a queen."

"You'd make a fine queen," I said, and kissed the top of her head. "I'd serve you."

She ignored me, and traced a finger down the page we were looking at. I almost imagined the image of the jackal-woman flickered in response, but decided not to. It was late, and I was tired.

"If this jackal had to guard the queen's tomb, I guess she didn't do a very good job."

"You're wrong," Annie said. "They found Anput had been damaged, but the seal on Nitocris' bedroom remained intact. They never got in. Obviously, they got out with the eye, but I don't imagine they lasted very long."

"Why? What do you think happened to them?"

She held my gaze, and didn't answer.

"You seem to know more about this than you're telling me," I said. "How do you figure all this? Where does your theory come from?"

"Glass is precious," she said. "The ancient Egyptians made glass because it was magic. I remember Egypt from when I was a little girl. I remember the old queens, and I remember the power of glass."

She caught my bewildered look. "You remember Egypt from when you were a little girl?" I wondered.

"It isn't possible, I know. Since I didn't quite dream it, I must have made it up. I'm crazy, after all."

Her chin had dropped, and her breathing changed. I touched her cheek, and felt a tiny wetness. I thumbed it away, and resisted the strange urge to taste her tears.

"You didn't make it up," I said. "I don't know where your ideas come from, but you don't make things up."

She stared at the pile of books, as if willing it to give up its secrets. I felt her frustration.

"Nothing is what it seems," she said. "Nothing is ever what I think it's going to be."

"I am," I said. "I'm what you think."

She glanced at me, surprised. She held my look for a long moment, and then a slow smile caught her mouth at the corners.

"Yes," she said, "You are, aren't you?"

Footsteps echoed again at the bottom of the stairs. I knew the librarian must be on her way up to throw us out.

"They had another reason to take her eye." Annie pointed again to the image of the jackal-woman standing beside the dark doorway. "The passageways into the pyramids were narrow, and pitch black. They knew Anput would see them. The first order of business would be to blind her, so she wouldn't identify them in the afterlife."

"They were afraid of her?"

"Terrified," she nodded. "With good reason. So, they pried out one of her eyes. Something made them flee before they got both."

"Being ancient Egyptian glass, would it be worth quite a lot?"

"It would be hard to sell it without identifying yourself as a tomb robber," she said. "Buying and owning it would be just as difficult. You couldn't pretend to own an artifact you came by honestly. They're evidence of a crime. Some collectors would be attracted by that."

It seemed plausible. "I wonder if that might make it worth a great deal."

"It might," she said, thinking about it. "Being forbidden often takes things from valuable to priceless."

"Fin probably brokered its sale to the senior Gaynor in the first place," I mused. "He acted as agent. Does that make you a little less fond of him?"

"He may have been an agent for good," she said. "Fin is more than he seems."

"Fin is a criminal," I said. "A powerful one. He's an agent

for nobody but himself."

"Why do you think he brought you into this?" she asked. "You're going to return the eye to Anput. You'll restore her."

"You think I'm going to hop on board a steamer and try to smuggle artifacts back into Egypt?"

High over our heads, the shadows moved. They swirled and then settled again, like a cloud of bats. Annie shook her head.

"You're going to throw the eye into the river," she said. "The river will carry it back where it belongs."

I didn't know what she was talking about, but when it came to Annie I seldom did. It didn't stop me believing in her, somehow. In this case, I had every intention of seeing the peculiar eye back in the blind woman's hand, and of never seeing any of the Gaynors or their entourage again.

"When you throw it in the river, don't get too close to the water," she said. "Remember what you promised me."

She pulled at me and pressed her face into my neck. Her skin felt warm enough to be feverish. Over her shoulder the librarian appeared and tapped pointedly on her wristwatch.

"Don't die first." Annie's voice sounded muffled. "Remember your promise. Don't die first."

Part Three

Egyptian Tides

-Eighteen-

Thursday, June 28, 1917
Santa Teresa County, California

The sun was already hot, high, hard, and bright. It turned the whole sky so white that it became impossible to tell exactly where it hovered overhead. Only at the edges, where the air met the tops of the canyons, showed the peculiar merciless blue that you see only in the desert. Down below, the avocado groves looked oily, a sea of thick green leaves baking in the morning heat.

A girl walked the access road, leaving the prints of her bare feet in the dust. Shade crouched between the rows of trees, dimness that probably still held some of the last night's temperature. The coolness didn't charm her. Rabbits were in there, and that brought snakes. Rattlesnakes liked the trees, and liked the rabbits even more. By now, the early morning mammals were asleep in their burrows, hidden from the heat, and so the snakes had mostly left, climbing the arroyo walls to find rocks in the sun. The girl stayed out of the rows anyway; leaving the trees to those that lived in them. It wasn't fear. Snakes did what they did, and rabbits did what they did. Sensible, natural things never bothered her the way they did most people.

Slenderness and bearing made her seem tall, though she wasn't really. Her hair and skin were nearly the same shade of amber, both the color of honey trapped in its comb. It had the curious effect of making her seem as though she had been cast from gold, all of one piece. She moved like an animal, in an almost invisible near-dance.

She was exactly what a girl should be, if left uninterrupted by lessons and mirrors and decoration.

Her name was Annie Kahlo. Today was her birthday, her eleventh, and she watched for her present. She knew that the universe would give her one, and it did. She stepped on it before she saw it.

The pain came in pure, all at once, from the arch of her right foot all the way up to her hip. The blood came right behind the pain, so close that it wasn't a separate thing. The girl took the weight off her leg, spun gracefully and sat cross-legged in the road.

The shards of glass that had pierced her foot stuck up in the road, two of them. Freshly broken, they appeared as though they had been hurled from far away and been embedded. The edges were clean and blue, even though they had not seen daylight for centuries.

"My birthday present!" she exclaimed, smiling. "I knew it."

She ignored her bleeding foot. When the shards had been pried loose from the dirt and cleaned with spit and the edge of her shirt, they showed deep blue, sapphire with other colors mixed in. The sunlight brought out black and purple, and the edges of rose and green. She had never seen anything quite like it. The ancient glass was smalt, though Annie wouldn't have recognized the word.

"Egyptian tides," she said.

The ground shifted slightly beneath her, a sideways slip. If she had been on her feet, it might have caused her to stumble. She had felt earth tremors before, but this seemed different. A covey of *quail flew up from the brush and wheeled against the sky. Annie glanced up at them, then returned her attention to her birthday gift.*

Her eyes were almond-shaped and dark. They stared fixedly at what lay in her palm, and then suddenly rolled up into her head. Only white slits showed. Her chin followed her eyes upward, and she faced the sky overhead. The cords on her neck stood out, and she struggled to speak. Her voice, usually sweet and clear, sounded as guttural as if it had not been used for a thousand years.

"Egyptian tides," she said again, through gritted teeth. She gripped the broken glass, and her fingers were bleeding now too, dripping dark spots into the dust. Her jaw opened and she screamed.

Then she screamed again, and the water came.

It started as a rivulet, visible far up the arroyo, a black snake nosing its way down to where she sat in the road. It ran so packed with dirt that it was really a thin stream of flowing mud. It got bigger, though, and the single thread of water broke into five, seven, and eight streams before again becoming a single one, much larger. By the time the water reached Annie, it had turned the road into a shallow creek.

The current rose, and flowed around the sitting girl. When it splashed her face, she coughed and staggered to her feet, her usual grace vanished. She stood with her arms spread wide, and didn't take her gaze from the sky above her. The water came first to her waist and then to her shoulders, and then slowed and rose no further. The flow was lazy now; it smelled curiously rich and green and alive.

It was a river, an ancient one.

Cleopatra would have recognized it. She had used its cinnamon surface as her mirror. Nitocris, the beautiful queen, knew its power; she had turned the tables as she died and killed her own assassins with its flood. Nefertiti would have known it, too. She had bathed in its coolness every day of her life.

"Egyptian tides," Annie murmured, a last time. Her head relaxed and fell to her shoulder. Her wet hair was plastered to her cheek. She closed her eyes. The current lessened and fell, from chest to stomach, and then to her knees. She stood in the subsiding flood, swaying slightly, regal in a way that no just-turned-eleven girl should be.

Her dark eyes opened again and saw things that weren't there.

"The sea to Rome," she whispered. "They come."

Eventually, the water went back entirely to where it had come from, leaving Annie shivering in the hot sun. Only the wet road showed that the great River Nile had come briefly to the California desert.

That evening, Grace Kahlo found her daughter sitting on the back steps. She had been gone for the whole day. When she tried to pry the shards of broken glass from her bleeding hands, the girl moaned and clutched them more tightly. Put to bed, Annie slept for four nights and three days. She didn't speak English for nearly a month, although occasionally she would look up from her reverie and comment in a language that her parents didn't recognize.

Annie was never the same afterward, her mother said, and that was true. Her eyes were often distant, and she sometimes said things that made no sense. She saw the world through bits and shards of colored glass; the eternal showed itself to her in bright, changing patterns. Anput, jackal-goddess of the seventeenth territory of ancient Egypt, had weighed the girl's heart and been satisfied.

On her eleventh birthday, Annie Kahlo became joined again to sisterhood. The blue glass fragments had been lost from a strange kaleidoscope, one older than memory. They were her birthday present, and the birthright of a queen.

Egyptian tides.

-Nineteen-

"This certainly took long enough," Mrs. Highland said. "I hope you don't plan to charge me for wasted time."

I slid the single sheet of paper that was her bill across the desk, followed by a manila envelope. She ignored the bill and opened the flap on the envelope.

"There are two prints of each photograph, and the negatives," I said. "They'll be sufficient grounds so that a judge will grant you a divorce."

She was a cool number, dressed in a lightweight gray suit, stylish in the way that got appreciated at country clubs and museum board meetings. Tangerine lipstick didn't quite go with her auburn hair, but she gave the impression of having chosen it for exactly that reason. She exuded female challenge, but it wasn't the kind I responded to. I liked confident women, but not when confidence got wielded like a machete. She managed to look wry. "Whatever makes you think I want a divorce?"

"Why else would you have asked me to take these photographs?"

She shook the photos into her free hand and spread them on the desk in front of her. I didn't look. I had seen them before. She picked one up, and discarded it for another.

"What the hell is this?" she wondered. "This isn't what I paid for—they're only *kissing*."

I didn't remind her that she hadn't paid me a cent, since I still hoped she would. "Evidence of infidelity in the state of California," I said. "They'll be ample grounds."

"I told you I don't want a divorce, you foolish man." She slammed the images on the desktop with a flat palm. I supposed she was angry, but it was hard to tell it apart from her normal state. "I wanted pictures of them—screwing. Are you stupid?"

"You don't need that. At any rate, I didn't see them do any such thing. Kissing is sufficient congress for divorce."

She stood up, braced herself on the desk, and put her face close to mine and spoke very loudly. Her lips were an inch from my nose, and her breath felt humid. If she hadn't been so generally dreadful, it might have been quite exciting.

"I don't want a divorce," she said, spacing the words carefully to account for my possible unfamiliarity with spoken English. "I want photographs of that slut in bed with my husband. I want pictures that are so clear and unflattering that every medical journal in the country will want to feature them for their anatomy sections. That's why I sent you to that seedy motel. Am I being clear?"

She stopped shouting into my face, pushed off the desk, and raised herself to her full height, which I pegged at about four inches over five feet.

"I will never grant my husband a divorce. He suits me fine where he is. I'm sure that he would love to be free to marry that common whore, and drag my name through the dirt. It won't happen."

"What do you want the photographs for?" I kept my voice mild. I knew it was a stupid question.

"Those photographs will follow her wherever she goes. When she loses my husband, she won't lose me. Whatever man she meets from now on will get a complete set, by airmail. I'll make sure no man will look at her without gagging. If she finds a job after he fires her, her new employer will receive a package of photos, as a personal reference from me."

I decided that her red face clashed with both her hair and her lipstick. I swept the photos into a stack and got them back into the envelope. She snatched up the bill, ripped it in half, and flung it. Half made it to my lap, and the other fluttered to the floor.

"I'll give you a week," she spat. "Do what you were contracted to do, or you'll be speaking with my lawyer. You're not going to get a penny from me until I'm completely satisfied."

She left the office door wide open behind her, and I listened until her heels had made an angry tapping all the way down the hall to the stairs. Then I picked up the rest of the bill and deposited it into the metal wastebasket beside my desk. I went to the sink in the corner of the office and made a small, careful bonfire out of the photographs and the negatives. When they were gone, I flushed the black bits down the drain and hauled the window open to air the place out. I closed the office door and sat back down behind my desk.

I puffed a few breaths from my cheeks while I thought about things. It didn't help.

"Oh, brother," I said, to nobody at all.

~*~

A coffee shop opened off the lobby on the ground floor of the Schooner Inn. It occupied an unused space that had stood empty for so long almost nobody remembered it had once been the hotel gift shop. It was a relic of a time long before the war, when the place had been swank. Oil people had visited Santa Teresa to work on being tycoons, and Hollywood types had escaped the crush to smell oranges and the fresh air blowing off the channel. They had all stayed at the Schooner.

That was a long time ago. Now the clientele didn't talk oil leases and movie deals. They met upstairs to buy and sell reefer and girls and fighting roosters, arrange truckloads of Mexican avocado pickers, barter stolen shipments of radios and mattresses. It was a safe place to talk about darkness in broad daylight.

Dusty hand-painted floor tiles were the only reminder of the good times. The rest of the small space consisted of cement walls painted dark yellow, a counter with a coffee urn and some pastry trays, a few scattered tables and chairs.

I picked the funny papers and sports page from an abandoned newspaper, and took my coffee to the emptiest of the empty tables.

A Greek couple owned the place. They didn't seem to be selling anything but coffee and donuts. Most people came to the Schooner for cheap draft beer at nine o'clock in the morning, not coffee, and the place usually stayed empty. They seemed happy, though, living the American dream. Some guys I knew caught a bullet and had been buried on shell beaches in the Pacific for them to have the chance of it, so it made me happy, too.

The man spoke only a little English. If the woman spoke any at all, she didn't let on. They were invisible to most people, a couple of foreigners, and I wondered if they liked it that way. I wondered if the people down in Corazón Rosa thought of Annie and me that way, as a couple of invisible foreigners. Annie had dark enough skin to pass as local, and she spoke Spanish like a native, but I knew the locals called her *la extranjera*. They couldn't make any mistake about me. I wondered if the Mexican city felt like home because I didn't belong, and was more beautiful to me because I couldn't understand it.

Beatrice Stone once lived in a hotel room upstairs from where I sat. She might have come in here between turning tricks. It was quieter than the bar. Nobody would be likely to bother her if she slipped a half-pint bottle from her purse to sweeten her coffee, and sit by herself for a while. I wondered if she had gazed at the putrid yellow walls and thought about fairy tales and lost love. I wondered if her ghost still came in here sometimes. I wondered about a lot of things, and never seemed to get any answers. I was used to it, and it didn't bother me.

There was movement at the door, and Harold Gaynor came in. He looked splendid, in a fresh seersucker suit with a gardenia in the lapel. He looked around and made a face like he didn't belong here, and felt glad about it. After letting his eyes adjust to the dimness, he came over. Eleanor Lane trailed him in. She wore an apricot-colored suit and appeared to like the place a whole lot less than he did.

"I was headed to your office, and saw you cross the street and come in," he said. "What an odd place to find you."

"Very odd," I agreed. "But no odder than anything else."

He pulled a chair out for Eleanor, without asking me if I wanted company, and they both sat down. She wrinkled her nose at me, by way of greeting. "Hello, peeper."

"I came to tell you something," Gaynor said. "I've fired the Parklane Agency. I'll no longer use their services on this, or anything else, and I've told them so."

I took a careful sip of my coffee. It was still hot, which somewhat made up for the fact that it wasn't very good.

"They have removed their operatives, back to Los Angeles," he said. "We won't see them around here any more."

"There's the matter of raping Beatrice Stone," I said. "They also may have killed her. Someone did, and I haven't come across any suspects more likely than them. Is leaving Santa Teresa and going home to Los Angeles good enough?"

"It has to be," he pronounced. "There's no proof of anything. I'm going on your word."

I thought about it. "I'm not done with them on the rape. They'll deal with me, sooner or later. If I find out they were the ones who put her in a bathtub, it will be sooner."

"There are more pressing issues," he said. "I need you to find the missing eye. You're the only one working on that now. I'm prepared to double the fee we agreed on."

"In that case, I can afford to treat you both to a coffee." I motioned to the Greek behind the counter. Eleanor stared at me, as if I had gone mad. She didn't drink coffee in places like this. She had probably never even sat down in a place like this.

"My mother didn't like you," Gaynor said. "Even more, she didn't like the woman you brought to her house."

"Miss Kahlo didn't much care for her, either. I think she liked your aunt a lot less. The blinded bird upset her."

I wondered how he would react if he knew how bad an idea it could be to upset Annie.

"The blind bird?" he asked, puzzled. "That's a pet. It's just a wild bird. Why would it upset anyone?"

"Miss Kahlo likes birds. She doesn't agree with sticking hot needles into their eyes."

"Be that as it may, it would be best if you left my mother out of things from now on," he said. "It only upsets her."

"I don't much care what upsets her," I said. "An innocent woman got murdered over her knickknack."

He didn't try to conceal his shock. "She was trash," he spluttered. "The very furthest thing from innocent you could imagine. And the 'knickknack' is a priceless rarity."

The Greek man brought a cup of coffee to the table. Gaynor ignored him. Eleanor stared at hers as though it was poison, and pushed it away.

"Yes, you've avoided mentioning that," I said. "I did a little research of my own. Tomb robbers pried the worthless bauble, which is now a priceless rarity, out of a statue. There's no possible way you can legally own it."

"How could you possibly know that?" He clearly turned uncomfortable. I held his gaze, and didn't give him an answer.

"As I told you, my father collected Egyptian antiquities for years." He shrugged. "In the early days, there was no such thing as illegal. Now that there are laws, it only increases the value of the items that made it out of the country. The Egyptian government isn't searching for the eye, I assure you."

"Maybe not," I said. "It still puts a bad taste in my mouth."

"Are you so very concerned, in your profession, about what tastes good?"

"Not particularly. I like to think I have limits, though."

"My family owns that piece of glass perfectly legally," he said. "The only crime that's been committed is its theft from us."

"That's true, if you don't count the fact the person who stole it got raped, threatened, and finally murdered."

"I tried to pay her to return my property," he said. "I tried my very best to reward her crime. It isn't my fault she complicated things so badly."

I wanted to punch him in the mouth. Eleanor stared at me, as if she knew it, and hoped I would. Her lips were slightly parted, as if the whole thing gave her a thrill.

"You're the only one on the case now." Gaynor stood up to leave. "I want you to continue."

"I plan to continue, but only because I want to run down whoever killed Beatrice Stone," I said. "If I find your eye along the way, so much the better."

"Two birds with one stone is agreeable," he said. "There's no reason one won't lead to the other, and I will reward you appropriately when the eye is returned. Double. I still don't care for your attitude."

"You shouldn't feel bad about that. Not many people do."

"Miss Lane will contact you about reimbursing your expenses to date. If you have any problems, you can always reach her on my home or office telephones."

"Oh, good. I'll see Miss Lane again," I said. "I can't wait."

She curled her lip at me. It was a luscious lip, made to be nibbled on. She was absolutely adorable, and knew it. He glanced at me curiously, but I had nothing to add. They left me alone, to finish my coffee and the funny papers.

~*~

Rex Raines caught me at my office, as I got ready to leave for the day.

"I was just leaving to go home," I said. "Aren't you lucky."

"I'm a policeman," he said. "Crime fighters never go home. Doubly so, since I spend my time gathering information for shooflies that nobody else will give the time of day to."

"Got three clients," I said. "All kinds of people are giving me the time of day."

"Any of them paying you?"

I paused to take inventory. Mrs. Highland wasn't likely to ever pay me a dime, since I was disinclined to take filthy pictures for her. Florence Nickerson had no money. Danny López had said he would settle the account, but he was my friend. If I didn't get any justice for the drowned boy I would be reluctant to call my time anything but a favor. I had an advance from Gaynor, and the promise of doubled rates, though.

"One of them is paying me," I said. "And I'm a little hopeful about the others."

"Planning to stick around then? No more fishing holidays down in Mexico to try to forget the Kahlo broad?"

"Not for a while." I didn't know why Raines suspected my trips south, but his constant mention of Annie wouldn't do, certainly not while she stayed in town. If the wrong person recognized her and blew the whistle that she hadn't died in the car fire, she would end up in the gas chamber. I felt relieved when he moved on.

"I took a look at the Allen Nickerson file," he said. "Nothing on the surface of it to raise anyone's hackles. Rocas Perdidas is a nice green place to have a picnic. Not supposed to swim in it, but people do, and kids have always liked to dive off the cement walls at the end. It's deep and dangerous if you're not a good swimmer, since it's not very easy to get out. There's either the one ladder, or a long swim away from the cement dam walls to find a place to haul yourself out."

"So, if he dove in to save a drowning cat, Joey O'Meaney could easily have shown him a gun and kept him away from the ladder."

"Could be." I could hear his shrug. "There's not a thing that says it's different, and not a thing that says it's so. Coroner determined accidental drowning. Only funny thing—the boy got pulled out wearing his shoes."

"That doesn't tell you anything? You think he went for a swim with his shoes on?"

"He might just as well have been horsing around on top of the dam and fallen in." I could hear the shrug in his voice. "O'Meaney's a twisted pile of garbage—everyone knows that, but no witnesses claim he was even there that day."

"Case closed?"

"The case got closed a long time ago," he said. "Never was a case. I just pulled the file like you asked me to."

I swung my feet off the desk. I felt myself getting angry. It wasn't a good idea, since Raines had been a kind of ally for a while now. It could be hard to get by in my profession without friends in the police department, especially for a known associate of Anne Kahlo, the cop-killer. Raines was the last person in the department still speaking to me.

"Case also closed on Beatrice Stone," I said. "She gets murdered in my motel room, and since she's a street walker and a lush, nobody cared. Now case closed on Allen Nickerson, a poor kid with a good heart who tried to save a cat. No rich parents, just an older sister who struggles to get by, so nobody cares if he got murdered."

His voice got ominously quiet. "You might have been charged with the Stone death," he said. "A lot of people would have been happy to see you put away. Watch your tone with me."

"I'm just frustrated…" I started, but I had already heard the click of the line dying in my ear.

I leaned back in my chair and scrubbed my face with dry palms. I would probably have to drop a dime on the thin man for something else, if I had the time and energy to settle for that. He wouldn't serve a day for the kid's murder. Too bad, but real life could be rotten that way. It wouldn't hurt to let him know I was breathing over his shoulder, so I decided to see if Annie wanted to come with me for a drink at the South Seas Room that evening.

-Twenty-

I walked across the green floodlit expanse of parking lot in front of the South Seas Room. Annie waited in the car. The lot was full tonight. At the front door, the same gunsel sat on the same stool. If he recognized me, he didn't let on.

Inside, the place was jumping. The Pacific combo onstage played an old swing number, and the dance floor boiled. I debated stopping at the bar to pick up a drink while I let my eyes adjust. The crowd pressed in three-deep, so I gave it a pass. I felt a hand on my elbow.

"He's at the same table you found him last time," a warm breath told me. Chessie Emerson put her lips against my ear, to be heard over the horns. Her perfume smelled feral, and she pressed herself against my arm. If I had never met Annie, I would have trumpeted like an elephant.

When I turned my head, her face came within an inch of mine. She didn't draw back. She had come across like a cold fish, the perfect personal assistant for Fin when I'd met her previously. This showed either another side of her, or she was a hell of an actress.

"Must be doing okay, if he rates a table like that with a crowd this size," I remarked.

"He probably thinks so. I put him where you could find him."

"You knew I'd be coming?"

She gave me a squeeze. "Let me know how you make out," she said, and disappeared into the crush of people. I elbowed my way through the smoke and music to the far corner. Joey O'Meaney indeed had the table to himself again. He was eating a plate of red pasta, with a cigarette smoldering and ready in the ashtray. With no chair opposite, I settled for looming over him.

"Clams again?" I asked.

"Spaghetti Bolognese," he said. "You think I eat the same thing every night?"

"I have no idea what you eat every night. Judging by your appearance, you need to be getting a lot more vitamins."

"Wise guy," he said, and put his fork down. "You want to be careful I don't get tired of you."

"Or what?" I felt the heat rise under my collar. "Your top gear is killing kittens and school kids. That's the limit for you."

"Says who?" He leaned back and smiled. His teeth looked rotten. "Do you know why I'm connected, pal? Because I'm useful in a lot of different situations, that's why. You might not want to try me out."

A couple of sequinned women passed the table, carrying drinks from the bar. One was light, the other dark. I didn't know if they were customers, or dancers who worked for the club. O'Meaney reached out and caressed the light-haired woman's backside as she went by. Both of them stopped in their tracks and turned around. The blonde stepped back, moved the plate of spaghetti an inch, and carefully set her glass on the table. When she had it settled, she hauled off and slapped the thin man across the cheek. It made a sound like a pistol shot.

On stage, the band faltered for a moment. In the pause, the brunette picked up her friend's drink and tossed it into O'Meaney's face. As the music rose again, he reached inside his jacket. I was faster. He pulled his hand out when he felt the muzzle under his chin.

"Okay, okay," he muttered, holding both hands up. "I had it coming."

I put the Browning away. He glared at the women, one side of his face visibly darkening. The blonde had a good arm.

"You think you can do that to me?" he asked. He sounded close to choking. "I know where you live, both of you. We have a date, wait and see."

He picked up the napkin beside his plate and patted his face with it. The blonde had her hands on her hips, ignoring him. She was visibly annoyed.

"Why did you throw my drink?" she demanded of her companion.

"It was your fanny he patted," the brunette said, in a reasonable tone. "No reason I should waste my own drink on him."

The two women wandered away, arguing amiably. O'Meaney watched them, the way a cat watches birds. He seemed to have recovered his good nature, and I wondered if the two of them had any idea of the danger they were in.

"I've got an eye on you," I told him. "Fair warning. This isn't over."

His laughter followed me toward the door. The trumpets played a riff from up on the stage, laughing too. Outside, in the silent night, the doorman ignored me again. The air felt cooler than when I had gone inside. I crunched back across the gravel and got behind the wheel of my Ford.

"I don't think I made much impression on him," I told Annie. "Best I can hope for is that he knows I'm watching him.

Maybe he won't kill anyone until I can figure out a way to trip him up."

"How old was the drowned boy?" she asked. "What was his name?"

We sat and watched the door of the nightclub from the darkest corner of the parking lot.

"His name was Allen," I said. "With an 'e'. He was fourteen. Not quite a boy, but not a man yet, either."

"And the cops did nothing?" she demanded. "For Allen with an 'e'? Who tried to save a drowning cat and got murdered for interfering?"

"Sheriff decided it was an accidental death." I shrugged at nothing. "Dangerous place to swim—he wasn't the first person they've pulled out of that reservoir. I talked to the Santa Teresa cops. Case closed, as far as they're concerned."

"You told me the boy's body had shoes on," Annie said. "Who goes swimming with shoes? This monster kills stray cats for fun, and now a stray kid—and he's sitting in there soaking up whiskey sours, free as can be?"

"I'm not getting paid for this," I reminded her. "I'm doing what I can. We'll follow him now, and see where he lives. I'll tail him for as long as it takes—until he trips on something that will put him away. He's twisted, but he's still a common hoodlum— sooner or later he'll do the wrong thing, and I'll drop a dime and have him locked up."

"The lesser of two evils is still evil," she said. "He'll get out eventually and start back up again."

"He isn't planning to stop drowning stray cats," I said. "There might be a law against that—at least if it's done in a reservoir where people get drinking water. I may be able to have him arrested for it."

She got quiet again, and I passed the time mentally listing the Boston Braves' decent pitching prospects for next season. That didn't take long, so I tried to figure out what Annie smelled like, instead. I had gotten as far as the ocean, rainbows, oranges, flowers, and clean skin, when the front door of the club opened and Joey O'Meany came out.

He walked across the lot and got into a familiar looking egg-crème LaSalle saloon, frosted green by the floodlights.

"The thin man himself," I murmured.

"Follow him," Her laugh was lovely. "Maybe he'll hold up a filling station on the way home, and you can call the cops and get him put away for a year or two."

"I don't make the rules, Annie," I said. "I can only work with what I'm given. I have to play by at least some of them."

"Well, I don't have to play by any rules, except the ones I make up," she said, and got out. "I like dogs more than I like cats, but I won't play favorites at a time like this."

She slung the strap of her bag over her shoulder as she walked away. The saloon's headlights came on and silhouetted her as she walked across the lot. She took her time, like a dancer walking onstage. She was beautiful when she moved, and O'Meany had time to get a good look at her. When she reached his car, she bent and leaned into the driver's window. I knew she didn't want an audience for whatever she had to say to him, but I also didn't think she understood how dangerous he was.

I cursed under my breath, got the Browning out and held it in my lap. I sat with one hand on the door handle.

There was a sharp cracking sound, and the LaSalle's windshield lit up whiter than the headlights. The flash disappeared as quickly as it had come, and then the headlights went out and the big car turned dark again. Annie got back in on her side, bringing a cloud of perfume mixed with burned powder. Her eyes shone.

"What did you do that for?" I asked. It was a stupid question, but the only one I could come up with on short notice.

"I told you I don't like rules," she said. "So, I don't play by them. As I also mentioned, I do like cats, and boys who try to save them."

Chessie Emerson had said much the same thing. She hadn't shot anyone to death over it though, as far as I knew. "Apparently a lot of people do," I murmured.

I held my hand out and she put the pistol into my palm. The barrel felt warm. I wiped the prints off with my handkerchief and got out of the car. I heard snatches of music from inside the club, and the far-off hum of traffic on the coast highway. Nothing else stirred. I crossed the lot and slid the gun underneath the LaSalle. I didn't glance through the open window at what slumped behind the steering wheel.

"I'm probably going to cry," Annie told me, after I got back in. "When I'm by myself."

I was in shock, but I didn't love her any less. Maybe I loved her more. I couldn't think of anything to add to that, so I let the clutch out and drove us home.

~*~

The next day, I had a summons from Fin, by way of a telephone call from Chessie. She told me, without any small talk, where to meet him that evening. Her voice sounded completely neutral. Most people showed up when he summoned them, and I ought to be no different. The old gangster kept his power and connections hidden, which made it generally better to play safe and do what he asked. She said I would find him at the overlook on Marina Drive. When I pulled into the empty turnaround, his Packard sitting at the rail, pointed toward the ocean.

We didn't greet each other when I got into his car. I waited for him to tell he what he wanted.

"Imagine being out on the water tonight," Fin said. "Picture it."

We sat and stared out the windshield, watching nothing. The Packard's engine was still warm and ticked occasionally. I didn't expect to catch dengue fever, but just the same I got a pint of bourbon out and rested it on one knee. Fin didn't ask for a taste, and I wouldn't have dreamed of offering. Across the bay, the lighthouse on Punta Desorden blinked and flashed, blinked and flashed. It looked like a low-flying star.

"Foolish boats bobbing around in the dark," he murmured. "Three hundred feet of dark water beneath them, strong currents, sharks and monsters. It's the stuff of nightmares—yet they have complete faith in an electric light spinning around on a rock, miles away. The lighthouse makes them feel safe—as if the world is in order."

He gave a series of small gasps, probably his idea of laughter.

"The world is entirely out of order," he said. "When the boats drown, the light is the last thing they see as they go under."

In the dim light from the dashboard, his profile appeared dreadful. His eyes were invisible under the hat brim, but I could feel them on my face.

"Is the strange and elusive Annie Kahlo your lighthouse?" he asked. "Do you love her?"

I turned away and stared out the windshield at things in the dark that I couldn't see.

"Of course, you do," he answered himself. "Of course, you do."

He took the pillbox from his breast pocket, slipped the tablet under his tongue with the ease of long practice, and the sickly-sweet odor filled the car. My window squeaked a little when I rolled it down a little. The fresh air was cold with the smell of ocean: salt and rot and fog.

"You want so badly to be a hero," he said. "With your gun and your bottle of bourbon, you go to the places no one else will, chasing 'no-such-things' like a child playing make-believe."

He spread his hands expansively and gave me a smile. It was rare and genuine; it broke from him like a wave, ghastly and unbearably sweet.

"You're an absolute fool, Mister Crowe," he said. "It's the best thing about you. Miss Kahlo killed our friend, the late Joseph O'Meaney, is that not correct? Did you put her in a position where she would attend to what you weren't quite ready to?"

"I understood I had *carte blanche* to deal with the thin man," I said.

"Of course, you did, Mister Crowe, and you understood right. I didn't expect you to involve Miss Kahlo, however."

"She came to the club to keep me company, nothing more. I didn't expect her to shoot him."

"Didn't you?"

I rolled the window all the way down on my side and lit a cigarette. I smoked it while he thought about things.

"I have no wish to interfere with Miss Kahlo," he said. "I have enormous respect for her. She reads the cards, and sometimes sees things that even I cannot. I hope she has not attracted the attention of the police, however. It would not be good if they learned she was alive, and back in this city."

"No doubt she's attracted a lot of police attention. One cop in particular knew I was sniffing around O'Meaney for the reservoir murder. He'll be around to talk to me."

"How did this policeman know you were interested?"

"I asked him for a favor—to pull the file on the kid's drowning, to see if he spotted anything odd about it. He didn't."

I felt the weight of his look.

"Does it occur to you that all of this may hamper your recovery of the Egyptian relic?" he asked. "Above all, you must focus, Mister Crowe. Miss Kahlo has returned from her safe hiding place to assist you in that. She is in danger to start with, and shooting common criminals does not improve her odds. Even angels can be captured by men with badges and guns."

"I didn't expect her to shoot him," I repeated. "Did you call this meeting to give me advice, Fin? I don't need it."

We lapsed into silence. I watched the lighthouse blink, and debated whether to get out and drive my car away from here. Before I made up my mind, Fin spoke again.

"The eye has surfaced," he said. "Perhaps."

"What do you mean?"

"An old man named Volpato owns a bicycle shop on Ocean Lane," he said. "He runs it with his daughter. Do you know the place?"

"I know the street," I said. "An alley, really. You can pass it a hundred times and not see it. Pedestrians only—closed to automobiles. Tourists like it."

He raised an eyebrow. "A certain kind of tourist, perhaps."

"I never noticed a bicycle shop."

"It's a front," he said. "I don't suppose Volpato has sold a single bicycle in the last thirty years. He is a dealer in curiosities—rarities of the kind that only attract an exclusive set of buyers. In this case, he has laid his hands on an Egyptian antiquity that has a startling resemblance to one we are interested in."

"Egyptian antiquities?" I asked. "He sells stuff robbed from pyramids? Here in Santa Teresa? Who would buy them? Tourists?"

"He sells magic, Mister Crowe." Fin's voice grew a little impatient. "He sells the arcane and the profane, to tourists or anyone else who knows how to find his shop. Monkey paws and crystal balls, elixirs and potions, gewgaws and kickshaws, curiosities and gimcracks. The antiquity you pursue has a magical element, does it not? Is it not believed to restore sight to the blind?"

"If someone in Santa Teresa had stolen artifacts for sale, why would they offer them to Volpato? Don't all the rotten roads in this town lead to you?"

He looked pleased, as if I paid him a compliment.

"Very good, Mister Crowe," he beamed. "Perhaps the seller is avoiding me deliberately, or perhaps it's coincidence. Volpato has his own reputation, and from time to time, we do business. I am a supplier. That doesn't concern you. What does concern you is that Volpato and Daughter has offered a jackal's eye, at a very steep price. They are advertising it to a small circle of clients as an exceptionally rare and powerful curiosity."

I was startled. "A jackal's eye? That's what Annie believes the glass eye is. She thinks it belongs to a figure named..."

The name wouldn't come to me, but Fin supplied it. "Anput? Is that who she mentioned?"

"Yes. She says it's a dog, more than a jackal. It guards dead queens and weighs hearts."

"Exactly right," he beamed. "Do you see now why I summoned Miss Kahlo to help you? She sees things clearly, while you blunder. The two of you are perfectly matched. It's no wonder you love her."

"How would this Volpato fellow have gotten his hands on it?" I wondered.

"Who can say? Perhaps Miss Stone gave up on ransoming the Gaynors' heirloom back to them. Perhaps she succeeded in selling it to someone else. Wouldn't it be strange if you were searching high and low for where she might have hidden it before her death, and it's right out in plain sight? Being advertised for sale?"

He rubbed his hands together, clearly enchanted with his own train of thought. "I've often thought that if I were to write a secret letter, the safest place to keep it undiscovered would be printed in the pages of a book, on the shelf in the public library. There is no more private place than a busy street. Miss Kahlo understands that. The authorities want her. In order to secretly return to this city, she lives in her own house, walks down the street with impunity, invisible in plain sight."

"Annie isn't wanted," I said. "She's been declared dead."

He waved my remark away. "If you find that Volpato possesses the eye and is offering it for sale, then resolution of the matter is a Gaynor problem. You will have discharged your duties. Miss Kahlo will return to Mexico, and you will get on with the rest of your life."

"I won't be done with the case, Fin. There's still the matter of who killed Beatrice Stone."

He treated me to one of his ghastly chuckles. "The wind blows, and the wind swings, Mister Crowe. Miss Stone is fast asleep, in the ground. She no longer cares who killed her."

I thought about telling him about the ghost in my living room, who wasn't asleep and seemed to care. I said goodnight and got out, instead.

-Twenty-One-

The telephone on my desk rang, just as I headed out to meet Danny López. He wanted to see me, and didn't like coming to my office. I hesitated, and then turned back to pick it up. I didn't have enough clients to ignore it.

"Is this the private eye?" a man wondered.

I allowed, modestly, that it was.

"This is Charles Martellus, from across the street."

It took me a second to place the voice's owner as the old man who had lived across the hall from Beatrice Stone.

"I saw the woman again," he said. "The one who broke into Bea's room after she died, looking for something."

"You told me you couldn't remember anything about her," I reminded him. "Other than she was a doll in a tan raincoat."

"That's true," he agreed. "I also told you that my drinking memory gets jogged later sometimes, and I might remember her if I saw her again. That's what happened."

"Describe her to me," I said. "Tell me where you saw her."

The receiver on the other end got covered, and I heard muffled voices.

"I'm using the telephone at the Schooner front desk," he said. "I can't talk to you this way. Come across the street."

I glanced at my watch and thought fast. López was waiting for me. I was interested, but not enough to miss my meeting with him. I had a good idea that a couple of burly operatives from Los Angeles had stuffed Beatrice Stone into my hotel bathtub, not some dish in a raincoat. I wanted to hear what Martellus had to say, but knew it was also the rambling of a professional drunk. Still, if there was any truth in what he had to say, it might be testimony in a murder investigation and needed to be reported.

"You cared for Bea, am I right?"

"She was the closest person in the world to me," he confirmed. "In her way."

"I'll come and talk to you tomorrow morning. In the meantime, if you want to help her, you're six blocks from the police station. I need you to get yourself over there and make a report on this woman you saw to a detective named Rex Raines. Can you remember that?"

"I'm not drinking," he said. "Detective Rex Raines—I can remember that for six blocks."

"Don't talk to anyone else," I said. "Wait around for him if you have to. He might not seem very interested, because they've closed Bea's case. It doesn't matter. What does matter is that you get what you saw down on an official piece of paper. If this ever gets to justice, I don't want your testimony disallowed because you didn't take it straight to the police. Tomorrow, I'll talk to you and we'll see where this goes."

He promised that he would walk over to the police department as soon as he hung up. I told him I would find him the next day. Then I forgot about him.

~*~

The wooden railing under my elbows was still hot from the fading day.

It would be dark soon, and the wharf shrugged off its burden of tourists, ice cream-strollers, and casual fishermen. Lines were reeled, pails collected, and people walked the boards toward shore without looking back. Behind us, the pier restaurant squatted in its smell of frying fish. I heard the quiet clink of silver and glassware, tables being set in the pause before the dinner crowd came.

López pressed a roll of bills into my hand. I tried to give it back, but he refused to take it.

"You did what I asked you to," he said. "The boy got justice."

"I didn't do anything," I said. "Maybe I got a confession of sorts, but Annie shot the thin man to death before there could be any justice."

"You did what I asked you to," he said again, and gave a small shrug. "Take the money. I have a lot of it, and it's *privilegio de la vejez* to spend it as I see fit. Use it go back to Corazón Rosa with Annie."

Privilege of old age. I wondered if I would ever see mine.

"Did you tell the boy's sister?" I asked.

"I told her," he nodded. "Revenge is usually empty once you have it, but he won't kill anyone else. She might find some comfort in that."

I told him about the two women who had insulted O'Meaney at his table in the club, and his face as he watched them walk away from his table. I had a strong sense that Annie might have saved both of their lives. Regardless, I didn't feel right about the money, and I tried again to give it back.

"It feels as though I'm being paid for killing someone," I said. "I can't live with that."

"You didn't kill anyone. You don't decide what Annie does. Only she decides that."

"It isn't the first time she's done this."

He raised one eyebrow. "Obviously not. Does it bother you?"

"Of course, it bothers me," I said. "She shoots people in cold blood. Then she goes to bed and cries herself to sleep. When she gets up in the morning, it's as though it never happened."

"She isn't entirely of this world, *amigo*. I think you have to decide if you can love her without understanding her."

"I asked her to marry me."

López stared at the water and drew on his cigarette. He held it between thumb and fingers, shielding the coal. The sinking sun painted his face orange and made his wrinkles deeper.

"When the sun goes down—*en el mismo momento*—as it leaves the sky, there is..." He struggled for the word. "...*un destello de luz verde.*"

"A flash? A green flash?"

He nodded, and I thought about Corazón Rosa, the sunsets seen from black sand beaches. All at once, I missed the place, a wet jolt in my chest caused physical pain. I swallowed it.

"I've seen it," I said.

"I thought so," he nodded. "You see things. Many people look and look and look, but they cannot see the green light. It is a failing, perhaps—a kind of blindness. Perhaps, like most blindness, it is also a mercy."

The ocean moved like gelatin, sluggish and glassy all the way to the horizon. The sun touched the water now, hissing violently, putting itself out, and its light grew brighter even as the sky began to darken. Scraps of cloud high overhead caught the explosion and were turned to peach and rose against the darkening blue.

"I will tell you a secret," López said. "Even if it is one you already know. There is a green flash when the light leaves and the sun sets, but there is another flash when the darkness leaves. There is another side to every card."

"At dawn, you mean?"

"*Amanecer*—the dawn," he agreed. "The dark flashes when it leaves. No one has ever seen it, it's impossible to see it in the blackness, but still—some people know what color it is. A very few people."

The drowning sun gave a last struggle and then surrendered. As it slipped beneath the surface, it melted and spread across the horizon, orange lava that flared bright. It ebbed away, and as it did, it changed into a flood of strange light that colored everything. I opened my eyes wider. Beside me, López stirred and I knew that he saw it, too.

I didn't really know why people called it a green flash. Maybe it was green, but it was also every other color, and no color that you saw anywhere else. Maybe it just couldn't be described, and green had to do. It was a color you remembered as much as one that you saw with your eyes—the color of childhood memory, the color of ghosts, the color of solemn promises that had been made and then forgotten.

When it all faded and the sea and sky came back into focus, López stirred. The show was over.

"It always feels like the first time," he said. "Everyone who sees that forgets to breathe."

He remembered the cigarette burning between his fingers, and puffed at it.

"You know what I'm talking about, don't you?" he asked. "You've seen it—the second color, the other side of the card, before the sun comes up. You've seen the dark flash."

I didn't want to know what he meant, but I did. I thought about Annie Kahlo again. I could hear her, whispering in my ear that you could only see in the dark if you closed your eyes. I took a breath, and tried to explain.

"There are colors that you can only see if you listen," I said. "There are colors that you can taste and smell. You have to close your eyes. The dark flash is like that."

He nodded and stubbed his smoke out on the railing. He shredded the butt, and watched the bits of paper and tobacco blow away.

"Do you want me to tell you what color it is?" I asked. "What I think I've seen?"

"No," he shook his head. "Don't ever tell me."

It was nearly dark now. The only memories of sun were just a few wisps of cloud dying pink over our heads. López pushed himself away from the rail, and turned to go.

"I will tell you the truth," he said. "I think the knowing would be too painful for me to bear."

~*~

Ocean Lane was dark; darker than the streets around it, darker than the sky or the time of day could account for. Too narrow for cars, really just an alley, punctuated by stairways and hemmed in by cement and stucco walls hung with railings. The shop windows were all lit with electric bulbs, even in the daytime. Bougainvillea climbed and flowered here and there, as though it didn't mind the gloom. It reminded me of somewhere else, probably a place I had gone to before the war. I couldn't put my finger on where that place had been, but I remembered it, just the same.

"I love cinnamon," Annie said, from beside me. "I wonder if it's possible to eat too much of it."

As if she had conjured it, I caught the oven-sweet smell of pastry from a bakery. A man sat on a bench by the door. A half-finished sandwich rested on a checked towel beside him. He played an accordion, bent over it and swaying as though it was trying to escape from him.

Three girls in matching school pinafores approached, arms linked at the elbows. They were singing. Their patent-leather shoes tapped the bricks under their feet in time to the song. Their voices were young and sweet, and the echoes from the walls turned them into an abbreviated choir. They ignored me, and smiled at Annie as they passed.

Two dogs ran by in a brown-and-white hurry to get somewhere. I looked back over my shoulder. They had stopped; the man on the bench had put aside his accordion and divided his sandwich between them. As if on invisible cue, a phonograph record began to play from a window above the street, dripping scratched saxophone notes down on us. I was startled. I took Annie's arm and stopped us.

"Do you hear that?" I asked. "It's all the same song."

She stood very still, watching me. She wore a half-smile, as though she knew things about me that I didn't suspect. Every time I looked at her face it appeared a little different. I always felt like I saw her, infinitely familiar, for the first time, and that she would be even more beautiful when she was very old.

"The girls, the accordion, the record—it's all the same song," I repeated. "Do you hear it? It's all 'I Love You Madly', but in different keys."

"Of course, you do," she smiled, and leaned in to kiss my cheek. "I depend on it."

We started to walk again. One shop sold postcards, and another sold spices. Some of them had strange names on their signs that gave no hint of what they were offering. One of them said "Volpato & Daughter: Bicycles" over the door, which seemed clear enough. Annie hesitated in front of it, and then made up her mind. An unseen bell jingled as we went inside.

Light filled the space. Chandeliers hung from the ceiling. There were lamps made from jade statues, from woodcarvings, from clocks. The store was a riot of cut glass and silk shades in every color imaginable. The walls shimmered and flickered as if on fire.

A very old woman appeared and tottered forward to greet us. She took both of Annie's hands, and craned up to say something in her ear. Annie bent down and listened intently. They seemed to know one another. When the woman had finished, they both turned to me and waited, as if they expected me to say something.

"You have a beautiful shop," I offered. "You ought to change your sign, though. It says 'Bicycles'. I don't think most people would realize you sold lamps."

"We don't sell lamps," the old woman said, clearly mystified. "We sell bicycles."

"I don't see any bicycles in here for sale," I said, puzzled. "Not one. I only see lamps."

"Did you come here to buy a bicycle?" she asked.

I shook my head, no, and her expression cleared.

"That explains it," she said, obviously satisfied. "If you had come here to buy a bicycle, there would be bicycles for you to look at, but you didn't—so there aren't."

She shook her head at me as though I was daft, and turned to Annie. "He's very strange," she said. "He doesn't make a bit of sense. I don't know how you deal with it."

Annie took my hand. Her laugh was warm, straight from the silver screen. "He has an eclectic mind," she said. "You never know what he'll blurt out, for no apparent reason. It's one of the things I like best about him. We're not here to buy a bicycle though, or anything else. We're here to see your father."

The old woman cocked her head and looked at Annie for a long minute. She had bright eyes, like a bird.

"My father?" she finally asked. "Is he expecting you?"

"Would we have come here if he wasn't?" Annie countered.

"It's been a long time since he expected anyone," the

woman said. "Business isn't what it used to be. Are you buying or selling?"

Annie tightened her grip on my hand, and silently willed me not to say anything. "Both," she said. The old woman considered things, nodded once, and disappeared into the back of the shop. I watched Annie's face, serene in the golden lamplight. She was serene. Annie could be sudden and unpredictable, but she was mostly about stillness, and she never seemed to mind waiting.

Several silent minutes later, the old woman returned, trailed by a man who she introduced as her father. He seemed no older than her, as if at a certain great number of years, the aging process maximized and could go no further. He took Annie's hand and then mine, with great formality.

"We've learned you may be in possession of an item that interests us," she told him. "Something of unusual value."

"Are you here to buy?" the man asked. "We are here to sell. Selling is what we do."

"The Egyptian eye. We aren't here to buy it," Annie said. She considered him very seriously. "In fact, I'd like nothing better than to see it returned to where it belongs. If I can do that without paying anyone, I will."

"You are always truthful." The old man smiled. "Even when it doesn't serve you."

"Always." Annie smiled back. "Even so."

"I don't have the item we are discussing. Not yet, anyway. I have a provisional agreement with someone who claims they will have it soon. They wish to sell it immediately when they do, and wanted an arrangement in place."

"Who is the person?" she asked. "Can you tell me?"

"Of course not," he said. "I wouldn't tell you if I knew, and I don't. It's a young woman. That's all I can say. I spoke to her once, right here, the day before yesterday. I don't believe I ever met her before that."

"Can you clarify what the item is, so we know we're talking about the same thing?"

"She claimed to have one of the eyes removed by grave robbers from a statue at the entrance to the burial chamber of Nitocris, the beautiful queen. It would be extraordinarily valuable, if it were genuine. Enough in her story that isn't common knowledge for me to take it seriously."

"The eye of Anput," Annie said.

"Anput." It clearly surprised the old man. "Do you know the story?"

"I do," Annie nodded. "Nitocris had a brother, a pharaoh who got murdered. She succeeded him on the throne. The young queen invited the conspirators who had killed her brother to a banquet. She held it in a room constructed to be sealed and flooded. She killed the assassins with the Nile River."

"She became herself a murderer," the old man nodded. "An alarm was raised, but she ran, and eluded her pursuers by running into a burning room. She never emerged. It was suicide, and she was mummified and given a royal funeral. Some accounts suggest it had been another trick—that she escaped, didn't die in the fire, and the mummy in her tomb belongs to someone else."

It startled me badly. Annie had caused the deaths of a number of men who were responsible for her sister's murder, and eluded capture by driving her car into a burning barn. When the fire burned out, the police had assumed her ashes were in the blackened shell of her convertible. The state of California had issued her a death certificate. The parallels were eerie.

"Anubis is the better known Egyptian canine," the man said. "He is also better suited to guarding tombs, because he specializes in it. Anput is his wife. A jackal."

"She weighs hearts..." Annie murmured.

"Quite so," he agreed. "She weighs hearts. Anput, not Anubis, guards Nitocris' chamber. The female guards the female. I can tell you for a fact that the likeness at the entrance is missing one of its eyes. It isn't well known, so it lent some credence to the young woman's offer."

"A female," she said. "Nitocris didn't want a male to guard her tomb, whether she lay inside it, or not. Tell me—would you recognize Egyptian glass if you saw it?"

He managed to seem slightly offended. "Of course."

"Then tell me—is this a piece of old cobalt? Or something else?"

She pulled a wad of tissue paper from her bag, unwrapped it, and placed a piece of glass into the old man's hand. He held it to the light. Somewhat dull, the long shard was dark blue, and caught the shimmering lamplight strangely.

"This is genuine," he breathed. His voice became reverent. "Definitely ancient Egyptian glass, containing smalt. Experts would have to authenticate it, of course. Do you have any idea in the power of this?"

Annie smiled. "I have some idea, yes."

"May I ask you a question? Where did you come by this? How do you come to know all of this so well?"

"I found this when I was a young girl," she said. "Or it found me. It gave me strange dreams—I dreamed of Nitocris. It's almost as if I lived there."

"Dreams," he nodded. "They can be more real than waking. The universe takes off its mask when we dream."

Annie laughed, pleased. "You understand. That's rare."

He turned to me, still holding up the glass shard. I glanced away. For some reason, I didn't like looking at it. Annie took it from him, gently, and put it away.

"What is your interest in this?" he asked me. "Are you also trying to return the eye to the rightful owner?" He smiled at the idea.

"I'm a private investigator. The owners have hired me to recover it..."

"They aren't the owners," Annie interrupted. "The eye belongs to Anput, obviously. It should be returned to her."

"More to the point," I continued, "A young woman got killed, likely because she had the artifact in her possession. She was a nice woman, and she didn't deserve the kind of death she got. Someone wanted the eye pretty badly. When I find out who has it now, there's a good chance I'll find out who killed her."

My own words surprised me a little. I hadn't clarified the idea in my own mind until now. I was more interested in tracking down whoever had killed Beatrice Stone than recovering the missing eye.

"I see. Is that why you came here, then?"

"What can you tell me about the young woman who approached you?" I asked. "Would you recognize her if I showed you a photograph?"

"She wore a mask," he mused. "Very beautiful, like something that would be worn at a Venetian ball. I would have made her an offer on that mask, had she not clearly needed it. She had long dark hair. She stood average height, I would say. She carried herself as if she was attractive."

"Did she wear glasses?" I asked. "With blue frames?"

"Of course not. It wouldn't be possible to manage glasses with the mask she wore. It was Venetian, with openings for the eyes. Very ornate, with sequins and black-and-white feathers—striking with her dark hair. A beautiful gown and shoes to go with it. No glasses."

Long dark hair and a good figure pointed at one person. Wanda Rice hadn't worn glasses in the photograph Bea had kept of her, so perhaps she didn't need them. She appeared the logical person to have kept the eye safe when her friend was being pursued and frightened by the Parklane boys. Her tears had fooled me.

"Do you have a buyer in mind yet?"

He shrugged. "That won't be difficult."

"I may represent a buyer. Save you looking. What is she asking for it?"

"She wants twenty thousand dollars, which is entirely reasonable. If the item is genuine, its value is priceless. Our commission is ten percent, also to be paid by the buyer."

"Twenty-two thousand—a ransom fit for a queen. How will you get in touch with her when you do? Did she leave a name?"

"You know better than that, I'm sure." He shrugged again. "If I know names, I forget them immediately. It's a condition of my business."

"I'll mention the price to my party," I said. "If he's agreeable, I'll get back to you and we can make arrangements."

I didn't need a name, not really. It was time to visit the Gaynor estate and have another chat with Wanda Rice, this time without tears and without lies. Annie and I thanked the Volpatos and left them to their invisible bicycles.

-Twenty-Two-

"What are you going to do?" Annie asked. "She can't sell Anput's eye, even if you're sympathetic because you like her. It isn't hers."

She played with a ribbon she held in her lap. She wore a matching one in her hair, a streamer of pink flowers.

"I only met her once." We were parked in front of the Sand Castle motel, facing the twilit ocean. I flicked my cigarette out the open car window, leaned back and closed my eyes. "At the cemetery, after the funeral. I found her quite disagreeable."

"Disagreeable doesn't mean you can't like her," Annie said. "I'm very difficult, and you love me."

"That's true. I do love you. I even asked you to marry me."

There was silence. After a minute, I cracked one eye open without moving my head and peeked at her. She appeared serene in the low light, gazing out at the water. She wouldn't answer, so I closed my eye again and listened to the surf and the occasional car passing on Cabrillo Boulevard.

"Do you smell that?" Annie spoke quietly. "Hau trees. Why do I smell them here?"

I did smell it, the same crushed leafy smell I had noticed the first evening I came here, about to be propositioned by Beatrice Stone. It came from the line of trees between the parking lot and the boulevard, and mixed with the odor of a bonfire somewhere out of sight on the beach.

"Those are Hau trees?" I asked. "How odd. I had never in my life heard of them, and it's a signature color for Gaynor Glass.

They call it Hau Tree Green. I wondered if it was a name they made up."

"They come from Hawaii," she said. "These trees are a long way from home. Like me."

I caught the sadness in her tone. Annie's father had come here from the islands, which accounted for her gold skin and almond-shaped eyes. Her mother had married Dr. Gardiner after the father died. She didn't talk about him. She shifted in her seat, and I followed her line of sight to where a Cadillac Sixty Special finished a sweeping turn into the lot.

"Right on time," I said. The car rolled slowly past us and stopped at the far end of the lot. Highland got out and headed for the office. He didn't glance our way. Once he had been inside for a minute or two, his secretary also got out and slowly drifted after him. Her movements were as awkward and graceless as a colt, even at a distance.

"She's beautiful," Annie said. "You didn't tell me that."

I didn't comment. I was used to Annie saying the exact opposite of what most people would say, and anyway, I thought the woman was beautiful, too. Highland emerged from the sedan and took her arm. They moved toward the wing opposite the one where I had stayed. I felt relieved. The bad memories of Bea looking up at me from underwater weren't going to go away for a while. I watched the couple move down a second floor balcony, and made a note of the room they disappeared into. After a moment or two, I got out and latched the car door behind me. Annie stayed put.

I went up the outside cement stairs in a hurry. If the pair had time to disrobe, it would be even more awkward. Awkward wasn't something I usually worried about, and I wondered if I was going soft. I knocked on the door and waited, a little out of breath. The woman opened the door and stared at me. She was clothed, but had removed her glasses. Her eyes were even more remarkable without magnification. They widened, slightly confused, and then her expression cleared.

"I know you!" she exclaimed. "I don't remember from where."

"We bumped heads picking up coins," I said. "We followed that up with a picnic of good sandwiches at the lookout on Marina Drive."

"I remember now," she said. "How nice to see you again."

Highland's face appeared over her shoulder, looking alarmed.

"I need to discuss something with you," I said. "It should be in private. May I come in?"

"Of course," she said.

"What for?" he sputtered, at the same time. I ignored him, went in and closed the door behind me. They were both dressed, as was the bed. An expensive bottle had been set out on the cheap table. I had landed at the door too soon after they came in for it to have been opened.

"We were just having champagne," the woman said. "We're celebrating. Will you join us, Mister...? If you told me your name, I'm sorry. I have a terrible memory for people's names."

"I don't think I ever told you," I said. "It's Crowe."

She put two fingers to her lips, contemplating the table. Her cheeks got visibly pink. "We only have two glasses—I'm so sorry. Do you mind using mine?"

"That's quite all right. When I tell you why I'm here, you won't likely want to drink with me. I didn't bump into you in the park by accident. I got hired to watch you."

I got a card from my wallet and held it out. She didn't want to take it, so I gave it to Highland. He sat down on the edge of the bed and stared down at it. I addressed him.

"Your wife employed me," I said. "I'm a private investigator. I was hired to dig up dirt. It's what I do sometimes—the nature of the job. Sometimes people deserve the trouble I stir up, and sometimes they don't. I don't get paid to think about it."

He stared up at me. His eyes were raw.

"What do you want with us?" he asked. "Why are you telling us this?"

There was no point in being here if I didn't tell the truth. "I thought I got hired to produce grounds for divorce," I said. "This is the opposite. Your wife doesn't want a divorce, and will never grant one. She wants to see you both miserable."

"Nobody determines whether another person is happy or not, Mister Crowe," the woman said, in a reasonable tone. "People make that choice for themselves. If she won't let us be free to marry, then we'll simply go on as we have."

"It isn't that simple." I told her that Gaynor's wife wanted intimate photographs, and she would use them to ruin the young woman's reputation. The air in the room got heavy. Gaynor stopped meeting my eye about halfway through.

"I don't care what she does," she said. Her expression became resolute. "She can't hurt me if I don't care."

"You need to think about it," I said. Elbows on his knees, Gaynor hung his head and stared at the floor. "She can affect your ability to make a living. She can end your chances of ever— marrying someone else, should you choose to do so. This will ruin your life."

She went and sat on the bed next to Gaynor. Her shoulders were turned away from me, making it clear she didn't want to hear anything else. She put a finger on his chin and gently tried to turn his face to her. He resisted, and kept his gaze on the carpet.

"I love you," she said, softly. "I won't leave you."

The room got quiet. It seemed indecent to move or to say anything, so I did neither. After a long moment, she looked up at me. Her lovely eyes were dry.

"Thank you for being decent enough to come and tell us."

"Good luck," I said. "I mean that."

I left the two of them, sitting side-by-side on the bed. He continued to stare at the floor. She looked as bereft as I felt. I crossed the parking lot to my black Ford and got in behind the wheel.

"It's over," I said. "So much for that. I warned them, and that's all I can do."

"How much did you get paid for this job?" Annie asked. Her smile was gorgeous.

"Nothing at all," I said. "I wouldn't take ten times the fee I quoted."

"My hero," she laughed. "Your heart has been weighed." She laid a warm palm against my cheek and pulled me into a kiss. When it was over, I put the key in the ignition and started the Ford.

"Payment enough," I murmured, and drove us away.

~*~

Miss Child had returned to her post, behind the reception desk at Gaynor Glass. She wore a cranberry-colored suit and gave me a nice, white smile. She looked swell. I had made her cry not so long ago, but she didn't seem to hold it against me.

"You weren't here the last time I came in," I said. "I thought you'd packed up and moved away, to someplace sunny and warm where everyone speaks French."

"Santa Teresa is sunny and warm enough," she said. "And I don't speak French. I've been in bed. A nasty bug wouldn't let go of me, for days and days. I'm better now."

"You certainly are," I said. "Your boss in?"

"He's off sick. I think I may have given it to him," she said, and seemed pleased about it. "He hasn't been here since yesterday morning."

"Really?"

I crossed the room to the display shelves of glass, to give her time to think about it. I gave even odds Gaynor was tucked into his leather office, and she had instructions he didn't want to see me. After I checked out some dark green bottles, I glanced over my shoulder at her. She twinkled at me.

"Cross my heart," she said, but crossed two fingers instead. I strolled back and re-joined her.

"What do you know about a missing glass eye?"

"I just started here, remember?" She made an innocent face. "I don't know anything about anything."

"I'll bet you know plenty, sister. Help me out."

She touched one rouged cheek with the tip of an index finger, and looked up at the ceiling. She was as cute as a basket of baby otters.

"Well, there's a valuable piece of glass that got stolen from Mister Gaynor and his mother," she said. "The family had it a long time, since his father was alive. The woman who stole it died, and it went missing. A detective agency from Los Angeles has been trying to get it back."

She glanced over her shoulder at the hallway leading back to the offices, suddenly nervous.

"Miss Lane is supposed to handle writing the checks out to them, and anything sensitive like that. She's Mister Gaynor's personal assistant."

"I've met her," I said. "You arranged for me to have a drink with her at the Montelindo Hotel, remember?"

"You were perfectly horrid to me about it, too." She wrinkled her nose. "I was just doing my job. Anyway, Miss Lane pawns off whatever she isn't in the mood to do onto me—which is most of it. I wrote out the checks to match the invoices. There were reports attached."

"Which of course you read, and memorized. Were they making any progress?"

"I think they managed some before the woman died," she said. "The reports were mostly about following her. They recommended 'appropriate force' to get it back, or else that Mister Gaynor turn the matter over to the police. He wouldn't do that, of course."

"Why not? Going to the police when something's been stolen is a natural reaction for most people."

"I don't know." She thought about it. "Maybe the Gaynors stole it in the first place. Anyway, I think it's second nature for the Gaynors to keep secrets. I think there's a lot of hanky-panky goes on in that house."

"He's a wealthy bachelor," I said. "Some amount of that gossip is probably to be expected."

"No, I mean his mother's house."

"His mother's house?" I wondered, surprised. I thought whatever had gone on between Bea and Wanda had probably been kept under wraps. "You mean rumors about the woman who stole the glass?"

"No, with the mother—the whole family really likes hanky-panky, from what I hear." She blushed prettily. "Anyway, I'm talking too much. You're cute, but I need this job. Anyway, I don't care what goes on in other people's bedrooms."

"Has Mister Gaynor ever been inappropriate with you? Said or done anything you objected to?"

"Never," she said, and then seemed perplexed. "I never thought about it. I'm not his type, I suppose. Miss Lane keeps an eye on things. I can't imagine she'd let anything improper go on here in the office. When you're rich, you can find your fun wherever you want to."

Eleanor Lane didn't strike me as someone who would recognize propriety if it hopped in a bus and ran over her, but I didn't say so.

"Anyway..." she lowered her voice. "Nobody comes out and says so, but it's my impression that Miss Lane and Mister Gaynor are engaged to be married. Eventually. It's the kind of secret nobody says out loud, but everyone knows."

"That could account for a lot of her attitude."

"It certainly could." She laughed out loud, and then clapped a pretty hand to her mouth and glanced over her shoulder, to make sure nobody had heard it.

"Mrs. Gaynor seems pretty upper crust to me," I said. "Not the kind to hold Greek orgies. What kind of hanky-panky does she like? Can you tell me?"

"I've told you all I'm going to. You're a detective. Find out for yourself. I promise you'll be shocked when you do."

It was all I would get from her, and she was too adorable to cause her trouble for gossiping. "Is Gaynor at home today?" I asked.

"I told you he got sick with a bug. Where else would he be?"

After I got my hat settled on my head, I gave her a knowing wink and made for the door.

"I think I'll bring him some flowers," I said. "Maybe a little soup."

~*~

I got off the highway at San Ysidro. As a rule, the flowers in Montelindo were a little brighter, the waves a little bluer, than they were just a couple of miles away in Santa Teresa. The palm trees appeared better watered than the ones the bums sat under at the foot of State Street. The residents of Montelindo enjoyed none of it, though, shut into their big homes behind vine-covered gates. I wondered at the mystery of having enough money to want broken glass-topped walls. You could afford to have a million-dollar view, and pay plenty to not see it.

Harold Gaynor's driveway, up the road from his mother's place, was crushed shell lined with masses of geraniums. It was hard to sympathize with it as the junior estate, just digs he put up with until he inherited the big house.

I shut the engine off at the edge of the circle in front of the house. Herb Robinson sat on the running board of the black Lasalle parked under the portico at the front door. He didn't polish it, or do anything at all to look busy. From a distance, he looked morose. When I waved, he got into the big car and drove it around the back.

The same squat woman as last time pulled open the front door after I had pulled the chime a couple of times. Like before, she examined my business card, front and back, before closing the door in my face. I had been left standing on the step long enough that I considered wandering out back and asking Herb what made him so sad, when the door opened again. The maid abandoned me on a bench in the front hall. I looked at the statue of the naked woman and speculated about her to pass the time.

Out of sight, the upstairs hallway echoed the sound of a door opening and closing. Eleanor Lane appeared at the top of the stairs. She wore a lavender robe, and her platinum hair was darkened damp. When she spotted me sitting below, her eyes widened and then narrowed. She spun off and disappeared without a word. After a moment, the door noise sounded again and then Arnold Gaynor came down the stairs.

He wore a robe, too, and his legs were bare.

"I'm not really receiving guests today, Crowe," he said. "I'm unwell."

"You had me fooled," I remarked, and glanced up toward the spot Eleanor had disappeared into.

"What's that supposed to mean? Are you being insolent?"

"Nothing at all." I indicated his bare feet. "I mean you look very sporty. Never know you were sick. Probably your breeding."

He eyed me, uncertain, and decided I must be giving him a compliment. "Probably so," he said, and gestured me to follow him. We went along the downstairs hall to his office.

"Drink?" he asked.

I couldn't resist checking my watch. It was early, even for me, and that was saying something.

"No, thanks. I'd have to go home and take a nap. I've nothing against naps, but I seem to be busy today."

"You don't mind if I do, then."

"Of course not," I said. "You're sick."

He crossed to the wet bar and got busy in the ice bucket. When he had splashed whiskey around, he turned to me.

"Do you have news for me?"

"Actually, I do. The eye has turned up for sale. It's on offer for twenty-two thousand dollars, which includes the broker's commission. Seller unknown."

"Buy it," he said, without hesitation. "I'll give you a check—or make cash available, if that's what they prefer."

"Just like that?' I wondered. "You're not even going to faint? You're willing to pay that kind of dough for something already belongs to you? It'd take me a couple years to earn that kind of money. And they'd be fat, happy years."

"I'd pay a lot more than that," he admitted. "I want this over with."

"You may have to. The people handling the sale have their own preferred client list, by the sound of it, and aren't worried about finding a buyer. They might not want to deal with a stranger, so the pot might need some sweetening. I'm assuming you aren't already a client, or this wouldn't be news to you."

"Who is it?"

"It's an old couple called Volpato, father and daughter. They have a bicycle shop on Ocean Lane—they sell expensive curiosities and magic out of the back. Genuine monkey paws and crystal balls."

He pursed his lips and shook his head. "Never heard of them. No reason I would have. I collect ancient glass, not voodoo. How did you find out about this?"

"As a matter of fact, Fin told me about it. I went to Ocean Lane and talked to the Volpatos about it. They don't actually claim to have the eye in their possession. They are representing the seller for a ten percent commission."

Gaynor's face got startled. He took a long drink from his glass, and crossed the room to fill it up again. He spoke with his back to me.

"I shouldn't like to think Fin is involved with this. He has made a great deal of money from my family over the years—he sold my father the eye about twenty years ago. He knows that it has become a family heirloom, since my aunt believes it alleviates her blindness. I don't deal well with being betrayed."

"I think he's only interested in helping you," I offered. "He's responsible for referring me to you, after all."

He turned around. His face got red, and twisted into the same angry mask I had seen the first time I met him. It was the expression of a child who is used to getting his own way, with something nasty beneath it. I wondered if he hadn't pulled the wings from a few flies in his time.

"And haven't you been a loyal, trouble-free employee, though?" he demanded. "Miss Lane has pestered me to fire you since the first day. As for Fin, he looks out for himself. He'd better watch his step around me."

I laughed, honestly amused.

"If Fin were to betray you, you wouldn't do a thing about it," I said. "Brother, you could hire all the Los Angeles tough guys you liked. It wouldn't be enough to go up against Fin, and you damn well know it. You're out of your league."

"He's nothing but an old monster," he shrugged, and made his face urbane again. "I've never liked him. Tell me—if these bicycle shop people are acting as brokers, who is the actual seller?"

I decided to keep the young woman Volpato had described close to my vest. If I told him I suspected Wanda, he would storm over to his mother's house to confront her. I wasn't ready for that.

"I've no idea," I shrugged. "Staying anonymous is the whole point of employing a middle man. We're not likely to ever find that out."

There was a sound at the door. It opened, and Eleanor Lane lounged against the jamb. Her hair dry, she had gotten dressed. She looked like a minor movie star. I didn't know how long she had been standing there, listening.

"Here's Miss Lane now," Gaynor announced, just as though I couldn't see her. "Shall I have her make a check, or is cash better?"

"Definitely cash," I said. "No offense, but I don't think these people will take your check. Like I said, I'd also be prepared to sweeten the deal a little. If the Volpatos have more than one offer, they are going to sell to a preferred client before they deal with an unknown."

He thought about it, nodded, and told Eleanor to arrange with the bank to have thirty thousand dollars in cash available the following day. The amount made me whistle.

"I just want this done with," he said. "I'm tired of the whole thing."

"It won't actually be done until I find out who killed Beatrice Stone."

"That's your business, Crowe," he said. "I couldn't care less about that. She shouldn't have started this whole thing."

"She got what she deserved? That your take on this?" I swallowed a lump of hate.

Eleanor stepped away from the doorway, into the room. She held one hand up, like the world's most elegant traffic cop.

"Let's not argue, gentlemen. Could I make a suggestion, darling?" She paused for effect, cast blue eyes first at him, then at me. I knew she wanted me to notice the 'darling', and be aware of her as more than just Gaynor's secretary.

"If this turns into a bidding war, you know you'll pay whatever it takes. If this glass eye is really so valuable, there's no telling how high the offers might go. Why not remove all doubt, before it even has a chance to get started? Offer fifty thousand dollars."

"Fifty thousand?" The amount wiped the nonchalant off Gaynor's face. "That's an absurd amount of money."

She crossed to stand in front of him, hipshot, and laid a hand on his shoulder. I felt as though I wasn't there.

"I'm tired of hearing you fret about this, darling," she purred. "It's taking your mind off more important things. If you're going to go that high anyway, why not make an offer they'll accept on the spot?"

He went silent for a moment, and then took a deep breath. He sounded as though he was surfacing from a deep dive. She stroked his hair, not caring that I saw her do it.

"Very well," he said. "Fifty thousand—plus five to the Volpatos for commission. We'll arrange things with the bank in the morning." He spoke as if it was a done deal, and peered at me, as if he were suddenly unsure of me handling so much money for him. "You'll communicate the offer, and handle payment?"

I said that I would, and stood up to leave. I wanted to get out of there before she pulled his robe off. At the door, I remembered something and turned back.

"Would you let your mother know I'll be out to her place for a visit?" I asked. "Today or tomorrow."

"Whatever for?"

"I want a word with Wanda Rice," I answered. "I don't necessarily want her to know I'm coming."

"I'll telephone Mother and tell her you'll be around tomorrow afternoon." He waved me off, not interested. I didn't much blame him. "She doesn't like surprises."

Out in the hallway, no sooner had the door closed gently behind me than I heard something being knocked over inside. I figured Gaynor had his robe off already. I did my best not to break into a canter on my way to the front door.

-Twenty-Three-

On Doctor Gardiner's birthday, we surprised him with an afternoon at Montelindo Park racetrack. We sat in wicker chairs perched high above the turf in the Hummingbird Club. The green oval below us stretched out empty, in the way that racetracks do between their brief, hysterical bursts of activity.

"You have to be a member to sit here," the doctor said, rather proudly. "They don't just let anyone in."

I looked around appreciatively. There were potted plants, and most of the women wore sunhats with ridiculous brims. It was a lot nicer than where I usually sat, down in the grandstand with my feet in a puddle of spilled beer.

"Swell place," I nodded. "How long have you been a member?"

"We aren't members," Mrs. Gardiner interrupted. "Annie is."

I stared at Annie, surprised. She had never mentioned any kind of interest in horse racing. She ignored me, watching the fountain in the infield. A waiter approached our table.

"Have a martini," Doctor Gardiner suggested. "We have plenty of time before the first race."

"I don't much care for them," I said. "I'd as soon stick to bourbon."

"They are an acquired taste," the doctor said. "Like so many things."

"One always starts with a martini here," Mrs. Gardiner said. "It's customary. Custom is very important at an old club like this one."

The waiter stood with poised pencil, resigned to waiting for as long as it took. I surrendered. I didn't want a martini, but it would be easier to drink one than talk any more about it. "Dry," I said. "Dry as you can manage." He nodded, wrote it down, and looked at her.

"I'm going to skip the martini," she told him, very seriously. "I'll have a glass of wine. I'll let you determine the color."

They regarded each other, pleased by her daring. The doctor ordered his usual vermouth martini, with a splash of gin. Annie asked for a small glass of water, without ice. I knew she wouldn't touch it. The waiter nodded and moved off.

"The Mariposa Stakes is next month." Mrs. Gardiner stared meaningfully at Annie. "It's exactly like the Kentucky Derby, except it's not in Kentucky. We have time to have bonnets made, if we do it now."

"I won't be here next month," Annie said. "I'll be home in Mexico. I've overstayed my time here. It isn't safe. I can feel my invisibility fading."

"Such a shame—now I'm sad." The old woman shook her head, and looked at me. "Does that mean your case is nearly solved? Are you leaving, too?"

"It isn't really much of a case at this point," I said, and hesitated. I had already told her almost everything about the body in my hotel room bathtub. I didn't keep scraping out a living at what I did by being a blabbermouth, but somehow, I usually ended up discussing cases over drinks with Mrs. Gardiner. It wasn't just because she was Annie's mother. I had confided in her before I became aware they were related, and somehow her odd insights always managed to get stuck things in my mind free.

"Of course, it's a case," Annie murmured. "An important one."

"Are you still planning to be arrested for murdering that poor girl?" Mrs. Gardiner wondered.

"Not at all," I said. "The police aren't treating me, or anyone else, as a suspect. They've closed the case. They don't care who killed her, and that's part of the problem."

"Then why are you still involved?"

"We're just being paid to broker a sale," I said. "The stolen glass eye has been offered to a dealer. The Gaynor family is sending me with a satchel full of money to recover what belongs to them."

"They are going to buy back what got stolen from them?" the doctor wondered. "How strange."

"It isn't about justice for them," I said. "They don't want the publicity. The eye was stolen by them in the first place, from a tomb in Egypt. It isn't the only thing they own that probably belongs in a pyramid, or a museum in Cairo. They have a big collection. A family like that can't afford the gossip."

"Most society people here are criminals," Mrs. Gardiner announced, loud enough for the silk crowd at the neighboring tables to hear. "They are successful thieves and swindlers from other places, hiding out and pretending to be cultured. Unless one is here to pick oranges or star in motion pictures, there's no other reason to come to California."

"I'm a criminal," Annie reminded her. "So are you."

"Of course, we are, dear." She put a fond hand on her daughter's arm. "We aren't thieves, though."

At the paddock entrance, a rider in a red coat raised a bugle and called the horses to post. After a moment, they emerged in single file, the horses numbered and colored, their jockeys in matching bright silks. Annie watched them, captivated. Her mouth moved, nearly imperceptibly. She talked to herself, or to someone we couldn't see.

"My client got murdered for the eye," I said. "She stole it from the Gaynors, and someone stole it from her before she could collect any ransom for returning it. Logically, whoever is offering it for sale now is her killer. That's why I'm still involved."

"That makes perfect sense," Mrs. Gardiner agreed. "When you find out who it is, you should arrest them, or shoot them."

A woman in a dark blue dress made her way through the tables at the opposite end of the club. She wore an elaborate bonnet to match. The somber color caught my eye, as odd among the bright pastel florals as a crow in a gathering of hummingbirds. When she turned her face toward us, it startled me. It was Beatrice Stone, or her twin. She didn't appear any more dead than anyone else in the room. I stood up to watch as she melted into the crowd.

"Somebody's keeping an eye on you," Annie murmured. The expression on her face told me she had seen the apparition, too. "Don't worry, she isn't real."

"That explains it, then," I muttered. "If she isn't real, then there's nothing to be worried about. I'm just hallucinating."

"I saw her, too." She put comforting fingers on my wrist, pulled me back into my chair, and turned my hand over to hold it. "We're having hallucinations together."

Shook up, I picked up my martini glass with the other hand and drained it. Luckily, the waiter passed by and I signalled him for another.

"You see?" the doctor commented, clearly approving. "You like it, after all. Martinis are the perfect thing, once you've gotten used to them."

Annie excused herself and wandered off, a drift of white. I thought she might be headed off to confront the apparition, but I knew better than to object or to follow her. Annie moved to her own music, and to interfere was a good way to lose her. To my great relief, she went in the opposite direction from the space the dark-dressed woman had disappeared into. She headed for the discreet betting windows situated along the far wall.

"How can you have a client who got murdered?" Mrs. Gardiner wondered. "How can you get paid anything, if your client is dead?"

"It's hard to explain, even to myself."

I would be surprised if anyone paid me a nickel. If I stirred up enough trouble, I'd probably have to leave town.

"Someone will pay him, I expect," Annie said, returning from the betting window. "When you do the right thing, there's usually a happy ending."

"I'm starting to believe the killer is someone who loved her," I said. "All the signs are pointing in one direction—I just don't know why. It makes no sense."

"When something makes no sense, it's almost always about love," Mrs. Gardiner remarked. "Remember that. Your mystery is likely about love."

"*Cherchez la femme,*" the doctor interrupted. "That's what they say. Forget about love. *Cherchez la femme.*"

"What a lot of nonsense," the old woman protested. "You're stuck in the last century."

"One doesn't rule out the other," Annie offered. "It might be both."

The waiter settled things by arriving with another round. He also brought a miniature frosted cake on a tray, with a candle stuck in it. The doctor made a show of blowing out the tiny flame. Mrs. Gardiner clapped, and Annie leaned over to kiss his cheek.

Out on the track, number eight, a filly named Dreaming Always, came in by a nose. Annie presented the doctor with his birthday present, the winning ticket she had just acquired at the betting window. My third martini tasted just grand. All in all, it became a nearly perfect afternoon.

~*~

I needed to talk to Wanda Rice. I went out to the Gaynor estate in Montelindo by myself. Annie was painting by the pool in her backyard, and gave me a vague wave when I stuck my head over the fence and told her where I was headed. When I had last talked to Wanda at Bea's funeral, we had been by ourselves, and I figured it might be best to stick with that.

The electric gate slid open just as if it expected me, and I piloted my sedan into the expanse of English garden that fronted the estate. The grass had been freshly clipped, and the giant ferns stood obediently at attention. It struck me as an odd contrast with the wild mess of spider plants inside the conservatory where the two residents spent most of their days. It was none of my business, though, and I didn't waste a lot of time wondering about it.

The blue-black Lasalle had been parked in the turnaround near the front door. Herb Robinson sat on the running board, smoking a cigarette. When my car came into view, he stood up in a hurry and got busy polishing a fender.

"Relax," I said, when I got out of the Ford. "It's only me. Just more hired help, come to call on the gentry."

He regarded me warily, and didn't answer. His open manner the last time we had met was gone.

"Heard your brother won rookie of the year," I said. "Pretty big deal—must make you proud."

"He don't talk to me much," he muttered. "Never did."

I got out my smokes and waved the package in his direction. He shook his head. I couldn't figure the sullenness. The last time we met I couldn't get him to shut up.

"I've been meaning to have a talk with you," I said. "I expect everyone knows I'm working a case for the Gaynors, and that their private secretary was found dead in my bathtub."

"She wasn't no private secretary when you found her," he said.

"No, she wasn't. She lived rough, on lower State Street, and had been for a while. That's why nobody cares who killed her. I care, though. You knew her, when she worked here. What can you tell me about her? What got her fired?"

He pointed at the LaSalle, and held out the polishing rag like a piece of evidence. "I drive Mister Gaynor to his office when he doesn't feel like doing it himself. I drive his mother where she wants to go, which is nowhere. She almost never leaves this house. I keep the cars clean and spit-shined. I don't know anything about what goes on with these folks."

"You knew Miss Stone, though. You must have. Did you get along with her?"

"She was a nice young lady. She was sad, though. She carried a burden before she ever came here, and she took it with her when she left. Some folks are just born to be sad."

"So, she was a nice young woman, and a sad one. Someone hurt her, though—they stuck her in a bathtub in a strange motel room and drowned her. Who wanted to hurt her?"

He puffed up and took a step forward. The whites of his eyes showed, and I thought he might be ready to slug me. I didn't react. All at once, he spun and hurled the wet rag at the LaSalle. It smacked the door and fell to the ground. He gave me a final glare and stalked off, disappearing around the side of the house.

I saw no profit in following him, so I went up the steps and rang the bell. A servant I hadn't seen before opened up. She stared at me without saying anything. I took it as permission and followed her inside. I knew the way to the conservatory, and got there without her help.

"I certainly hope you've brought me the eye," Olive Gaynor called out. "We don't appreciate uninvited company."

"Your son said he would telephone you," I said, crossing the stone floor to where she sat. The spider plants seemed more cloying than the last time, a jungle that nearly clocked the light from the glass roof overhead. "I spoke with him about it yesterday."

"My son informing me of your plans, and my agreeing to issue you an invitation are two entirely different things. Surely you see that."

The sparrow in the gold cage cheeped, and the blind woman touched the slender bars as if to quiet it down. It surprised me to see it still alive. It occurred to me that it might be a different one, and I found myself not wanting to know.

"I'm working for you, Mrs. Gaynor. This isn't a social visit. I can't wait around on the off-chance you might invite me here."

"What do you want?" she snapped. "Get to the point."

"As your son likely explained to you when he called, I need a private word with your maid. She may have information I need, whether she realizes it or not."

"Out of the question," she said. "I won't allow it."

"If you want me to locate the missing eye…"

"Stop it," she hissed. "Do you think I'm entirely stupid? Do you imagine my son keeps things from me? The eye has been located. It's been listed for sale in some trashy pawnshop. My son has chosen you as the errand boy to ferry our money to buy back what belongs to us—nothing more. How dare you come around here asking to badger my employees?"

Clearly shaken, she poured herself a glass of sherry and tilted it to her lips. Her color was high, and I noticed again what a handsome woman she was. Good breeding, I imagined.

"This interview is over," she said. "I don't care for you, Mister Crowe. I didn't like you the first time I met you. My husband would never have allowed a private detective in our home, let alone a crass, cavalier one like you. I care less for the strange woman you brought in here, uninvited."

"One of your employees got murdered. The person who did it might well be living under this roof. It's almost certainly the same person who is selling the eye back to you. Once the sale is complete, the trail will disappear. The guilty party will run, but with over forty thousand dollars cash, they will be able to vanish before you realize they've gone."

"There was no murder, Mister Crowe. If you're referring to the degenerate who used to be my assistant, she lived a life that was bound to end with her dead in the gutter. The police aren't after any murderer. This is your invention."

Her arrogance made me angry. I was tired of rich people.

"The police having an open case doesn't decide whether something happened or not. A young woman is dead, and it's because of your goddamned eye."

"We don't expect to see you here again, Mister Crowe," she pronounced. "Do your job, and deliver the money. Then go away. Do you know your way out, or shall I ring for someone to show you?"

I knew my way out. Nobody met me in the long hallway, or the grand entrance hall. Out front, the LaSalle had disappeared, leaving my shabby black Ford all alone on the circular drive. Someone had an elbow hung out the open passenger window.

"Get yourself thrown out?" Wanda Rice asked when I got in. She wore her black-and-white uniform and a hostile expression.

"You could say that. I came here to talk to you, actually."

"I heard you say that to them," she said. I must have looked surprised, because she curled her lip. "Didn't see me in there? Good domestic help is invisible. It's one of our hallmarks, didn't you know that?"

We both stared straight ahead, at a hedge in front of the car, as if we were driving too fast and about to crash into the greenery.

"You don't like me much, do you?" I asked.

"Why should I like you?" She glanced over at me. She seemed genuinely surprised by the question. "I don't like you, as a matter of fact—not that you mean anything to me. You're smug. You put yourself above all the nonsense that the rest of us muddle around in."

"Maybe I've given up on trying to figure any of it out," I said. "Maybe what strikes you as smug is just—tired. For the record, I don't like you much, either. I'm not sure what Beatrice saw in you."

Her eyes got stung, as if she was cutting onions, and she looked back at the hedge. I felt instantly bad for saying it. I had no reason to. Maybe I felt bothered more than I wanted to admit by her dislike.

"You strike me as honest, though," I said. "I'm going to be straight with you. Do you have the glass eye? Is it you offering it for sale through Volpato and Daughter?"

"That's absurd," she spat. "Through what—daughter?"

"More to the point—did you, accidentally or not, kill Beatrice Stone?"

The slap stung my cheek and rang loud bells in my ear. I caught her wrists as she scrabbled for the door handle. She had pulled my left hand to her mouth before I realized she intended to bite it.

"Wait!" I hollered. "Hear me out! I'm trying to help her!" She struggled wildly. My hand was slick with spit, and I slipped it free. "If you cared about her, listen to what I have to say."

It got through to her, because she released my other hand and twisted quickly away, her back against the door. She glared at me through a veil of hair that had come unpinned. Her face had gotten red, and I could smell her perspiration.

"I don't give a damn about the eye," I said. "Listen to me. All I'm going to do is carry a satchel of cash to the person who has it, make the exchange, and the whole business can go to hell. There's a damn good likelihood, however, that whoever hands me that piece of glass killed Bea, and I'm not going to let that go. Volpato says he's dealing with a young woman, and you're the young woman who fits the bill. If it's you, you're better to tell me now."

"Nobody has that eye!" she shouted. "She hid it. If she were going to give it to anyone, it would have been me. She didn't, because she asked and I wouldn't take it. She hid it where she could get to it later. She knew the streets, and nobody's ever going to find it."

"Well, a young woman seems to be offering to sell it."

"Nonsense. Nobody has it. It's gone with her to the grave. I guarantee it." She sat and glowered at me. I had a good instinct for the truth, but I had no idea if she was telling it, so I felt flummoxed. I had been certain I would break the case with this conversation, and I just seemed to have deepened the mystery. I didn't have much else to say to her.

"Was she ever happy?" I wondered, for no reason.

"She was happy with me." She wiped a tear away angrily. "She was happy with her job at Darling's. She came here to be a movie star, but she would have been happy working there forever. All the nice things, all the customers who dressed well and smelled good. She wanted a small house for the two of us, and a job at Darling's—nothing more."

"I heard she had some trouble there."

"She worked the cosmetics counter when she moved out here, and loved it. Someone complained they smelled liquor on her breath, but nothing got proved. They moved her to glassware, and the same thing happened so they let her go. I got her the job here."

"You knew her before she worked here?"

"Yes, we met..." She visibly changed her mind about telling me. "It doesn't matter. I knew her, and recommended her to the Gaynors. For a little while it worked out, but then their spies found out about us, and the bitch fired her. Once she left, she drank more and things went downhill. She felt sure she could get her old job at Darling's back, but they wouldn't even let her in the door."

"Not even as a customer?"

"They accused her of shoplifting, and told her never to come back. She couldn't stay away. They didn't want a woman like her wandering the aisles, so they stopped her every single time she went in."

"Seems to me she would have learned to stay away."

"No—that isn't how she saw it. She loved the place more than anywhere else in the world. She talked constantly about how she would turn things around and get her old job back, and eventually be promoted to department manager. I got tired of hearing about it, and told her so. Now I wish I hadn't been so mean."

In the rear-view mirror, I saw Herb Robinson wander around the corner of the house, and stare at my car. He did a double take when he saw who sat in the passenger seat, and quickly reversed direction, out of sight.

"She was supposed to take care of the two of us," Wanda said. "In the end, she couldn't even take care of herself."

I played my hunch again. "Did you play any part in what happened to her? Because she betrayed you? It would be understandable."

"Betrayed me?" Her expression got bitter. She shook her head, and barked a small laugh. "She didn't betray me. I betrayed her."

"I'm sure you didn't…" I started. The look on her face shut me up.

"That old bitch found out about us, and fired Bea. She gave me a choice, or she would fire me, too. She would expose me and make sure I didn't find another job."

"What choice? What are you talking about?"

She barked a laugh "What do you think I am to Olive Gaynor? Just her maid? I'm her—lover."

I did my best not to let my mouth gape open.

"I need this job," she said. "Where would I go? What would I do? Do you think I should end up like Beatrice? As a whore? Strolling the streets? Olive was—insistent, and I let her insist. I gave in, without any kind of fight. I still do."

I felt stunned. I couldn't imagine giving in to such a thing, but I knew it happened all the time. If she had inserted a male employer into the story, I wouldn't have raised an eyebrow. Something stunk about that, but I couldn't make it clear in my own head. Beside me, Wanda stiffened and hunched her shoulders.

"I told her," she said, in a near whisper. "I punished her with it. Bea knew what the choice was, and what I did. It just about killed her. If she ever had any hope for any kind of happiness, I ended it."

Suddenly, she yanked the door handle and got out. After she gave it a good slam, she leaned in the open window and glared at me.

"Do you understand? I gave her what she wanted, and I still do."

After she spun away, I turned in my seat to watch her march up the steps to the front door. When she had gone in, I sat and stared at the hedge. This changed everything. The trouble was, I had no clue what it changed it into. After a few minutes, I thumbed the starter switch and the engine came to life.

"Oh, brother," I said.

-Twenty-Four-

I sat with Annie beside the swimming pool in her back yard. It was nearly dark. The pool had been lined with dark rock, and the lessening light made the water black. A rubberized blow-up mattress floated in one end. It had been made to look like a pink flamingo.

"Is that thing big enough for two people?" I asked.

"Why?" She ate sunflower seeds from a bowl, slipping the kernels from shell to tongue as neatly and elegantly as she did everything else.

"I thought we could pack light, and take it around the world," I said. "Stop in strange places, and pretend to speak different languages. Maybe never come back."

"Maybe never come back," she echoed. She nodded, and watched the floating pink raft. "We could throw popcorn off the stern, so we'd have a trail to follow back if we wanted to."

"Good idea," I agreed. "Just in case."

"Just in case," she nodded. "Remind me, forever."

Her eyes were luminous. I watched her, trying to memorize her face. That funny thing about Annie struck me again, that she never looked exactly the same to me twice. I told her about Wanda's assertion that nobody had the eye. Beatrice had hidden it somewhere only she would ever know about, and it was still on the loose.

"Now you don't think that the young woman dealing with Volpato and Daughter is Wanda?" she asked. "You've changed your mind."

"Wanda is aggressive and often unpleasant," I said. "She isn't lying, though. I have a nose for it."

"You do, don't you?" She smiled at me, full force. "I don't lie, and that's one of the things you love about me."

"One of them," I agreed. "Even if it makes things harder sometimes. If Wanda says she doesn't have the eye, isn't the young woman the Volpatos are dealing with, and had nothing to do with Bea's murder, I tend to believe her."

"Then who is the young woman? She has to be someone."

"I haven't a clue," I said. "I also trust Wanda's instinct that the eye is still missing, whether this woman is offering it to highest bidder or not."

"How can Volpato and Daughter be brokering a sale for it?" she wondered. "They have a perfect reputation. They wouldn't offer the sale if they weren't convinced they represented the real article."

"Anyone can make a mistake," I shrugged. "If the money's easy enough. If she says she has it, they're probably taking her at her word."

It was fully dark now. Fireflies began to flash, green-yellow sparks in the far corner of Annie's yard. I lived right next door, and never saw them in mine. I had rarely been here in the evening when they weren't putting on a private show for Annie.

"So where is the eye, if nobody has it? It has to be somewhere."

"Bea had nobody to trust with it," I said. "She might have loved Wanda, but Wanda lived in the Gaynor's house, and had betrayed her once. Her room at the Schooner Inn wasn't safe, and even if she trusted Charles Martellus to hold it, his room was no better. She could hardly afford to rent a safe-deposit box at the bank."

"What about the thousand dollars she got from Gaynor as a ransom down payment? Nobody could have burned through that much money so fast."

"That's a good question. I suspect she gave some of it to Wanda. She might have been robbed. In any event, I don't think she would have asked for more if she was still flush. She wasn't the type."

"If she had nowhere safe to keep it, and nobody she trusted to hold it for her, she hid it." Annie sounded certain. "It's the only possibility. She hid it somewhere that only she knew about."

"But where?" I wondered. "She practically lived on the street. She would have had to hide it in a public place. Did she bury it on the courthouse lawn? Cover it with sand at the beach?"

"How do I hide?" she asked. "In plain sight. I live in my house, and I drive the same color Mercury convertible that burned up in the crash. It would never occur to anyone that I died in a burning car. I hide in plain sight. Everyone can see me, but nobody looks. Where did she like to go? What was her favorite place?"

"I don't think she had any favorite places," I said. "She lived a hard life. The Schooner Inn represented a place to sleep, and to bring customers. Everywhere public is dangerous for a woman like her. I can't imagine her being fond of the beach or a particular neighborhood. She had no car, and no way of getting out of town."

I had a sudden thought.

"Wanda told me Bea loved Darling's department store. She used to work there. It represented the kind of life she wanted, and lost. She liked to go in there and wander the aisles. The store watchman threw her out every time she went in—had her marked as a shoplifter, and threatened her with the police every time he caught her, if she ever came back. She always did, anyway."

"I don't imagine the police scared her very much," she remarked. "Once you've been frightened badly enough, it takes more than the police to keep you away from a place you need to be."

She talked about herself as much as Beatrice Stone, and I hated the sadness in her voice.

"What department did she work in?"

"Cosmetics," I said. "She got let go for drinking on the job. Wait a second—they gave her a second chance, and transferred her to—"

We stared at each other.

"—glassware," I finished.

"Glassware," she echoed, and nodded.

~*~

Through my open office window, I heard sirens coming down State Street. They got louder and then growled to a stop across the street. Something was going on at the Schooner Inn. Something always went on there, so after a cursory glance at the pair of black-and-white radio cars pulled onto the sidewalk, I went back to what I was doing.

I sketched Krazy Kat on a yellow pad. It didn't look much like him, and I figured I needed a sharper pencil. Undeterred, I balled the drawing up and started a new one. I sketched the mystery woman dealing the Volpatos, to see if it looked like Wanda. I had a hunch the person didn't have the eye. Maybe she thought she knew where it was, could make a deal with a buyer, and come up with it in time to collect.

There were footsteps out in the hallway, the waiting room door banged open, and Rex Raines stuck his head into my office.

"Filing your nails again, Crowe? You should get a secretary to watch your office, so you can go out sleuthing from time to time."

"I had a secretary, once. She didn't stick around very long."

"Imagine that. Know a guy named Charles Martellus? You sent him to me a few days ago, and I took a report from him."

I said that I did, and realized with a start that I'd forgotten about him. I had been so sure of Wanda's guilt, I hadn't paid much attention when he last called me. He might hold the key to the whole thing.

"I've been meaning to get over and talk to him, but I got busy. He thought he recognized a woman he saw break into Beatrice Stone's room right after she got killed."

"You got busy," he nodded. "Good thing you've got us civil service types to take reports on closed cases for you."

"He tell you anything useful?"

"Didn't amount to much. He saw a good-looking number in a tan raincoat, the kind that belts tight at the waist, come out of the room across the hall from him. Then he spotted her again. She wore a scarf over hair. Whole lot of attractive women in this town—you could put a raincoat and scarf on any one of them and they'd make a fine line-up. Besides, he was a drinker. No judge would ever listen to his testimony, even if he caught someone in the act."

"I still need to talk to him."

"You can't—not any more. He's dead."

I swung my legs off the desk and sat up straight.

"Notice the ruckus across the street?" Raines asked. "Hotel called in an apparent homicide, about an hour ago. Found in his room."

"Somebody killed him? Over what?"

"Doubt we'll ever know, unless some honest citizen needs future considerations from us and wants to blab. Whoever killed him, robbed him. I don't have a clue what he had, but they tore his room to pieces—slashed his mattress, ripped the backing of pictures on the wall, even tore the lining on the curtains."

I picked up my hat from the desk. "This isn't any coincidence, Raines. The same person who killed Beatrice Stone searched her room, and Martellus could identify her. She either killed him because of that, or because she thought he was holding onto whatever she stole. I need to see the scene."

"Sit down." He waved me back into my chair. "There's nothing to see. It's a hotel room with a bed, a dresser, and the body of an old man. No place to hide anything. Probably no evidence, and probably no case. The Schooner is one of the roughest dives in Santa Teresa—this could all be over the price of a pack of smokes."

"Were there any witnesses?" I asked. "Did anyone see a young woman matching the general description go in or out of his room?"

"Witnesses—in the Schooner Inn?" He laughed. "Anyhow, no woman did this. Martellus was an old man, but he was no lightweight. I recall him as a pretty rough customer."

"I don't think he had an easy life."

"He got beaten to death. A strong man did it, not a woman."

"And nobody saw a damn thing."

"Oh, come on, Crowe. Does the Schooner strike you as a den of Good Samaritans? You learn to mind your business pretty quick in there. I have to say, it's pretty funny how you keep popping up in this. Beatrice Stone found dead in your bathtub, her hotel room searched. Now this Martellus fellow you send over to give a statement, beaten to death and his hotel room across the hall, his room likewise searched."

"You cops aren't interested in Beatrice Stone's murder. She's in the ground, already forgotten. Ten will get you twenty the old man will get filed and forgotten by tomorrow."

"Don't get cute with me," he snarled. "These people live risky lives."

"Not by choice, in most cases." I looked out the window. A black panel wagon had parked in front of the radio cars. The coroner moved quick today. A uniformed cop had been stationed at the front door of the hotel, keeping gawkers back. I felt suddenly sad. Martellus hadn't seemed like such a bad guy.

"Keep me posted, Crowe." Ready to leave, he reached up a hand to make sure his hat sat good and tight on his head. "I know you will, as long as it suits you."

His steps were halfway across the waiting room, when I heard them stop and come back. He stuck his head back in the office, an innocent expression pasted on, as if he had just thought of something.

"Someone told me they saw you at the racetrack," he said. "You like the ponies?"

"Now and then."

"They said you were with someone looked a lot like the Kahlo broad."

"What about it?" I shrugged. "I like the type, I guess."

He stared at me a long moment. I imagined I saw something like pity in his expression.

"You like the type," he echoed, and shook his head. "Dead is dead, Crowe. Get over her—you can't bring her back. You have enough problems."

I sketched a salute. When his footsteps were gone, I got up and closed the door behind him.

~*~

The sidewalk at the front entrance of Darling's department store was concrete, colored and poured into pink-and-green geometric patterns that made me a little dizzy. I loitered on it and waited for Annie. At a quarter to five in the afternoon, it was near enough to closing that most of the snooty clientele drifted out, headed for drinks and dinner.

The store was a landmark, anchored at the point where the seedy lower part of State Street turned to swank upper. For the California transplants, it represented an island of civilization, a reminder of back East, and a place to remind society women that they weren't from here. Even the mannequins in the front windows were higher class than the people walking past them. The big front doors were glass, polished wood, and brass. It wasn't quite Gimbels or Macy's in New York City; maybe it was better.

My elbow got touched, and Annie appeared beside me.

She wore a loose cotton number, printed black-and-white, like handwriting. Her hair had been pulled back, pinned with a small pink flower. Dark eyes and honeyed skin set her utterly apart from the flow of pale, well-dressed women leaving the store. A funny thing about Annie; it didn't make my heart go faster when I saw her. I never got breathless butterflies. Whenever she showed up the world slowed down and the air felt cool and sweet, as if I had been holding my breath without realizing it. Every time I went near her, it became a plunge into blue water, deep relief, as if I had been stuck and could now move again.

"Am I late?" she wondered.

"No such thing. We won't have much time to look around, though."

"I don't think we'll have much looking around to do," she said. "I think it will be right where we think it is."

"This is the craziest long shot I've backed in quite a while."

"I'm the craziest long shot you ever bet on." Her smile was lovely. "Everything else is a piece of cake."

Inside, the place smelled like most stores do, no matter what they sell: a peculiar mix of new fabric, frying doughnuts, and hair oil. It all came across as very expensive and tasteful. The concrete floors were polished to look like marble, and the light sconces were painted gold. A fountain flowed and sprayed in the middle of the first floor, with a wishing pool to catch any stray pennies when all the dollars were spent. The air was ten degrees cooler than outside, and full of closing time. Customers hurried, apprehensive, and employees were suddenly energetic and focused on the business of shutting things down.

The store directory had been displayed on a pillar. It told us glassware was on the second floor, and we headed for the escalators. A young woman at the perfume counter stared at us insolently as we passed.

At the top of the escalator, Annie pointed at the glassware department, straight ahead, a sparkling maze of plates, bowls and glasses. Past the shelves of brandy snifters and champagne flutes, a display of decorations and knickknacks gleamed. I followed her straight to it, and stared at the hundreds of tiny colored elephants and horses, miniature flower vases and bottles.

"There it is," Annie said, almost right away, and pointed at the corner of a middle shelf.

The pinkish ball sat innocuously between a crystal lotus flower and a cut-glass ashtray, appearing as though it had a perfect right to be there. It appeared slightly rough, and not perfectly round, but even so had a certain genuine authority. She picked it up and weighed it in her palm.

"I don't think anyone even saw it," she said. "It was probably invisible."

"It might as well have been invisible," I agreed. "She left it right in plain sight. Nobody would ever buy it. If anyone picked it up, it doesn't even have a price tag."

A uniformed watchman strolled by, and eyed us incuriously.

"We're closing in five minutes, folks. Have to ask you to finish up—cashiers don't like to stay a minute past their shift. You know how it is."

He smiled to take the offense from his remark. He was an older fellow, undoubtedly a retired cop stretching his pension. I nodded to let him know we were agreeable. Annie held the eye up. The orb appeared dull, with a black blemish floating beneath the surface. It looked like translucent stone.

"Egyptian glass," Annie murmured. "Isn't it beautiful? The Egyptians were the first to discover how to make it, and the best. Look—it's alive."

The more I watched it, the more the glass appeared to be a living eye. I didn't want to handle it; I had the idea it might be warm to the touch.

"Let's pay for it, and get out of here," I muttered. "The sooner this is over with, the happier I am."

"Pay for it?" she asked. "It's not for sale, in the first place. Even if it was, there's no price tag on it. They won't know what to do at a cash register. They'll call a manager."

"So, put a price tag on it." I checked the other items on the shelf. "We'll pick a nice, expensive one, so nobody will think twice."

"No." She sounded definite, and touched my arm to stop me. "We can't buy it. Money can't change hands. I can't explain it to you—we just can't."

"What are we supposed to do then? I'm not going to pocket it." I pointed my chin toward the uniformed guard, loitering nearby. "Not in front of him."

I needed to think fast. The eye wasn't Darling's regular merchandise, and we weren't going to get past the cash register without drawing attention I didn't want. The cashier would undoubtedly call a manager for instructions. With the security guard hovering, anxious for us to leave the store, I couldn't risk slipping the eye into a pocket. A shoplifting charge might get Annie identified, and end up with her in the gas chamber.

"Put it back, Annie." I made up my mind. "We'll have to come back for it."

She raised an eyebrow, but didn't comment. I picked up a snow globe, and examined it. Inside the globe, a miniature pine-covered island floated in a puddle of blue. The globe's base had been lettered: *Echo Island.* I shook it until the tiny snowflakes whirled.

"Now," I murmured.

She slid the glass eye back onto the shelf beside the crystal lotus. It made a gentle clink. I lifted the snow globe to the light, to show her. She gasped with feigned delight.

"It's wonderful," she exclaimed. "My mother will love it."

"It's settled then," I said, loud enough for the watchman to hear. "The perfect gift. Let's find the cashier and then get out of here." He nodded as we passed, already forgetting us before we were gone from sight.

We paid for the snow globe, and joined the final trickle of customers headed for the street. I steered Annie down one side of the steps, and stopped her in front of an inconspicuous wooden door set to one side of the grand entrance. 'Security' had been spelled out at eye level, in plain black paint. I tried the door. I found it as unlocked as I expected it to be, and I slipped in behind Annie and pulled it closed behind me.

A metal desk, a swivel chair, and a cabinet on rollers filled up the room. The wall sported a duty log and a pin-up calendar from last year. A faint odor of cigars and stale coffee filled the space. Faint light came from a small window high up in one wall.

"We'll wait in here until the store is closed," I said. "Then we'll go get the eye, and let ourselves out."

"Isn't this exactly the wrong place to wait?"

"It's exactly the right place to wait," I smiled. "A night watchman routine is the same everywhere, so it's easy to figure out. The managers stay an hour late to count their tills. Cleaners will run mops, and stock clerks will be busy in the shelves, making sure the store is ready to open tomorrow. The watchman will be busy for that hour, checking doors and windows, and then he'll let them all out. When they've gone, he'll settle in here with a newspaper and a flask of coffee, but not until then. Between now and six, this is the one place in the building he won't be."

"I'll take your word for it," she said. "It sounds like an exciting adventure. I have candy, to pass the time."

She sat behind the desk and rummaged in her bag, looking for something. She pulled out a silk scarf and a Colt New Service revolver and laid them on the desk, out of her way. She found a roll of cinnamon Lifesavers and thumbed one free for me. The lozenge made a tiny burn on my tongue.

"I see you got yourself another gun," I said.

"You keep losing mine," she answered, unperturbed. I had slid her last murder weapon under Joey O'Meaney's car. "Between ruined Mercury convertibles and lost pistols, running around with you is expensive. I like this Colt, though. I should have switched to a bigger gun a long time ago."

I didn't have much doubt she had gotten this latest weapon from Danny López, and I mentally cursed him.

"Keep it in your bag, Annie. We have enough trouble."

"There's no such thing as enough trouble."

Her laugh made a small shiver in my chest.

-Twenty-Five-

We sat together in the shadowy office, and didn't say much. The sunlight up in the tiny window stayed bright, even if it struggled to come inside. I passed the time looking at the pin-up calendar. Annie stared at things I couldn't see.

Just after six o'clock, there came a flurry of noise. Voices and footsteps told me that the last employees were being escorted out the front door. Then came silence, and I knew the watchman would make his final rounds before he settled into the office for the night. He might do a cursory walk around in the small hours of the morning, but for the most part he would read the funnies and snooze. It was time to go.

We left the office. Outside the front door glass, the late afternoon sun still glared. Inside, the store was mostly dark. Single bulbs here and there struggled with the gloom. I eased the latch shut, and we headed for the escalators. Upstairs, there were no windows, and we paused to allow our eyes to adjust to the gloom. Occasional electric bulbs made counters glow, providing the only illumination.

I followed Annie through the wide hallways. The departed crowd had left behind the odors of cigarette smoke and perfume, and we moved through their ghosts. The glassware department glimmered in front of us. Annie went directly to the right shelf, plucked up the Egyptian glass and held it up toward me, like she was offering it.

"Let's be done with this," she said. "Let's take the eye, and go back to Mexico. We'll never come back."

It was the closest Annie had ever come to speaking of a future with me. The temptation to take her hand and run for the border became sudden and enormous. I shook it off.

"Somebody is going to get away with murder if we just leave," I said. "This eye is bait, and whoever takes it is almost certainly Beatrice Stone's killer. I can't just leave things this way."

She gave me a glance that was unbearably sad, shrugged and put the eye into her bag.

"We play the rest of the game holding four aces," I said. "We know whoever is selling the eye doesn't have it, because we do. We're going into this holding both the eye, and Gaynor's ransom money. Whoever shows up to collect is Bea's killer, and almost certainly beat Charles Martellus to death. Once that's resolved, we're done."

"Something terrible is on the way," she insisted. "We're both going to die."

"We're not going to die, Annie. It will be over soon— probably within the next day or so. Then we'll leave."

"I don't care about any of it." She shook her head. "We're in danger, the bad kind, and the eye belongs to Anput. It has to get back to her."

"You're going to take it to Egypt?" I smiled at the thought.

"No. You're going to take it to the river, and throw it in. The river will carry it back."

"Whatever you say."

"I do say." She gave me a sad, contained sort of smile. "Some things I already know."

"Let's get out of here," I said. "We'll have to leave the front door unlocked. Someone will find it and assume the watchman forgot to lock it. I hope we don't get the poor bastard fired."

We retraced our steps, down the escalator to the front door. I twisted the big latch, which gave with a startling thump. I froze and put a finger to my lips. After a long moment, the coast still seemed to be clear. The guard still wandered somewhere in the depths of the huge store, likely on another floor. I pushed on the door, but found it solidly shut. After a moment, I saw why. There was a second lock higher up, the kind that needed a key. We were locked in.

"We'll have to find another way out," I said. "We can probably go upstairs, and use a fire escape."

"Why would we leave?" Annie asked. "We have the whole night, and the whole place to ourselves. Let's play."

"I don't want to get arrested," I said. In fact, everything that put Annie close to a brush with the law was dangerous. She walked the streets of Santa Teresa with impunity, convinced of her invisibility, but if she got picked up on a break-and-enter, certainly someone at the police station would recognize her. Her face was too memorable.

"We won't get arrested," she said. "The cards say there's trouble ahead for us, and the cards won't let us miss it. Tonight, I want to play."

She pulled me back up the steps and into the deserted store. Here and there, mannequins stared accusingly at us. From the direction of the escalators, the sound of hard black shoes echoed from the marble floor. We ducked behind a pillar, to wait until the watchman passed. Enough light filtered in to see by, but a flashlight beam bobbed around, probably giving the man a sense of his own security and authority in the darkened, empty building.

"He won't be back," I said, when the footsteps were gone. "I've done the job. He'll be in an office, reading the funny papers and drinking from a flask until morning."

"Time to go, then," she said. "Let's explore."

We passed a darkened confection counter, and Annie stopped. She rummaged some coins from her bag, left them beside the empty register, and picked out a small bag of cinnamon red-hots. As we walked away, she popped one into my mouth.

"You see? We have everything we need."

She pulled me by the hand to the fountain, still running in the dark. The splashing seemed loud. In the daytime hubbub, you didn't hear it at all. We sat together on the rim.

"I have money, you know. Enough for both of us to live on. That's not the problem."

"That's not the problem," I agreed. "I couldn't live off your money, though."

"I just never thought about not being alone," she said. "That's the problem."

"You aren't alone now."

"That's true," she mused. "I talk to you twenty-four-seven, and I see you when I dream. Do you believe me?"

"I do the same." I thought about it. Annie colored my world. Even when I wasn't with her or thinking about her, I was with her and thinking about her.

Forty feet away, a herd of white mannequins had frozen, showing off their new clothes. The shadows rendered things colorless, but one of them wore a dark dress and matching hat that might have been navy blue. Something in her posture seemed familiar to me, for no reason I could have put a finger on.

"There's a 'nine' on my kitchen calendar, written in pencil." Her hand tightened on my arm. "I'm not the fainting type, but something terrible is about to happen."

I didn't know what a nine in pencil meant, but I had learned that when Annie read her peculiar tea leaves out loud she didn't explain them. From the corner of my eye, I caught movement in the gloom. The mannequin in the blue dress had shifted from one side of the group to the other. I was sure of it. Mannequins were made of wire and plaster. They didn't move by themselves, but this one had.

"I don't feel good about this," she said, again. "I told you—something terrible is going to happen."

"It's going to be all right."

"Remember what you promised me."

I put an arm around her. The light from the fountain rippled. The blue-dress mannequin had gone, as vanished as if it never been there. Maybe it hadn't.

Annie spoke under her breath, like an incantation.

"Don't die first."

She shifted herself on the fountain edge, and turned into me. The kisses started. After what seemed like hours, she stood up and pulled me to my feet. Without letting go of my hand, she led us deeper into the store, until we reached the furniture and bedding section. She stopped us beside a display bed, and in one graceful motion pulled her cotton shift over her head. It floated to the floor.

She was glorious. Annie was always a miracle to me, but tonight she presented herself by turns fragrant and regal, then savage and elemental. Ancient and brand new, she took my imagination by the hand and ran with it. In the dark furniture section of an empty department store, I shared a bed with a queen.

~*~

I got into my office before noon, bright-eyed and ready for the day. The night spent in Darling's furniture department hadn't hurt me a bit. We had the bed made, and were wandering around looking at men's hats when the store opened. Nobody gave us a second glance, and we went out the front door into the bright morning with the glass eye safely tucked into Annie's bag. Back on Figueroa Street, I had kissed Annie good-bye on the sidewalk in front of her house, and then I had walked on air next door to mine.

Now, freshly showered, shaved, and resplendent in light gray and white seersucker, I put my feet on the open window sill and smelled State Street below me; cigar smoke and ocean air. A box full of cinnamon-sugar-covered Mexican donuts called *churros* sat on the corner of the desk, and the coffee bubbled and gurgled in the corner. The Browning sat loaded on the blotter. I was ready for anything.

I heard a noise in the waiting room, and stuck my head in. Eleanor Lane stood gazing at a hunting print the previous tenant had left on the wall. One elegant finger twisted a lock of platinum hair. Her sleeveless green dress matched her wide-brimmed straw hat and open-toed sandals. She looked nearly as good as I did.

"Your office is just as dreadful as I imagined it," she said, without looking away from the picture. "It suits you perfectly."

"Come in," I said. "I have fresh coffee, made with an electric percolator. I also have Mexican donuts, called *churros*."

She rolled lovely blue eyes at me.

"*Churros,*" I said again, showing off my correct pronunciation.

I followed her into my office. She took the client's chair and lounged elegantly, crossed knees draped over the arm. She wasn't wearing stockings.

"I don't want coffee or anything else from you, peeper. I came to tell you that Mr. Gaynor's offer of fifty thousand has been accepted. You have one last job, and that's to deliver the money."

"Fifty grand," I whistled. "You have the cash with you?"

She smoothed her dress with one palm, accentuating hips and breasts. "Do I look like I'm carrying a lot of extra cash to you? There's a meeting tonight, at the bicycle shop. Eight o'clock. You'll get the money and instructions then."

"If you're not here bringing me a suitcase full of money, then what can I do for you?"

Her face changed, and I got an unpleasant idea what she'd be like when she really got angry. The expression disappeared in an instant, but I didn't care for it.

"I want you and I to be on the same side," she said. "Try not to be horrible, for once."

"What exactly is it you want me to do?"

"I want you to do your best to make sure this all goes without a hitch." She widened her eyes. "I know you've been making noise about solving an old murder, but none of that will make a difference to people who are alive. It could put a big screw in the works."

"Why would it matter to you if it did?"

She puffed her cheeks at me, as if she were explaining things to a complete idiot.

"Because Harold has been terrible to me." Her expression changed again, and she seemed as if she were going to burst into tears. She made a hell of an actress. "He's obsessed with this business—thinks about nothing else, and bites my head off whenever I come near him. Here's the thing—it's the world's worst kept secret that Harold and I are going to marry. I have to put up with him, and ever since this eye got stolen his mood has been impossible."

"When's the happy day? I assume I'm not invited."

"He wants to wait until his mother dies. She doesn't approve of me. Point is—I'm not married yet. There's no law I can't have a little fun."

"Fun?"

"I just want everything to go smoothly, without a lot of complications. Getting this whole thing over with, and Harold back to normal, would definitely put me in the mood to have fun. I'd have you to thank for it."

"I'm spoken for, when it comes to having fun."

"That strange woman you run around with?" She glanced at my left hand. "She's pretty enough, if you like the type. You're not wearing a ring, though. You can't tell me you believe in all that 'until death do you part' silliness."

I gave it some thought. The Krazy Kat clock on the wall stuck out his tongue and told me it was already lunchtime.

"I think we were hoping it went past 'death do you part'. Why should we stop?"

She stared at me, puzzled. She clearly wasn't used to being mystified, and she patted a stray hair into place to make up for it. She stood up and stretched, so I could get a good look.

"You're a peculiar man," she said. "Turning me down. I hope you aren't sorry."

I didn't think I would be sorry. I wasn't entirely sure I understood what she had been trying to buy. I wasn't sure she knew, either.

"Volpato and Daughter, eight o'clock," she said. "Do your very best not to be screwy and mess this up, peeper."

She flounced out, leaving me a ghost of her perfume.

~*~

Ocean Lane got even stranger at night. Annie held my hand while we walked. With the shops closed, it was mostly dark except for the occasional night light in a display window and oddly spaced electric bulbs on poles. It was full of people, though. They didn't appear to be tourists. I had no idea who they were, or why they were congregated here. I saw a man in a striped shirt, juggling oranges. A young woman sat with her back against a wall, nursing a baby. Another man spoke to a crowd of about thirty people, exhorting them in earnest whispers. I couldn't make out what he told them.

The sign reading 'Volpato & Daughter: Bicycles' was unlit, and the shop windows were dark. The old woman opened the door before I could knock. Annie and I were hurried inside, and the door closed behind us. The light from a hundred lamps bathed the room. It should have been much too bright, but it was warm, gentle, and golden.

My wristwatch said seven minutes before eight o'clock, but a group already waited for us. Volpato's daughter was clearly delighted to see Annie, and hugged her as if they had been separated for years. The old man waited politely, hands behind his back, for them to finish.

Eleanor Lane smirked at me. She had dressed to the nines, as usual. Harold Gaynor stood beside her, one hand at the small of her back and the other gripping the handle of a leather satchel. Fin sat in a velvet armchair, in a pool of his own shadow. I didn't know what he was doing here, but I never felt surprised when I saw him.

I wondered what the reactions would be around the room, if the gathering knew that Annie had the eye in her bag.

"We begin."

Volpato cleared his throat. His tone seemed deferential, nearly apologetic, but made it clear he was in charge.

"This is an auction," he said. "Everything sold by the firm of Volpato and Daughter is sold by auction. All sales are final, and there are no returns. Payment will be made directly to the seller. Our fee is ten percent of the selling price, and is not refundable."

He glanced at Gaynor, who nodded. Then he went on.

"For sale is a piece of glass, once the property of Nitocris, queen of the Fifth Dynasty of the Egyptian Old Kingdom. Its provenance is a private matter, between buyer and seller. We will be happy to provide our opinion of authenticity, or lack of such, once the sale is complete."

He looked around, to make sure we all understood. Everyone except Fin nodded.

"This item has magic attached to it, as does everything we sell. When you buy the arcane and the profane, anything attached to it is your responsibility. We make no claims."

Everyone nodded again. Fin smiled, and Volpato seemed satisfied. He closed his eyes, swayed a little, and began.

"Fifty-thousand-dollar bid, now fifty, now fifty, will ya' give me fifty? Fifty-thousand-dollar bid, now fifty, now fifty, will ya' give me fifty?"

Eleanor raised her hand, and he immediately opened his eyes.

"Sold! Fifty-thousand to the lady and gentleman. Merchandise can be redeemed at midnight tonight, at the Rocas Perdidas reservoir dam."

"You got that, Crowe?" Gaynor asked. He sounded strung out. "You know the place?"

"Rocas Perdidas? I know it quite well. Had some business there recently." From the corner, Fin grinned at me. His eyes glittered beneath his hat brim.

"Good." He thrust the leather satchel at me, and I took it from him. "Do your best not to screw this up."

Volpato's daughter let us back out onto the dark street. I looked over my shoulder before the door closed and saw Eleanor counting bills into the old man's outstretched palm.

"Ridiculous," Annie said. "Volpato announced he might be selling a phony. An auction with an agreed price, only one bidder, and no merchandise—ridiculous! But, it was exciting, wasn't it?"

"It was exciting," I agreed. "Volpato brokered a chance at the eye, not the eye itself."

"He also said 'once the property of Nitocris'. It still belongs to her."

"I'm glad you didn't correct him."

The satchel weighed more than I expected. I wondered if Beatrice had ever imagined her impulsive theft would be worth this much. I wondered if the trouble she had caused made her happy, or if she was beyond such things. When we got to the Ford, I locked it in the luggage compartment before I got in.

"You don't need to come with me," I told Annie.

"Of course, I do. I have the eye."

Her tone was pleasant, the kind that warned me not to argue.

We took Cabrillo along the beach. A set of headlights in my rear-view mirror got too close, and unsettled me. I wheeled the Ford into a hard right and pulled over. The trailing car kept going.

"I don't like this," I said. "There's someone else beside Wanda Rice involved. She might be a tough cookie, but she didn't beat Charles Martellus to death. I'm wondering if the Parklane boys are still mixed up in this. I believe Gaynor as far as that goes, but I wonder if Bea annoyed Wanda enough to arrange a rape."

"Why would she?" Annie asked. "It makes no sense."

"Love," we said at the same time. We looked at each other and laughed, even if it wasn't a funny subject.

"Logically, they're planning to pull a robbery," I said. "We know they don't have the eye. I don't really like running around with fifty grand in cash in my trunk. It's too early to go to the reservoir, and I feel like a sitting duck going back home to wait."

"Should we wait in your office?"

"I have a better idea," I said. "I can think of a handy place nobody would think to look for us."

I drove to the office, and found a parking spot in front. I got the satchel from the trunk, and Annie and I watched State Street for a few minutes until I felt satisfied nobody had followed us. Then we crossed the street to the Schooner Inn.

Tonight's crowd of beer-drunks spilled out onto the sidewalk from the bar, and we disappeared into the middle of them. I was glad of them, because the milling group made it likely watchers wouldn't see us go in. If they cruised by later and saw my car, they'd figure we were in my office.

I got us a room for the night; up on the third floor, room 303. I knew Annie didn't like the number, but we wouldn't be there for long. When I got the door open, we left the lights out. It smelled stale. Enough light came from the street to make out the bed and a dresser against the wall. A pitcher and glasses were set out on a tray.

I took the pitcher to the ice machine at the end of the hall, and filled it with water in the men's room. When I got back, the room was still dark. Annie stood at the window. She parted the venetian blinds with two fingers, and stared out at the city night below. Neon light, striped with shadow, bathed her face in pink. Her lipstick looked black.

"We're safe for now," I said. "If they planned to pull something early, they won't now. Too public, even if they spotted us coming in here. They'll wait until the meeting at the reservoir."

"The cards say we're both going to die tonight."

"Nobody's going to die tonight, Annie." She didn't respond, and I began to worry. Bad things happened when she came unglued. "This might not have been a good idea, after all. We should maybe go out—go for a walk. Come back later when things cool off. This room's an oven."

She shook her head, no.

"You feel sure it's Wanda Rice who will show up tonight?" she asked.

"Call it a strong hunch." I poured ice water into a glass and handed it to her. "We're going into this holding all the cards. We have the money, and we have Anput's eye."

"Have you thought about letting her go?"

"How can I let her go?"

"She doesn't have the eye. We have it. She might be bluffing, and have nothing at all to do with Bea's murder. If she's punishing the Gaynors for the way they treated Bea, then maybe she's one of the good guys. Maybe she deserves the money."

"Let her walk away with fifty grand, return the eye to Gaynor, everybody's happy?"

"Well, I can't let you give the eye back to the Gaynors. It doesn't belong to them. Otherwise, it sounds about right."

"We're avoiding the obvious," I said. "Or at least I am. Technically, I work for the Gaynors. I have the eye, and I have their money. The right thing to do might be to return everything that belongs to them, and walk away. Leave whoever is trying to scam the ransom dangling. Case closed."

"You can't," she said. "There's more than Bea's murder. She was raped. An old man was killed. There's too much damage for you to allow this to end, and you know it.'

"Wanda didn't rape anyone, and she certainly didn't beat Charles Martellus to death."

"Maybe she involved those men from the Los Angeles agency. Gaynor said he fired them and they were gone. Do you believe him? When Beatrice slid into the gutter, it doesn't seem like Wanda did much to slow her down. I don't think we have her figured out, at all."

"There are parts of this that might never get solved, no matter what happens tonight. We might have to live with it."

I wondered if I could walk away, and live with it. If it meant living with Annie, I thought I could.

"What say we get on the midnight train to Los Angeles?" I asked. "First leg of the trip to Corazón Rosa could be done by morning. I can leave instructions for Danny or Fin to sell my house and car—get the money to me down there. We can leave together, and never come back."

I waited a long heartbeat, and then another, but she didn't answer. When I spoke again, it hurt my throat.

"You don't have much to say."

She sipped her drink; the ice cubes chimed softly. She held the cold glass to her forehead for a moment, and then set it on the dresser without looking away from the street.

"I never do," she finally said.

Crossing the room, I stood behind her and looked over her shoulder. I couldn't see what she was staring at. I caught her fragrance, sugar and salt, something with ginger and lime, sweet against the smoke and the heat from the night outside. I turned away, and went back to sit on the bed.

"You show me things," I said. "I can't explain it. It's like I never saw beautiful before. I can't just forget about it."

She finally turned to look at me. I felt glad that I couldn't see her eyes.

"That's the trouble with beautiful," she said. "Once you've seen it, you can't go back to what you were before."

-Twenty-Six-

Dark greens and navy blues shaded the night, like underwater. The moon switched on, and lapped light on the reservoir surface. I drove the Ford past where the marked surface ended, all the way to the top, overlooking the dam. I wheeled it around and reversed, so it faced the road that had taken us up. I had no intention of getting very far away from the car. Whoever met us would arrive with nothing to trade, but expected to leave with fifty thousand dollars.

We sat in silence. I smoked two cigarettes out the open window, and Annie stared at the water and thought about whatever Annie thought about. We heard the other car before we saw it, as it strained up the hill. I started the Ford's engine and left it running. A lot of guys have tried to escape trouble in a hurry, and gotten killed trying to crank a flooded engine.

The other car crested the hill and the driver hit the dipper switch and turned on the high beams. Then it stopped and waited.

I got out and stood in the glare of lights, the satchel held by my side. I had moved the Browning from holster to waistband, and it dug into my abdomen. I didn't want to draw attention by shifting it, so I gritted my teeth and left it alone.

The car opened on the passenger side, and a woman climbed out. She stood behind the door for a moment, and then stepped out where we could see her. Her elegant black dress clung to her hips and breasts. Her features were hidden behind the Rio de Janeiro party mask. The spray of black-and-white feathers reminded me of some exotic, faraway moment I couldn't put my finger on. Her dark hair fell over one shoulder. It was all a long

way from a maid's uniform, and I was impressed with the lengths Wanda had taken to disguise herself.

"Bring the money over here," she called. "Walk slow, and don't get too close."

Her voice grated strangely, like she had something sharp and unpleasant in her throat. I knew she was disguising it, but the sound nonetheless chilled me.

"Her poor voice," Annie murmured. "It can't be good for her vocal chords."

"This is a trade," I called back. "It doesn't work that way. We're here to collect the eye. I'll turn over the money when I have the glass eye in my hand."

"It works the way I say it does, peeper," she answered, and lifted a hand to show me the pistol she held. "Send the woman over here, with the money."

"Look, I know it's you, Wanda." I kept my voice gentle. "I can't let you go. You see that, don't you?"

She either didn't hear me, or ignored it. "You have three seconds to send the woman to me, or we leave."

"Where's the eye?" I called. "This is a trade."

"Three..." she called back.

"Just talk to us," Annie said. "This isn't what you think."

Annie removed the satchel from my hand so quickly I didn't react, and walked across the bright stage of lights toward the other woman. I stood frozen, and watched the two of them, in silhouette. When Annie got to her, the woman made a sudden lunge, and grabbed for the satchel. Annie hung on to it.

"We have the eye," I yelled. "We know you're here with nothing. It's over— give it up! Do you hear me? We have the glass eye!"

Both women stopped dead, frozen in the yellow light.

It was a terrible mistake, one I would live with for the rest of my life. Without any warning, the woman swung her gun toward Annie. The muzzle flashed. It made a tiny, terrible coughing sound, and Annie fell. She went to the ground so slowly she seemed to float, and I imagined she looked at me as she went down, her lovely eyes infinitely dark.

The pistol in the woman's hand followed Annie's flight down. The woman set herself, and her posture stiffened as she braced to fire again.

The Browning came out of my waistband already firing. It barked three times, with no sense of space between the shots. The woman's dress fluttered as she spun a terrible last pirouette. She threw her gun in a strange jerking convulsion as she fell, and it clattered away across the rocks. On her back, she raised one knee and then went still. All of it was over before the smell of gunpowder reached my nose.

I registered from the corner of my eye the driver's door on the other car opening. A large man emerged and began firing. Even a little deaf from my own shots, I heard the ugly sound of bullets hitting the Ford behind me. The engine at once began to rattle, and the radiator made a thin screaming sound. I fired back without aiming. One of the big car's headlights flared white, made a popping sound, louder than the gunshots, and went dark.

The driver got back behind the wheel. The engine roared and stalled. He got it started again and ground the clutch as he wrestled it into reverse. I moved toward Annie, and didn't watch him leave.

She lay motionless. I slid to my knees beside her, brushed her hair back and saw the end of my own life in her face. Relief flooded me like cold water when she opened her eyes.

"I told you, didn't I? The cards don't lie. We're both going to die."

"You're going to be fine, Annie. I'm going to get you to a doctor."

Behind us the hissing noise from the Ford continued, and the engine started to rattle louder. The sound grew more distressed, until after a rapid final clatter the motor quit. The silence rang, definite and final. The ghost of a smile played at the corners of Annie's mouth.

"Sounds like your car got killed, too. Can you carry me?"

I told her that I would carry her across the world if she needed me to.

"I believe you could," she said. "You might have to. Let me try to walk a little first, to save your back.

Her dress, under her breast, was wet. The blood looked black in the headlight glare. I tried to check the wound, and she brushed my hand away.

"Leave it. I think it looks worse than it is," she said. She sounded brave. "Check to see if she needs help."

"I hit her at least three times, Annie. There's no help for her."

"Check anyway, Nate."

I went to one knee beside the woman and slipped the black-

and-white mask upward. The feathers caught dark hair, and the wig pulled away with the mask. The woman's real hair shone so platinum blonde it was nearly white. Eleanor Lane's eyes were slitted, and her beautiful mouth had frozen into a snarl.

"God damn it to hell," I said. "God damn this."

It wasn't much of a eulogy, but I had no other words for the situation, so I went back to Annie.

"It's Eleanor Lane," I said. "Not Wanda. I don't understand."

Annie nodded, like she had expected it. "I dreamed it was her," she said.

I tried the engine on the Ford, got a brief clunk and nothing more. It wouldn't be going anywhere. I got an arm around Annie, and helped her to her feet. She let out a small cry of pain, a puff of air against my face, and then she set her face and started walking, leaning on me hard enough that I had to pay attention to my balance.

"What are you afraid of?" Annie asked, as though she could read my mind.

I glanced over my shoulder, back at the broken car behind us. The headlights were already going yellow as the battery drained. The nearest telephone would be at least five miles from here.

It took an interminable time to negotiate the hillside road down from the dam, but eventually we reached the road that would eventually get us to the highway, and hopefully some traffic.

The sea grass gleamed pale in the dark; it whispered in the wind, but I couldn't feel it on my face. The horizon stretched into black, empty space. I knew there must be beach and ocean, because I could smell the wet sand and the cold water that never stopped moving, but I couldn't see any of it. Every ten seconds or so the noise of a wave crashed and spread and faded, and I got startled by it every time. The asphalt gritted with sand, and I could sense the road under my feet more than I could see it. Annie squeezed my hand, and I jumped a little.

"What are you afraid of?" she asked, again. "Tell me."

I wasn't afraid of any of the things moving in the night around us, the things that swam in the sea and prowled the sand dunes and trailed us on the road.

Nothing much bothered me, not anymore. I walked on streets that were wet with neon and almost never touched the gun in my pocket. I wasn't afraid of being by myself, or the things I pretended were lost and couldn't be remembered. I wasn't afraid of filling stations or empty diners in the middle of the night. I wasn't afraid of bad dreams or empty bottles, reflections in dark windows or the kind of crying that was hard to stop. I wasn't afraid of the endless stars that stretched on and on and on, once you left behind the comfort of the moon.

I wasn't afraid of my own face in the mirror, awake at three o'clock in the morning.

I wasn't scared of the things that crept out of my childhood at night, even when they stood beneath my bedroom window while I slept. Real as real, they turned up big heads with blank faces to bask in the cold yellow streetlights. Their feet shuffled a little, dancing with the joy of waiting for me to die, but they didn't scare me.

"Tell me," Annie whispered, and I could hear the smile in her voice.

A seabird rose from the grass, startled into flight by our passing. I heard the brief sound of its wings overhead. I strained, searching for its whiteness in the dark air, but it was gone.

"There's nothing to tell," I said, but it wasn't quite true.

I took a breath and held it. I was afraid of losing her, and only that. I was afraid of a time when she wouldn't be around anymore. I was afraid of a world without any colors. I wouldn't ever say it out loud, though, or even think it. Especially not now, with her bleeding.

"Nothing," I said, and let the breath out. "I'm not afraid of anything real."

Her laugh was delighted, dark and sweet.

"Very good!" she cried. "How could anything be real, anyway? When it's all a dream in the first place?"

She took my hand and pulled me along, a little faster. The beach road stretched away, black and then silver as the moon emerged from the clouds. It seemed endless; we had always been walking, and we would walk on forever. After a while, Annie's breathing became audible, and I could hear the strain in it. She began to labor, and when she first slowed and then stumbled, I knew she had reached the end. I caught her behind the knees, straightened up and carried her. She didn't talk any more.

From a long way off, the road got illuminated a little brighter than the moon could account for. The glimmer resolved itself into the bobbing lights of a car, coming fast. About the time I could hear engine noise, I could also make out only one headlight. Unless it was wild coincidence, I had shot out the other, back at the reservoir. The big man was coming back.

I couldn't get my gun out without dropping Annie. I decided not to bother. Without her, none of it was worth the trouble. I kept walking.

The car drew abreast and stopped. I made out the familiar silhouette of a LaSalle limousine. The driver's window came down with a series of tiny squeaks, and I braced myself for the shots. Herb Robinson stuck his head out.

"Get in," he said. "I'll take you to the hospital."

I stood there, Annie in my arms. Her eyes were closed. She felt warm, but I didn't know if she was still breathing.

"We can't go to a hospital," I said.

"She might die, if you don't."

"She'll definitely die if we do."

~*~

Danny López lived in a two-story brick house with a wide veranda across the front of it, on a strange Santa Teresa avenue full of houses just like it. The whole street appeared as if a builder from Akron or Toledo had come here with only one set of plans, and transplanted a little of the Midwest here to become part of the *barrio*.

The trouble was, I didn't know exactly which house belonged to him. They all looked the same, especially in the dark. I told Herb to stop the LaSalle halfway up the block to let me out. I went to the nearest house, and banged on the front door. After a long minute, a porch light came on, the door cracked, and a woman peered at me from the opening.

"Do you speak English?" She started to close the door, and I quickly dredged up the bad Spanish I used in Corazón Rosa.

"Va rápido y busca señor López. Nesecitamos un doctor."

The woman's expression got confused. *"Quieres al señor López o prefieres un doctor?"*

"Ambos—apúrate por favor!"

"Oh, mi dios. Se morirá?

Annie's eyes fluttered, and opened. Her voice made a croak. *"Yo estoy muerta hace mucho tiempo."* I died a long time ago.

Mention of López' name had already swung the door wide open. A sudden flurry of family members swirled around us, roused from sleep. Two young men pulled on shoes, and left to find the doctor. I turned to go back to the car, but Herb Robinson was already framed in the doorway, an unconscious Annie cradled in his arms. He held her as easily as a sleeping child.

A man motioned for us to follow him back to the kitchen. An old woman spread a clean bedsheet on the kitchen table just as Herb carried Annie in and settled her. The sheet got immediately bloody. I took her hand; still slack, warm, and dark with grime from the reservoir.

Danny appeared beside me. The crowd in the kitchen melted away. He laid gentle fingers, as brown and gnarled as roots, on her neck.

"She's alive, at the moment," he murmured, gazing down. "The doctor is on the way. *Ai, chica—que hiciste?* What did you do?"

"The woman we met at the reservoir shot her out of the blue," I said. "Annie had her gun out, and so did I. Neither of us managed a shot until too late. It just didn't seem like a dangerous situation. I killed her before she could shoot Annie again."

His face changed, grew hard. He turned black eyes my way. "She should never, ever have come here. She was safe, where she was. You need to leave here, quickly. Take your friend with you."

It took me a moment to realize he was talking about Herb. I glanced at the doorway. It was empty; he hadn't stuck around.

"I'm not leaving."

He looked up at me. "You have no control over this situation. She killed a policeman, remember? You'll have to make a report, and you'll have to account for where you went. If you lead them here, they'll let her die before they call for an ambulance. Get out, now."

"I won't leave her alone."

"You must." He shook his head, vehemently. "For her sake. Whether she lives or not, she doesn't know you're here. Don't endanger her by being sentimental."

I took a last look at her face, trying to memorize it. Annie never appeared the same way to me twice, and I knew I wouldn't recall her exactly as she was now. I said goodbye under my breath, like a prayer, kissed her hand, and left.

My Ford sat abandoned at the reservoir, so López instructed one of his men to give me a lift home. Back on Figueroa Street, the lamp in my living room glowed in the front window, just like nothing had happened in the last few hours. One sleepless light burned upstairs at the Gardiner's house. Annie's windows were all dark. I figured they were going to stay that way, and that stabbed me in the heart.

My suit coat was soaked with blood. It didn't much matter, but I went inside and changed into fresh clothes. Then I followed the sidewalk, through streetlight and shadow, the two blocks to the police station.

-Twenty-Seven-

"All right, Crowe, DA says self-defense," Raines said. "You're sprung."

Roused from an uncomfortable nap, I sat up in the hard chair and rubbed my face. The interrogation room looked like the same one I had sat in after finding Beatrice Stone in my bathtub, but they probably didn't vary the decor much.

"I figured I'd at least have to explain myself to a judge."

I had walked into the Santa Teresa police station three hours earlier, saving everyone the trouble of searching for me when Eleanor's body got discovered. I told them I had shot a woman to death, who she was, why it happened, and where they would find the body. I probably saved some unfortunate early dog-walker a nasty shock.

"Herb Robinson came in and confessed everything. He showed up before you did—he's in a cell downstairs. He'll certainly get the gas chamber."

"What did he confess to? I shot Miss Lane."

"He's the one beat our friend Martellus to death in the Schooner Inn. He's also trying to cop to murdering Stone, but that one's a little muddier."

"Be a lot of trouble for you people to open the file back up, since you never called it a murder."

"Right." He didn't bat an eye. "Doesn't matter. He beat a white man to death. No need to gas him twice."

I felt an irrational surge of anger, and swallowed it. I liked Herb, and felt like I owed him one. He had turned his car around and gotten Annie to a doctor. If she survived, it would be because of him. It wasn't very noble, but compared to that I didn't care how many people he had killed.

"He say why he did it?"

"He was sweet on Eleanor Lane, thought Gaynor gave her the run-around. Says she told him Gaynor had promised for years he would marry her, and didn't. She hoped to get some of his money a different way—get back something Stone pinched from the Gaynors when she worked for them. There was a reward, apparently. He agreed to help her with her little scheme. I don't think he's too bright."

He stopped pacing, and stared at me.

"You know about this, right? What got stolen?"

"I can't tell you." I shook my head. "It's still a case, and I'm still on the job."

"I'm still on the job too, Crowe, and I just finished talking the DA out of charging you with murder."

"I'll tell you when it's all over," I said. "For now, trust me that it doesn't matter."

"Miss Lane got him to help abduct Beatrice Stone and give her what she claimed was truth serum. Idea was, she'd tell them where she hid the stolen item. He didn't realize until she stopped breathing that the dose had been too high, or else it had been poison."

"It was poison, all right," I said. "I happen to know so. You going to exhume the body and check?"

"County's not going to pay for that, Crowe." He shook his head. "What's the difference? All the actors are dead anyway, or will be soon."

"It fits for me, now. They knew she liked to stroll the motels on the beach, the Sand Castle in particular. Lane rented a room to use for questioning, probably left the door ajar to get back in quickly after they snatched her. In a hurry, they saw my door ajar, got into the wrong room. The bathtub was a desperation move—make it look like maybe she had passed out from drinking and drowned."

"Might even have worked, if it wasn't the wrong room. You never would have gotten involved. You wouldn't have even read about it in the papers. You're always griping that nobody cared about her, and in this case, I concede your point."

"Course it would have worked," I agreed. "Who would think different? Just a dead hooker, drunk in the tub."

"Lucky for us you're around," he said. "Like all murders, it got more complicated. With the woman dead, they figured they'd toss her room at the Schooner before she got discovered. I gather they didn't find anything, but Martellus saw the Lane broad. It worried them enough that Robinson went back to shut him up. I don't know if he meant to kill him—he seems a little bit simple."

"He's not a bad guy," I said.

"He ever tell you who he thinks his brother is? Most ridiculous thing I ever heard."

"No more ridiculous than everything else."

He went to the door. "Don't leave town until the coroner's given his verdict. After that? I think you really should leave town. Get a fresh start somewhere else. I don't think Santa Teresa is good for you, and I know you're not good for Santa Teresa."

Halfway into the hall, he turned around.

"One last thing, Crowe. Robinson says you had a woman with you, and she got hurt. Want to tell me who she was? Am I going to find another body?"

We watched each other for a long moment. I hoped Annie was safe.

"There was no woman with me. There are no bodies left to find."

He stared at me for a long moment. I held his eyes, and wondered if he guessed the truth.

"If you say so." He shook his head. "I'll be pretty happy if I never see you again. Good luck, wherever you're going."

I didn't feel like that deserved an answer, so I put my hat on and didn't give him one.

~*~

Danny López's wife sat across from me at the kitchen table. She didn't speak any English, and had never spoken to me. I didn't know if she minded having me in her home. Danny stood at the stove, frying bits of meat and serving them to us on small flour tortillas, one at a time so they would be piping hot when we ate them.

"I think she's going to make it," he said. "It's too soon to be sure, but the doctor is optimistic. Annie is a strong woman."

"Where is she? I'd like to see her."

He turned to glance at me. He was stooped and wrinkled, but something in his eyes made me understand why so many people were afraid of him.

"You know better than that," he said. "You've just been released from a murder charge. Do you think you're so free and clear the cops aren't watching you? You told me only a moment ago that a witness reported a second woman got hurt in the gunfire. Do you want to lead them to her?"

He must have seen that I felt stricken, because his eyes softened.

"She's in a safe place, *amigo*. She's being looked after—the best care I can arrange, and I can arrange plenty. When she is well enough, I will get her home—back to Corazón Rosa, where she belongs. When things are quiet here, you might go and see her there."

"She'll be glad to get there." It made me feel unaccountably sad; perhaps abandoned. "She left behind a dog named Button—our dog, but really hers. I imagine she's missed him terribly."

"Tell me how you are feeling," he said, changing the subject.

I was caught off-guard by the sudden sting of tears. I didn't know what to do with them. Friend or not, I wouldn't cry in front of López, so I froze and concentrated on my breathing.

"This business with Annie..." He shook his head. "Too much for any man. Too much for me—you know how I feel about her."

"It isn't just Annie." I wanted the beautiful, broken image of Eleanor out of my head. Her sprawled body and feathered mask came at me in waves. "It's also the woman I shot and killed."

"Tell me." Danny said, almost too softly to hear.

"I spent a dozen years in uniform," I said. "I was a military cop, and I walked a beat in St. Louis. I never fired a shot. Putting on a gun in the morning is as normal to me as putting on a tie. I sleep with a pistol on the nightstand. I always accepted I might kill someone someday, and always knew I wouldn't do it without a good reason. It never occurred to me that if it happened, I'd feel terrible."

"You had a good reason, in this instance," he said softly. "Annie's life was the best reason."

"I know, and I'd do it again." I struggled to lasso my thoughts. "I'm just saying it never dawned on me to think about how it would—feel. It never seemed possible it would be a woman."

"A very beautiful woman," he nodded.

"It shouldn't matter that she was good-looking," I said. "I'm older and smarter than that. It seems like more of a shame, somehow, and that's all wrong."

"You're a man," he shrugged. "You want to be an angel, and I admire that most of the time. In the end, you're a man like me. Killing a beautiful woman seems worse than killing a hoodlum who hasn't shaved his beard in three days."

"I don't think I'll ever walk outside when the weather's beautiful," I said, "and not think Eleanor Lane will miss out on the whole day, because of me."

He crossed the kitchen with the frying pan and served his wife. She smiled and touched his hand. He smiled back. After he set the pan back on the stove and turned off the gas, he sat down with us.

"Do you believe in Heaven?" he asked me.

"I don't think about it much."

"I do," he said, softly. "I think about it all the time. They call me a gangster, *amigo*, at least in your part of town. I like to tell myself in the mirror I'm better than that, but maybe I'm not. I've killed a lot more people than I like to remember, and one or two of them have been women. Several of them didn't deserve it."

His wife got up from the table, and carefully pushed her chair in. She left the room. Maybe she spoke more English than she let on.

"I don't know if I can be forgiven," he said. "I go to confession because it makes her happy." He nodded at the doorway his wife had left through. "The priest says I am forgiven, but I don't believe it. *Me volvería loco si lo cryert.* I'd go crazy if I did."

"You're a good man," I told him. "You'll go to Heaven if there is one."

"I don't believe in Heaven," he said. "I believe we go somewhere, though. In the end, I think we all go to the same place. I think the people I've killed will decide if I'm forgiven, not some priest. If I'm right, you'll see this Eleanor Lane again. From what I saw, she loved you a little—but she also didn't like you much, did she. It will be interesting, *amigo*. I hope I'm there to see it."

We stared at each other for a moment, and then his face split into a wide smile. We both laughed.

"Oh, brother," I said.

~*~

Harold Gaynor refused to return my calls. Nobody answered the buzzer at his front gate. He wasn't at his office, and they didn't know when he would return. I had his satchel, filled with his fifty thousand dollars, but no Harold to return it to. I drove out to his mother's estate. Maybe I would give it to her, and maybe I wouldn't.

I also had the glass eye. I supposed it belonged to Anput, and not the Gaynors. If there was justice, it should be put back in Egypt where it belonged, and anyway I had made a promise to Annie. She had told me to throw it in a river. I kept my promises, even when I didn't know how. If it came down to it, I would take the eye back to Mexico with me and let her deal with it.

My Ford had been towed from the reservoir into town. The Mexican mechanic acted horrified that the transplanted Zephyr engine had been ruined, but vowed to find me another. I didn't much care. Annie's green convertible sat in her garage, but it felt somehow wrong to disturb anything at her house. In the end, I went next door and borrowed the keys to the neighbor's car. Mrs. Gardiner knew about Annie, and became hollow-eyed with worry. The doctor insisted on escorting me to the driveway and demonstrating the Cadillac's controls.

At the Gaynor estate in Montelindo, I talked into the same squawk box as before. There was no answer, but the same electric servomechanism slid the gate back. I rolled through the same lush, barbered grounds, past stands of ferns and green lawns.

A lazy English, with specific affectation.

Annie's voice sounded so clear in my mind that I glanced over. The empty seat beside me stabbed my heart.

I didn't look forward to meeting Wanda, even if she didn't know I had gone to the reservoir with her tried and convicted in my own mind. I felt as though I owed her an apology. She didn't answer the front door however. The squat maid let me in without a word, and abandoned me in the hallway. I found my own way to the conservatory.

The two women were seated at their usual table at the far end. Olive laughed loudly as I approached.

"The intrepid Mister Crowe returns in failure," she called. "The eye remains missing, a great deal of money is unaccounted for, and my son needs to bury his personal secretary. Is there any further way to ruin us, any greater embarrassment you can cause?"

"I have every penny of the money," I growled. "Do you want it?"

"Oh, I'll let you return it to my son," she said gaily. "You can do it when you explain how you shot and killed his lovely, beloved Eleanor. It should be a conversation to mark in your calendar."

"Indeed," I said. I dragged a wicker chair out from under an umbrella of spider plants and to the other side of the table. I was through with standing at attention for this woman. She went to a sideboard for a glass, and made an elaborate fuss out of pouring a glass of her ruby port for me.

"I see you eyeing my medicine every time you're in here," she said. "Since this is the last time we'll meet, a small celebration is in order. I'll be generous."

She clinked the glass sitting in front of me with hers. I didn't want it, but I tossed it off in a gulp to annoy her.

"I'll look forward to telling your son that you caused Eleanor's death."

"Do tell." She cocked her head, feigning rapt interest. Her smile was charming, and I realized again what a strikingly good-looking woman she must have been before a life of bitterness and cheap sherry had their way.

I addressed the two of them. "You're closer than sisters," I said. "Much closer, and you have been for years. Did old Mister Gaynor enter matrimony as a favor, so you could be together?"

Olive bared her teeth, and picked up her sherry glass, ready to throw it. I held up a placating hand. "I'm sorry, that's not my business and has nothing to do with this."

"How dare you?" she hissed.

"You hired the murderers. Eleanor conspired this with your chauffeur—for you. Not at the end, mind you—at the end, I think she tried to cash in on a rich payday. She had given up on your son's promises of marriage and simply wanted something for the wasted years. Herb went along, because there's nothing Eleanor could have suggested he wouldn't have gone along with, the poor sap. You hired them to kill Beatrice Stone. They simply didn't know they were going to kill her until she suddenly died."

We bared our teeth at each other. I wanted to finish this and go. I felt worn out.

"They didn't know they were going to kill her—but you did. You supplied them with a deadly poison, knowing Beatrice Stone had no chance of surviving it."

She sat back in her chair. "I assume you can prove this slander."

"I'm not planning to prove a thing," I said. "I'm not taking this to the police. I'm going to walk away and leave you people to your wretched lives. I just want you to know that I know."

"Then please continue." She clapped her hands together and poured herself another drink.

"You wanted the eye back—for her." I nodded at Chamomile. "You were probably a little impatient at how the negotiations were dragging out, but then Bea contacted you. She told you something that made her death more imperative than recovering the eye. It mattered a lot more than this woman having a bauble she thought made her see. Bea knew a secret, and keeping her quiet mattered more than someone else's eyesight."

Chamomile interrupted. The black veil pinned to her hat blurred her features. "Do you believe my sight got restored when I held the eye in my hand?"

I was startled. "I thought you didn't talk."

"You assume a lot, Mister Crowe. That ought to be a dangerous habit, in your profession. I may not see, but I can speak when I feel the need to. Now tell me—do you believe in the eye?"

I thought about it. "I believe I do. I'm willing to allow there was more to the eye than I understand. If I could, I'd give it back to you. I can't."

I had made a promise to Annie, whatever I believed. I would throw it into a river, when I found one. Also, the blinded sparrow huddled in its cage on the table made me feel a little less sorry for Chamomile.

"You knew Eleanor had expensive tastes, and that Herb would help her," I said. "You gave them a little something to slip into Bea's drink. Not hard to get her to drink something, right?

You told them it was a truth serum of some kind, and when it took effect they'd find out where the eye was and get it back. How much did you promise them?'

I glanced at the nearly empty glass on the arm of the chair, and felt a small shock at my own stupidity. Olive had poured it from the same decanter she was drinking from, though. I didn't imagine she'd do anything to me in her own house, not in broad daylight with servants present.

"It wasn't truth serum, though. It was deadly poison. They rented a room at the Sand Castle, because they knew Bea did steady business there. They planned to dope her and then get some information, but she died before they got her back to the room. Couple of amateurs—best they could think of was a clumsy attempt to make it seem like she passed out in the bathtub and drowned."

I got unaccountably tired, all at once. The women and the house were pressing on me. I needed to finish this, and leave.

"They undressed her and ran a cold bath," I said. "It wouldn't fool any reasonable coroner, so they hoped the cops wouldn't care so much about a dead hooker. You know what? The cops didn't care. They were free and clear, except they were in the wrong room."

"Ridiculous!" she spat. "Do you really think I would do all of that to get the eye returned to me?"

"No, I don't. You had a more pressing reason. You seduced your maid, Wanda Rice. I don't think you loved her, because I don't think you love anybody. You fired Bea, and forced her out of this house so you'd have Wanda to yourself."

"You are filthy. Obscene."

"That worked for you too, like most things do when you're rich. What you didn't count on was Wanda and Bea loving each other. Eventually, Wanda came clean. Bea didn't care about getting a few thousand for the eye any more. She would spill the beans to anyone who would listen, and ruin you. She wanted revenge, and you knew you had to stop her."

I addressed Chamomile. "She hated you, too. I don't know why. Maybe because you'd been betrayed, too, and she couldn't stand the reminder."

"What about the eye?" Olive demanded. "If any of this was true, why would so much time and trouble be wasted?"

"Getting your lover her eye back seemed a waste of time to you?" I raised an eyebrow. "Anyway, it was never about the glass eye, not really. We were chasing the wrong thing. Beatrice asked your son for a thousand dollars, figuring he'd refuse. When he gave it to her, she asked for ten thousand more. When she found out the truth about you and Wanda, she never planned to return it. She wanted Miss Chamomile to suffer, too."

Olive brought the decanter over, and refilled my glass to the brim. I didn't plan to touch it.

"When your son sent the Parklane boys after her, and they got rough enough to rape her, she got worried. She got rid of the eye. If they recovered it from her, she figured they'd have no reason not to kill her. You beat them to it."

I felt more and more fatigued. I tried to remember the last decent night's sleep I had. I had slept well with Annie in the department store, but enough. I hadn't slept much since.

"I'm sorry she never got a chance to ruin you," I said. "I guess that's about all I have to say."

Olive laughed. It sounded genuine, but I knew it wasn't. "Do you really think I'd care?" she scoffed. "Do you think anyone in my circle would listen to a common prostitute? Who would she tell her stories to? Other prostitutes?"

"Chamomile would have listened to her," I said. "She threatened to expose you to Chamomile. Maybe you do love someone, in your small way, because you weren't going to let that happen. Beatrice loved Wanda, and you got her into your bed. You ruined them, and Bea planned to ruin you back, by telling Chamomile here about it. She knew it would destroy you."

"She didn't destroy you, my love, did she?" The blind woman spoke up, her chin tilted in Olive's direction. "She destroyed herself, and me. It cost her life. The guilty always escape, while the innocent destroy each other."

"You caused the death of an old man named Charles Martellus, too, if you're keeping final score. Martellus spotted Eleanor in the hallway outside Bea's room in the Schooner Inn. He was a harmless drunk—nobody would have listened to him as a witness, but he represented too much of a threat. Herb Robinson confronted him and ended up beating him to death."

"Fantasies," she sniffed. "You are amusing yourself at my expense. Finish whatever this is, and get out of my house."

"Worse than all the misery you caused Beatrice Stone— you broke her heart. You broke it a long time before she died. Sometimes I wonder if dying was a relief to her."

"You broke mine, too," the blind woman murmured. "It's what you like best. Breaking hearts makes you powerful."

"He's a liar, my dear," Olive said. "He's a cheap, whiskey-guzzling private detective. He's going to leave us in just a few minutes, and we'll go on like always."

"You couldn't be faithful, could you?" Chamomile asked. "Time after time you betrayed me, and I always believed you when you swore it would never happen again."

"None of this has anything to do with us," Olive said. "This dreadful man won't be bothering us any more. I've already made sure of it."

"Take my hand," the blind woman said.

Olive obliged, and shifted in her chair as Chamomile pulled her closer.

"Thirty years I've loved you," Chamomile said. "That's a long time, don't you think so?"

"A long time," Olive agreed. The puzzled expression on her face changed to horror as she saw the pistol the blind woman brought up from her lap. She struggled to get her hand back.

"Long enough, I think," Chamomile murmured. "It ought to be long enough to really know another person. Just think, the next time I see you, I'll see you as you truly are. I wonder what you'll look like."

I heard the hammer snap before the roar of the shot filled the conservatory. Olive Gaynor's blouse puffed and settled, and a red stain began to spread. She lowered her chin to her bosom and slumped in her chair. The blind woman brushed the veil back from her pale, sightless, eyes. She stared at me and didn't let go of Olive's hand.

"Don't really need to see, to aim a foot away," she said. "See you in Hell, Mister Crowe."

She put the barrel under her chin, and pulled the trigger.

Her head flew back. Her gaping mouth made it look as though she was singing an aria, accompanying the echoes of the gunshot. Then the room got perfectly still, and the three of us sat companionably in the ringing silence.

I supposed I ought to get up and do something, but I felt very strange, and exhaustion washed over me in waves. The glass of port dropped from my hand, and I watched the spreading red stain on the floor. It reminded me of the one on Olive's blouse. Everything had a pleasant synchronicity, and I closed my eyes and smiled.

I felt a hand on my shoulder, and dragged them open once more. Fin stood over me. His face appeared more morose than usual, if that was possible.

"Where did you come from?" I asked him. My words were badly slurred.

"I got summoned, of course." He gestured toward the dead women. "What have you done here, Mister Crowe?"

He moved away from me and surveyed the scene.

"Forgive me," he murmured. "You didn't do this at all, did you? What a sad ending to a sorry affair. The wind blows, and the wind swings—it pays no attention to our little hopes and schemes, does it? Blows and swings—oh, my!"

He stood with his hands clasped behind his back, and contemplated the two dead women.

"Fig's a dance," he murmured. "Isn't that what I always say, Mister Crowe? Fig's a dance."

-Twenty-Eight-

There are a lot of different kinds of poisons that do a lot of different things. The one that Olive Gaynor gave me did what she expected it to. It killed me.

The two dead women sat, holding hands, and watched me die. Olive stared steadily at her lap, and Chamomile pretended to look up at the ceiling, but I knew they were peeking at me. I watched them too, just as carefully. I would tell them I was no fool, and that I knew damned well Olive had slipped something into my drink.

Fin stood before them, staring back at me, puzzled. My eyes still worked, and I slid them over to where Wanda stood in the doorway, one hand raised to her mouth. Her black-and-white uniform looked crisp and clean, like a nurse's. I wondered if she might be willing to moonlight as one, because I had a feeling medical attention wouldn't reach me in time. Inside its golden cage, the blinded bird cheeped, over and over.

The ghost of Beatrice Stone stood behind her, and watched all of us. I winked at her. If she caught it, she didn't react. I had a lot to tell her. My mouth didn't work, though.

Fin's expression grew concerned. "Are you quite all right, Mister Crowe? You look peculiar."

I couldn't answer, so I slid out of my chair and onto the floor instead. I did it as gracefully as I could. The glass eye rolled along the floor beside my head. I didn't know how it got there; I supposed it had come out of my pocket. It sat on the tiles and watched me from up close. I didn't want to see it, so I looked up. A light was set into the ceiling above me, an electric bulb behind frosted glass. Staring straight up, I watched it get much too bright, and then fade to orange and red. It got steadily dimmer until it became a spot floating in a black sky. The bird's cheeping faded away to nothing.

I found out later that Wanda called for an ambulance, and while they waited for it Fin administered an antidote, which didn't cure me, but at least blunted the poison. They both tried to save me. There was a lot of commotion, a gurney ride and a scramble of white coats.

I didn't know a thing about any of it, because I wasn't there.

~*~

I was all at once far away, in a desert, behind the wheel of a nice car that wasn't mine. I saw mahogany trim and an emblem that said 'Hispano-Suiza' in fancy gold handwriting. There was lavender twilight outside the windshield, and the black bulk of an immense pyramid. I seemed to have finished parking the car, so I shut the motor off and got out.

It was a nice evening. I felt sand under my feet and a cool, steady wind that played with my hat brim. I left the car and walked toward the pyramid in the growing dark. A large structure at the base was lit up by a lot of torches; their light looked pretty in the purple dusk. I went through a big stone arch into an open space.

Three priests in black cassocks loitered in the courtyard, smoking. I knew they were talking about baseball to pass the time while they waited for whatever was going to happen inside. One of them caught my eye as I went by, and I thought about asking him for a cigarette. The look on his face changed my mind.

"Check your pockets," he suggested.

I did. A fresh pack of Pall Malls had been tucked into the breast pocket of my jacket, with a new book of paper matches to keep it company. I checked the cover in the light from the guttering torches. The printing on it said, 'Surrender, Dorothy.'

"You'll like it here," he said. "You generally find what you need—as long as you know what you need, of course."

I lit up, and we stood together companionably enough and smoked. I hoped they would start talking about baseball again, because I knew a lot about it. Nobody said anything, though. Finally, I spoke up. "Where am I supposed to go?" I asked. "What comes now?"

"We don't write your material for you, bub," he said, gently. "This is your gig."

"You can follow the bouncing ball," another of the priests offered. "If you see one."

They both looked at the third priest. He was a lot older than the first two, with a craggy, handsome, face, like the kind of movie star whose name you can never remember. He held the last of his cigarette between thumb and finger; he took a final drag and threw it away before he glanced at me. His eyes were dark and mournful.

"Some people see a white rabbit," he said. "Personally, I don't know how to feel about that, but to each his own."

I looked up. The pyramid loomed huge; its shape blocked whatever little light remained in the sky, black against dark blue. Clearly, it was old, as old as the stars, older than my imagination could ever account for. At the far end of the courtyard, an iron gate stood illuminated by torchlight. People went though it and inside, some in a hurry, and others more slowly. Nobody came back out.

"I'll walk in with you, if you like," the old priest offered. "Save you waiting for the white rabbit."

I thought about it and nodded. When I had finished my cigarette, we left the other priests behind to talk more about baseball.

"Who's going to win the Series this year?" I asked, when we were close to the pyramid entrance. "Can you tell me?"

"The Yankees are going to win it," he confided. "I'm allowed to tell you that, and it's only fair that you know. They'll beat the Dodgers in seven games. Al Gionfriddo will make one of the greatest catches of all time. It will be the last catch of his career—even though he doesn't know it. 'Forty-seven is his last year in the majors. It will save the sixth game for Brooklyn, but it won't be enough."

"I appreciate it," I told him. "It's not really a surprise, now I think about it, but it's a relief to know."

I stopped to put a hand on the gate, to see if it was real. The metal felt rough with corrosion beneath layers of paint. The old man touched my elbow, and we went through. It was warm inside, and dark. The rough-cobbled floor sloped gently downward. Huge wooden beams and stone columns supported whatever hung over my head, unseen in the dimness. Canvas tents on either side were lit gold, stalls full of people shopping. We didn't stop to see what was being sold. Soft voices and footsteps echoed.

"I know what this is," I said. "It's a train station."

"The only way to cross the river is by train," he agreed. "I'm impressed. A lot of people don't put two and two together so fast."

"I'm a private detective," I said, modestly. "Or at least I was."

"Your license is still good," he said. "Things don't change much, just because you're here."

"I thought there would be music, somehow."

"There is," he nodded. His face was solemn. "On the other end—music and color. This is in-between."

There were occasional signs posted, black letters painted on white board. Most of them were written in a language I didn't understand, but I could read one of them. It said: 'Danger, Unseen Currents'. A fancy-looking arrow pointed straight ahead. I figured it was meant for me.

"That's your platform," the priest said, as if he could read my mind.

"The dangerous one?" I smiled. "Unseen currents?"

"Every day of your life has been dangerous," he said. "Did you ever get up in the morning and known what the day would bring? Ever? 'Danger' is another word for hope."

"We live for risk?" I smiled.

"Hope is dangerous, and the only thing that matters," he said. "Your life would have been dreary and infinitely gray, were it not for the unknown and unseen. The thrill of possibility—a dream come true or the bitterest disappointment, ecstasy or disaster, every single day. You never knew, but you hoped."

The train loomed out of the dark. We walked past the black locomotive, leaking steam from a hundred places, the wheels taller than we were. The cab windows high above us were black and empty.

"What do people fear more than anything else?" he asked. "What shakes them awake in the middle of the night, unable to breathe?"

"Death," I guessed, and gestured around me at the dark station. "This."

"Death is hope," he said. "There would be nothing to be afraid of, if it was an ending. You were always afraid of this because it isn't the end. It's the beginning."

He pointed at a bench, situated under a pole lamp. A woman sat on it, in a pool of yellow light. "I'll leave you here," he said. "Someone wants a word with you, before you board your train."

The woman watched the train, and didn't look at me as I approached. Her hair was pinned up over her slender neck and perfect profile. Shadow did nothing to blur the loveliness of her features. It was Annie. When I reached the bench, she turned her face to me and smiled.

"Don't die first," she said.

"What's that supposed to mean?" I asked.

"Don't die first. You promised."

"One of us goes first," I said. "That's the deal. It's how things work. We won't have any control over who goes first."

I thought about surviving Annie, and instantly didn't want to think about it. She shook her head once, an impatient flick.

"I know that," she said. "I'm talking about intention, and right now you do have a choice. You can go back. Don't take the train. Get on the streetcar, instead."

She pointed, and I saw a trolley car on the opposite track, pointed the opposite direction from the train. It appeared tiny compared to the enormous locomotive. The windows were lit. The driver gave me a small wave, as if to let me know he would wait.

"You promised, but I won't lie," she said. "It would be easier for you to just get on the train. I'd still find you, later, if you died first. I wouldn't hold it against you."

"Show me," I said.

She nodded and rummaged in her bag until she found a deck of cards. She shuffled expertly, and laid one card between us. She touched the back of it for a moment, with the fingertips of both hands, as if she had second thoughts. She had artist's hands, improbably strong, long and elegant, with the nails cut short. They were purposeful; their beauty was incidental. I moved her fingers away, gently, and touched the bicycle picture. The card felt ice-cold.

When I turned the card over, I saw gray days. I saw streetlights struggling through fog. I saw long nights alone at a kitchen table. I saw a long line of empty bourbon bottles, and tasted the oily steel of the Browning against the roof of my mouth. I didn't want to see anything else. I reached out and touched her cheek. She turned the card face down and slid it back into the deck.

"Do you love me enough for that?" she murmured. "Do you love me enough not to leave me alone? Can you be braver than I am?"

"*A promise is a promise,*" *I said, and started toward the streetcar. At the bottom of the steps, I hesitated. The driver put his hand across the top of the fare box, to show he didn't need a ticket from me.*

The guy sitting across the aisle from me wore a forage cap that told me he was a carrier pilot, but I didn't recognize him. He looked a lot like Clark Gable, if Gable was twenty years younger. He kept himself busy watching the woman in front of us. She was a younger version of Annie, one I had never met. She wasn't hard to look at. The light hair tucked into her service hat went well with gold-colored skin and dark eyes. She stood in the aisle, with one knee on the seat beside her and an elbow crooked around a chrome pole, as if she had too much energy to think about sitting. She stared out the window and paid no attention to us.

The trolley rocked and moaned a little as it approached the end of the line. The car was nearly empty, just the three of us behind the driver, all wearing the same uniform. Behind round etched glass lenses, the yellow bulbs in the ceiling were too bright. The seats were red leatherette, and the walls were metal painted the same pale green that one saw everywhere these days. They designed it to be soothing. I figured whoever thought up the color must have made a mint by now.

When the streetcar stopped to let us all off, the darkness outside was a relief. We stood together for a moment, as if undecided about going on. The seaport spread out across acres of macadam, the hulks of cranes and ships disappearing into the black. It didn't matter that midnight had come and gone; lights hurried here and there, busy getting ships ready to cross the Pacific to nameless coral islands. At the edge of the darkness, there were two enormous dirigibles moored to gantries, both nose-in, with their tails out over the water.

"Aren't they perfect?" the woman asked.

Her voice sounded happy, and startled me a little. It had a kind of breathless, silver quality that I usually heard coming from a movie screen. Just like that, the sound of it moved her in my books from not bad-looking straight to beautiful.

I gazed up at the gray-skinned airships, side-by-side twins, floating in the dark. Standing beneath them made me feel tiny. There were spotlights on them, here and there. The lights were white, but they colored when they moved. The engines churned, massive and loud, propellers a blur. A tiny jet of flame blew back as one of them backfired, and the sound echoed out across the water.

"Blimps are yesterday's news," the pilot said. "They hunt for subs, but they're too slow for the job. Somebody sitting behind a desk dreamed them up. There's no reason for them—they're foolish."

I saw the hurt flicker across her face.

"Why does there have to be a reason for them?" she asked, her voice trailing away. "Why can't they just be..."

He looked at her, dismissive, and walked off. I looked again at the airships hanging above us, ghostly in the night sky. I thought I had an idea what she was trying to say, and I felt bad for her. They were so big and so powerful, but they were fragile at the same time. In a few minutes, they would be out over the dark ocean, and in a few years, they would be gone for good. They made me terribly sad, in a way I couldn't put my finger on.

I cleared my throat and said, "They're so goddamned beautiful, they make me want to cry."

She stared back at me without expression, and I thought maybe she hadn't heard me over the noise of the engines. I said it again, louder.

"They're so goddamned beautiful, they make me want to cry."

I wiped at my cheek to illustrate the point, and the gesture made me feel all at once stupid and awkward. Worse, I was shocked by the wetness of my own tears on my fingertips. She stared at me, and I turned to go, embarrassed.

"Wait—do we know each other?" she asked. "Did I see you somewhere?"

"I don't think so," I said. "If we ever met, it was a long time ago, and I don't remember it."

She nodded 'yes' at the same time I shook my head 'no'. Neither of us said anything for a minute. Her face went completely still, etched in the lights from the docks. Her eyes were so dark they were invisible.

"Maybe a long, long time from now," she said softly. "Maybe it hasn't happened yet, and that's what I'm remembering."

"Maybe," I agreed. "Maybe heartbeats are only where it begins."

She took my hand and led me to the edge of the nearest dock. We stood over black water. The airships thrummed over our heads. She cupped a hand to my ear.

"This goes to the river," she said. "Take what's in your pocket and throw it in. Don't get too close to the water."

I held a smooth orb, nearly hot to the touch. I pulled it out and held it up to the dark sky. I didn't need any light. The glass eye glimmered from within, alive and staring at me.

"Throw it," she said. "The tides will take it back where it belongs."

I reared back and threw the eye as far as I could, into the darkness. It simply disappeared. If there was a splash, I couldn't hear it over the blimp's engines. Anput's eye was finally on its way.

"Egyptian tides," she said. "Bye for now."

She left then, headed back to whatever her life was. I thought she was a strange woman, but I stood for a long time and looked at the place where she had been. Eventually, the airships left their moorings and floated off into the dark. When sound of them had disappeared, I began to get cold, and started walking.

It was over— just like so, and just like that. Anput's eye got lost, and found again. I hoped Nitocris, the beautiful queen, would appreciate getting it back.

I was so tired that my eyes hurt. At this hour of the morning, I had no hope of getting a cab, so I started walking. The rain had stopped, but the brick buildings were still dripping onto the wet pavements. The air smelled as clean as it ever does in the city, of old cement and electricity, dead cigars and yesterday's newspapers. Here and there, neon signs insisted it wasn't too late to find some fun, if I hurried a little.

A few blocks up, I passed a concert hall. The sidewalk and the flight of stairs were flooded blue by the lit marquee over the entrance. The doors stood propped open, and music came from inside. A saxophone tried to be heard over a bunch of crying horns; it kept getting lost and then finding its way back. I recognized the song; "I Love You Madly". I liked it all right, so I stopped to listen.

A woman was selling cakes from a wooden booth set into an alcove by the stairs. Pale and pretty, she followed me with her eyes as I walked over to have a look. I realized with a start that it was Beatrice Stone. She wore the same blue dress, but she appeared different, fresher than I remembered. The small cakes lay set out in rows, frosted with blue light from the sign overhead. I didn't know who would buy cakes at three o'clock in the morning, but I didn't know a lot of things.

I put a dollar bill on the counter and watched her as she carefully arranged eleven of them into a flat box. She held my eyes when she gave me my change and didn't answer when I thanked her. I turned and nearly bumped into a man standing on the sidewalk behind me. The face under the hat brim belonged to Fin.

"You blunder, Mister Crowe," he said. "It's what gets you into trouble."

Hunched into his overcoat, head cocked, he looked like he belonged to some species of large bird. He stared at the cake booth.

"Do you know what's different about that woman?" he asked. "I think you do."

I didn't answer, and he shifted his gaze to me.

"She's a ghost, Mister Crowe."

I handed him the box of cakes while I lit a cigarette. I was interested.

"She isn't real?"

"Oh, she's quite real," he said. "I didn't say she wasn't

real. I said she's a ghost. "

Beatrice glanced at us, and then back at the stairs. She was waiting for the people to come out.

"A ghost selling cake in the middle of the night?" I asked. "Is that what ghosts do?"

"Ghosts are everywhere, Mister Crowe, busy doing the things they do. When it's quiet, you can see them from the corners of your eyes. You move among them very comfortably, don't you?"

"You don't say." I took the box back. "Is that what you think?"

"The wind blows, and the wind swings," he said. "Through cemeteries and empty schools, hospital hallways and flower gardens. You see things that aren't real, because you aren't afraid to see them. It's the best thing about you."

He touched his hat brim, and turned to go. As if he had a sudden thought, he turned back.

"Right now, you're in an ambulance," he said. "Miss Rice heard the gunshots, and found you. I know a lot about poison, and I administered an anti-venom. It wasn't exactly the poison I would have chosen—you were given asp venom. I have better antidotes, and I'll bring them to you as quickly as I can manage. I won't get to the hospital fast enough to prevent a certain amount of damage, but since you've chosen to live, you shall live."

"You think doctors at the hospital will let you give me an antidote just because you say so?"

"I do, indeed. I have a great deal of influence in this city, as you know." He paused, lost in his own thoughts. "The Gaynor family likes to collect other things, beside glass. Olive Gaynor had a fascination with rare, exotic poisons. I might bear some

responsibility."

"You supplied her," I guessed.

"I buy and sell many things, Mister Crowe—things people cannot find elsewhere. I don't decide what they do with the things they buy from me. Still, I feel I should intervene in this case."

"You don't want me to die," I said. "You have a soft spot for me."

"Perhaps. I may not want to explain your demise to Miss Kahlo. She has a certain way of dealing with what she perceives as injustice. A way that even I can fear, and respect."

He gave me one of his slow, sweet, ghastly smiles. It made him beautiful.

"Goodnight, Mister Crowe. Fig's a dance."

He crossed the street to where his dust-colored Packard waited on the curb, painted blue by neon. I finished my cigarette while I watched him disappear.

The woman still watched me from her booth, her chin propped on an elbow. I realized that I hadn't said goodbye. She smiled as I walked over to her.

"Thank you for everything," she said. "Thank you for acting as though you cared. It made me feel good."

"I did care. Caring is what I do. I'm just good at not showing it."

"You have to admit, we had a hell of a date."

"It certainly was," I agreed. "One hell of a date."

"Why not stay here?" she asked. "I get off soon. Why not buy me a drink? Maybe get a little dinner? It's nice here."

Her lips and eyes were painted black by the blue light. She was tempting, and it did seem nice here, on this strange, neon-tinted street. "I have to get back," I said. "I made a promise."

"Do you always keep your promises?"

"Practically never," I said. "I always try, though."

"You're wrong," she said. "You do keep your promises. It's going to hurt, though, going back. It's going to hurt a lot. There will be days you'll wish you were back here—with me."

"I already wish that," I said. "It doesn't change anything."

I sketched her a small wave. She didn't give it back, so I started walking again. The sky over the street began to show some light, and I wondered how much time had passed. I went to a phone booth on the next corner, fumbled out a nickel, and dialed a number from memory. Annie Kahlo answered on the fifth ring.

"Were you asleep?" I asked.

"I always hear you," she said. "Asleep or awake."

"I bought you some cakes," I said. "They look good, but they aren't real. A ghost sold them to me."

I could hear the pleasure in her voice.

"Those are the best kind," she said. "You always know the perfect thing. You can wake up, now. You're back, and it's time to wake up."

"Am I asleep?"

"Yes, and no," she said. "Mayonnaise, ocelot, tomato, orange, raspberry, drawer—remember? Magic words. Mayonnaise, ocelot, tomato, orange, raspberry, drawer. You aren't dead, and it's time to wake up."

-Twenty-Nine-

I knew it was a hospital room. I had seen them before. The white tubular bed frame was a dead giveaway. I looked around the room without moving my head at walls painted pale green, and unadorned by any attempt at artful decoration. The bare window showed a glimpse of hard, blue sky. I saw no activity. The room stayed quiet and empty, which probably meant I had been there awhile. I contemplated nothing much, until a noise at the door got my attention.

A nurse came in, and did something at a rolling table down at the foot of the bed. I heard the scratch of her starched uniform when she moved. She glanced over at me, and her eyes perceptibly widened when she saw mine open.

"You woke up," she said. "I'll get the doctor."

I woke up again when he pried up one of my eyelids and shone a bright light into it. He repeated it with the other before he spoke.

"Welcome back," he said. "Do you know why you're here?"

He was a neat-looking man, carefully barbered. He had a collection of pens in one breast pocket of his white coat. The top of a cigarette pack peeked out from the other.

"Could I have one of those?" My voice hurt my throat, and didn't sound like me. He looked perplexed, and then realized what I was staring at.

"Let's get some fluids into you first, and then see about smoking a little bit later. You've been asleep for quite some time."

"How long have I been—gone?"

"You've been unconscious for . . ." He checked his wristwatch. "Just about sixty-nine hours. Nearly three days. Do you know what happened to you?"

"Poison."

"Yes. Luckily, you were discovered quickly. The scene was violent, and the police are anxious to speak to you. I'll try to keep them out until you're feeling more alert, but they can be persistent."

"What was I poisoned by?"

"Quite honestly, I have no idea. They don't bother us with details. Did you experience any pain during the event?"

I thought back, remembered sitting and watching the two women, unable to move or speak. I didn't remember any pain, and told him so. He nodded, seemingly satisfied.

"The extreme lethargy, the depression of breathing and heartbeat, were consistent with the venom from certain snakes, yet there were no puncture marks anywhere on your body. We deal with rattlesnake bites from time to time, but this presentation appeared entirely different."

"It came from an Egyptian asp," I told him. "They don't have them around here, usually. I was in good company—one of them got Cleopatra."

If that surprised him, he hid it well. He likely chalked it up to delirium.

"A very strange man came in here, not long after the ambulance brought you. He said something similar. He claimed to have dosed you with an anti-venom."

His face grew suddenly long. Uncomfortable, he went to a sideboard and came back with a glass ashtray, which he placed on the bed between us. He got his cigarettes out and lit one for me. I expected the first mouthful of smoke to make me cough, but it tasted wonderful. When he was satisfied I could manage it on my own, he lit one for himself.

"The police escorted the man," he said. "I didn't recognize him. They were nearly deferential."

"He owns a lot of Santa Teresa," I said. "His name is Fin. He might own this hospital, if you check the deed."

"I don't know why I did it," he said, growing more uncomfortable. "It goes against the oath I took, and I could still lose my license to practice medicine for doing it. I had lost you twice, you see. We got heart and breathing going again, but I knew it would be a losing battle. You were dying, and I didn't know what else to do. The man said you needed more anti-venom, and I went out of the room and left him alone with you."

"You did the right thing," I assured him. "I'm here, after all. You won't lose your license. Fin won't let that happen."

He nodded, not appearing any happier. "Anti-venom or not, you have a long recovery in front of you," he said. "The effects of the poison may stay with you for quite a while. Some of them might be permanent. There may be dizzy spells, disorientation. There is muscle and nerve damage that I can only guess at."

"I need to go to Mexico."

"You won't be going anywhere for quite a while, Mister Crowe. The first time you try to stand up, you'll see what I mean. You aren't able to travel to the other side of this room, let alone Mexico. Ask me again in six months time."

We both finished our smokes, and he took the ashtray away and went to the door.

"You should let someone in your family know, so they understand what to expect."

"I don't have any family."

"Who is going to take care of you?' he asked. "Someone has to attend to your recovery."

"I'll take care of myself," I told him. "I always have." We looked at each other for a long moment before he gave up and nodded.

"You should let someone know," he said again, and left the room. I closed my eyes and drifted off again.

~*~

Rex Raines wheeled me around the grounds of Cottage Hospital. I sat back in the wheelchair and enjoyed the play of light and shade. Even though the grounds were inside Santa Teresa city limits, it felt like the countryside back east. They kept the grass watered, and there were live oaks.

"I could get used to this," I told him. "Keep a brisk pace, would you?"

"Fat chance. You want to wrap this up for me, fill in the blanks, or should I take you downtown and get out the truncheons?"

I told him the murder-suicide had nothing at all to do with anything. I thought that the two women had been heading for a scene like it for a long time, and the missing eye had pushed the blind woman to the brink. She had nothing in her life but Olive, and Olive was unfaithful.

"In the end, Chamomile Gaynor just got tired of living. Life cheated on her, and Olive cheated on her. She just got pushed too far, and she went bonkers."

"They weren't married," he commented. "A woman can't cheat on another woman."

"I expect that from someone stupid," I snapped. "I don't expect it from a cop. Not one who's been around."

"The whole thing makes no sense."

"That's love for you," I said. "When something makes no sense, it's almost always about love."

A quarrel of sparrows flew up from a bush, disturbed by our passing. The birds settled in the next one down the path, and waited for us to approach so they could do it again. I wondered what had happened to the blinded bird in the cage. It made me a little sad, thinking about it.

"Family's well connected, but they're having a hell of a time explaining this to the newspapers," he said. "Public story is that Olive Gaynor was cleaning a pistol she kept for protection, and it discharged and killed her sister-in-law. The poor woman got so distraught she turned it on herself. Too many people know about it—cops, ambulance attendants, and house staff—to cover it up completely. It's a scandal, no matter how much dirt gets thrown over it."

"Rich people problems—nothing you or I would know about."

"Brother, ain't that the truth."

~*~

A couple of days later, when Danny López took me on the same stroll through the grounds, I had been in the hospital for nearly a week. I had traded the wheelchair for a cane. We stopped often, so I could rest.

"Fin came in to the conservatory, just as the poison was taking effect on me," I said. "I thought I dreamed it, but he gave me some sort of anti-venom that probably saved me. What was he doing there, in the Gaynor house?"

"He shows up everywhere, that one," he said. He forked two fingers at the ground. "I don't like to think about him. He is darkness."

"He's also a kind of light," I said. "Annie loves him."

He smiled at the mention of her. "Annie is safe now, back in Corazón Rosa," he told me. "I sent her across the border in a truck full of melons. My people drove her the whole way in three days."

"With a gunshot wound?"

"Three men dressed as farm workers were in the truck with her." He shrugged. "My two best gunmen riding in the back, with Thompsons under the melons. The driver is a doctor—a very fine one. He took care of her the whole way down. He said the bullet went through-and-through. *Herida limpia.* She is a strong woman, and recovering nicely. *Ella es también más que un poco mágico.* Nobody tells her what to do—not even death."

"Did she send any kind of message for me?"

"She didn't mention you—at least not to me." He gave an elaborate shrug. "You know how she is, *amigo*. She doesn't always say what she is thinking."

"Or else she says exactly what she's thinking, out loud and fearless. Depends."

"Fearless." He seemed to like the word. "That's what Annie Kahlo is—fearless."

"I miss her."

He put a hand on my arm, and stopped us on the path.

"It's time for you to go to her, *amigo*. You have both fought all the battles here you're ever going to. It's time to leave Santa Teresa behind. Walk on the beach in Corazón Rosa, fish a little. Maybe she can teach you to paint pictures. Hers are very beautiful. When you are well enough, my people will take you, the same way we took her."

"Will I ever be well enough?"

His eyes went liquid with pity. "Of course, you will, one day not so very far away. I am sure of it, *hermano*."

I gazed up at the hospital building. My bones ached strangely, and I still got suddenly exhausted. I didn't know if I would ever walk without the cane. My thoughts moved in peculiar directions. Part of me seemed to have been left behind, back at the pyramid, smoking and talking baseball with the three priests. I wasn't sure I would ever come all the way back from wherever I had gone.

I thought about Beatrice Stone, selling cakes by the blue light of a theater sign. *"I get off soon. Why not buy me a drink? Maybe get a little dinner? It's nice here."* I shuddered, despite myself. I touched Danny's elbow, and started walking again.

~*~

I stayed in the hospital for three weeks, and then I left against doctor's orders. If the white coats had their way, I would have remained in an institution, probably forever. Mrs. Gardiner came over to my house to check on me several times a day. She referred to me as "The Patient", and took pretty good care of me.

She brought me soup, and recommended martinis. I tried one, with great ceremony, in her lovely back garden, under the green-and-white striped umbrella. It was a celebration, but I wasn't ready for booze yet, and it made me violently sick. I told her I might try a little bourbon one day, but I was done with martinis for good.

A month after the reservoir shootings, I called Gaynor at his home from a pay telephone in the lobby of a hotel across from the beach. The place stood less than a mile up the strand from the Sand Castle, where this whole sorry business had started. I watched the colored amusement park lights while I listened to his line ringing.

"Leave me alone, Crowe." He sounded as if he'd been drinking, a lot, without much sleep. "You killed my secretary. You're responsible for my mother's death."

"I killed her," I agreed. "I wish I hadn't been forced to, but I was, and I did it. I can't change anything. If you can't refer to Eleanor Lane as anything more than your secretary, even after all this, I don't blame her for trying to get what she could from you. I would have done the same."

"Go to hell."

I wondered if he had anyone left to look after him, in his big house. I supposed he could sell it now, and move into the family estate, now that his mother was done with it. He might be grieving now, but he would bounce back. His kind always did.

"I have fifty thousand dollars that belongs to you," I said. "I'll need to return it in person. Should I bring it to you there, or at your office?"

"Go to hell," he said, again. "Keep it. I don't want to see it. Consider it your fee."

"I can't keep it. It's too much. I didn't do anything to earn even a fraction of that."

He snorted over the line. I didn't know if he was laughing or crying.

"Keep it, you fool. It's cursed money. If you contact me again, I'll have you killed. I'm already thinking about it, believe me."

"That's already been done," I said. "I came back." I was talking to a dead line.

Fifty thousand dollars would buy me some good years in Corazón Rosa with Annie. Truthfully though, Annie had her own money, and it was more than cash keeping us apart. I didn't mind hanging on to a good chunk of it, but I didn't feel like spending the whole thing would bring me any kind of luck. I decided I would hand most of it over to Danny López. The old gangster would see that it found its way to some people who needed it, and maybe the end of this horror would do some good.

I left the hotel lobby, and went outside, into the warm night. The air smelled like good seafood. I needed a long walk, but I knew I wouldn't get far before the pain turned me back.

A white dance pavilion faced the beach. Couples floated up and down the steps; faint music and shadows moved behind the screens and railings. I had never danced with Annie. That struck me as strange, because it seemed like the kind of thing she would have liked to do. The chance of it had just never come along. Sudden sadness made it a little hard to breathe, so I shrugged the thought away and kept walking, into the amusement park.

The lights were bright and everywhere; they spun and twirled, thousands of hot bulbs sparking and flashing. Behind me, the roller coaster rattled and roared. The sound of the calliope fought with the dance band, the buzzers, shouts and bells. I moved through the crowd and smelled hot dogs, sweat and cotton candy. I turned my shoulders and hips, stepped forward and sideways, and a kaleidoscope of frantic faces flowed past me. Over it all, the Ferris wheel rolled pink and green, taunting the night sky.

I didn't belong to any of it, and I passed through the color and heat and noise to the beach. It was dark all at once, and I crossed the sand and went to a flight of wooden stairs.

The pier was nearly empty, the darkness interrupted only by the naked bulbs on poles that marched out over the water to the end. There were occasional strollers and huddled pairs of lovers at the edges, but they all stayed close to the shore. No one but me was going very far out, and nobody looked at me as I passed. When I had gone as far as I could, I leaned on the rough wood railing and lit a cigarette.

Twenty feet beneath me, the ocean moved in, huge and silent. The dark waves were not-there and then suddenly there. They rolled and whispered toward the beach, massive and nearly invisible, and the timbers under my feet ached with the weight of them. Lines of phosphorescent foam moved along their tops, riding them all the way to the distant sand where they finally broke in a long shushing spill of pale against the gloom. The whiteness spread and then faded away until the next one.

Eleanor Lane had loved Harold Gaynor, and now she was dead. Beatrice Stone had died because she loved Wanda Rice. Charles Martellus loved Bea, and it cost him his life. Chamomile had loved Olive, perhaps too much, and they were both dead. Herb Robinson loved Eleanor, hopelessly, and he was headed for the gas chamber, as good as dead.

On the other hand, I loved Annie Kahlo enough not to die. None of it made any sense, and when something makes no sense, it's almost always to do with love. I knew that, even if I didn't know anything else.

There were no stars tonight, no horizon, and the blackness over the ocean was total. Japan and Samoa and Hawaii were somewhere out there in the dark, but the distance between me and those tiny lights and people was so huge that it became meaningless. I wondered if someone far away looked out at the dark sea, this very moment, and if they sensed me looking back.

We play the music loud, and turn on as many lights as we can. We pretend that it isn't really night at all, and that we aren't alone. The universe is only as big as we imagine it, and no bigger. Someone important is in charge, and they are on the telephone right now, giving directions. Our make-believes will be enough to get us through, and someone knows exactly what all of this is about.

Trouble was, I didn't believe in any of it anymore. I finished my cigarette, and started the long walk back. My footsteps sounded small on the boards. I saw my own moving shadow come and go beneath me.

I watched the lights, and wished again that I had danced with Annie Kahlo, even once.

-Thirty-

All the other café patrons sat inside this morning. I could see the bustle of servers through the windows, moving in and out of gold light. I imagined the breakfast noises and smells, the soft clatter of china and cutlery, the heavy scents of eggs and pastry. Out here there was none of it; just me at a small table, by myself.

I had two envelopes with me; one yellow, from Western Union, the other plain white. The telegram came from Corazón Rosa, Mexico, and I opened it first. It had only one line.

'It's been raining and I don't want it to stop.'

There was rain here, too. The downpour pattered the awning over my head. The air shone silver, and the passing cars threw up curtains of gray. It looked nice. It smelled the way warm rain always does, like wet cement, asphalt and iron, but with a broken-heart promise that it would all wash away to reveal the wet dirt and green underneath it, if I could only wait long enough. I had been waiting a long time.

I folded Annie's telegram and put it carefully back into the yellow envelope that it had come in. Her messages came every day. I never read any of them twice, but I saved all of them. I put it on the table where I could look at it whenever I wanted to, and picked up my cup. It was empty.

The white envelope carried my name and address, made out in a woman's handwriting. It had been left in my box, without a postage stamp. I slipped the letter out from inside, written on plain white paper.

Dear Mr. Crowe,

I have the glass eye, as you might have surmised. I found it on the floor beside you when you were unconscious. I think you'll agree Bea earned it, and would have wanted me to have the benefit of it, whatever that might be. I also think you mostly catch whomever you pursue, so I'm asking you not to chase me. I dream about Bea sometimes, and she speaks kindly of you in those dreams. Remember, I called an ambulance for you, and I believe that puts me in your good graces.

Sincerely, Wanda Rice

P.S. I put the blinded bird outside, in a bush. It won't have survived for long, but better to die in a garden than a cage.

"Egyptian tides," I murmured. I wished Wanda Rice well, and I had no reason to chase her. I hoped she would be able to sell the eye for a lot of money and find some happiness. I didn't think she had much chance of it, but that wasn't my business. I could have sworn I had thrown it in a river, but maybe there was more than one world.

A Boxer dog went by, casting left and right on the wet sidewalk. A woman in a blue dress trailed behind, under an umbrella. Since the Boxer didn't have a leash, I didn't know if it was her dog. Maybe she was just following it. I kept an open mind, since I was supposed to be a detective. The dog didn't mind the rain. It kept busy, looking for something and not finding it. I didn't suppose the woman was much help.

They were too far away for me to see the woman's face, but the blue dress looked familiar, so I sketched a wave, just in case. If she saw it, she didn't wave back. I watched them turn the next corner and go out of sight.

The waitress came outside, carrying a coffee pot. If she thought I was strange, sitting outside on a wet morning, away from the warmth and light, she didn't show it. When my cup was full she went back inside.

'It's been raining and I don't want it to stop.'

Mock orange and bamboo grew on the other side of the railing. The heavy air didn't move, and except when a drop hit a leaf and made it shiver, it was all perfectly still. I put some sugar and a little cream in my fresh coffee carefully, and stirred it.

'It's been raining and I don't want it to stop.'

After the war, I had seen cities bombed to rubble. The streets were dark and damned, ruined forever, still shaking with fear. It made you hurry a little, to get through before twilight left. Occasionally though, you'd see candlelight in a blasted-out window, or hear the sound of a woman's voice. You knew everything would come back, given time. Even the worst disasters fill up again with soft color, light, the odors of evening meals, the shouts of playing children, silky laughter. It all just needs time.

Time is what I had. I would get to Mexico, eventually. For now, there was coffee and the rain. I didn't need anything else, and I could wait.

The End